Fabricated Lies

He Thinks He's the Hunter
Patrick Hanford

Savoy House Publishing

Other Books from Patrick Hanford:

The Creation of Marla Adams

The Desperation of Marla Adams

Chapter 1

They called the killing chair 'Yellow Momma.'

At Holman Prison, Alabama, another inmate got the lucky job of slapping on another coat of paint for today's show. Splattered bright yellow paint on the concrete floor surrounded the electric chair, the same color as the 'Do Not Pass' stripes down the middle of a road.

After eleven years, Jake Washington had lost his last legal battle. A rock the size of Gibraltar stuck in the middle of his throat. His dry tongue scratched across cracked lips while heartbeats thrashed inside his chest. Every few seconds, he blinked, hoping for something better.

Strapped to a hard wooden chair inside a brick room with two square windows, he swore to anyone listening he would never kill anyone again.

The warden stood outside a window with arms crossed. Behind him, the mandatory witnesses shuffled in their chairs. Women swept their hands across their dresses. Men straightened their ties and jacket collars.

A sponge soaked with saltwater sat trapped between Jake's shaved scalp and a metal bowl. An electric cord jutted toward the wall. Cold sweat and water dripped from the sponge down his cheeks to the leather straps on his wrists. He shifted his eyes toward his family. His chest heaved as dry lips opened to stuttering gasps.

Jake looked out at his wife, who stared back at him outside the death room while rubbing her pregnant belly. He'd been incarcerated for years and didn't know who the father was. He didn't care anymore.

Eighteen-year-old Clarice stood next to her mother. There were chairs, but she didn't want to sit. She held her mother's arm tight. Her eyes frozen, unblinking on her daddy. She felt heat rise up her neck as she watched him mouth at her, "I'm sorry, Princess."

Her olive-colored skin was unblemished, except for a small white spot on the left side of her forehead. Her mother tried wiping the whiteness away every day for the last decade.

Clarice wrapped her arms around her mother's neck. "Mama, stop this."

Her mother's words faltered. Tears ran down her cheeks.

A round government-issued clock with a white face and black numbers hung on the wall. She heard each incessant second-hand click pound in her head. She wished for it all to go away.

Clarice stared at the warden aiming a Kodak camera at her daddy. She flinched when the picture snapped. The motor whined and pushed an image out the front of the camera. Watching him take the corner of the photograph with his thumb and index finger and fanning it dry, she wanted to steal it and tear it apart.

Inside the death room, an officer stood next to the wall and held a phone receiver to his ear, waiting for a governor's reprieve. His left hand adjusted the chrome-plated police badge on his chest. The brightness of the badge flickered against Clarice's eyes. He glanced toward the black curtain pulled halfway back.

The executioner stood motionless behind the curtain, waiting for his turn. His fingers slid sideways on the red switch. The volt and amp meter needles pointed toward zero. He smelled fear. He'd smelled it yesterday.

The minute and hour hands waited at twelve. The warden tapped his watch. Clarice mumbled, "No."

The officer shook his head, hung the phone back on the cradle, and slipped a black hood over Jake Washington's head.

The second-hand clicked past 57, 58, 59. All three hands snapped together in one row.

Clarice turned away.

The black curtain shut. The voltmeter jumped to 2400, the amp meter swung to 8. A heavy buzz instantly filled the room as a bolt of lightning seared from Jake's brain to his leather-strapped ankles.

Clarice closed her eyes. Tears flowed. Ears roared. Her prayers disappeared.

The man with the badge killed her daddy.

She never forgave her daddy for dying in the electric chair, she never forgave the man with the chrome-plated badge, and she's no princess.

✦

Fifteen years later, Clarice's vitiligo spread from a small white spot on her forehead to warped white patches across her face. Children called her Jersey because of her facial patches. It stuck, and no one remembered her actual name for the rest of her life. Her mother taught her how to use knives, stand up for herself, and live off bribes and graft, then left her when she died in a police shoot out. Her half-sister, Rosie, landed in juvie for assault and battery.

Clarice left Alabama behind, and Jersey headed for Chicago. At six-foot-one and two hundred pounds of lean muscle, she likes Goose Island beer, sharp knives, and killing, especially cops.

Chapter 2

Chicago Police Officer Remo Wolf charges through crowds. He pulls the White Sox cap down farther on his forehead while drumbeats of rain bounce off his hooded jacket. His sweatpants stick to his wet legs.

He runs every day from the Navy Pier, crosses a Chicago River bridge, and through the tunnel under the rail line to the Cedar Tree Tavern three miles away. Rhythmic footfalls pound the wet sidewalk one foot in front of the other. He maneuvers between cars rushing through intersections, constantly visualizing potential cover as his captain taught him in the Afghan hills. His heart pounds inside his chest while deep exhalations billow warm mist into the icy rain. He runs from his past, and it never leaves.

A man wearing water repellent clothing and riding a mountain bicycle turns at the corner and cuts Remo off. He spins like Walter Payton and charges past the bike, feet splashing water across his pant legs.

A block away, he spots the green awning of his destination. His pace quickens.

Remo hand butts the green-painted door and stands at the entrance. Rain splatters the concrete sidewalk behind him. "Jimmy." With one hand on his hip and the other in the air, he points at the bartender. "I make it this time?"

With a stopwatch in his hand, Jimmy, the bartender, shakes his head. "Nope, eight seconds slower."

Officer Bobby Lynch, Remo's partner, sits at the bar with half of his beer gone. "Slow. Very slow. Try harder tomorrow."

Remo pushes the wet nylon hood back from his head. "What are you doing here? Thought you said you had stuff to do today."

"I did. After our shift ended this morning, I went to the credit union, got a haircut, bought ammunition, went to the grocery store, and then stopped by Becky's house and... well, you know." He points to a full mug of beer. "And now, here you are, gasping for air. Drink up, partner. You want me to find a wheelchair for you?"

"You should stay away from your brother's wife." Remo points at a keg tap handle. "You got PBR?"

Jimmy smiles while wiping down a century-old bar counter with divots and chips along with a few names carved into the wood from years past. "Yep. Five fresh kegs of Pabst Blue Ribbon delivered this morning."

Remo finishes his beer, points for another, then scans the room. The only other patron, a muscular woman with deltoids like armor plating and white patches on her bronze-painted face, sits alone at the other end of the bar. She takes another drink from her beer bottle with her left hand while a small knife twirls between her right fingers. Remo leans toward Jimmy and asks, "Know her?"

Jimmy shrugs his shoulders. "She comes here a couple of times a week for an hour or so."

"Got a name?"

"Calls herself Jersey."

"Jersey—she do anything besides drink alone?"

"Sometimes a person comes in and sits next to her."

"Yeah? And does what?"

"Talk, drink." Jimmy pulls a shot glass out of the small dishwasher and wipes it dry.

"Same person?"

Jimmy shakes his head. "No. Different people. They talk and then sometimes they slide an envelope to her."

"An envelope? That's important information. Don't you think?"

"All I care about is her buying beer."

"Then what?"

"A few minutes later, two others come in. Always the same two guys. She tips good, so I don't say nothing."

Remo glances at Bobby. "Doesn't smell right." Remo looks back at Jimmy. "Can you describe the two?"

"The two guys? Sure. A skinny little fart with an Irish accent, and the other is a fat guy someplace south of Texas."

Jersey holds an empty bottle in the air. "Another Goose."

"Goose?"

"That's all she drinks, Goose Island IPA." Jimmy snaps the cap off a bottle.

"Let me have her beer," Remo says as he grabs his mug with a fresh draw.

Her eyes glance at him as he places the bottle in front of her. "One Goose IPA on me."

She rubs her left hand across her lips while the knife continuously flips between her right fingers. "Do I know you?"

"No." Remo waves his hand in front of him. "Just thought I'd buy you a beer."

She takes the bottle in her left hand. "Thanks."

"Got a name?" Remo asks.

She stares at him for a few seconds, then says, "Jersey."

"Jersey. That's an unusual name. From there?"

Her eyebrows furrow while the knife continues to twist between her fingers. "No, I'm not. I just like Jersey. Fits me."

Remo taps his forehead. "Oh, you mean because of..." He points to her forehead.

She jabs the knife tip into the wood countertop. "You got a problem with my name?"

He clicks his mug against the knife blade stuck in the wood. "No, not at all. Let's change the subject. Come here often?"

"Is that your pickup line?"

Remo smiles. "No. Of course not. I use others."

She drinks from the bottle, then wipes her sleeve across her mouth. "So, what do you want?"

"You work?" Remo asks.

"Yeah, I work."

Remo leans against the bar. "What do you do?"

"I clean up garbage. Why do you care?" She takes another drink.

"Yeah? Me too." He takes a long draw from his PBR and puts the mug near her bottle. "I clean up my own garbage pretty well. Maybe we work for the same people."

"No. I work for me, and *you don't*."

"If I need the garbage cleaned up some time, you think you might help?"

"Thought you said you cleaned your own garbage."

"Big city. Can't clean everything by myself."

She finishes her beer, stands, and slides a twenty-dollar bill under her empty bottle. Pulling the knife point out of the wood, she closes it and puts it in her pocket. "Well, thanks for the beer."

"If I need help, can I call you?"

"You can catch me here some days. Got to go." She struts out the front door as rain pounds the concrete.

Bobby looks at Remo. "What the hell was that?"

Remo shrugs as he sits back on the stool next to Bobby. "Think I just made friends with a hitman or woman."

Chapter 3

Remo rubs shrapnel buried deep in his thigh. "Are you coming back with me to the pier?"

"Got my slickers on and my running shoes for rain." Bobby licks the last drop of beer off the rim of his empty mug. "You've already run three miles, rubbed your thigh, and you're old. Andrew Jackson in my pocket says I got you beat by fifty feet. You ready?"

"A Jackson? Fifty feet? Let me think about it. Besides, I'm only four days older than you." Remo holds two fingers in the air. "Jimmy, two more PBRs and two shots of Bulleit."

"That's what I said. You're old and worn out. Bet you've got knees and ankles cracking when you move."

Jimmy pushes two shot glasses full of Bulleit Bourbon between them.

"Mine don't." Remo holds his fist near Bobby's face. "But I could make yours crack if you want me to."

Two beers slide down the bar. Eye-to-eye, they gulp the bourbon, then clink the mugs.

"We finish the beer and go," Remo says. "First one to stop in front of the Navy Pier entrance wins, and my Jackson says you're just a kid with a big mouth."

Standing in front of the Navy Pier entrance, hands on their knees, Remo and Bobby take deep breaths. A bright sun cuts through clouds, making rain a short-term memory. Hundreds of people appear outside, as if Star Trek transported them there all at once.

"Are you trying out for the Olympics?" Bobby asks.

"Trying to stay ahead of your scrawny ass. You got skates on those shoes?"

Bobby feels a tap on his shoulder. "Hi, stranger."

He turns to see Becky's smiling face inches from his. Her husband, Belly, Bobby's older brother, steps to her with a transparent bag of cotton candy in each hand.

"Here you go," Belly says. "Hey, Bobby. Why are you running in the rain?" He pats his stomach. "Can't keep this big boy hanging over your belt if you run every day."

She ignores her husband and smiles at Bobby. "Haven't seen you lately."

"Becky?" Bobby's eyes shift between her and Belly. "Right, it's been...it has been a while."

After she takes a bite, she says, "Belly, honey, would you get me a pink lemonade? I'm parched." After Belly steps away, she leans into Bobby. "Don't you ever leave my house like you did this morning. I made you breakfast, and you snuck out the back door." She points at Remo. "Were you in such a hurry to get back to your buddy?"

Chapter 4

Just after eleven o'clock at night, Remo turns the steering wheel of his police car. Headlights swing across locked buildings.

Bobby glances out the window. "I can feel your thoughts." He shifts his weight in the seat. "Black as night."

"Yeah. Pretty black outside."

"Come on, tell ol' Bobby what's bothering you."

"Same shit. Dead buddies in Afghanistan, idiots on these streets, and assholes in the department. Chicago's not right for me. I should head back to hometown."

"Don't give me that crap. Ignore everyone. I'm here for you, and I want you to stay in Chicago. You need to slow down on the alcohol. You get moody with too much of that stuff."

Remo's right hand taps Bobby's chest. "Thanks."

"Besides," Bobby smirks, "I backed off so you could win this afternoon. You probably need the twenty."

"Oh, no you don't," Remo snaps back. "I saw you running your ass off."

"I slowed down so much I stopped at Gino's for a slice of pizza."

Camilla, the dispatcher on the radio, interrupts them. "2516."

Bobby grabs the microphone. "See? Even Camilla wants you to stay." He snaps the button. "2516 here."

"Green motorcycle making too much noise in the 7100 block of West Dickens. Also, an assault and robbery on 7000 block of West Grand by an eighteen-to-thirty-year-old on a green motorcycle."

Bobby replies, "Probably the same person."

"Check it out."

"10-4." Bobby hangs the mic on the clip. "We're not going to find this motorcycle. It's on the other side of town or hidden in a garage."

"Right. We're three blocks from Dickens Street. We'll do a drive-by and show the neighbors we're close, then head north to Grand Avenue."

Seconds later, a Yamaha motocross motorcycle zips past them.

"Looky here." Bobby grabs the mic again. "2516. We got a green motorcycle in front of us at Cortland and Nordica."

◆

The motorcycle swerves in front of the police car. The rider's head, covered with a full-face helmet, turns back toward them, raises the left hand, and shoots a single finger in the air.

Remo flips the toggle switches. "What the hell is with this guy?" Their siren wails as blue lights flicker across sleeping houses.

The bike leans hard right at the intersection, then pops a wheelie.

Bobby's hand tightens around the grab handle above the window as he leans away from his door. "Look at this guy. Reckless driving, unsafe speed, ran a stop sign. Maybe drunk or high or both. I can finish out my ticket quota tonight."

Remo's back stiffens. The two-stroke engine whines high as it jumps forward in a blink. "I didn't catch the little shit's license plate number. Did you see it?"

"Maybe if your grandmother was driving, she could get a little closer." Bobby points at the rider. "And that is not a little shit. Look at those thighs, frickin' linebacker legs. You sure you want to mess with that?"

The rider sticks a leg out for balance and leans left through another intersection.

Remo taps the brake twice and cuts across a curb. Tires rip nine-inch ruts across a manicured corner yard and shoot a rooster tail of mud and grass.

"Call dispatch for backup." Remo's mind flashes back to his Humvee charging toward Taliban soldiers.

"Come on, Remo. We're right behind him. He'll slide somewhere. We can pick him up then. We don't need help with a single motorcycle."

"Call, damn it."

Bobby pushes back into his seat and grabs the radio microphone. "2516, motorcycle turned on Armitage Avenue. We are in pursuit. Just turned north on Sayre, heading toward the railroad crossing. Traffic is zero."

"10-4. Need assistance?" Camilla asks.

Bobby clicks the microphone button. "No, we got him."

Remo white-knuckles the steering wheel at the ten and two positions. "We do *not* got him. Tell Camilla we need assistance."

Bobby's lips curl into a smile. "Hey, you told me to call. You didn't tell me what to say."

Remo turns hard and feels the back tires slide. "Twenty minutes into our shift. I need a drink." Turning left on Grand Avenue, he looks for the bike. "Damn, we lost him."

"Stop the car." Bobby rolls his window halfway down. "Turn off the siren." Blue lights shoot in every direction from the roof bar. He strains for any sounds. "I hear that whiny piece-of-shit engine revving. It must be getting closer."

From behind, the bike zooms past them, brakes and skids to a stop a hundred feet in front. The motorcyclist waves a middle finger at them again. *Come get me.*

Bobby steps out of the car, pulls his service weapon from the holster, and aims. The bike jumps forward like a horse out of a racing gate.

"What the hell are you doing?" Remo calls out.

Bobby holsters his weapon. "Don't worry. I wasn't going to shoot him. I was aiming at the bike." He closes the door. "Hurry up. He's starting to piss me off." Bobby buckles his seatbelt and snaps the shoulder strap against his chest, then pulls the mic off the clip. "2516, motorcycle heading south on Nordica Avenue back toward the rail line."

"Look ahead. The road narrows with construction near the rail," Remo says.

"We'll lose him if he gets into the neighborhood streets again."

The bike crosses the tracks and turns onto a gravel trail along the side of the tracks. Red lights flash while the railroad crossing arms lower. Clouds open, rain pounds the car.

"Hurry up and get across the tracks. We need to catch this bastard," Bobby says.

Remo floors the accelerator pedal, and the car bounces across the tracks. He spins the steering wheel ninety degrees right. Tires spit gravel while the vehicle slides and bangs against a metal garbage bin. The car speeds down the trail with a long brick fence to their left and the track to their right. A heavy downpour throws sheets of rain on their windshield. The wipers sweep back and forth while blue lights bounce off the brick to their side.

Bobby looks behind him. A headlight the size of a yacht charges down the rail line. The brightness of two hundred thousand candelas fills the rearview mirror. Heat rises in the car. A horn with steel wheels blares.

"Remo, we got a big-ass train bearing down on us. It's moving fast." Bobby looks out his side window and watches the gravel trail narrow. "Hey, buddy, we got a problem. This rail is about twenty feet from the car and getting closer."

A lightning bolt cracks open the darkened night with three seconds of light. A tree in a backyard explodes one hundred yards in front of them. The burning branch snaps off the trunk and falls across the brick wall to the ground, blocking their path.

"Bobby, duck."

The branch slams against the grille and bounces against the windshield. Cracks streak across the glass. The broken wiper flaps in the air. Remo's hands squeeze the steering wheel tighter.

"Headlights out." Bobby looks at the brick wall. "Remo, there are no blue lights. We're running dark, and the train can't see us."

"And I'm driving down the width of a bowling ball gutter." White heat sears the back of Remo's neck. He focuses on the round motorcycle taillight forty yards ahead.

"The bike's getting away. I don't think I can catch him."

The train horn blares loud.

"I don't care about the bike anymore," Bobby yells. "This hell train is going to shred us. We got to get off at the Neva Avenue intersection. It's the next crossover."

Remo flashes back to Afghanistan. An RPG hit the Humvee in front of him, throwing white light and searing heat around him.

Remo snaps back and watches the horizontal railroad crossing arms on each side drop at the crossover. Red lights flash. The motorcycle speeds through the middle of the gravel trail, passing the intersection. "He didn't turn."

"Neva Avenue ahead." Bobby glances behind him. "Forget the bike. We got to get off this trail."

"Can't," Remo yells. "The crossing arms on the right are down, and a damn semi-truck is on the left. If I try to get off, I'd T-Bone it."

The horn from hell blows long and hard behind them.

"It's on our ass." The headlight, as bright as day, shines through the car. "It has to be less than fifty yards from us. It's going to rip off my half of the car. We're dead."

Remo's fatigued fingers spasm on the bouncing steering wheel.

"Look ahead. Not good," Bobby says. "At the Harlem Avenue intersection, the trail dead ends. We *have* to turn. Remo, we have to get off here." Bobby turns back. He can't stop looking at the light like a moth attracted to a bug zapper. His eye muscles twinge, eyelids spasm. "Oh God, forgive me for all I have done. I confess all…"

"Shut the hell up." Remo focuses on the Harlem Avenue railway crossing pole two hundred yards ahead. The wooden railroad crossing arms on each side of the track start to lower. Red lights flash at the intersection.

"You got to get off, now!"

Remo turns the wheel hard right. The car spins and broadsides the crossing arm, shattering it into a hundred pieces. The car slams into the corner of a dumpster with a hollow echo. The horn bellows down the tracks. Train wheels clackety-clack as they pass over the crossing.

Remo turns the engine off. They listen. The bike is gone. The train is gone. The rain is gone, plunging them into silence. Bobby opens his door, leans out, and loses the roast beef sandwich he ate thirty minutes ago. Remo's shoulder shoves his door open, and he steps out and leans against the car with his hands and head on the roof. "I need a drink. A big drink."

"What the hell are you talking about! You're on duty. We just started."

"Don't care." He slips a small bottle of Bulleit Bourbon from his jacket. "Look, it's only a pint, and half is already gone." He takes a drink.

"You wrecked the car. Someone might run a breathalyzer on you."

"Shut up. That's not enough to do anything to me."

"That looked like fun," a voice from the sidewalk says.

Chapter 5

Remo turns to find a weathered man with a dirty sheepdog face. He smells like he lives in the dumpster they hit. Legs crossed, he sits on a wet, broken concrete sidewalk. A bottle of gin, almost empty, stands between his legs. His life crammed in a stolen shopping cart. "You chasin' that motorbike?"

Remo slows his breath down. "Not now, old man. Not anymore."

"I saw where he turned. Wanna know?"

"Sure, where?"

The old man holds his hand out. "That'll be a buck."

"A dollar? Listen, old man, I should bust you for..." Remo scans the stuffed shopping cart full of the old man's life. "You been here all night? In the rain?"

"This is my spot. I like the trains, and I know when every one of them comes by here, and I know who walks the track every night."

Remo flips out a five from his front pocket. The derelict snaps it up as fast as a cobra strike. His eyes squint at the nametag pinned on the shirt. "Thanks, Patrolman Wolf." The bill disappears inside his shirt. "And now I know you too."

"It's Officer Wolf, and don't drink that five. Get some bread or cookies. At least buy something to eat, old man."

He scratches his sheepdog beard and points down the street. "That motorcycle went up the ramp of that parking garage. Got to go out the same way he went in."

◆

From the second level of the parking garage, the motorcyclist pulls the helmet face shield up. A woman stands at the edge and taps the Bluetooth button on the side of the helmet. "It's Jersey. I have both cops close by me. You want me to kill them? I like killing cops."

The motorcycle engine pings as she watches the old man point his finger toward her. Remo and Bobby turn toward the garage as she listens to her call.

"How the hell do I know what they look like? They're over two hundred yards away, and it's dark outside." She slides out a six-inch-bladed knife from the inside of her boot. "Yeah, I know the deal. I bring them to you, but I won't charge you any more if you let me do it right now—fine, I'll bring them." Jersey slides the knife back into her boot and watches one cop open the trunk. "Looks like you two get to live a little longer." Jersey snaps the face shield down, climbs on the bike, and pops a long wheelie up the concrete ramp to the top floor.

◆

Remo opens the trunk and grabs a rope. He turns toward the two-stroke engine noise in the distance. "Come on, Bobby." Remo flips the Bulleit bottle upside down as the bourbon disappears down his throat. He rubs his sleeve against his mouth. "We got an asshole to arrest."

"Yeah? Do not fire that weapon. They'll check you if you do."

Remo pitches the empty bottle into the dumpster. "All good." The glass bottle whangs inside. He shakes the cobwebs from his vision as he paces ahead.

A three-foot concrete wall surrounds the garage. Remo stands between metal pillars on each side of the entrance/exit way and rolls out the rope. "Here, tie this around each pillar. Make it chest-high. If he makes it back here, the rope should stop him."

"We should call for backup," Bobby says.

"Backup? Oh, you want backup now, but not when a train was up our ass?"

Bobby ties the last knot. "Well, yeah, so what? Okay, okay, you were right. Backup would have been helpful."

Remo tightens the rope. "This should knock him off his bike when he comes by here." Remo turns back toward Bobby. "How are you going to call for backup? No car, no radio."

"So, it's the two of us, buddy. Don't worry, we got him." Bobby smiles.

"Yeah, we got him." Remo checks the magazine in his pistol.

"What's the plan?" Bobby asks.

"You stay here, and I'll walk up the ramp until I find him. If he makes it back down, then stop him."

"Stop him. How? He's on a motorcycle. My guess is he's not stopping at the toll booth. He'll fly by past the posted speed limit sign of five miles per hour."

"That's where the rope comes in. If the bike gets past the rope, then you got a gun—use it."

Bobby smirks. "Oh, so *now* use the gun. How about giving me the KA-BAR knife in your boot?"

Remo's hand scrapes across Bobby's hair. "I should pull out the KA-BAR and give you a haircut."

"No thanks. Remember? Told you I got it cut yesterday."

❖

Remo's fingers wiggle around the pistol handle. He steps toward the ramp while his eyes search the first floor. He hears nothing. Second floor, the same. His boots step slowly up to the third level. The overhead lights are out with broken glass on the ground. The moon hides behind blackened clouds; stoplights rotate green and red on empty street corners.

Afghanistan bore blackened nights during Remo's patrols. The misty air chilled their bones. Corporal Lowery, who constantly smiled and kissed a picture of his brand new wife every night before sleep, took the lead. A kid, not over ten, jumped out from behind a car and shot Lowery in the head. The kid was the son of the tribal leader and escaped justice.

Remo scans the top floor of the garage. Four cars sit with few places for a motorcycle to hide. He pulls out his flashlight and sweeps the light underneath the vehicles. There are two motorcycle tires behind a car. Remo turns the flashlight off. His arms straight, his hands tight around the pistol, his finger fidgets around the trigger guard. He steps forward.

The cycle kicks on, the engine rat-a-tats.

Three quick steps to the front of the car, Remo calls out, "Freeze. Police."

The engine revs high and the bike shoots out over the trunk and hood. Remo ducks and rolls on the concrete and then watches it charge down the ramp.

Bobby hears the whine coming toward him. His fingers spread wide as they brush against the pistol grip in the holster. Where is it? His hand slips the pistol out with the barrel pointing at eye-level. The engine grows louder. No headlight, no movement. He kneels in the middle of the exit row with the rope in front of him. Either the rope or a bullet will stop the bike. The transmission shifts while the engine noise peaks coming straight at him. An obsidian night hides everything.

The bike jumps over the concrete wall to Bobby's right as the headlight pops on in midair. A single taillight disappears in the night.

Remo races down the garage ramp. Bobby stands alone with his gun at his side. He turns toward Remo and glances at the dirty uniform. "You roll around in the dirt up there?"

Another train passes by the wrecked police car as the motorcycle engine fades away. Remo brushes the dirt off his shirt. "This will be a lengthy report, and the lieutenant is not going to like any of it."

Chapter 6

In the police locker room, sweat and deodorant hover in the air. At the opposite end of the lockers, Sergeants Miller and Jackson laugh while they glance back and forth at Remo. Reaching inside the top shelf of his locker, Remo twists the top off a pint bottle of Bulleit Bourbon and gulps down a third. Remo is shirtless, with several small eagle tattoos on his muscular chest and arms.

Bobby tucks his shirt in his pants. "How many?"

"How many what?"

"Tattoos and bullet holes," Bobby asks.

"That's the first time you've asked me."

"Okay. Let's get down to it. How many pints today?"

"Pints? Hmm, not sure."

"I want you to stop."

"Stop? Why?"

"Did you leave that bottle in the car?"

"No." Remo replaces the cap and pushes the bottle to the back of the shelf. "To answer your first question, too many bullet holes, not enough tats."

"All eagles? Why?" Bobby asks.

"I got all of them while in the 101st Airborne Division." Remo points at his deltoid. "Like this one, my first, the best. Me and the tattoo artist were sober...mostly. After that, each bird is not quite perfect. One or both of us were drunk when he put them on." Remo sits down on the wooden bench. His index finger pushes on the center of his deltoid. "Afterward, every time I got shot, it was in the eagle's head."

The sergeants' metal doors clang shut. "Wolf." Miller adjusts his utility belt as he steps closer. "You're out of uniform. You need to cut your hair. It's too damn long for a cop."

"I'm still regulation. Get your eyes checked."

Jackson points at Remo's chest. "Damn ugly shit tattoos you got. Get something respectable, like a clown. Oh, wait," he chuckles. "You already got clowns."

"Thanks, Sergeant Asshole." Remo stands and points to his lower abdomen. "I wanted to put a tattoo right here of the girl that went down on me last night, but I couldn't find a picture of your mother."

Jackson shoves Remo against the lockers. "Better watch your back."

Bobby steps in between them. "All right, back off." He waves his hand toward the two cops. "Go on, get out of here."

"What the hell is wrong with you, Bobby?" Miller asks. "You could've had anyone for a partner, and you pick this drunken trash instead." The two sergeants leave out the side door.

Chapter 7

A few hours later, Remo and Bobby find a replacement car, the oldest one on the lot. Remo pushes his coarse black hair back as his thick hand turns the steering wheel. His light blue short sleeve shirt has a perfect crease down the middle of the Chicago Police patch.

White condensation puffs into the icy wind from the exhaust of a cold engine. The odometer rolls past one hundred eighty-two thousand as the car turns west on Cermak. Their headlights streak an arc across a mattress shop with a blow-up gorilla on the roof announcing 70% off. It's four in the morning.

Remo glances at Bobby. "What are you looking at your watch for?"

"Me?" He lays his arm back on his lap. "Nothing. Just need to be somewhere after shift ends."

"You seeing Becky again after work? I can't believe she was at the Navy Pier. You're going to get caught one of these days." The dashboard lights reflect off his square chin. The front tire pounds through a Chicago-size pothole.

"She is a lot of fun, but you saw her at the pier. She wants me to stay with her every day. Not just breakfast, but all the time. My dumb-ass brother won't take care of business in his own house, so someone like me has to. He'd rather drink at the bar."

Remo slides the heel of his hand down the right thigh where Afghan shrapnel is buried. Captain Remo Wolf saved fifteen trapped soldiers and killed over thirty Taliban. They awarded him a Silver Star, a Purple Heart, and a medical discharge, along with his PTSD and alcoholism—all for allowing hot metal to tear into his legs and back.

"That doesn't mean he doesn't care if someone else is screwing his wife, and you shouldn't talk about your brother like that. He's a detective. You need to be careful."

"Yeah? If he's so smart, why are her two kids looking more like me every day?" Bobby shifts his vision from the windshield to his right. "But that's not the reason." He looks through his reflection in the side window. Drab buildings with plate-glass windows float by along the sidewalk. "Got a package I need to pick up after shift."

"Bullshit. You messin' with drugs again? I don't need a dead partner. I got no one else on the force that wants me around. Besides, you promised me you stopped the drugs weeks ago."

"Yeah, I know…I did…I mean…yeah."

"And what? Are you shooting or snorting, or both?"

"I don't see you cutting down on the booze. You quit, I quit."

"Booze is different. I need it. The war was bad. I need it to forget."

"Bullshit. A drug is a drug. Snort it or drink it. We're both screwed over." A quick wave of his hand. "No more needles. I promise, only the nose, just coke." Bobby rubs his lips. "There was this chick Saturday night, damn gorgeous and all, and she stuck her arm out, and a white line called me, and, well, I don't know what happened next. I woke up Sunday morning, and she was naked next to me. She told me I owed her two hundred dollars for last night." Bobby combs his fingers through his short hair. "I told her I didn't have it and would pay her later. She said she'd send her pimp after me."

Remo slams on the brakes. His fist pounds Bobby's chest. "Stop screwing the prostitutes. They're gonna get you in more trouble than the drugs."

Bobby grabs his chest and gasps between coughs. "Come on, not necessary."

A stoplight clicks red. Remo turns into an all-night store drive-through and stops at a small glass window. He listens to it slide open. "Hey, Jaldeep, a pint, please."

The man takes the folded bill between Remo's fingers. "I can get in big trouble for this." He holds a small brown paper sack out toward Remo.

"Any problems tonight?" Remo grabs the sack.

"Yes." Jaldeep crosses his forearms on top of the windowsill. "That little shit on the skateboard stole a bag of chips again. You need to put him in jail."

"Right. If I see the kid, I'll pull him over and talk to him. Thanks." Remo pulls the bottle halfway out of the sack and sees the Bulleit label. The bottle slides back down. He cracks the seal and drinks half.

"Hey, at least get off my property before you do that."

"Got it. See you tomorrow night."

Their car turns down the street and passes a kid wrapped in an oversized black parka and hoodie on a skateboard. Wheels click on the sidewalk.

"That's Datreon." Bobby points at the kid. "We should stop and ask why he took the chips."

"Because he's hungry. Leave him alone and don't change the subject. You got to stop." Remo rubs the top of Bobby's head. "You going to forget about that package?"

Behind them, Datreon turns at the corner.

"Hmm, maybe."

Remo whacks Bobby's chest again. He gasps for air.

"Not fair. I wasn't ready for that."

The dispatcher calls over the radio, "2516."

Bobby's thumb snaps down the microphone button as he struggles for breath. "2516."

"A green motorcycle doing donuts at the intersection of Cortland and Nordica."

Bobby turns toward Remo. "I want this bastard."

"If it's your drug dealer on the bike, I can beat the shit out of him." Remo whips the car around.

"You said you were a scout in the army. Go track him down."

Remo shakes his head with a half-smile. "How about I track my fist up your ass?"

Bobby scoffs. "Let's not get personal." The microphone button snaps again. "10-4, we are half a mile out, on our way." Bobby rechecks the time on his watch. "Was that Camilla on the other end? She sick?"

"Camilla?" Remo replies. "Didn't notice. Why?"

"She sounded different from earlier. You know, before the train."

"Look ahead at the intersection," Remo says. "There's a single red taillight spinning in circles." His thumb flips the light bar switch. Bright blue lights scatter across building frontages. "It's that green motorcycle from earlier." Remo finishes the bourbon and pitches the bottle out the window. Broken glass scatters against the curb.

Down the street, Jersey taps the side of her motorcycle helmet. "I got them. You owe me an extra five hundred for not killing them at the garage." She pops a wheelie and shifts into second. "Five minutes. Be ready."

Remo says, "Tell dispatch we found the bike."

"2516," Bobby calls into the mic.

"Go ahead, 2516."

"We're here and see the motorcycle. It's at the intersection of Cortland and Nordica."

"Who?" the dispatcher asks.

"Camilla? That you?"

"Don't call out names over the radio."

"You sound different from a minute ago."

"A minute ago? This is the first response from you since you tried to catch a train out of town. Thought you two were sleeping the rest of the night. You need assistance?"

Bobby looks at Remo. "What the hell happened?" He pushes down the microphone button. "You called us to check on a disturbance."

"No, I didn't."

"Then who did?" Bobby asks.

"Don't know, but not me."

"This is 2517. We can be there in ten minutes to help."

"10-4," Camilla replies. "2516, you got that?"

"Yeah, but you got someone else in dispatch?"

"Negative."

"Motorcycle leaving the scene," Bobby calls out. "In pursuit."

"2517 approaching area."

Jersey turns left and right, staying ahead just enough to not lose the police car. She taps the Bluetooth. "You got the gate open? I'm twenty seconds away."

"Whoa, hold on," Bobby says. "The bike went into a self-storage facility. There's only one way out and look at the overhead lights. They're out. Don't like this without backup."

"No." Remo turns the steering wheel. "We need to go now."

Their car passes through the gate. Headlights pierce the night as random blue lights illuminate the ten-foot-high metal fence. He turns down the row, then slams on the brakes—tires screech to a halt. A large garbage bin sits in a corner. The rider stands next to the bike lying on its side with the engine idling.

"We should wait for 2517."

"Bullshit on that." Remo pushes his officer's hat on top of his head. "We'll lose him if we wait. Let's go."

Remo opens the door and advances to the front of the car. His flashlight aims at the perp.

"Police. Put your hands in the air."

"This is not a good idea." Bobby grabs the radio microphone. "2516, we pulled into Manny's U-Store It. Need backup, quick." He drops the mic on the floorboard and pulls out his flashlight.

Remo and Bobby's lights fixate on the full-face helmet with a black shield. Jersey hops on the garbage bin against the fence and puts her hands in front of her face mask.

"Hands up in the air," Remo calls out.

Jersey turns her head away from the light and raises her hands.

"Step down from there. No reason to get hurt."

"That is one big mother, Remo."

Afghanistan flashes inside Remo's head again. He should have shot the kid. He didn't. Instead, the kid blew himself up and killed three soldiers. He should have shot the kid.

Remo partially raises his pistol out of the holster, elbow back, feet separated. The bourbon blurs his vision. Ready. "Don't mess with me." Moth wings flutter in his head. The kid in Afghanistan. He should have shot him.

Jersey drops her hands. "Which one of you is Bobby Lynch?"

They both draw their weapons.

Chapter 8

Bobby points his pistol at the motorcyclist. "Get down from there."

"I'm done." Jersey jumps over the fence.

"Hey, look what we have here." In the dark, a voice calls from the storage units.

Remo and Bobby's flashlight beams sweep across the metal units and land on two kids with big smiles across their faces. Their heads and pistols turn at an angle. They can't be over twelve or thirteen years old.

Remo has never seen them before. He thought he knew every teenager in his section. "Why don't you boys go home to your momma and watch cartoons or eat some gummy bears?"

"You don't want to do this," says Bobby.

Remo's eyes search the two for anything different about them. "You're going to jail if you don't put the guns down and leave now." Damn sneaky kids. At least in Afghanistan, you can smell the Taliban a hundred yards away.

"What about me?" another voice from the other side of them asks.

Bobby pivots until he is back-to-back with Remo. His left hand aims the flashlight on the kid in front of him while his right index finger eases against the trigger. Every muscle in his body twitches. "Don't be stupid," Bobby says. Three guns surround them.

"2516, a motorcycle doing donuts at the intersection of Cortland and Nordica. Sound familiar?" The kid laughs while his gun points at Bobby.

"What's going on? You called that in?" Bobby's hands tighten around the grip. "Then you heard another unit will be here in less than a minute." Bitter liquid creeps up Bobby's esophagus.

"Ambushing two cops? What the hell are you thinking?" Remo's vision widens as he searches for an escape. "You'll have twelve thousand cops hunt you down until they have three ball sacks hanging in the police station."

Bobby whispers, "Got your vest on?"

"No, I left it in my locker after the interaction with those assholes."

"I got mine on," Bobby whispers. "Switch, I'll take the two. You take the single." He steps in front of Remo. "On one, we fire."

One kid in front of Bobby makes a deadly mistake; he drops the barrel down. "You ain't got shit, man—"

"One," Bobby says.

Remo fires. A bullet rips through the kid's chest. Bobby hits the one with the barrel still pointed at him first, and his second shot hits the blabbermouth.

Flashes of gunfire come from a dark corner. Remo and Bobby fall to the ground. Blood pours from a bullet hole in Remo's thigh. A second from his chest. Bobby lies on his side with blood oozing out the corner of his mouth. He touches the bullet hole in his abdomen. Two more kids step from the dark with their pistols aiming toward the cops on the ground.

A shadow in a long black coat and a black fedora hat slinks forward, silhouetting in front of the headlights. A red pin reflects on the left side of the hat.

The silhouette aims a gun at Remo's chest, a high polished chrome .38 Special revolver gleaming across Remo's eyes.

A graveled voice uncoils. "I've been waiting for you."

A young gun tears open Remo's shirt. Over his left pectoralis, an eagle tattoo has a fresh bullet wound.

The guttural voice proclaims, "You got it coming. You shouldn't mess with people's lives."

Strange how crazy thoughts dominate at death's door. Remo's mind wanders while lying on the ground. His childhood dog running for a stick. Is anyone from his patrol near Kabul still alive?

From inside their car, a police radio belches, "All units, all units. Shots fired near Cortland and Harlem. Any units nearby?"

The chrome barrel rises to Remo's chest.

Bobby yells, "No," and lunges toward the revolver as it fires. A bullet pierces Bobby's skull.

Headlights race across the metal fence inside the storage facility. Shadows disappear in the night.

"2517 on site. Officers down, send an ambulance."

Chapter 9

Three months later, Remo stands at a park entrance.

A golden sun rises above Lake Michigan's horizon; crystal light flickers across whitecaps in the water. Cool breeze shuffles through leafy crowns of evergreen trees. His fingertips rub his shirt hiding the most recent round scar on his chest.

Large metal swings with long chains connected to empty rubber seats gently twist in the breeze. Remo steps across dew-covered grass, stops at a dark blue painted park bench, and sits with elbows resting on his knees. In the distance, shoes crunch across a gravel trail at an even pace. They slow. A man wearing baggy gray sweats and a backpack stops next to Remo.

"Good morning, Officer Wolf." Captain Kimball sits on the other end of the bench.

"Morning, Captain."

"You willing to do what we talked about last week?"

"Why me?" Remo leans against the back of the park bench.

"I know the force admonished you for the ambush. Since then, there's been a pattern. Three more police officers have been killed, along with several bystanders in the way."

"I've heard."

"Need to find who's responsible." Kimball raises his eyebrows and stares at Remo. "You agree?"

Remo rakes his fingers through his jet-black hair hanging below his ears and nods his answer.

"Your job is to get in, find the financial backer, and eliminate the group. A one-man assassin inside an assassin group."

"How do you expect me to get in?"

"That's your problem."

"Any names, any leads?"

"One unconfirmed. A person who goes by the name of Jersey."

Remo's eyes light up. "We've met." He leans back against the bench. "That could be my in. I would need the use of the department's computers."

"I've arranged for your release from therapy and psych this week. You do this, and I'll promote you to detective."

"I'll do this on the condition you re-open the investigation on Bobby Lynch. He didn't die because of the cocaine in his system. He died from a bullet to his brain."

"I'll do my best. Are you in?"

Chapter 10

Later that day, inside a physical therapy center, overhead speakers quietly play Florence and the Machine's "Dog Days Are Over." Therapists work with five other patients on tables, each at least thirty years older than Remo and recovering from strokes or heart attacks. He completes his yoga class and lifts the bottom of his sleeveless Chicago Blackhawks t-shirt to wipe the sweat off his face. The healed bullet hole scar on his chest still shoots electricity whenever it wants. Thick fingers push his hair behind his ears, which he hasn't cut since before the ambush.

He steps to the front desk and leans across to Danielle, the receptionist. "She'll be here in a few minutes. All set?"

She stares into his eyes. "I'll be ready at eight o'clock. Don't be late, and don't be cheap."

"Have the perfect restaurant picked out for you."

"You never told me why you want me to cancel her appointment and give yours to her."

A car door closes at the handicapped spot in front of the glass doors.

"She's here," Remo says. "I need your best performance."

A woman that looks like she should try out for the NBA or NFL opens the door and pushes an elderly woman in a wheelchair to the front desk.

A few minutes later, Danielle shakes her head. Jersey raises her voice. "She damn well has an appointment. You better look again."

Remo steps up to them. "Need some help, Danielle?"

Jersey turns toward Remo. "Who the hell are you?" Her finger pushes against Remo's shoulder. "This ain't got nothing to do with you."

Remo points his finger at her. "Jersey, right?"

"And who the hell are you?"

"We met at the Cedar Tree Tavern a few months back. We talked about garbage collection."

She raises her head and slowly nods. "Yeah, okay."

Remo points at the girl behind the desk. "Danielle is very good at what she does."

Danielle says, "I'm sorry, ma'am. I don't see an appointment for her today. Are you sure it was for today? I can look at one of the other days this week."

Remo says, "Listen, I got things to do today. I could give up my thirty-minute slot with Tony to her."

Danielle glances at each of them and sighs. "Okay, thank you." She points to the row of empty plastic chairs. "It will be a few minutes."

"I can show them the way, Danielle." Remo holds his hand out. "You can push your grandmother's wheelchair down the center aisle."

"She ain't my grandmother. She's my neighbor."

"Jersey," the elderly woman says. "I'm all right. This boy seems nice."

"What the hell happened to your face?" Remo asks Jersey.

"Nothing, but something's going to happen to your teeth. I'm going to knock them down your throat if you don't shut up."

"No, really. What is that?"

"It's fucked up skin." Jersey glances at Remo's arms. "Like those scars on your arms. What's your name?"

Remo hadn't thought of an undercover name. He changes the subject and bends down to the wheelchair. "And how are you today, ma'am?"

She smiles and brushes the large Chicago hockey logo on his shirt. "That's a pretty picture. Do you know his name?"

"I think his name is Black Hawk."

"You mean like the Indian's?" She pats Remo's chest. "The only Indian name I know of is Apache. I think it's an Indian tribe."

"Yes, I believe you are right."

"I can only remember somebody's name if I connect it to something." She looks behind her. "Like Jersey. I'm from New Jersey, so I remember her name." She looks back at Remo. "I should call you Apache, but that might be rude." A smile returns to her face. "I could remember you if I called you Che. You see, Che could be short for Apache, and that wouldn't be rude." She pats Remo's shirt again. "I can remember Che."

Jersey nods her head. "Yeah—Che."

Remo stands and steps closer to Jersey. "Che...okay, call me Che. Jersey, I need some cash. You got any garbage you need taken out?"

"Thought you said you took care of your own garbage?"

"Did. My backer skipped town. Need something quick. I owe somebody money."

"You're lucky. A contact has disappeared, and I have a friend that doesn't want a particular person going to trial. You want it?"

"This person needs to find an accident?"

"I was going to give this to someone else, but here." She slips an envelope out from the inside of her coat. "I'll find you if you steal from me."

Chapter 11

Remo steps down a long sterile hallway and stops at the door. A bronze plaque says, 'Dr. Morgan, Physical Medicine.' He knocks twice, a voice invites him in. The doctor snaps papers together, smiles, and points to a chair.

"It's been three months, Mr. Wolf, and you have passed all the physical tests, OT and PT."

"I'm good, doc. See?" Remo rolls his arms around and twists his back. "I'm ready."

"I can't hold you back, but I'm worried about your mental aspect. You know what I'm talking about—grief, guilt, revenge. I think you need to continue with counseling."

Remo's hands rub back and forth across the armrests. "I'm okay, doc. No more pills."

"I was hoping for a little more response than that."

"I'm good, doc."

Dr. Morgan taps his pen on a piece of paper. "What would you say if I needed you to blow in a breathalyzer right now?"

Remo crosses his arms and inhales deeply. "I don't think that's necessary."

"Why would that be? Have you been drinking this morning?"

"I don't need a breathalyzer because I'm not driving, and I'm not officially back at work."

Dr. Morgan pushes his chair back, walks to the front of the desk, and sits on the edge near Remo. "I'm worried about you, my friend. You're finished with all the therapy here, so I must release you, but I'm not part of the mental health division. You will need their clearance before you can return to work."

Chapter 12

After a hard workout at the gym and a high protein dinner at his downtown apartment, he grabs the envelope from Jersey off the kitchen countertop. He wraps his hand and fingers around it and sighs. There's no way to turn back after this. He opens the flap again and empties a stack of one-hundred-dollar bills with a note stuck on the front with RICHIE KING and PROOF NEEDED written in red ink.

Remo knows him, but he's not a cop. Richie King killed twelve-year-old Tywon Aguilar and beat his younger brother, Kelvin, near death almost a year ago. Remo knew the two kids from his old district before the ambush. A rival gang shot their parents months before. Homeless, the two boys wandered the streets like many others. Richie King's trial is scheduled for tomorrow, and the rumor is Kelvin won't show. The chance of conviction drops significantly without a witness. Since he's not a cop, is Jersey testing him? Maybe she's not the cop killer?

Music blares out the open front door of a converted warehouse. Even at 1:40 in the morning, there's a line to get in. Partiers stumble through the parking lot. Remo pulls his Cubs cap lower over a blond, shoulder-length wig and strides down the sidewalk. He taps the pocket of his black leather jacket once. Bypassing the front door line and turning at the corner of the building, he walks around to the back parking lot. Several men, drunk and high on whatever, stand around as they talk and laugh. The back door is open. Music blares out the second-floor open patio above the back entrance.

A man wearing a black t-shirt with the club's name on the front and the word 'SECURITY' on his back holds a whiskey bottle, blocks the entrance, and shakes his head while he takes a drag off his cigarette. "Got to go through the front, man."

Remo slips a plastic baggie half-full of weed out of his jacket pocket and holds it out in front of the man. "This gets me in?"

"Sure will." He steps to the side.

Inside, a string of lights shines behind the "top shelf" booze at the bar while multicolored lights hang from the ceiling and swirl over the crowd. Dancers hold their drinks and jump in unison to the pounding of the bass. A waitress places two fresh bottles of beer on a tall table. A man and a woman are too busy kissing to notice. Remo nonchalantly snaps up the bottles and walks away, not missing his stride.

A metal staircase climbs up next to the red brick wall with second-story seating above the dance floor. Remo mixes in with a crowd going up the stairs. He glances at Richie King celebrating with a handful of women around the table who beg for attention and free drinks. Two bodyguards stand beside the table, arms crossed, looking like they could scare the weak and timid, of which Remo is neither.

Richie wears blue nitrile gloves. Since his last incarceration, he's been a germaphobe when his cellmate never washed his hands for two years. Now, he never takes his gloves off except for the shower and sex. There is no shower at the bar. Sex with one woman tonight would be possible if he ever made it to his or her place.

One woman climbs back up the stairs from the bathroom. She notices Remo leaning against the rail, smiling and holding the two bottles up. She smiles back and stops next to him.

"Hi," Remo says. He hands a bottle to her.

She grabs it. "Hi, back at you."

"Have a proposition for you," Remo says.

"Hmm. Bye."

Remo stands straight. "No, no. Nothing dirty, not looking for sex."

She takes a drink. "Good, because that's not happening."

Remo nods at Richie. "Him. How well do you know him?"

"Richie? You want a piece of him? He doesn't go that way."

Remo scoffs. "No, thanks. I want to talk to him. Have a business offer he might like."

She sips the beer and then says, "See those two guys standing next to Richie? You need to ask them."

Remo holds a folded one-hundred-dollar bill between his fingers. "One more of these if you have him meet me over at the upstairs patio, without Dumb and Dumber."

She stares at the money, then back at Remo. She takes the bill and stuffs it inside her blouse. "I want two more."

Remo nods. "Two it is."

A few minutes later, at the patio, Richie taps Remo's shoulder. "You looking for me?"

Remo turns to see the girl has one arm wrapped around Richie's waist with her hand holding onto his belt and the other hand holding straight out for the cash.

"You said two." She pulls up on his belt. "And you need to hold on to him. He's too drunk to stand on his own."

She scampers down the stairs with the balance of the transaction stuffed in her blouse.

Remo wraps Richie's arm around his neck. "Need some info from you."

"What do you want?"

The two stand near the wrought iron railing. "Where is Kelvin Aguilar?"

"How the hell do I know?"

"You ready for twenty-to-life?"

"No."

Remo leans slightly over the rail. Ritchie almost loses his balance. "I've got friends that don't want you to go to court tomorrow."

Richie slurs his words. "Good. Tell 'em to take my place."

"Tell me where you're hiding Kelvin."

"I'm going to cut..." Richie's knees give way. Remo pulls him back up. "He's a fucking rat. I'm gonna cut that piece of shit's tongue out."

A bodyguard calls out, "Hey, buddy. You need to leave Mr. King alone."

"Just talking and holding him up." Remo squeezes Richie a little closer. With his free arm, Remo waves his hand in the air. "He's stinking drunk and can't stand."

The bodyguard grabs Remo's wrist. "You need to let him go."

Remo releases Richie, grabs the bodyguard's shirt, and headbutts him. Stunned for a second, the guy shuffles back a step. Remo sweeps his foot behind the guy's legs, and he falls flat, knocking Richie against the railing, and rolls backward. Remo grabs Richie's hand, but the glove slips off, and Richie screams until everyone hears a thud on the ground.

Remo pulls his cap low over his blond wig and disappears out the front door with the blue glove in his hand.

Chapter 13

The next morning, Remo sits on a metal folding chair across from Dr. Hendricks's large oak desk. Incense burns in a small ceramic holder on his desk.

"I think I'm good, doc. I'm hoping for a release."

Dr. Hendricks, a psychiatrist who works with the CPD, Chicago Police Department, leans back in his overstuffed chair. "Mr. Wolf, we've worked extremely hard the last several months, and I think we are close. How's your sleep?"

Remo nods. "Much better. That melatonin you gave me has helped."

"And the duloxetine medication?"

"Great stuff."

"I checked with the pharmacy. You refilled it only once."

"Well, I might have missed a few. The pills make me feel...a little funny. Not good if you're out on the streets."

"You're not out on the streets. You've not been released to work." Dr. Hendricks points to the incense. "You should try this. It helps."

Remo nods.

"Still concerned about your anger issues. You haven't let go of your partner's death."

"Like what?" Remo stands up and scrapes his jet-black hair behind his ears. "You want me to forgive and forget? I should let the murderer of my partner off, scot-free? Maybe we should let all the murderers out of prison and sing kumbaya with them. Sometimes shit just happens. People slip out of their gloves and die anyway. Not everything is my fault."

Dr. Hendricks stares at Remo for several seconds. "The police have not found the person with the…" The doctor flips a page in his booklet. "The black fedora?"

Remo gazes at the floor and sweeps imaginary dust off his thigh. "No. Not yet. He'll pop up somewhere. They always do."

"And then what?"

Remo sits down and crosses his leg over his knee. "And then we arrest him. He goes through the normal process of going to trial and, hopefully, conviction."

"What if he's acquitted? What would you do?"

"If he's not the right man, we let him go and keep searching."

"What if you're sure he's the one? The man with the black fedora. Would you let him go?"

Remo wiggles in the chair. He's uncomfortable talking about Bobby's death. "Doc, if the judge and a jury say he's not the right person, who am I to say anything?"

Dr. Hendricks's fingers slide across his graying beard. He looks back at his notepad. "Mr. Wolf, I'll release you to return to work, but you must continue therapy with me." Dr. Hendricks writes on a business card and hands it to Remo. "Expect you will return to nights, so our next visit will be in two weeks at eight in the morning. You should take your medicine every day."

Remo strolls down the hallway and drops the business card in the waste can. A staff member smiles and holds the glass front door open as Remo steps through to the outside. He is the last patient of the morning. The woman in dark blue scrubs locks the door behind him. He needs to find Bobby's killer and give him the justice he deserves.

A mile south of his apartment and two blocks from the CTA, Chicago Transit Authority, rail station, Remo carries a plastic bag full of Chinese takeout, stops at an old house, unlocks the door, and steps inside. Like his mood, it's cold and dark, nothing extra.

He places the sack on the countertop, opens the refrigerator, and pulls out two PBRs. He finishes the first one in a few seconds, then opens the second. A train full of people rolls past the house.

Chapter 14

That afternoon, Remo sits in the police HR department office in another folding metal chair against a blank wall. He looks at his watch again. Three hours have passed with people walking in and out of the doorway. He is the last one in the lobby, and it's four minutes until five o'clock. The countertop's glass window slides open, and a piece of paper sticks out from the window. "Officer Wolf," a voice calls. "Your request has been approved. You've been reassigned to the Bureau of Detectives. You need to see Captain Kurt Maxwell right now. He's waiting."

Across town, upstairs at a decades-old, two-story redbrick police station, Remo steps to the front of a frosted glass and wooden door with 'DETECTIVES' ROOM' etched in black paint. He opens the door and steps in. The chatter stops. Several detectives stare at him as he walks to the back of the room. He knocks twice on Captain Maxwell's door.

"Enter."

Remo sticks his head past the clear glass door with an ear-to-ear grin. "Got a minute, Truk?"

Captain Kurt Maxwell matches Remo's stature and muscle. Everyone calls him Truk, Kurt spelled backward.

Slapping hands and a very brief man-hug, Truk says, "Sit down. Three months has been a long time. I'm glad you're back."

"Thanks. I've been reassigned to your station."

He slides Remo's badge and service weapon across his desk.

Remo drops his hand on top of Truk's, still holding the badge. "I'm only back because of Bobby. He deserved better."

Truk slides his hand away, leans back against his chair, and snaps his knuckles. "Word is Captain Kimball asked the chief to assign you here. It must be nice to have friends in high places to promote you to detective under the circumstances. I will warn you, Bobby Lynch was well-liked in the force, and several officers blame you for his death." Truk points out past his office. "There is not a single person in that room on your side. Don't forget about Belly over there. He's said many times you will pay for his brother's death."

Remo turns toward the other detectives. Belly stares him down. "I want Bobby's killer just as bad as Belly."

"I know you do, but the chief told me he expected you to ask for that, and he said no." Truk leans forward. "You understand what I'm saying? I cannot officially give you the case. You cannot officially investigate it, nor officially give me any reports on the investigation. You understand me?"

Remo sits straight up in the chair. "Sure. What do you officially want me to do?"

"I can't start you on a desk out there. You'd be a piece of raw meat thrown into a lion's den. Only one place you can go. The chief directed me to put you undercover. You have contacts out there. Find yourself a new name and a different life. This office is not the place where undercover officers work from. Still, he agreed with me to let you stay under my watch," Truk leans back in his chair, "being that no one else wanted you."

"I couldn't ask for a better spot, Truk." Remo's fist taps the desktop. "Besides, there's no one else in the force I want to work for."

"If you run across anything interesting, let me know officially in a report that the chief could read. Nothing about Bobby. Understand?"

"There's some bad criminals out there. I could arrest them and put them in jail. Murderers sit behind bars in comfy beds, fed three squares a day, daily exercise, and free medicines. It may take months to get them to court. Need a conviction before dirty money is paid to lawyers and criminals are released only to kill, rape, and steal again. I've seen it happen in Afghanistan and Chicago. Murderers roam free within the home of the brave."

Truk pushes his chair back behind his desk. "That sounded like a practiced speech."

"Thinking with nothing else to do for three months. After I do my job, it all depends on the prosecutor. Some good, some not so good."

"I guess you're talking about the CCSA, Cook County State's Attorney's Office. True, Richard Watters has struggled with his cases the last year or so. Some acquitted that should have gone to prison. Maggie McCall, the assistant State's Attorney, has been there for a few years. She's good, almost a hundred percent conviction rate. She's running for the CCSA position, and I think she'll beat Richard Watters in the election next month. Have you met her?"

"No. Should I?"

"I think she is exactly who you need to know, officially—and unofficially." Truk swings his chair around and pushes one of the six buttons on the face of the desk phone. He taps the speaker button when it rings. "Maggie? Truk here. I have someone you need to meet."

"I was supposed to be in court this morning. Everything was set for a quick conviction and send this guy up for twenty years. Somehow, this asshole gets killed in a bar last night. I have a fundraiser tonight. I'm busy. I've got no time for bullshit."

"Maggie, I know you got a boatload of stuff. This guy could help you."

"Help to do what? Filing? Got interns doing that."

"He's a cop, a good cop. He can bring you more cases. You want more, don't you?"

"Not if the perp miraculously dies a day or two before the court date."

Remo leans forward in the chair and combs his fingers through his hair. Richie was partying on his last free night, not because he had the conviction beat.

"You will thank me later if you meet him this afternoon," Truk says.

The sound of paper shuffles on the speakerphone. "As a favor to you. A short time this afternoon. Who and where?"

"His name is Detective Wolf, and meet him at Nat's Bar near the corner of Wabash and Harrison."

"Truk, that's several miles away!"

"Four o'clock sound fine?" Truk asks.

"That's thirty minutes in a taxi, only if traffic is bearable. I have a stack of papers on my desk that need finalization."

"So, your answer is yes?"

"This better be worth it." Her phone goes dead.

"You got one chance, my friend. She can be an ally or a foe. One chance."

Chapter 15

Remo shoves the glass door of the police station open to busy street noise. His pager vibrates. It's Jersey. He calls her. "Yeah."

"Had someone watching you last night—nice touch making it look like an accident."

"Okay. Any bonus prize for the show?"

"No, but now that you're in, don't expect to get out."

"All right. Now you tell me, who do you have?" Remo strolls down the sidewalk.

Jersey replies, "A guy named Massa."

"I only know one. Joey Massa, a cop."

"Yeah, but a dirty cop. Killing cops is always fun."

Remo knows Internal Affairs has watched Massa for over a year on suspicion of trafficking. "Rumor is he has a shipment coming in." Remo glances at his wristwatch. His meeting with the female prosecutor is in fifteen minutes, and he needs to call Truk about the Massa hit.

"Shipment?" Jersey asks. "Maybe I should take his shipment. What is it? Drugs, guns?"

"Young girls."

"Girls? No, don't want no girls."

"I could help, maybe meet the guy with the cash."

"No," Jersey snaps back. "Nobody wants to meet you. Tuesday, come to the house in Lawndale and bring proof of King. You show up, you get more work."

"Got it. Just you and me?" Remo enters Nat's Bar, a fifty-year-old establishment, and points two fingers at the bartender.

"No. Two more will be there," Jersey says.

Remo remembers the Cedar Tree Tavern bartender telling him about the skinny Irish dude and the fat South American meeting up with Jersey. "You got a little club going on?" He steps past several people and takes an empty booth.

"Club? Yeah, a club—a Killing Club," Jersey replies. "Are you in?"

The waiter places two draft beers in front of Remo. A bright light enters the room as the front door opens. Remo stares at an absolute goddess. An aura of sunlight surrounds her. He wouldn't be surprised if she floated across the room.

"I said, are you in?" Jersey yells on the phone.

"Yeah, I'll be there."

The door slowly closes behind Maggie McCall. Her fingers streak through her windblown hair while she scans the room with her no-bullshit look toward perverts, killers, and anyone offering extended warranties.

Remo forgets to call Truk. He forgets everything. His hand rises in the air. Her stare turns to a smile. "Got to go." Remo snaps his phone closed. This may be the best day of his life.

Chapter 16

The south side of Chicago harbors Joey Massa, a thriving drug dealer, a mean pimp, and meaner cop. He buys and sells international runaways like stocks on Wall Street, but he's also a cheat. Skimming off the top from his boss, Georgio Chronos, Joey's secret coffer is full of hundred-dollar bills.

A fist pounds on the metal door of a warehouse converted room and awakens Joey from a drunken stupor. He reaches across the bed for his watch, 5:20 AM. He mumbles to himself, "Who's up this time of the morning?"

"Why someone knock on your door?" asks the ninety-five-pound Asian prostitute lying next to him. She pulls the sheet above her breasts. "Go on, see who it is."

"Shut up. Ain't nothing but trouble that knocks this early. You go answer it."

"You not man enough?" She points to his pillow. "Pistol make you man enough."

He pulls his plaid boxers on, then slips a .45 caliber semi-automatic from under his pillow. His thumb cocks the trigger back as the left hand grabs the almost empty bottle of vodka off the nightstand.

"You stay there," he says as she flips him the finger.

"Maybe you invite friend into bed but need more money for that."

The wood-slatted floor creaks as his bare feet step to the metal door. He scans the outside from the door viewer but sees no one.

"Who's out there?" No answer. He steps back and wipes his face with his forearm. A quick swig of the vodka bottle brings two more knocks. "I said, who the hell's out there?"

"It's Georgio," Jersey says in her best low male tone. "Let me in."

"It's five in the morning. Come back in six hours."

"Got some new girls for you, can't take them with me. Open up."

His thumb lowers the hammer back down as he swallows the last of the vodka. The safety bolt snaps open, the door unlocks.

Jersey runs full speed as the doorknob turns. The door flies off the hinges like a Frisbee launched across the hallway and landing on top of him. She snaps to her feet and jumps hard on the door. He takes the full brunt with each pounding and drops the gun. Jersey's fingers grab his hair and drag him back across the empty floor to the middle of the room.

He screams. His arms reach for something, trying to grab anything. "What the hell!" he yells.

A fist hits him against his temple. Jersey's knees pin his arms down. "Know why I'm here?"

"No." He tries to clear his head. His hand sweeps the floor for the pistol.

"Wrong answer." A three-inch tactical knife springs open in her hand. "Try again." Jersey stabs the blade through his right hand into the wooden floor.

He screams in pain. "Damn it. I didn't do nothing to you! Who are you? What do you want?" He tries to focus on the white patches on her face.

Another knife springs open. "Look at me. Don't you know who I am? With this face? Wrong answer." The second blade pierces his left palm into the floor.

"I'm a cop, damn it," he cries out. He screams out loud. "Shit, you want the girl? She's all yours. Take her."

"Girl? You got a girl in here?" Jersey turns toward the bed. The prostitute sits quietly with her back against the headboard and the sheet pulled up to her eyes. Jersey slings a six-inch knife sleeved in her left belt loop across the room. Her backhand slams across Joey's face. "Wrong answer, shithead. Georgio sent me. Tell me why."

"What the hell did you do that for?" He stares at a knife sticking through the dead prostitute's chest. A red patch grows on the bed-sheet.

"Tell me why Georgio sent me."

"Georgio?" The fog lifts while he focuses on Jersey's face. "That old man's got nothing on me."

Both her hands clasped in a fist slam down on his chest.

With a shallow gasp of breath, his broken sternum doesn't move.

"Last chance, asshole. Tell me why I'm here. If I have to tell you, it's gonna really hurt."

Struggling with a whisper, "You can have all the money. I'll cut you in. We can work together." Knives stuck in his hands, a fireball of pain burns as he twists to free them. "Give me a second chance."

Her hand reaches under her shirt, slipping a six-inch knife out from a sheath attached to her bra. "I don't give nobody a second chance. Bad business." She slams the blade through his larynx and trachea.

Eyes bulge, his breath wheezes around the blade.

"Told you it was going to hurt."

Blood flows from his mouth, his chest spasms for a breath.

"Don't think you can skim Georgio Chronos without repercussions. He don't give nobody second chances either." With a twist of the blade, his neck cracks like a boot on a pecan shell.

Chapter 17

On the west side of Chicago, grassless yards surround brick-and-mortar carcasses. An abandoned house stands with neighbors of concrete slabs. Dehydrated grout crumbles between dark red bricks, fifty-year-old paint curls away from a splintered porch. The unlocked weather-warped front door bears a sloppy red KC painted across it, the Killing Club. The house sits empty every day. Decades ago, like countless other pristine mass-produced suburbianas of the short-lived euphoric 1960s, it once was a thriving neighborhood.

The abandoned house is a perfect place for invited guests to embellish their accomplishments, successes, and murders. Remo, now as Che, contemplates each person. Did they help kill Bobby?

Solido, well, he's big. Really big. At over four hundred pounds, he's a Chicago steamroller on legs. He swears he won Central America's strongest man competition twice. Storytelling tats on log-sized arms and neck project from his XXL wife-beater shirt. His shaved head hollers a bright green F on the left side and a U on the right. Long wrinkled camo shorts cover half his ass.

Euro is as skinny as Solido is grande. Can't miss his bright yellow shirt and pants. A white belt, as wide as a loaf of Wonder Bread, wraps around his thin frame. He wants to be Linc Hayes from the 1968 *Mod Squad* TV show, except Euro is as white as his belt, with gold front teeth and a heavy Irish accent.

Jersey stands on the north side of six feet and two hundred pounds packed full of one hundred percent grade A beef. White hypopigmented patches cover her face from the ever-expanding vitiligo. She dominates a room when she enters.

Che pulls down on his tight black Cubs t-shirt hiding tattoos across his chest and deltoids. His white Indian Springfield motorcycle with padlocked saddlebags sits outside. It feels good to be back at work. A different method, but still... His dead partner, Bobby Lynch, flashes across his mind. Who killed him and who's bankrolling this?

After a hefty amount of alcohol, lies, and bullshit, it's time to start. Jersey raises her hand. "Everyone has met our newest member, Che." She places her paw on his shoulder. "The rules are simple. I pay you and you take out who is on the paper I give you. You got a month to do it. You take the money and don't show up, you're my next target." Jersey holds her arms out. "Here at our little get-together, you talk and show proof of your work. It requires physical proof to count, meaning something from the hit: a ring, a watch, an ear, an index finger."

Che nods once.

Jersey steps toward the table. "All right. I'm first for this month's show-and-tell."

Jersey stands behind a tabletop podium. Like an actor changing characters, her face changes, her body expands. She grasps the sides of the podium like an angry preacher, shoulders up and eyes burning straight ahead. She's center stage. Taped on a wall behind her is a fifty-yard pistol target sheet with a human silhouette in the center.

Her hand, the size of an NBA forward, slips inside her size-eleven thigh-high boot, revealing a knife with a tinge of blood still on the blade. "I took this knife and shoved it through Joey Massa's neck." She laughs. "Got to know how to stick that knife in." The ends of her smile careen toward high cheekbones. "Can't go sideways, uh-huh." Jersey looks straight ahead. Her right arm swings around behind her, and the knife pierces the silhouette horizontally across half the neck. "You cut his carotid and all you get is a red squirter and dead in seconds." Her eyes pop forward like a hyperthyroid rage. She slides the knife out of the target. "Hell no, that be messy." Her laughter consumes the room. "Don't like messy. I like *clean* cuts." She swings around and shoves the blade entirely into the wall. "Like a butcher cuttin' pork chops." The knife pierces the middle of the throat, vertical, chin to sternum, with the handle butting against the wall. Hatred cuts deep. "This here is the way to do it. He ain't gonna talk no more, but he ain't gonna die fast neither. That is, until I twist it." With a quick turn, the drywall crumbles to the floor.

Solido calls out, "Jersey, where's the proof?" He turns to Che. "I got mine. She ain't got shit."

"You want the story?" Her head rocks back and forth. "I got the story. Joey Massa thought he was a big man, but he ain't no more. He ain't *nothin'* no more."

"No souvenir, no hit, no money," Che says. He knows the story. He read the police report about Joey Massa with his body spread like an X, knives in each hand and foot, in his throat, and missing one ear. Unfortunately, another girl had been found dead in the room.

The last of Che's beer slides down his throat. He flips the empty bottle in the air, two somersaults, and the bottom of the bottle lands on his palm.

"Bollocks, girl. Let me see your pressie," Euro yells out in his Irish accent. He leans to Che. "She ain't got it, I bet."

"You're on. A hundred says she does," Remo says to Euro.

"You've been flappin' those lips and you showed me nothin'." Solido pours over a metal chair like a Salvador Dali painting. "You say you got an ear. Show me the ear, Jersey."

"I'm not finished with my story, Solido."

"I knew it. You got nothing." His beer bottle turns upside down, and the beer disappears down his throat. "You ain't got shit, girl." His bottle crashes against the wall. "Show me the damn ear."

The front door creaks. Remo swings his pistol behind him as a knife flies by his head. A rat, the size of a cat, crossing the threshold, has a blade stuck in its guts.

"You want the ear, Solido?"

He turns back toward Jersey as dead flesh flies across the room and slaps him on the head.

"Eat it like everything else in front of your face."

Solido jumps to his feet; his oak-barrel legs shove the metal chair backward five feet, ready for what comes.

Her long fingernails with perfectly painted Chicago Bears logos click across the top of the podium. Her hand slaps it off the table, and it lands on the floor with a loud crash. Her half-drunk beer bottle flies toward Solido's head. He head butts it like a crackerjack box. She hurdles the table and lands on top of Solido. Blue and orange claws swing left and right. The big man swats her to the side of the room like an annoying fly.

Che's eyes are wide open. He'll remember that if he ever lines up against Solido.

"Come on, Jersey." Solido reaches for her arm. "You hurt my feelings."

"And you broke the heel off my boot. These are new. I stole them last week from the Gucci store." She unzips the boots and pitches them in the corner. "You gonna give it back or eat it?" Jersey asks. She dodges a flying beer bottle as it crashes against the wall behind her.

Euro walks around the room and straightens the chairs. "Christ on a bike. We only have three chairs, don't be a gobshite and smash 'em." He places the podium back on the table.

Jersey brushes the dirt off her bare feet. "Damn it, Euro. Speak American. Can't understand half of what you say."

An hour later, after everyone's told their stories, Jersey's hand clasps Solido's shoulder. "I got someone for you next month. It'll make Euro envious." She hands him a slip of paper and an envelope of hundred-dollar bills. A quick nod and a smile say yes.

Che steps toward the door. Jersey's arm blocks him.

"Che, I got ten large for you."

"I got someone in mind just for you." He opens the envelope and flips his thumb over the bills' edges. "Where's the money coming from?"

"Don't worry about where, just take it." Jersey watches him step out onto the porch and down the concrete stairs. She chugs the last bit of Goose Island IPA. "Okay, everyone had their fun, told their stories. I got work to do before daylight. Bring me body parts next month."

Che shoves the kickstarter down on his Indian. The engine roar resonates down the street. Five minutes later, he pulls into a restaurant parking lot. He opens his phone and taps T. The phone rings.

"CPD. Captain Kimball here."

"Found them. There are three with the leader, as you described. Her name is Jersey."

Chapter 18

Aweek later, the digital alarm clock buzzes with progressive intensity as a red 6:30 AM projects on the ceiling. With one blurred eye open and the other still stuffed in the pillow, Remo Wolf swings and misses the clock and slams the small lamp on the night-stand against the wall. The alarm buzzes louder; his head pounds from last night's alcohol toxins. A serrated hunting knife slides out from under his pillow, stabs the clock, and pins it to the nightstand, killing the sound. The woman lying next to him rolls over and sticks her hand under the sheets to check if he is ready for a morning round.

"Jesus, girl. What the hell?"

Maggie McCall finds what she's feeling for. They connected instantly at Nat's Bar. "Remo, darling, just checking if you want a little breakfast before you get out of bed."

Not in a hurry, he allows her fingers to investigate for a few seconds, then sits up and swings the crumpled sheet over her head. "I'm out. My pager buzzed all night." He stands as she takes in his nakedness. His head spins from too much bourbon. "My snitch told me a big heroin shipment is rolling in town in the next few days. Got to find this before it hits the streets, or there will be too many kids dying. I need to call Truk this morning."

Maggie's thin fingers catch the sheet floating down and flip it off her head, revealing Dublin red hair and porcelain shoulders. With her knees pulled to her breasts, her hand brushes bedhead hair from her eyes as the sheet drops just enough to show what he's missing. His fingers slide jet-black hair behind his ears.

"Who has it?" she asks, fishing for information as any Cook County Assistant State's Attorney should. "I can help you. Did the snitch that hangs at Kedzie and Lexington tell you about the heroin?"

He grabs his jeans from the chair next to the bed and pulls his pants up, sans underwear. He buttons the five-button jeans and turns toward her. "Yeah, how'd you know? A guess?"

"Oh, how sweet. You think I'm guessing?" she asks with an innocent face.

"Not ready to tell yet."

She playfully flips her shoulder-length hair back. "Bet if you get back in this bed, I could make you ready."

Keloids protrude from the thick, raised bullet hole wounds on his chest and arms. The scars remind them both of the ambush that killed his partner, Bobby Lynch. Too many people Remo has cared about have died, and the killers didn't get their due. Remo's blue Chicago Cubs t-shirt slips over his head and covers the physical scars.

Alone on the bed, she rolls onto her stomach, knees bent, feet dangling in the air. Her fingers play with his buttons. Her thumb and finger undo the top one. He tries to act like he doesn't care what she is doing, but his feet slide closer to the bed. Her fingers tug on the front of his pants. "Come here, Che."

He pushes her hands away and chuckles at her. "Don't call me that. I shouldn't have told you my undercover name. You're going to slip up one day and call me that in public."

She swings around and sits up, wrapping her legs around him. She pulls up his shirt to see his eagle tattoos with bullet hole scars. Her fingertips trace the tattoo on his left pectoral. "I know you hate the scars. I love them." Her palm rubs across the chest scar. "How did anyone shoot this tattoo perfectly hitting the center of the eagle head?" She releases her legs around him. "And remind me about these others where the eagles were hit."

"Guess I didn't think about the eagle being a magnet for lead. Why can't someone shoot somewhere else besides here?" He points to the chest. "This one was from the ambush with Bobby." He points to both deltoids. "These two were from the Taliban." Remo pulls the shirt back down. "Lucky for me I didn't tattoo one over my heart, hmm? And don't call me Che." He slides the shoulder holster on with a Remington 1911 inside, then pats the pager on his belt and burner phone in the pocket.

She snickers. "You look like Sonny Crockett from the 1980s *Miami Vice* with that pager."

"This pager has saved my life many times over. No phone beeping or vibrating from a particular girl I know who calls me during a bust. If my phone is off, no one can track me. Burner phones change each month, more often if needed. I should have bought out all the burner phones from Radio Shack before they went under. If you need me, page me. Remember, I'm undercover—don't tell anyone I was here."

"Nobody ever knows you're here. Don't think voters want to know you're in my bed." She stands on her knees at the edge of the bed while holding the sheet above her breasts. He places his hands on her cheeks, his thumb brushes across her bottom lip. Her tongue swirls across his lips and she purrs, "Stay a little longer."

He smiles. "See you in a few days. I'm off the grid for a while." He flips the empty Bulleit Bourbon bottle into the wastebasket.

"No calls?"

He shakes his head, she knows the answer. As he leaves, the front door snaps shut behind him.

She lies back in bed with the sheet covering her. Nobody at city hall pays enough attention to her, especially Richard Watters, Cook County State's Attorney, but not for long. She has the highest conviction rate in Cook County. As a State's Attorney candidate, an alcoholic cop in her bed doesn't sit well with the media or the voting public. She sits back up, reaches for the half-full shot glass of bourbon on her nightstand. "You be careful, my little Che."

Neon orange and black boxing gloves round out her matching sports bra and workout shorts. A heavyweight bag hangs from her ceiling. A picture of Maggie's younger sister's convicted rapist, Gerardo Hernandez, is taped on the bag, shoulder-high. Her gloves pound his face. Hernandez is why she crawled out of the pigsty in the Chicago South Side and went to law school. After passing the bar exam, all she ever wanted was to be a prosecutor. Each punch and kick produces a resounding thud and a swoosh of air. After twenty minutes, it's time for core exercises. She hates core exercises. She hates her trainer. He wants cores done every day, seated trunk twists, ab twists, side twists, leg lifts, and planks. The bastard, she hates him with each rep she completes.

After her shower, makeup, breakfast, and three cups of coffee, she pushes the remote. A woman speaks on the local news channel. Maggie swears at Little Miss Split Ends, Brenda Nielsen, who can't say a four-word sentence without a teleprompter in front of her, while she congratulates Richard Watters on his most recent conviction. Another fifteen-year-old kid who last saw his mother two years ago as she was being sent to prison herself. The kid's house might as well have a vacancy sign out front for a forgotten father. "One down, two thousand to go, Richard." Maggie pushes mute on the television. "At that pace, taking seven months and spending eighty grand for a conviction, you can wrap up the kiddie crime in Chicago by the end of next century. I want something bigger, much bigger."

On the kitchen table, Maggie's finger spins the mobile phone around and runs through the contact list to a picture of a pickup truck, then presses call and speaker.

"Hello," Truk says.

"You know about the heroin coming into town?" Maggie asks.

"Yeah."

"Why didn't you tell me?"

"Did Remo tell you that? Thought you said you were trying to back away from him until after the election."

"I am, unless he shows up at my door looking like he does."

"Anyway," Truk says. "We're trying to find the heroin, and he was supposed to shut up about that. The fewer people that know, the better. Don't want any leaks."

She feels his avoidance of the subject. "Listen, Mr. Big Shot Captain of the Chicago Detectives, am I not paying you enough to tell me everything as soon as you hear it? Besides, he can't keep a secret from me."

"You think he can't keep a secret?"

"Truk, let me rephrase that. He can't keep a secret from me when I have no clothes on."

After a few seconds of silence on the phone, Truk says, "Yeah, I'll remember that."

Chapter 19

The midday's warmth is welcoming, but Chicago nights can still freeze your ass. Remo's Indian motorcycle rumbles down an older section of Chicago with spotless roads. His black leather jacket fringe flutters in the wind. Thirty-foot elm trees drape branches over the street like green archways as sunlight flickers between leaves. Squared hedges and carpet grass adorn every yard; Norman Rockwell lives. Remo swings up the driveway of an inconspicuous house and turns one hundred eighty degrees in the driveway. An unattached garage has a padlock the size of a grapefruit. He shuts the engine off as his heel clicks the kickstand out, and the engine pings heat away. His fingers slip through his hair behind the ears.

Motorcycle boots clomp across the wooden porch, announcing his presence at the door. He presses his personal six-digit code on a digital coder on the doorjamb. Electronic locks click, two stainless steel deadbolts snap open.

He opens the door and stares at a living room mess with papers on the floor, clothes thrown everywhere, and the couch flipped on its back. Remo slips the pistol out of his shoulder holster and racks the slide. With each step, the ball of his foot is slow and quiet. Cautious eyes shift across the empty room as the pistol barrel scans the room.

Next to the couch, cat feces sit inside one shoe. Past the living room, the bedroom is immaculate, with not even a wrinkle in the bedspread. Inside the kitchen, the stand-up coffee pot's guts are clean and dry, and the dishes are in perfect order on the drying rack, large to small. Remo checks the back door—locked. Davy, the owner of the house, is nowhere to be seen. He has one more place to look—the basement.

Another digital coder on the basement door waits. He pushes single buttons with his finger, waiting each time for a beep and a red light to change green before touching the next number. A row of green lights appears. Remo's eyes look up to the red light under the surveillance camera in the corner. If Davy is downstairs, the red light under the surveillance camera will turn green.

Remo glances above his head at a fisherman's netting holding large rocks. Last year, an intruder attempted to enter his basement. As soon as he tried to turn the doorknob, the stones dropped and crushed the intruder's skull.

The light turns green. Remo turns the knob and opens the basement door to reveal bright lights and electronic beeps below. He slides the pistol back into the holster. The soles of his boots echo with each step down the bare wood stairs while remembering to miss the almost invisible tripwire across the second step.

In the basement of Davy's house, walking down the stairs is always intense. The bipolar man in his thirties changes the passcodes and booby traps weekly, sometimes hourly, when he is in hyper-mode.

From below, Davy calls out, "Don't step on the third to last. You won't like it, you know."

Remo stops inches from the step. "Thanks for the warning. What would happen if I had rushed down here?"

The basement looks like a command post with strange websites, radar screens, and tiny red dots flashing on digital GPS maps. "No big deal. I saw you from the time you pulled your bike in my driveway. Those passcodes don't work anymore. I just let you in, you know."

Remo winces when Davy says 'you know.' He says that each time he stops talking—if he's stable. When off the meds, he is the most hyper-irritating man Remo has ever met.

"Yeah, expected that." He shrugs his shoulders. "What's with the mess upstairs?"

"Damn cat. Chased him all over the house after he pissed on my favorite jeans last night, you know."

"Forgot to feed it again? I think he left you a present in your shoe."

No answer.

"So, Davy, what have you got for me?"

Davy's pale white skin begs for sunlight.

"You got the info on Euro? I need more about this guy."

Davy taps a key on one of his laptops. The screensaver pops on, the Wheel of Fortune spins. Davy asks, "How long do you think you will go before Jersey figures you out, you know?" He shoves his Buddy Holly glasses back up his nose. Davy's chair rolls across the floor straight to a 26-inch monitor with a split screen showing a rap sheet and a birth certificate. "His actual name is Bram O'Toole Wilde, you know."

"What kind of name is that?" Remo asks.

"Crazy Irish. I called Harry, my friend in Dublin. He works at the National Archives of Ireland and found the birth certificate. Euro was born in Galway, Ireland. His mother's last name is Jones. Did you know they call their mothers 'mam,' you know?"

"Davy, focus for me. What about the father?"

"The father's name was left blank. The mother, the mam, she made it all up with a bunch of Irish names, you know."

"Well, that explains why he calls himself something else, but why Euro?"

"His mam gave him a big gold Euro-sign necklace for his twelfth birthday. Days later, she was involved in a botched Galway bank heist, and the police killed her. A judge sent him to an orphanage school, and he bounced around several foster homes until he was fifteen years old. That was when he jumped on a merchant ship and headed to Chicago. Ever since then, I can't find anything with his real name, you know."

Remo scans the photo from the Cook County Jail website on Davy's laptop. "That's him, crooked teeth and all. This picture was before he started putting gold caps on his teeth." Remo sits down and says, "Okay, so what else you got on him?"

"He's not as dumb as you think. Graduated from a two-bit trade school, he knows electricity. Worked for a small-time contractor until he got caught stealing tools. Three months in the county jail for that, you know." A picture pops up on the screen of Euro with county orange scrubs and only one gold tooth. Razor wire fence surrounds the metal buildings behind him.

Remo looks hard at the picture. "How did you get that? That's inside the jail compound."

Davy's head nods. "I got friends there, just like you. Euro came out knowing how to pick locks and shut down alarm systems. He got out and started small-timing house break-ins. He pawned everything for five cents on the dollar at Big Jim's Pawnshop for about two years and then quit, you know."

"Quit? Why?"

"He and Big Jim had a falling out. Big Jim has moved permanently to the cemetery, you know."

"His first kill?"

"I think Euro planned it. That was his first real taste. He must have liked it 'cause he changed his MO to killing for hire, you know."

"So, he uses his knowledge to knock out the electricity, breaks in, and then takes out whoever his mark is. He mentioned he makes his kills look like a robbery gone bad," Remo says.

Davy shakes his head. "Sounds like it, you know." A click on the keyboard reveals another photo. "Took these pics of Euro in an all-night bar, you know."

"Where? Recently?"

"Last night, when you told me to look him up. He walked into a small bar, so I turned on the parabolic microphone. No one else in there except him and a guy with a black fedora, you know."

"A fedora? Was there a red pin on the side of the hatband?"

Bobby Lynch took his last breath in a dark alley. A faceless man holding a chrome revolver stood over Bobby and him.

"Yes, how did you know, you know?"

"Zoom in," Remo says. The picture on the monitor expands and focuses on a blurry red pin. Flames spiral up Remo's neck.

"The guy gave a picture and a white envelope to Euro. Euro called him Fedora. He wanted Euro to do the hit tonight, you know."

Remo's fists tighten into burning stones. "More interested in the mystery person with the black fedora. Did you get his face?"

"No. Very careful, never raised the head, whispered the whole time, you know."

"Damn it." Remo slams his fist on the table. "He's still out there, and I want that bastard."

"One more thing. Five minutes after Fedora left, a girl came in. She plopped down next to Euro and laid a wet one on his lips. Euro showed her the picture and said he had a hit tonight. She ordered two shots of whiskey and told Euro she would be close by his side the whole time. She said it was perfect for her. Killing law enforcement was her favorite, you know."

"Law enforcement? The hit is another cop?"

Davy expands the picture of the girl. "Recognize her?"

Remo scans the photo and stops. "Impossible. Is that...Jersey?"

"They hugged and kissed on each other for an hour, you know."

Remo shakes his head. "Jersey and Euro, never saw that coming. Where did this happen?"

"East Thirty-Seventh Street at 2 AM, you know."

"What the hell are you doing out at two o'clock? Are you looking to die soon? Even I don't walk down that street by myself."

"Never said I was by myself, you know."

"Davy, who do you know that will hang out with you at two in the morning?"

Davy spins around in his chair and smiles. "Hey, Mr. Big Shot Detective, maybe you don't know everything, you know."

Chapter 20

The next morning, someone bangs on Jersey's door. A knife slips out from her back pocket. "Yeah? Who is it?"

"Rosie."

Jersey opens the door. Her sister stands wearing the same clothing she wore five years ago when she went into prison. "Oh, Lord." A thousand ants rush across her body.

"You gonna let me come in?"

"Yeah, yeah, sure." Jersey looks out the door after Rosie steps in, then closes the door. "Heard you were getting out early. Aren't you supposed to stay in Alabama? Your parole board better not find out."

"Screw the parole bastards. I'm here now, and I need money."

"Okay. I can scrounge up a few hundred for you. Where you going?"

"Going? Nowhere. Here. I need money, ten K." She drops the nylon sports bag onto the floor. "Nice furniture, sis. Two cable spools, plywood, and bean bags. A couch with a broken leg. You go to the dump grounds for this?"

"Drop the attitude, Rosie. Beats the hell out of where you were the last five years."

They laugh at each other. The two sisters hug for the first time in years. "Damn, I missed you," Rosie says.

"Glad to see you too, but we got to keep you out of sight. Hungry?" Jersey asks.

After a sandwich and two beers, Rosie walks around the house. "Nice place. How'd you get it?"

"I pay the old man cash each month, twenty percent more than he asks for, and it includes everything, gas, electric, water. He don't ask no questions, he don't ask no names."

"You got a con going? Ain't lyin' about money. Need ten big."

"Ten? You just got out. You lose a bet?"

"Cost me ten to get out early. Got in this fight and cut a bitch. Wild Willie took the fall for me. I was up for the parole board in two weeks and that woulda killed me getting out of there. Need to send it to her in two weeks, or I die." She pops the cap off another bottle of Goose Island IPA. "Need a con, quick."

"No more cons. Contracts now."

"Killin'? No shit." Rosie picks up a knife on the plywood table and flips it twice in the air. A pistol target page with knife holes is stapled to the wall. "With these?" The knife spins, blade over handle, and hits the center of the head.

"Five years," Jersey says. "You haven't thrown a knife in five years and you hit the center of the head."

"I was workin' in the kitchen, stole a ladle, shaved it down, and practiced with that. I need money, girl."

Chapter 21

Two men in cheap black suits step into a dingy restaurant, blocking anyone from leaving through the front door. Jersey sits alone at the corner table. One holds an icy stare on her as the second checks the six tables and booths and then waves his hand, all clear.

The restaurant owner quickly steps through the kitchen's swinging door. He holds his hands up in the air. "I don't want no trouble here. I'll call the police if I have to."

Jersey spins her fork in a bowl of spaghetti and stuffs a round glob into her mouth. A thin noodle slips past her pursed lips like a snake tasting the air. She pushes the bowl to the side and reaches for a knife out of her boot. When she stabs the point into the table, the handle wobbles back and forth.

One man reaches into his inside coat pocket. Jersey quickly stands and pulls the knife from the table. He unfolds his police badge in front of her. "Got a minute, miss?"

The owner says, "Please, Jersey. Don't tear the place up."

When a third cop steps past the kitchen door, Jersey's eyes glance back and forth at each one as she slips the knife back into her boot, sits down, and spins the fork in the spaghetti again. "Sure, always happy to donate to the policeman's ball."

✦

Outside the second-floor interrogation room at the station, Detective Roland stands in front of Remo. "You sure you want us to do this, Wolf?"

"It's a favor I will owe to you," Remo says. "I need you to hold up this girl for a few hours. Talk about the cash in the box and the list of people I texted you. She knows who they are. Tell me how nervous she gets. Keep her busy while I check out a few places she has been to."

Roland's finger jabs Remo in the chest. Usually, Remo would grab the finger and twist it until he heard a crack. Instead, he lets it slide this time. He needs Roland's interrogation skills.

"I'm only doing this because you kept my nephew from getting busted last month. You should take my suggestion and clean up."

"I'll keep that in mind," Remo says.

"You won't owe me shit. This makes us even. I'll page you when I let the bitch go," Roland says.

"Here's a list of things I found in her house two days ago. Ask her about each one."

Jersey sits on a wooden chair that looks like it's been through the chipper and glued back together. Her elbows rest on a steel table bolted to the floor with fist-sized dents on top. She smells stagnant mold and sweat while fluorescent lights buzz above her head. Angled shadows make her eye sockets look deeper and white patches brighter.

On the other side of the one-way picture window, Remo stands and watches Jersey sit alone. His nineteen-inch arms fold across his chest. Remo counts three options Jersey can take. She can make up a story to get out quick enough to help Euro with the hit tonight, ask for a lawyer, or sit tight and play with the two cops all afternoon and night and let Euro do his own thing. The last is not likely if she wants to collect any money. Remo's not liking this one bit. This interferes with the purpose of the Killing Club, but he needs her flustered. Roland needs to keep her in the interrogation room for a few more hours, and maybe she will make a mistake. Remo needs to know where and who Euro's hit is. He leaves the room on the other side of the two-way mirror.

The two detectives bring in day-old donuts and vending machine coffee. "Would you like a donut? Some refreshments?" Roland asks Jersey.

"Thanks, I had my lunch."

"Oh, right. Sorry about the interruption. Let me introduce ourselves." He bites half the donut and shoves it in his cheek. "This is Detective Winslow, and I'm Detective Roland. And what do you want us to call you? Clarice?"

"Who?"

"Clarice Washington."

"That's your name, right?"

"Don't know what you're talking about."

"You remember, I took your fingerprint when you came into the station." Roland pulls a sheet of paper from a file in his hand and slides it across the table. "There is this new digital thing that can ID fingerprints in a few seconds. You can do the damnedest things with the internet and websites nowadays. The name Jersey didn't pop up, but the name Clarice Washington did. It only took another minute to see you were born in Alabama, moved to New Jersey, and now live here in lovely Chicago."

"Clarice died fifteen years ago when Momma died. Jersey's my name."

"Jersey. Right."

"Listen, Detective Roland, I got stuff to do this afternoon. What do you want?"

"I'm sure you can clear up this confusion pretty quickly. You see, it looks like you may owe the IRS about one hundred thousand dollars."

She leans back in the chair. "The IRS? A hundred Gs?"

"Well, that plus interest and penalties."

"And why do Chicago cops care about the IRS and my *alleged* back taxes?"

Roland sips from his paper cup. "Well, we figured if you owe that much to the IRS, you must owe quite a bit to Chicago. You know, city business tax, sales tax, state tax. That would be federal and state laws broken. But Winslow has a brother-in-law with the IRS, and I bet he could get you off with giving just the hundred grand. That is, of course, if you have some info for us, that is worth something."

Winslow turns his chair backward and straddles it across the table from her. "Your sister, Rosie, is she still in Tutwiler Prison?"

One eyebrow slants in disapproval. "Rosie? What's my sister got to do with anything? You need to leave her alone."

"I'm concerned about how your family is doing. I'm a cop, serve and protect and all that," Roland says as he sips his coffee.

Her finger wipes cold sweat beads from her forehead. "She got out a few weeks ago. Don't know where she is."

"Sure about that? She's on parole and not supposed to leave Alabama." Roland slips another picture from the manila folder. "Looks like her, doesn't it? She stepped on a bus with Chicago on the heading. Have you seen her this week?"

"No comment. What's this got to do about the IRS?"

"Not paying taxes and harboring a fugitive. Big mistake. That would be two federal offenses."

"She's not a fugitive. She got released from prison."

"Your mother is our next stop. I'll bet she knows where Rosie is."

"Is this why I'm here? This all about Rosie? Why do you care about where she is? And I told you Momma's dead. You damn pinheads killed her in Alabama years ago."

Winslow shifts his coffee over as he bites a donut. "Rosie has a history of violence. Five years in the pen for almost killing someone will hang with her forever. A parolee with an attempted murder rap will never have a good job, much less checking groceries, mopping floors, or even a fry cook. Couldn't get a job with the city cleaning bathrooms. She'd never pass the first five minutes of a background check."

"What do you want, dickwad?"

"Are you giving her some of that hundred thousand that belongs to the IRS?" Winslow asks. "That's accessory. Twenty more years for her."

Roland pretends someone sent him a text on his phone. "Tell me about the knives in your bedroom." Roland slips his phone back into his pocket.

"What? Bullshit. You got no reason to be in my house. You got a warrant?"

Roland leans toward her. "We found over fifty brand new twelve-inch hunting knives, still in plastic bags, sitting in an opened cardboard box on your bed. Red letters URGENT and OVERNIGHT stamped across the top."

"Why do you need all those knives?" Winslow says.

"I'm scared of the dark. Bad neighbors. I got a right to protect myself."

"Why do you have six knives soaking in bleach in the bathtub? The water was tinged pink. Do you think it was human blood? Whose blood, Jersey?" Roland asks.

"You got no right doing that. I was cutting pork chops."

"With the bleach, there's no way to confirm someone's blood. DNA destroyed by the acid." Roland snaps back, "Guess you know that, don't you, Jersey?"

"Any guns in the house? Maybe we should gain a warrant for a more thorough search," Winslow asks Roland. "If we find any guns in the house and Rosie is living there as a convicted felon, it will send her back to prison."

"I don't like guns."

Roland holds another donut up in the air and offers it to Jersey. She slaps it against the wall.

"Why was there a shoebox full of hundred-dollar bills in your closet, Jersey?" Roland asks. "Winslow, did you know even criminals hide their money in a bedroom closet?" Roland looks back at her. "Did you claim that money on your taxes yet? We might need to let the IRS know about this."

Her ass pushes back in the chair. "I ain't no criminal, and that's not my money. Someone planted it there. How many boxes did you find?"

"Boxes? You had more than one?" Winslow asks.

Damn, Rosie. You're here a few days, and you steal ten K from me?

Roland leans across the table. "Where have you been this last week, Jersey?"

"Last week? You mean as in, where was I a few days before Sunday? I'm sorry, are you including Sunday as last week or this week? You know, preachers think Sunday is the beginning of the week, and everyone else thinks Sunday is the end of the week."

"Cut the BS, Jersey," Winslow says. "We can make this hard on you."

"Hard? You can't make it hard enough for me. I bet that tooth-pick between your legs never gets hard. Is that getting you hard, Winslow?"

"Answer the question, Jersey," Winslow says.

"Detective, you already frustrated with this interrogation? I bet that pencil stub gets frustrated every night."

"Enough," Winslow says. "Let's throw her in the drunk tank for twenty four hours."

"Chicago."

Roland turns to her. "What?"

"Chicago. Did you already forget the question?"

"Never mind that. Ever heard the name Joey Massa?" Roland slides a picture of Joey Massa with four knives stuck in him and a hole in his throat. "He was the third police officer murdered in Chicago in the last two weeks."

Her elbows rest on the table. A few days ago, she knelt over Joey Massa in his apartment. The hunting knife in her hand slammed into Joey Massa's throat. She rubs her temples with the heels of her hands. "No. I don't know him."

"What about Giorgio Chronos?"

"No."

"We're looking for him too. I'll bet he can tell us a little more about you."

"Hey, Roland. You think Rosie knows where all these people are?" Winslow shoves the last bite of fried bread with chocolate and sprinkles on top into his mouth. "You hiding her here in Chicago? Has she been to your house? Anything there you want to talk about?"

"No comment. You damn well better leave my shit alone. I need to pee."

Roland slides another picture out from the folder and turns it in front of her. "Know this guy? Where is he? He goes by Euro. Are you hiding him too? We've been looking for him. I need to ask him a few questions. Maybe you got yourself a Chicago secret cult going on, Jersey. Are you hiding Euro, and Rosie, and Chronos?"

Chapter 22

Truk stands on the other side of the two-way mirror. He pushes 'Remo' on his phone.

"What's up, Truk?"

"Why is this Jersey girl here? You know something about her I don't?"

"Her? No, not especially. Just, uh, you know, just trying to get some intel from her."

"Intel? Like what?"

Inside the bar where Euro met Fedora, Remo says, "Hold on, Truk. I'm asking someone a few questions. I can be there in a couple of minutes. Keep her there until I get back to the station."

"Make it quick. This girl's not telling us anything." Truk disconnects the phone.

Remo holds the phone in one hand and with the other flips a photo of Jersey to a bartender. "Recognize her?"

"Yeah. She and another guy kissing on each other all night."

Remo flips a picture of Euro on the bar. "Him?"

The bartender nods. "A strange guy from somewhere else."

"Ireland."

"Yeah, maybe. The guy had gold front teeth. Strange looking man. Before she came in, he met someone completely covered with a hat, coat, gloves, and a scarf. Never saw the face."

Looking through a two-way mirror, Truk uncrosses his arms in front of his chest and shuffles his feet. He stares at Jersey sitting on the chair. A speaker hangs from the corner of the room.

"No," she says.

"No that you know him or no that you know where he is?" Roland asks.

"No to both. I need to pee, now."

Jersey opens the ladies' room door across the hall from the detectives' office. Roland steps right behind her.

Jersey turns back to him. "Are you coming into the bathroom with me?"

"Yeah. Don't worry, I'm not going into the stall with you," Roland says. "I don't trust you. You might try to sneak out that window up there."

"That window?" Jersey points to the rectangular window at eye level. "That ain't big enough for me."

"You're right about that," Roland snickers. "No way you'd ever squeeze your ass through..."

Her fist connects square to Roland's jaw, and he drops like a Jenga tower. Winslow's black baton slams against her temple. Dazed, she swings back but misses. Roland sweeps his legs behind her feet, and she flops onto her back. She rolls to her side as two batons pound her head, arms, and legs. On his belt, Roland's badge flashes against her eyes like the badge that pulled the lever on her daddy's electrocution chair. She lunges at Roland. Her fist sinks into his stomach, slamming him against a metal partition door. The electronic eye triggers the toilet flush.

The snap-click sound of a Remington shotgun stops the action, cold. A man fills the empty space of the doorjamb and stands with a shotgun in his hands. "You move, and I will blow a hole the size of a bowling ball through your chest," Truk says.

Jersey fluffs her hair and smiles like she won the lottery. "You, I like." Her finger points at the shotgun. "And you can put that away. I'm done with these two squirrels, but not with you, baby." She winces at the captain's chrome badge stuck on his shirt pocket.

The shotgun barrel stands firm, still aiming at her chest. "Go back to the interrogation room...please."

She shoves Roland and Winslow away, steps toward the shotgun, and speaks in her best siren voice, "That is not the barrel I want pointing at me." Her eyes flash at his name tag. "Captain Maxwell, you got any other big barrels you want to point at me?"

"No." He lowers the shotgun. "Boys, take her back to the interrogation room."

Five minutes later, back in the cold cinder-block room, Jersey says, "I want to go back to the IRS crap. And who is that massive hunk with a captain's badge?" The chair creaks as she shifts back.

"IRS?" Roland says as he dabs blood off his swollen lip. "No, I think we need to talk about your friends and relatives. Let's go back to Euro. You remember him, right?"

"No. Who had the shotgun pointed at me?"

"That's Captain Maxwell, Truk."

"Truk, like a big Mack Truck? He got a girlfriend? Married?"

Roland ignores her question and slides the third picture across the table of Euro and her in the bar. "Jersey, you're lying. That is a state offense, lying to a cop. Two feds and one state offense so far. The years are adding up fast."

"Need to add assaulting two dumbass cops in the ladies' bathroom."

Jersey raises her voice like a damsel in distress. "I had to defend myself, officer. I thought you were going to take advantage of me." She leans back and laughs. "You two think you're pretty smart. Well, you got nothing on me. Not against the law to see people on the street. What if I did see him? I like kissing strangers just for the hell of it. Not against the law to kiss someone in Chicago."

"You need to tell Euro he's being watched. We know he's up to something, and he can't go far."

Roland slips his baton out of the belt loop and slams it against the table, inches from her fingers. "Broken fingers, all swollen and bleeding, you won't be able to hold a knife anymore. That would be a shame, wouldn't it, Jersey?"

"Next time I see you, you're going to find out how well I can hold a knife. Are you going to charge me? If not, then let me go, or I want my lawyer."

❖

The police station lobby downstairs is full of victims and accusers. Past the entrance and the sergeant's desk is a wall with two metal doors. A large white arrow on one points up to the detectives' office while the other points down to the basement.

Remo steps past the glass front doors and maneuvers between people as he holds a paper cup of steaming coffee. A prostitute notices his standard attire, faded jeans, a Chicago Blackhawks hockey t-shirt, and a black leather jacket with fringe on the arms. With black mascara and lipstick as thick as tar, she stands at the sergeant's desk and calls out at Remo. "Hey, baby. I'm done here in a little bit. Meet me outside?" He walks past her.

The downstairs metal door snaps open. A police officer in uniform takes the last step up from the basement.

"What's going on down there?" Remo asks.

"Wolf, do you own a uniform anymore?"

"Hmm, I don't know. This is undercover, man."

"Yeah, right. Anyway, Truk wants us to take all evidence ten years old and older downstairs. Running out of storage room up here," the cop says.

"Haven't been down there in forever. Still a mess?"

"Yeah," he chuckles. "Can't believe the basement is as big as this corner lot and all the way across the street. Nothing but crap." His finger jabs Remo's shirt. "Big enough the Blackhawks could play a game down there."

"Still got all that old furniture from the seventies and eighties?"

"With six inches of dust on top of everything."

The upstairs metal door opens and hits against Remo's back. He turns around and watches Jersey walk to the glass front door and disappear down the street. His cover would have been blown if she had turned around. His pager vibrates. *She's gone.*

"No shit, Roland."

Chapter 23

Upstairs, Remo opens the door and enters the detectives' office. Six wooden desks are lined up two by two with the captain's office in the back. Remo nods to a few detectives until he sees an asshole standing alone next to a desk.

Detective "Belly" Lynch steps in front of him. "What the hell you are doing here, Wolf? Only legitimate detectives belong upstairs." Belly stretches in his lift shoes to reach five-foot-five inches. The pale Irishman, with multiple age spots covering his face and neck, considers himself a cool detective. A cigarette is lodged behind his left ear. His thinning comb-over attempts to cover multiple brown scalp patches of actinic keratoses. Adipose hangs three inches below his belt thanks to his nightly six pack of Irish red ale. Not the classic look the Chicago Bureau of Detectives is proud to stick out in front of the public.

Almost a foot taller than Belly, Remo reaches to scratch his nose while the fringe on his jacket scrapes over Lynch's balding head and turns the Brylcreem-laden hair into a mess. "Oh no, Belly. I didn't mean to move those three long hairs on your ugly scalp. You know, you should transplant some of that back hair on top of your head. That way, maybe Becky would jump back in bed with you."

"Don't talk about my wife. I'll kill you right here."

A single gold-colored plastic trophy sits on Belly's desk. Remo flips it in the air.

"Leave that alone. It's mine," Belly says.

"Must be proud of it." Remo acts like he almost drops it. "Only trophy you ever got, right? Third place in a high school motocross. Was that the time you ran over the spectator and he almost died?"

"None of your business. At least I didn't get my partner killed."

The back of Remo's hand swings hard across the Irishman's jaw, and Belly bounces to the floor. Remo drops to his knees, pinning Belly's twig-thin arms against the floor. A switchblade pings open next to Belly's head.

Remo leans toward Belly. "I got a friend who likes to stick her knife in pompous shitheads' ears. I'm going to send her your name."

Two detectives pull Remo back. Truk steps out of the captain's office. "Damn it, Lynch." He pulls Belly off the floor with one hand and stands him up like a ragdoll. "You dumb son of a bitch. Pick on someone your own size...if there is one."

Belly straightens his JC Penney jacket like he won a fight. "Yeah? Listen, Truk, that drunk's got nothing on me. I can take him anytime I want. He got my brother killed, and I ain't forgetting it."

Truk grabs a fistful of Belly's shirt. "Remo and Bobby were ambushed. It was not his fault."

Two detectives hold Remo back while he swipes his hand toward Belly. He shuffles behind Truk and pulls the cigarette from behind his ear. Reaching for a wooden match from his side coat pocket, Belly's thumbnail snaps across the match head. A flame rolls over the tip. The end of the cigarette turns red as Belly flicks the match at Remo.

"Told you," Truk says. "No smoking."

"Yeah? Maybe I'll throw another match at that drunk. All that alcohol in him, he'd go up in flames."

Truk slaps the cigarette out from Belly's lips. "Somebody will smash you like the cockroach you are, and all that will be left are those long stringy hairs." Truk walks back to his office and asks, "What are you looking for, Remo? A favor or forgiveness?"

"I need to talk to you for a minute, Truk."

"All right, come on into my office."

"Nah, let's go down to the corner."

Truk glances at his watch. "A little early for a beer, don't you think?"

"You had lunch yet? I'm buying."

Remo quickly raises his fist toward Belly, who flicks another lit match head toward Remo. Truk steps into his office and snatches his coat from the rack behind the door. Remo hears Belly yelling on the phone, probably at Becky.

The bar door swings wide as Remo and Truk step inside. "Percy," Remo calls out. "Is it happy hour yet?"

The thin, weather-beaten man behind the bar swings his towel over his shoulder. "For you, Detective Wolf, anytime is happy hour."

"You're still my favorite bartender. Two tall drafts." They sit down at a small table. "Got any fresh pastrami?"

"Of course."

"Two sandwiches," Remo says. He turns back to Truk. "How'd it go with Jersey?" Remo already knows the answer.

"Jersey left," Truk says. "Had to break up a scuffle between Roland, Winslow, and her."

Percy slides the beers on the table. "Two pastrami sands' in a minute."

"Good thing you did," Remo snaps back. "They would have lost. Cheers."

"Sorry about upstairs." Truk spins the handle of the mug around. "I had to do the dog and pony show for them."

"I know, we're good." Their glasses clink and then tap the table for luck. They both gulp half down.

"You know, she ain't half bad-looking." Truk wipes his sleeve across his mouth. "Get past that shit on her face and all."

Remo snickers. "I'll tell her to expect your call." He leans forward on the table. "All kidding aside, you need to be incredibly careful with her. It means nothing for her to kill. Cops seem to be favorite targets."

Truk finishes his beer. "What do you want, Remo?"

"I have a guy named Euro, and he has a hit on someone tonight. I need help to find out who."

"Why is that my problem?"

"Did Jersey say anything suspicious?"

"Jersey was no help." Truk pushes his mug to the side of the table.

"I want you to put a tail on Euro."

"Can't. I don't have anyone to spare tonight. Everyone in my department has their own case to work on." Truk's thumb spins his Super Bowl ring around his finger.

"Two sands'," Percy says as he places the plates in front of them. "And extra-crisp pickle, just like you always want, Detective Wolf."

"You're the best bartender in town." Remo bites the pickle in half.

Truk holds up his limp pickle. "What the hell?" He drops it on the plate, grabs the sandwich, and bites a man-size chunk out of it. "I got no one to spare."

"Come on, Truk. Volunteer someone with nothing important to do. It would be a straightforward job. A simple tail."

"Listen, Remo." He bites the limp pickle. "I got enough work for twice as many detectives out there. I got no one to spare. Why can't you do it?"

Remo looks behind to make sure no one is listening. "I got that drug bust all set up for about three in the morning. I've been working my snitch hard, and he promises Rolly Chang will drop at least a kilo of heroin tonight. I can save a lot of lives with that heroin off the streets."

"Chang? You think you got Rolly Chang in a bust tonight?" Truk's hands wave a negative. "You ain't got shit, Remo. We've been trying to bust him for over a year with nothing to show for it. Nobody is willing to give him up. And why did you tell Maggie about the heroin coming into town?"

Remo downs the rest of his beer. "My snitch has never been wrong about drugs coming into town. And why are you bringing up Maggie? When did you speak to her?"

Truk glances left and right. He wants to say more about the morning call but doesn't have the time. "Nothing gets past me. Got it? Nothing. Besides, you don't need to talk to Maggie McCall unless she has a dress on."

Remo holds the mug up for another. Confused eyes look at Truk. "What?"

"Never mind. You bring Rolly Chang in, and you can have an extra man."

"Euro has a hit tonight, not tomorrow." Remo spreads his hands in the air. "Listen, I heard you need to pay off a big gambling debt, and my snitch also told me about the third race at Arlington Park this week. A sure thing."

Percy slides two more beers on the table.

"Your sure thing don't mean shit." Truk gulps more beer down.

"Have I ever told you wrong before?"

Truk counts on his fingers. "Lots of times."

"Yeah, well, my snitch is right about this one." Remo swallows a significant part of the second beer. He puts the mug down and bites into the sandwich. "Okay, I didn't want to worry you, but I have a recording of Jersey talking to Euro. She said the hit was someone in law enforcement."

"Law enforcement? Damn it. This would be number five."

"I'll take anyone. A janitor would work for me."

"Okay, okay, maybe I got someone." Truk leans against the back of the chair. "This rookie came to me a couple of days ago. His name is...hold on, it's somewhere." Truk pulls several business cards out of his shirt pocket. "Here, his name is Donovan Fillard. He's asking everyone for extra duty."

"Thanks, Truk. I know which car he can use, and the horse is Artsy Full in the third. Guaranteed."

Chapter 24

Donovan Fillard stands in his spotless dark blue police uniform with the standard checkerboard band police cap. His smile stretches ear-to-ear. One floor underground in the police garage, a confiscated 2016 black Mustang Shelby GT 500 sits as the motor rumbles. Remo's motorcycle pulls between Donovan and the car. "You think you're ready for this?" Remo asks.

"Yes, sir. I love this car."

Remo hits the kill switch on the motorcycle. The Shelby hums alone. "It's just a car. Four tires and a steering wheel."

"More than that. I used to race the semi-pro tracks along the east coast before becoming a cop. Six hundred horsepower and over six hundred pounds of torque. This is one bad-ass car."

Still sitting on the bike, Remo reaches inside his saddlebag and flips a manila folder open. "Donovan Fillard."

"Yeah, heard of me?" Donovan asks like a fan walked up for an autograph.

"No," Remo says as he climbs off the bike and walks to the front of the Shelby. "They confiscated this from a dumbass who stole it in Canada last week. He got busted for running a red light in Schiller Park, south of O'Hare Airport. The owner in Canada wants it back yesterday, but US Customs is taking their sweet time. Lucky for us."

"Sweet. Anybody else driven it?"

"No one, except tonight. It's all yours. It's all stock except the front bumper has two black four-inch-diameter metal pipes welded to the chassis. Somebody in service must have been bored and thought it was funny to make it look like a cop car bumper. The owner back in Canada will scream about the modifications."

"Like a two-pipe grille guard for knocking shit out of the way. Always had fun shoving cars off the track," Donovan says.

"Quit gawking and pay attention." Remo holds up a picture of Euro from the folder. "All I want you to do is follow this guy. I don't want you to engage him. I don't want you within fifty feet of him. He doesn't look it, but he is a professional killer." Remo points to a cell phone stuck on the dashboard with Velcro. "There is a GPS on this phone, and Captain Maxwell can see where you are at all times. The phone is a direct link to him. All you got to do is push the Bluetooth button and talk."

"Captain Maxwell. You mean, Truk?"

Remo closes his eyes and gestures a quick wave off. "Yeah, Truk."

"Wow, I get to call Captain Maxwell. When I call him, can I call him Truk?"

"Sure, call him Truk. No skin off my nose."

"Wow. My buddies from the academy will go ape-shit when I tell them."

"This is important. No one must know you are driving this. Especially Truk. He thinks you're in a CPD unmarked car. He would go berserk if he knew I took this out of storage. Euro can pick out an unmarked car in a second. That's why you have this."

Donovan takes a selfie with the Shelby behind him. He looks at Remo. "This is to show to my buddies later."

"Focus, Donovan. Euro hangs out in the loop with the young chicks, so be careful. He knows every bartender in every bar and every crack on the sidewalk. He can pick out a cop two blocks away. His normal MO is to show up around midnight. If he bounces bar to bar, that's fine, but you call Truk if he gets in a car. Tell him what kind of car he is in and how many are in the car. After that, you leave. Your job is done. The cops on the street will pick him up."

"Yes, sir. I can do that, but I may have to take this baby out for a test drive."

"I don't give a shit what you do before you see him, as long as you don't wreck it. You got your vest on? Give me that cap, and we need to cover that bright shiny badge on your shirt pocket. It's like a beacon for every crook in town." He reaches inside his saddlebag again and pulls out a black cotton jacket, skullcap, and sweatpants. "Put this on, and you are unofficially an undercover cop."

Donovan zips the jacket up and covers the shield. "You sure I'm cleared to do this? Cover up the badge and all."

"Listen, rookie." Remo bends toward him and speaks softly, "Heard you're a decent flatfoot. This is different. This is your first undercover action. If you are a good little cop and keep up with Euro without getting caught, we might think about you in the detective world later, much later." He pulls the skullcap low on Donovan's head. "Are you proficient with your service weapon?"

"I was top of my class. I've shot pistols, rifles, and shotguns most of my life."

"Ever shot a man?"

Donovan's lips squeeze tightly together as he nods. "Yeah, a man climbed through my parents' window. I fired once with my dad's revolver. Hit him in the chest."

"When was that?"

"I was fourteen."

"You feel bad about that?"

"Oh, hell no," Donovan snaps. "He wanted my mother's jewelry. I gave him some of my dad's lead."

Remo gives Donovan a quick pat on his back. "I think Truk picked out the right man for this job."

Donovan's white teeth shine out of a broad smile. "I've been a cop almost a year, and I'm going undercover with a Shelby GT 500! The guys at the track would go crazy."

Remo looks at his watch. "It's 11:17." He opens the car door and reaches across the front seat for a small black nylon bag, and with a quick zip, he opens it. "A Sig Sauer P320 .40 cal is in here with two clips of fourteen. Any trouble, use it, but remember, you're not supposed to be in this car."

Donovan's hand reaches for the pistol. After a quick look at both sides, he flicks the magazine release, checks it, and snaps it back in place. A red dot skims across the wall. "Nice laser on it. Do I have clearance to use this?"

"Yeah, I talked to yo momma, and she said it was okay."

Donovan pitches the bag with the gun back inside on the passenger front seat. "This is going to be a great night."

"Go on and hustle up." Remo opens the door. "Find a parking space and watch for him. Don't play games on your cell phone, no lights inside the car, and keep the windows up and doors locked. Stay awake and in the car. You may be there 'til the bars close at two in the morning."

Chapter 25

As Jersey walks up the concrete steps to the door of her South Side house, she hears a creak and a bang next door. A woman next door blurts out a few cuss words.

"Agnes?" Jersey hurries over to the other house. The woman stands on her porch, holds a sack full of groceries in each hand, and kicks her wooden screen door.

"Agnes, let me help you. What are you doing out here this late?"

"I got this. I don't need no help."

Jersey steps around and grabs the thin, rusted handle to the screen door. "Can I open this for you?"

"No. I said I got this. I don't need no one helping me."

"Right, of course, it's just that I came over to ask for a cup of sugar."

Agnes glances at Jersey. "You the girl next door?" She smiles. "Are you going to bake another cake?"

"Yes, that's right." Jersey touches Agnes's hand. "Could I help you with those bags?"

"Why, sure. What did you say your name was?" She hands one bag over.

"Jersey."

"Oh, that's right. I forget. Yeah, Jersey. I was born in Jersey. Is that why you got that name? You're born in Jersey too?"

"Maybe."

"Have you been cooking? You have flour on your face."

"That's not flour, Agnes. That's my skin."

Agnes places her bag on the small dining table and turns toward her bedroom. "Excuse me, I need to freshen up a bit."

Jersey empties the bags and puts the quart milk carton next to another quart carton in the refrigerator. She halfway closes the door, reopens it, and stares at the quart carton that hasn't been opened. The date expired two weeks ago. She closes the door and throws the expired carton in the trash. Jersey pulls the contents out of the bags and notices the first has three cans of dog food and a box of dry cereal. The second bag has a loaf of bread, marked down because it's stale, and a large bag of potato chips.

"You wanted some sugar?" Agnes says as she walks back into the kitchen.

"You know, I think I'll pass on the cake tonight." Jersey looks around the floor. "I didn't know you have a dog."

"Dog? I got no dog in here, just me." Agnes avoids looking directly at Jersey.

"I thought maybe you did with two cans of dog food here."

A few plates clatter together as Agnes moves them from the drying rack next to the sink. "Oh, those? I like the chicken n' rice and the beef n' gravy. I fry up the chicken with some salt and pepper and it's pretty good."

Jersey looks back into the trashcan with several empty dog food cans inside. Her hands rub across her face. She pulls a wad of money out of her front pocket and counts out three fifty-dollar bills. She looks around the kitchen. "Girl, where's your purse?"

Agnes avoids looking at Jersey. "My purse? Oh, I must a' took it to my bedroom. Don't worry 'bout me. I be fine."

"What do you mean?" Jersey steps in front of Agnes. There is an abrasion across the left side of her face. "What happened to you?"

"Nothin'. I'm all right."

"Did somebody rob you? Is that what happened? Did they take your purse?"

"Oh, no. Those boys said they needed some help, so I gave it to them."

Jersey dabs the dried blood on Agnes's face with a washcloth. "Do you know them?"

"Them two 'cross the street. Some days, they nice to me. Some days they just mean."

"You stay right here, Agnes. I'll be back in a minute."

Jersey marches across the street and kicks the gate open at the side of the house. She charges around to the back where both boys sit on the back porch steps looking inside the purse.

"Give me that," Jersey announces.

They both stand up and flick their knife blades open. One says, "You better leave, or I'm going to cut you up."

"Listen, you little shit. You're going to hand that to me, and your brother is going inside and find me fifty dollars."

"I ain't got no fifty dollars, and I ain't givin' you shit."

One boy steps to the side of Jersey while the other swings his blade toward her face.

The knife fight lasts three seconds, resulting in a broken forearm with one boy, and the other has a knife stuck into his palm.

She yells at the one with a broken arm. "Get your skinny ass inside and take fifty dollars from the coffee can in the kitchen. Now!" She looks at the one with a knife in his hand. "You touch that old lady across the street, you get near her, you even look at her, I'll come back and cut your throat. Got it?"

The boy comes out of the house with money in his hand. "I promise, we won't do nothin'."

Jersey grabs the good arm and snaps the money from his hand. She squeezes hard and grins at him. "I like killin'. I might sneak in and…" She snaps the other forearm. He screams out loud. "Kill you in your bed." She shoves him to the ground and walks back to Agnes's house.

The wooden screen door shuts as Jersey strolls into the kitchen. She holds up the purse in one hand and two hundred six dollars in the other. "Those boys were deeply sorry they bothered you. In fact, they wanted you to forgive them, and they gave me this money to give to you."

Agnes counts out the bills. "I ain't never seen this much money in a long time. Maybe I should go back over there and tell them this is too much."

"No, I don't think that's a good idea. Those two boys want to leave you alone, so maybe you should honor their wishes and let it slide."

"Jersey, right? Jersey, I thank you for helpin' out an old lady." She sticks the money in her purse. "You still want that sugar?"

Chapter 26

A modicum of office lights shoots out the glass skyscrapers downtown. A black Shelby charges out the police garage ramp onto the street. Alone at a red light, Donovan Fillard drops the two windows down. The exhaust rumbles a mean moan. Echoes bounce off glass buildings as red lights turn to green. He shoves the accelerator to the floor. The turbocharger's six hundred horses scream in the black night while the back tires boil white smoke in the air. "This is a whole lot more fun than putzing around in a patrol car."

The Shelby idles down Wabash Avenue as the phone on the dash pings. Truk says, "Pull over past the next corner." Truk's computer screen has a street map with a green dot on it, Donovan's car. He watches the dot stop on Wabash Avenue.

With the engine off and the headlights darkened, Donovan waits. The street is busy; overhead lamps light up the sidewalk. A semi-organized circus of people, drunk and high, marches up and down the avenue.

Three skinny early-twenty-something boys step down the sidewalk wearing DePaul University sweaters and look for some late-night action. A girl carries a guitar case over her shoulder. Two couples talk and laugh while they cross the street in front of the Shelby. Drunk tourists scatter about the night.

The front door of the club closest to Donovan opens with music blaring. A hundred people walk past the car during the next hour.

He can't play games on his cell phone, no music in the car, no calls to his buddies about the muscle car. It's past 12:30, and his eyes grow heavy.

A bright yellow cotton eyelet shirt and hip-hugger bell-bottom pants catch Donovan's sleepy eye from the edge of the right side mirror. Euro's twenty-eight-inch white leather belt wraps tight around his waist. With a girl under each arm, they walk together and tell jokes. The girls laugh in unison. Euro's smile exposes his gold teeth.

Two big men follow behind. They look like six-foot-seven, three-hundred-pound Samoan offensive tackle twins. Flowing hair halfway down their backs bounces with each step. Bright red, tight-fitting t-shirts try to contain bulging steroid-induced pecs and biceps. Large white block letters across one chest spell 'FRANK,' in case anyone is curious. The other t-shirt broadcasts the name 'UMI.'

Donovan scoots down in the seat while his left index finger flips the remote side mirror adjustment switch. The electric motor hums as the mirror turns, putting Euro in the middle.

Two cars in front of him, Euro watches a right side mirror tilt on a black Shelby, eyes reflecting at him. His arms wrap around the girls' necks. Pulling the one to his left closer, he kisses her forehead while watching the eyes in the mirror. The three pivot into a bar behind the black car, with Frank and Umi following. Donovan sits quietly.

Twenty-five minutes later, Euro steps out of the bar with different girls under each arm but no tackles behind him. Euro ignores the Shelby and laughs out loud as they pass by. They disappear into another bar.

Two hard taps sound on Donovan's driver window. One of the Samoans stands next to him. The window rolls down halfway. Three big white letters, UMI, block his vision of the street.

"'Sup, man?" asks Donovan.

Umi snaps the window off and pitches it into the middle of the street. "You a cop?"

"Hey, don't mess with my car." Donovan's back muscles stand at attention as he slips the black nylon bag on the passenger seat under his legs.

"Go hang out somewhere else, 'fore you get hurt."

"I can stay here if I want to. What's wrong with me being here?" Donovan unzips the bag under his legs.

The right passenger window explodes, glass spews across the passenger seat. Frank sticks his head inside; his long hair covers half his face. A fetid breath rolls out his mouth. "'Cause you gonna get hurt."

The engine rumbles. "Got it."

Frank reaches across the seat, grabbing the stick shift. "Go now."

Donovan shoves the Sig barrel against Frank's enormous head inside the car. "I'll be leaving now if that's okay."

Frank releases the shifter and leans back. His hand pounds the roof, leaving a dent the size of a basketball.

Donovan drops the pistol on the floorboard, turns the car out onto the street, and shoves the pedal to the floor, leaving two black strips while the thunder of exhaust bounces off the buildings. Donovan's thumb pushes the only phone number listed on the cell stuck to the dashboard.

"What do you got?" a voice asks.

"Is this Truk?"

"Yeah."

"I got spotted. Euro's two bodyguards ran me off."

"That didn't take long to pick you out."

"I did nothing, promise. I sat in the car and counted skirts walking by."

"Park around the block, get out, and watch from across the street."

Donovan turns the corner. "Get out? No. Remo said not to get out of this car."

"What car?"

"Um, nothing...I meant just a car."

Truk watches the green dot on the screen turn the corner. "Get out, sit your scrawny ass in a dark corner, and don't lose him." The phone goes dead.

Donovan hides in a dark corner across the street from the bar. At two AM, Frank and Umi step out of the bar and look up and down the curbs for the black Shelby they ran off. Umi steps into the middle of the street and turns back to the bar. A quick nod of his head gives the okay for Euro to step out. Frank whistles one long shriek to a dark gray Mercedes E550 convertible, top down, parked a half block away. Headlights pop on, and the car pulls in front of the bar. The two tackles squeeze into the back seat as Euro settles in the front passenger seat. Two girls with short skirts and long legs blow kisses and wave goodbye.

Donovan taps his Sig Sauer in his pocket, sits in the shadows, and watches the convertible roll away. He sprints to his Shelby around the corner and jumps in, fires the engine up, and pops the clutch. His thumb presses a phone button on the top of the dashboard.

Truk answers, "Talk."

"I'm following them, four in all, in a gray Mercedes convertible."

"Okay, I got you on the GPS," Truk says. "Just follow them. Nothing stupid."

"He is already two blocks in front of me and has green lights ahead of them. If you want me to follow them, I need you to turn the lights all red around here. I'll lose them if they turn the corner. Can you do that?"

"Yes, we can turn all the downtown lights red," Truk says.

Three seconds pass, all the lights flash red, and the Benz stops. The Shelby, with headlights off, hovers a block behind the Mercedes. He squints at the license plate, KRUL BENZ.

Donovan sizes up the situation. Both cars face south on Wabash Avenue, with a few scattered parked cars against both curbs and two empty lanes going both ways. A full moon glows overhead above the skyscrapers and makes it easy to see the Benz. Do they see him? People letting out of the bars look for nonexistent taxis. He places the pistol between the console and passenger seat. "Truk, you sure you want me to follow?" Donovan asks.

"Stay back a block and quietly follow."

"Can I follow if they run? I told you I got racing experience."

Chapter 27

The Benz stops at the intersection for the red light. Euro watches every light turn red. "Look around, Jamal. Red lights mean we got ourselves an Irish shit sandwich." His fingers check the full clip in his Glock. "We don't need to dodder here." From the right side mirror, Euro watches the black Shelby sit one block back with the lights off. "I must be thick as a plank for being here. That cop is behind us." Euro yells, "Go!"

◆

"Don't give a shit what Detective Wolf said," barks Truk. "I said, stay back and follow them. Stay on the phone, and I'll talk you around the area."

"This is my area. I know downtown."

Tires squeal as the Benz turns left.

The Shelby's bright lights burst on as Donovan shoves the gearshift to first. "Green flag time," he says with a big smile. The car leaps like a horse out of a racing gate. "I needed this little baby in the championship race last year." He slams the gearshift into second as he drifts around the corner.

On the monitor screen, Truk watches the green dot turn off Wabash. "I'm calling for backup," Truk says on the Bluetooth. "Give me five minutes."

"In five minutes, this is all over," Donovan yells.

A couple, arm in arm, scurry back onto the sidewalk and watch the two cars turn hard down the road. Metal scaffolding lines along the right curb in front of a partially renovated building. The Benz flies down the dark street. Bystanders and cars angrily wait for the lights to change green. Donovan's side mirror shatters as the right side of the car bangs against the scaffold. "Remo is not going to like that." His foot shoves the pedal to the floor. His head snaps back against the headrest as the tachometer ramps to 5000 RPM in seconds. He slams the stick into third gear. The Shelby's two front pipe grille guards bounce hard against the Benz's rear bumper.

Jamal shouts, "What the hell is he doing? Cops don't do that."

"That's not a cop car. Turn right," Euro barks.

The tires on the Benz screech around the corner. Donovan downshifts to second; the RPMs jump to the 8000 red line as he follows inches behind the Benz.

"I can't lose this guy," Jamal yells.

"Turn left," Euro says.

The Benz rear slides wide and clips a parked car.

"Oh baby, I'm feeling homesick for the racetrack," Donovan says. "Let's play touch-and-go." The black pipe protrudes from the Shelby's front bumper and taps the Benz's back quarter panel. The left taillight shatters.

Frank turns around and climbs over the convertible boot onto the trunk, hair flowing like a shampoo commercial. Umi holds Frank's feet as he pulls out a pistol stuffed between his pants and the small of his back.

Storefronts fly by in a blur. The Shelby jams to third gear and surges to seventy-five, ramming the back end. The Mercedes bumper looks like a bent elbow. Frank's body swings wide across the trunk. Umi, crammed between the seats like a bloated water balloon, pulls hard on Frank's feet. Donovan rams the back bumper, throwing

Frank into the street. Umi aims his pistol at the windshield and fires twice.

Umi jettisons onto the Shelby hood. His left hand grabs the cowl induction scoop of the hood, the edge closest to the windshield. The butt of his pistol pounds the center of the glass, spidering across the windshield.

People along the sidewalk aim their phones at the two cars. Fingers point at the big man in red splayed across the hood.

Umi's bent fingers pull his body to the cracked windshield, now face-to-face with Donovan.

Donovan glances at Umi's face with a nose leaning heavily right and missing teeth. Apparently, he'd lost at least one fight; he's about to lose another tonight.

Jamal slams on the brakes of the Benz and turns right down a side street.

Umi's pistol swings around and aims at Donovan's head.

A quick downshift to second shoves the Shelby's front end low. The tachometer fast-forwards to the right, the engine screams to the breaking point, and the exhaust trumpets a loud 8500 RPMs. Umi's massive body slides down the hood, hands and arms stretch to their limits. His size-fourteen shoes scrape the concrete in front of the Shelby while thick left fingers still clutch the hood. Umi's gun fires, the phone explodes off the dashboard. Donovan dodges the plastic shrapnel as he turns right.

Truk's screen goes blank. "Where the hell is the car?" He swings around and yells, "Get this screen back up, fast, now!"

Chapter 28

The owner of a food cart pushes it across the next intersection. He sees wavering headlights speeding toward him; the Benz flies past. Donovan swerves toward the cart. "Are you hungry?" He shifts back to third and shoves the gas pedal to the floor as the Shelby lunges forward. Six hundred horsepower screams ahead as Umi slides against the windshield.

The owner desperately tries to push the cart safely to the sidewalk. At the last second, he dives away. The two-pipe grille guards ram the cart forward, flip it into the air, on top of Umi, and smash the windshield. Yellow mustard and hotdogs spew on top of him. The two-hundred-pound cart bangs the top of the roof and rolls past the trunk. Umi drops the gun and grabs the loose windshield by the corner, rips it off the car, and shoves it away, crashing to the ground.

Donovan swerves left and right, trying to throw the clinging maniac off the car. Umi's legs swing wildly back and forth. He grabs onto the hood with both hands.

Barricades and flashing yellow lights announce construction on the street two blocks ahead. Jamal slams on the brakes, a single taillight glares red. Tires screech past the intersection as he turns the wheel hard right. The Benz bounces over the curb into a corner parking lot and bangs against a parked car. Four other parked cars sit quietly under the overhead lights.

Donovan shoves the stick back to second, the engine whines. The Shelby turns hard right at the intersection before the parking lot. Foot to the floor, Donovan rides the emergency brake. White smoke billows from the back wheel wells as the rear drifts around the corner. Umi's legs are splayed across the hood with his feet clamped on the quarter panels. His hands hold the edge of the hood.

The Benz slaloms around four parked cars and jumps the curb to the street forty feet in front of the Shelby. Umi hangs across the hood with no windshield while Donovan shifts the Shelby up to third gear and charges at the Benz. Euro turns and aims his Glock behind Umi's head at Donovan.

In a second, the Shelby pulls even on the right side of the Benz at ninety-four miles an hour. The Benz shoves the Shelby toward the parked cars on the right.

"Oh no you don't," Donovan yells at Euro. "Jimmy Wilcox tried to squeeze me out at the championship race. He didn't get me then, and you're not getting me now." Donovan taps the brakes and turns the steering wheel left. The Shelby front end bangs against the Benz rear quarter panel. Euro fires wildly as the back end of the Benz bounces against parked cars. Donovan roars forward, now face-to-face again with Euro. Donovan turns the wheel hard, hits the Benz, shoving Euro against Jamal. Euro drops his Glock between his feet.

The convertible scrapes parked cars on the left curb. Broken glass and side mirrors explode in the air. The left side of the Benz looks like it's been through a cheese grater. Jamal turns hard right. Euro ducks. The Benz bounces the Shelby back in the middle of the road.

Streetlights still red, angry cars wait for a change to green. Two battered vehicles, door to door, fly through the intersection at ninety miles per hour. Sparks erupt between them.

Donovan quick-turns the wheel left, then straight. Umi's hands desperately grasp the edge of the hood. His body slides over the hood and across the front quarter panel with shoes scraping the asphalt.

Scaffolding grows out from the sidewalk again along the left side. An enclosed wooden pedestrian walkway narrows the street with multiple cars parked along the right curb. Only enough room for one car to pass. The speedometer points at eighty-five. The Benz jumps ahead. Umi lurches for Donovan and grabs the steering wheel.

A car from an alley turns right onto the street, twenty yards ahead. Donovan slams on the brakes. Umi turns the steering wheel. Donovan watches the scaffolding charge at him. There is nothing he can do. The Shelby flips and slams into a wooden walkway, shattering wood in every direction. The car slides on its roof and knocks over a fire hydrant. It settles against the storm drain at an intersection. A geyser of water shoots in the air and drops down on top of the smoking mass of bent metal.

Umi is buried under three stories of scaffolding. Donovan, belted in, hangs upside down. The Mercedes turns a corner and disappears.

Chapter 29

Remo's motorcycle coasts around the corner of Garfield Park. It looks like an open tomb of black nothing. A baseball field in disrepair has a bent chain-link fence behind home plate. The corner overhead streetlamp is dark, likely a result of a flying rock. Remo parks the motorcycle behind diseased cedar trees fifty feet away and grabs the duffle from his saddlebag, stuffed with everything he needs. He swings the strap over his shoulder. As he walks down the dark street, he pushes the light on his watch. It's 2:35 AM, twenty minutes after Euro's escape from Donovan and an hour before Rolly Chang's scheduled appearance for the heroin exchange.

Italian cypress trees, thirty-foot-tall green pencils, align down the street curb. They have doubled in height since the last time Remo was here. Broken flood lamps hover above a storage building; once upon a time, they beamed false protection onto the field.

Memories flash of double plays and home runs in high school. Remo's cleats once echoed down this same pathway.

He stops at the storage building with two rusted, full-length metal doors, one facing south and the other east. There is a bubble skylight on top with a roof that should have been replaced a decade ago.

After fifteen seconds of playing with the deadbolt lock, Remo opens the south door. His flashlight scans a room full of equipment. Two t-shirt air guns are attached to CO_2 tanks. Fifty white t-shirts with a Garfield Park logo on the front are rolled and stacked neatly in a corner. A sledgehammer and blue painter's tape are in a plastic Home Depot bucket next to twenty cans of white spray paint. A twenty-foot folding ladder lies on its side, and five six-foot metal tables with legs folded lean against the wall. A red plastic one-gallon container of gasoline sits next to a handheld string edger.

He places the duffle bag down on the floor, empties it and separates the contents: night vision goggles, a Sig Sauer P220 pistol with a suppressor, a sawed-off 12 gauge shotgun, and three hand grenades. He slips a pint bottle from inside his jacket and drains the last of the Bulleit Bourbon.

From outside, he pounds the red brick with a sledgehammer until a ragged hole emerges. Back inside, he slides the t-shirt air gun easily in and out of the hole. Remo fires two t-shirts from the air gun to fix the distance.

He straps five tables stacked together with painter's tape and leans them sideways, catty-corner from the doors. The ladder, open and locked, stands in the middle of the room with spray paint cans taped together under it. He douses gasoline on the spray cans. The smell is heavy. "This could go bad for me." He climbs up to the skylight on the roof and opens it. Silence meets black again. He steps back down.

Remo sits inside, in the dark, against the wall, and waits. Gasoline penetrates the stale air. Remo's watch slides across his wrist; it shows 3:42 AM. Chang is late. A rush of air chills his shoulders. His lips crave another bottle of bourbon.

His mind skims back to Afghanistan. Remo captured a teenager after an ambush. Days later, nine soldiers and the teenager were inside an MGPT, modular general purpose tent, conducting a trial. He didn't know how the tent exploded, but it killed everyone inside. Remo should have shot the kid.

Bringing in six kilos of heroin, a boatload of cash and a dead Rolly Chang will give Remo another star on his list. Chang needs to die tonight.

Remo looks through the hole in the wall as two headlights from a black Cadillac Escalade approach. Four twenty-six-inch-high gloss-black wheels turn slowly at the corner of the Garfield Park baseball field. The headlights go dark as the Escalade tires bump over the curb and roll down the pedestrian walkway in front of the building where Remo waits. The SUV stops. Two men dressed in green camo-colored Hawaiian shirts and army pants step out from the front seats, each with a shotgun strapped over their left shoulder. Remo recognizes them, Jiang and Yung Rui. Maggie said they skipped bail last month for armed robbery.

Jiang sees something white near the cypress trees and steps to a rolled-up t-shirt on the ground. He picks it up off the ground, flips it in the air, and catches it. The left back door of the Escalade opens. Expensive Italian shoes crunch the gravel. Rolly Chang snaps his lapels from his suit, straight out of page seven in *Esquire Magazine*.

"I don't like this, boss." Jiang holds the t-shirt up.

"What?" Rolly asks.

"Why are these here?" Jiang asks.

"That's okay, some kid probably dropped them."

He steps to the back of the Escalade as the back lid rises. Yung Rui grabs two small carry-on suitcases in the back.

Remo smiles. The snitch was right. Rolly has the heroin.

Seconds later, two Hispanic men, each with an automatic rifle, appear from behind the trees near the baseball field. One holds a strap on a stuffed duffle bag. Remo recognizes them. Johnny Rivera and Hector Ramirez have hidden from the cops and the cartel for three months. They need the heroin. Two million dollars on the street is enough for the cartel to forgive late payments. The bag drops in front of Rolly.

Johnny's breath mists in the icy air. "Eight hundred K."

It's Remo's lucky night, five scumbags ready for a fall.

Remo adjusts the night vision goggles, then checks the tightness of the suppressor on his pistol. The five light up neon green. He crouches down and takes a quick look at his sawed-off 12 gauge shotgun at the top of the ladder. He pats the three grenades in his cargo pants in case things go wild. The suppressor centers at the prize of the night, Rolly Chang. Remo's thumb eases the hammer back.

"Police," Remo yells out from inside the storage building. "Put your weapons down."

Jiang and Yung Rui turn toward the voice and answer with two shotgun blasts. Chunks of brick spray across the grass.

Remo ducks and then swings back. Rolly is gone. Remo fires, a bullet rips through Johnny's thigh. He drops next to the SUV like a cold sack of potatoes next to the duffle bag and cries out in pain.

"Wimp," Remo says.

The others scatter in the trees like mice.

With the goggles on, Remo watches three runners light up along the line of Italian cypress trees. Chicken shits, Remo thinks. I want to play cops and robbers, and you want to play hide and seek.

Two silent pops from Remo's pistol land in Yung Rui's chest with a sick thud. He falls backward, dead.

From behind a tree, Hector rips a line of bullets across the brick building.

Remo grabs the t-shirt gun and stuffs a pre-rolled shirt inside, and then a grenade. He turns the CO2 tank on, slips the plastic barrel through the hole in the wall and aims at the trees and fires. A fireball seventy feet away explodes a tree trunk to shreds, throwing metal and wood shrapnel in every direction. Another grenade explodes. Distant sirens wail in the air.

Bullets bounce off the metal door, and a gun butt pounds against it. Hector calls out, "Come out, ass wipe. I'm gonna kill you."

The gravel crunches under Hector's boots to the right as his legs cross the hole next to the door. Remo pulls the pin of the third grenade and rolls it five feet outside. Two seconds later, the explosion silences Hector.

Remo's pager vibrates. He pushes the automatic response, *Leave a number, I'm busy*. The pager vibrates again. The same scenario, *Leave a number, I'm busy*.

Jiang's shotgun barrel sticks inside the hole. Remo jumps behind the six stacked tables taped together. A shotgun blast rains down shattered brick above Remo's head. He answers the phone. "Maggie, can't talk now..."

"I have a hit on me!" she screams. "Remo, did you hear me? I have a hit on me! What the hell am I supposed to do?"

He climbs up the ladder. The sirens blare in the distance.

The metal door explodes open from a shotgun blast to the doorknob. Jiang calls out, "Come on out, you piece of shit. I'm gonna cut your balls off." Jiang rushes into the room. A shotgun blast blows a hole in the middle of the tables on the floor. His eyes follow the ladder to the ceiling as Remo's feet disappear.

He stands over the skylight and says, "Hey, Jiang." Remo fires his shotgun at the paint cans; they explode like popcorn in a hot pan. Jiang drops the shotgun and covers his head. Remo fires again, and the metal door slams shut. Buckshot ricochets, hitting Jiang and knocking him down.

Remo pitches the shotgun to the grass and stuffs his pistol down the waistband of his pants.

He pulls a Zippo lighter out of his front pocket and flicks the wheel across the flint. A red-yellow flame rises. With his phone in his left hand and lighter in his right, he tells her, "Hold on, girl." He drops the lighter inside the building.

"Damn it, Remo. Talk to me," Maggie yells.

On his hands and knees, Jiang struggles to stand. He watches the lighter drop from the roof to the floor. "No. No," Jiang yells as he covers his head.

With a whump, the gasoline and paint ignite. A blast of heat shoves Jiang against the door. His arms rise in front of his face, and he screams in pain. His nylon shirt melts against his skin, his black hair flames like a torch at night. Hands sear against the hot doorknob as he opens it and charges outside.

Remo runs across the roof. Emergency red and blue lights bounce off buildings three blocks away. He turns his attention back to Maggie. "What do you mean, a hit? Who told you about a hit?"

"An informant told one of the undercover cops about twenty minutes ago. What am I supposed to do?"

"Stay there." He closes the flip phone and stuffs it in his pocket.

Remo jumps to a tree limb and drops to the grass as fingers of fire envelop the burning building. Smoke billows out of the skylight like an angry volcano.

Rolly Chang hurries toward the street with the duffle bag strap over his right shoulder while he drags one of the wheeled suitcases with his right hand. Johnny Rivera hangs on to Rolly's left shoulder as blood flows out the bullet hole in his thigh.

Remo marches around the building. Flames roar from the open door and the skylight. White powder is spread across a bullet-shredded suitcase. Hector's mutilated body lies on the ground. Jiang is down on his left side next to the Escalade front door with most of his hair burnt off, face half melted away and clothes still smoldering.

Remo's boot shoves Jiang's shoulder. He moans as he rolls onto his back.

"That didn't go like you thought, did it, Jiang?" Remo points his pistol at Chang. "Hold up, Rolly," he says. "You too, Johnny."

They stop. "Are you going to shoot me in the back?" Johnny asks.

Damn it, not the way I wanted this to go down. "No, I'm going to arrest you. Put your hands up."

"Is that Detective Remo Wolf?" Rolly asks. He pushes the suitcase to the side. "You here alone? No one else? No friend, no partner? Shame to hear about Bobby Lynch."

"Shut up, Chang. Put your hands up."

"We all need friends. Some are close and some are distant. Friends help. I have a friend that wears a black fedora. You know anyone like that?"

"I said, shut the hell up," Remo yells.

Fedora hides behind one of the cypress trees, holding a mobile phone head-high, and records flames ravaging the roof while Remo stands with his gun pointing at Rolly and Johnny. Fedora's chrome revolver rises toward Remo. A thumb pulls the hammer back.

"Some of my best friends are inconspicuous. You have any of those, Detective Wolf?"

"Shut up, Chang. Drop the bag. Turn around and put your hands where I can see them."

Remo steps back from the heat and fire. The Escalade is between Remo and Fedora without a clear shot. The video zooms in as Fedora steps toward the Escalade to get a better angle. A fire truck horn blares closer.

"Hear that backup, Chang? You got less than a minute. Turn around and give it up."

"I don't think so." Rolly slips his Glock out of his shoulder harness.

Johnny nods as his hand moves to the gun inside his belt. "Ready," Johnny says.

Before they can turn around, a bullet pierces Johnny's back, and he falls forward, dead. Chang drops the bag and runs. Remo spins around. Jiang is down next to the Escalade, his pistol in hand. Jiang's bullet missed Remo and hit Johnny.

A flash of an exploding tent in Afghanistan rushes through Remo's mind.

He aims the pistol toward Jiang. "Put the gun down."

Jiang lies on his side and rolls to his back, still holding the pistol.

"Put it down, Jiang. You got no place to go."

Jiang swings the gun toward Remo.

Two bullets rip into Jiang's body.

Police cars jump the curb and charge across the grass. They find four dead men, two suitcases of heroin and a duffle bag full of hundred-dollar bills. The storage building burns as flames jump to the cypress trees.

Fedora disappears into the dark, missing the chance to kill Wolf.

Remo runs to his motorcycle while he pushes 'recall' on the phone. Before he can say hello, Maggie's voice charges through the phone. "Don't you ever hang up on me again."

He decides it's best not to argue with a screaming woman. "Pull your ladder down from the ceiling and climb up into the attic. Still got the pistol I gave you?"

Her voice quivers, "Yes."

"Good, I'll be there in twenty minutes."

"I'll be dead in twenty minutes. I need to call Truk and the SWAT team now."

"Go up in the attic, cover yourself with whatever you have upstairs. Remember our code we have?" His boot shoves the kickstarter down as the Indian engine roars. "I think I know who it might be."

"I'm scared, Remo."

"Go upstairs. If you don't hear the code and someone pulls the ladder down, then shoot to kill."

Chapter 30

The increasing RPMs vibrate his arms as the Indian charges down East 290. Head down, his black hair flaps in the wind as the speedometer needle crosses 100 mph.

West of the Chicago Kenwood District, behind a large mansion, Maggie's house is a twelve-hundred-square-foot converted pool house with a front room, kitchen, hallway, and bedroom/bath. Her house once held caustic pool chemicals, so it is the only house on the block with commercial overhead fire sprinklers in the ceiling.

A grateful man came to her after she prosecuted his daughter's killer nineteen months ago. The killer got fifty years, she got the pool house.

This is not the first time she has been threatened. Last year a crazed gangbanger escaped Cook County Jail and went straight for her house. He got as close as twenty yards to her front door before the mansion owner's guard dogs almost ate him for a midnight snack. Maggie thought the owner would make her move, instead he laughed, praised his dogs, and threw her a pool party.

Chicago wind is cold, especially turning the corner onto I-90 as the icy mist from Lake Michigan slaps Remo's face. The Indian rapidly downshifts on the exit ramp and slows to sixty-five. Remo rides the bumps on Forty-Seventh Street like a motocrosser.

A blanched yellow 1987 Mazda with two brown quarter panels sits unattended at the corner of Forty-Ninth and Vincennes, out of place in this high-priced neighborhood. Remo stops and searches the car. A picture of Maggie McCall sits on the passenger seat.

This is what Euro and Jersey had talked about at the bar. 'The Law' was not a cop. 'The Law' was a prosecutor.

Remo rides his bike up the driveway of an empty house for sale. Lights and engine off, he rolls to the unattached five-car garage and hides his bike behind the house. He unlocks the saddlebags and pulls out his pistol and two more magazines, a twelve-inch sawed-off 12 gauge shotgun and three grenades.

Remo speeds down the alley as barking dogs announce a stranger is nearby, nothing he can do about that. His pager vibrates in his shirt pocket—*someone here, front door open. Lights cut off.*

Remo climbs over the vine-covered wall surrounding the mansion complex. He has been to her house many times, but never over the fence at four in the morning. Remo will have to apologize to the owner for what is about to happen. He runs toward Maggie's house. He hears a Doberman running full speed as it barks incessantly. How did Euro and Jersey make it to Maggie's place without being chewed up by the dogs?

Euro hears dogs outside. He turns and steps to the front window, but the darkness lends nothing to see.

The dog charges toward Remo. Thirty yards away, Remo stops and stands arms wide apart. He orders, "*Arretez,*" French for stop, like the owner taught him to say. The dog stops in front of him. "*Asseyez.*" It sits like a statue. Remo charges for the front door as the dog turns its head and watches.

Chapter 31

Maggie's house is dark. Euro cut the electricity before entering through the front door. He steps into Maggie's bedroom and raises his Uzi with a suppressor on it. A quick burp from the Uzi rips through the pillow and the bed.

Maggie hides in the attic. Slow footsteps tread below her in the bedroom. She doesn't know who is in her house. Maggie bites her hand to quell the mounting fire in her spine as she pulls her knees up under the blanket. Her thumb flips the safety off the pistol. Is Remo close?

Euro looks behind him to Jersey with a disappointing nod that Maggie McCall was not in her bed. Someone must have tipped her off. He feels her somewhere in the house.

"Hey, little Miss DA," Euro calls out. "I got a pressie for you. Have a think and let's get this over."

His flashlight points toward the kitchen. The Uzi's rapid, suppressed sounds rip through every glass and plate in the cupboards. Broken marble flies off the countertops. Just as quickly, total silence returns. He looks at the refrigerator and smiles at Jersey. Stacks of cold food sit on the counter next to the fridge. Did she pull them out? Is she hiding inside? Bullets shred the stainless steel front. Jersey pulls the door open with hopes of her dead body inside. Instead, nothing but an orange cloud of OJ and milk pours on the floor.

"Don't be a posh, girlfriend," Jersey calls. "Come out and talk to us."

Euro barks out orders. "Maggie McCall, get your ass out here now!" His white platform shoes clomp on the tile just like Euro's favorite TV character, Linc Hayes, in the 1968 show *The Mod Squad*.

Jersey's smile returns. "If you come out, I won't make it hurt so much."

Euro nods. "Right, that be grand."

Remo squats next to the front door. He recognizes Euro's and Jersey's voices.

Euro's flashlight shines from the kitchen across a large open front room with a couch and two thick leather chairs. "Heard you got a bit of Irish in ya. I'm gonna need to ride that fine thing before I leave."

"Talk American, Euro. I can't understand that crazy Irish shit," Jersey says.

Remo takes a quick glance around the doorjamb. He must separate them. He aims his shotgun at the couch in the front room and blows a hole through it. The stuffing smolders while embers float down.

Euro drops against the wall. Jersey's not in control anymore. She slips to the bedroom, out the window, and disappears.

"Euro, what the hell are you doing here? This is my job!" Remo yells past the open door.

He turns to the voice in the front room. "Che, baby. What's the craic?" What the hell is he doing here? "Come on out and let's take this bitch down." He swings the Uzi toward the front door. "Heard she's got a bit of Irish in her. It'll be a shame to kill her."

Euro rips another round in the hallway closet, then reaches for the ceiling pull-down rope slowly swinging in the air. He hears a snap-click of the shotgun being racked in the other room. Euro flinches as another blast sprays wood shrapnel against the wall. A curtain catches fire.

"Thought I saw some movement behind the couch," Remo says. "Is Jersey with you?"

Euro spins around to an empty hallway. A head nod to Jersey, but she is not there. "Jersey? It looks like my sweet bean left me." A black taped double magazine slips out and flips back into the Uzi. A full mag is loaded. "It's just you and me, Che." A quick burp in the ceiling drops white fiberboard to the ground. "You sure this is where you want to be, Che?"

"I came down here to help you, you son of a bitch. My contract said to follow you and make sure it's done right," Remo says.

"Your contract? Did that gobshite Fedora send you?"

Fever rushes Remo's spine. "You call him Fedora?"

Euro's eyes beam down the hall. "You've never met Fedora, have you?" He feels Che on the other side of the wall. "You're a bit of a chancer coming here tonight."

"Euro, I got no beef with you."

Euro's Uzi shreds the drywall on the front of the house. "Show your face." Another curtain laps across the burning one. Red and orange flames roll up the wall to the ceiling.

Overhead fire sprinklers hanging from the ceiling pop on, soaking them both.

Smoke billows inside the attic. Maggie's bare feet are hot from the fire piercing the ceiling. She holds a towel over her mouth to hide her cough.

"It's me, Che. Give me a break." Remo sees Euro's dark reflection off the mirror at the end of the hall. "I'm just here to help you."

Euro hears an odd thump bounce off the wall and on the floor, rolling to a stop. It's a hand grenade just a few feet away from him. Euro jumps into the bedroom, but there is no explosion. Instead, a dull burst releases billowing smoke.

Remo raises his 9 mm pistol with a silencer, it pops twice. The mirror shatters. The frame falls to the ground, revealing bullet holes in the wall.

Euro's Uzi burps a long two seconds. Fire jumps off the curtain to the leather chairs. He jumps out of the bedroom window.

Distant sirens bounce off low clouds. Deep horns moan their approach.

"Maggie, stay up there. Don't move. He's outside and coming around to the front."

Another Uzi burst explodes the front doorknob off and sends it flying across the room. Remo replies with a shotgun blast the size of a football through the middle of the door. The top hinge rips off from the wood molding. Uzi bullets charge back through the shredded door.

Water pours from the sprinklers above. Head down, Remo runs through the raining water into the kitchen and fires his pistol behind him.

Euro aims through the shadows flickering from the fire. He hears a growl behind him. Euro spins, his eyes wide with fear as a Doberman charges like a bullet train. Black lips separate as a blitzkrieg of white teeth finds its mark into Euro's left forearm. He screams, falling to the floor as blood spews and spasms rip through his muscles. The dog pulls, teeth grind, its head twists back and forth. Euro's Uzi barrel sticks in the dog's ribs and he pulls the trigger. The dead dog flies against the wall.

Water pours from the overhead sprinklers. Blood splatters from Euro's arm to the floor as his Uzi burps a line of black holes neck-high across the hallway. He gasps for air as he rushes the kitchen entrance.

Remo's 9 mm sticks up over the counter; two bullets hit Euro's injured left arm.

"Damn it, Che." Euro slithers away on the other side of the wall between the kitchen and hallway. Like a mop slopping through blood, a red streak follows Euro's limp forearm.

"What the hell are you doing, Euro? I told you I'm here to help you get rid of the girl." Remo snaps the empty magazine out and shoves another in the handle. He fires again and pierces three more 9 mm bullets into the kitchen drywall. He hears a thud on the other side of the wall. "Euro? You still there?" Remo sits up. "Come on, man. Let's stop this silliness and do the job."

The Uzi sprays another line across the wall. Remo drops to the floor as blood flows from his right shoulder. His pistol slides across the floor, out of reach.

Red and blue lights swirl across the front of the house. A fire engine's horn blows long. Blood charges down Euro's yellow sleeve and flows past his hand to the floor. He steps around the corner of the kitchen. His face is paler than a clean sheet. "Che, baby. You look hurt."

"I'm a cop, Euro. Put the Uzi down. It's over."

Euro pitches the empty Uzi on the broken countertop as he slips out a knife from a leg sheath. "Jersey always said killing cops is fun. Maybe as good as getting gold teeth." He touches the tip of the blade to a molar. "Got another one of those this morning. Today is my lucky day." He aims the point toward Remo.

"Had your chance," Remo says as he sits on the floor.

Euro's curious look turns wide-eyed.

Two bullets hit Euro's back and head. Blood splatters forward as he falls inches from Remo. The smoke clears with Maggie's two hands holding her gun, pointing at the dead man. Behind her, fire crawls up the ceiling.

"Get out," Maggie yells as sirens whirl in the distance.

"What? I saved you," Remo says. "He would have killed you if I didn't show up."

"Get out of the house before Miss Split Ends and the news media show up. If she finds you, your cover is blown." Maggie slides the pistol across the countertop. She pulls on his arm as Remo stands. "Go out the back door and do what you always do when you get shot. Call Truk, find Doctor What's His Name at the hospital, and I'll see you tomorrow."

❖

White nurse's shoes step quickly down the white tile floor. A woman in blue scrubs opens a door marked Private. The head of the bed is raised sixty degrees. Remo has never asked Nancy her age, but with cigarette wrinkles around her lips and eyes, he thinks a rough fifty years.

"Back again, detective?" Nancy asks.

"Nancy, I just can't stay away from you."

"You know, if you used your airline credit card for all these visits, you'd have enough points you could fly to Tahiti and stay a week for free."

Remo holds his hand out. "I promise, I'll try to slow down."

Two hard knocks on the door, and a reporter pushes the door open. Nancy does her best impression of a linebacker and rams her hands into the solar plexus of the skinny man. They both disappear into the hallway.

"No one is allowed past this door," Nancy says to the reporter. "It's my job to make sure all patients are resting; you will not mess with my care plan. Now, you need to move out of the way, or I will stick this long needle between your legs."

A few seconds later, Nancy steps back into Remo's room and shuts the door. Thank God for Nancy. Anyone else would have let the reporter take his picture.

She changes the bloody ABD pads as if nothing happened. "Dr. Turner will be here in a few minutes. Need anything?"

"Shot of bourbon?"

Nancy points at the door. "Across the street at the bar. Watch out for reporters."

Chapter 32

The next morning in the hospital room, Remo recovers from the bullet wound in his right shoulder. Maggie's hands fluff the pillow under his head as she intentionally shoves her cleavage in his face. His favorite perfume rolls out of the low-cut sweater.

"Thanks, Maggie. You're really good to me," he says.

Standing straight again, her cleavage disappears. Remo flinches when she pushes on the bandage a little too hard.

A nurse steps in and smiles. "Looks like Miss McCall has everything under control. If you need anything, push the call button." She disappears out of the room.

"Another eagle with a bullet hole. How many more do you have left without a hole in the middle?" Maggie asks.

"One on my right deltoid, why?"

Her fingertip traps a falling tear against her cheek, then she steps to the third-floor window and slides the white curtains open. "Want to know how many more times you're getting shot." Children play tag in the park across the street. Maggie watches people walk and laugh along the crisscross sidewalks. "Why were those people trying to kill me?"

"Not sure. Killing an assistant DA makes no sense." Remo is trying to figure out why there was a hit on Maggie. "Euro called him Fedora."

"Who?"

"The man with the black fedora, he called him Fedora."

"The same man that ambushed you and Bobby?" Maggie asks.

"Right. Who is this 'Fedora' person, and why did he want you dead? And why ambush Bobby and me?" Remo wondered if Fedora knew about the Killing Club, or was it a coincidence he picked Euro?

"Why me?" Maggie's arms stretch out. "Do I still have a hit on me?"

"I'll investigate more about Euro and the hit tomorrow."

Maggie turns back to him, her arms folded across her breasts. "This guy Euro, you knew his name. The two of you talked to each other during the shooting. How did you know him?"

"Just knew of him. I know a lot of people in my undercover work."

Her arms spread open. "No, I heard you when I was in the attic. You *knew* him. You were speaking to him about sharing the hit on me. Why?"

Remo pushes back against the pillows and sits higher in the bed. "Can I trust you with a secret?"

"Don't forget, I am a prosecutor."

"And I was in your bed two nights ago."

Her eyes glare, lips tighten. She checks to see if anyone else is in the room. "So, tell me."

Remo punches the pillow behind him a few times. He scoots back against it. "I know the group who are shooting the cops." He crosses his ankles and then uncrosses them.

"You know?"

"Euro was part of that group."

"You mean like a vigilante group? Are you in this group?"

"Come here, sit next to me, please."

"No. Did you know he was coming after me?"

"I figured it out after you called me. I thought it was on another cop. Never imagined it would be you."

"You knew he was going to kill someone?" She steps back. "You need to be careful what you say to me."

"Might as well tell the whole story," Remo says. "I'll claim temporary insanity, head injury, concussion, PTSD, something while saving your life."

She sits in the chair and crosses her legs. "Go on."

A few minutes later, Maggie rushes out of the hospital room.

Remo sits in his bed. "Well, that didn't go as I hoped."

❖

"Truk, I'm in trouble," Maggie says on the phone as she walks out of the hospital.

"Yeah, heard someone tried to kill you."

"I need protection. A bodyguard. You."

Truk leans back in his office chair. "I work for the Chicago Police and don't have time to be your personal bodyguard."

"This Euro fellow is dead, and some woman named Jersey was in my house. She ran out when Remo got there. I'm worried this woman may want to finish the job. I'll pay you two weeks of vacation until the election is over. I know you need the money."

Truk sits up. He calculates his winnings from the odds on the next bet. "The Bears play the Saints in New Orleans on Sunday. I could take Jersey there for a few days."

"Send that big guy you have over to my office now, and I want someone near me anytime I am outside my office. You take the bitch out of town for two weeks, not two days, and I will pay you double your two weeks off."

"Double? Deal."

Chapter 33

Remo sits on his bike a block away from Jersey's house. His snitch said Rosie, Jersey's sister, is hiding out in the house. She jumped parole, and there's a BOLO, be on the lookout, for her. Instead, Remo waits and watches from his binoculars as two thugs step to Jersey's front door. One looks like it may be a woman.

A knock on Jersey's front door startles Rosie. Her finger pushes the window blind down. A man and a woman are on the porch; both wear wife-beaters and brown camo pants. The woman is bald, and the man looks like a hairy alien.

"We know you're in there, Rosie. Come on out."

"What you want?" Rosie asks from the window.

"The money, now."

With a knife held behind her back, she opens the door. "Not ready yet. Still got a week."

"Effey doesn't want to wait another week. She wants it now." The hairy alien slips a pistol out from his waistband and holds it close to his chest. "Understand?"

"Yeah, I understand. A deal is a deal. I got one more week."

"How about I shoot you in the head and take a picture? Effey would be good with that."

Rosie spins the serrated hunting knife handle in front of them. "How about I cut your balls off and stuff 'em down your twin sister's throat?"

"Time to be Che again," Remo says. He fires up the bike.

A white Indian motorcycle streaks across the driveway and pulls up inches from the front steps. The bald woman turns toward the bike and sees a wide man in a tight Chicago Bears t-shirt.

"And who are you?" the bald woman asks.

"Me?" The motorcycle engine dies. "Name's Che." He gazes at their outfits. "Must be Match Your Partner's Clothes Day." He steps off the bike. "I'm a close friend of the family. Rosie, these guys bothering you?"

"You need to leave before I kill you," the hairy alien says.

Che slips two pistols out of his shoulder holsters under his black leather jacket and steps up to the porch. "Listen, Bigfoot. Take Miss Potato Head with you and move on. Time for you to leave us alone."

"I'm going to break your neck," the man says.

Che shoves the gun barrels against the intruder's stomachs. "Let's see if I can make both of you dead before you hear the gunfire. Can you count to three? One, two—"

"All right. Okay. You want to play Clint Eastwood and save this trash, go ahead." The bald woman turns back to Rosie. "Money in six days, or we come back."

❖

Inside, Rosie holds out a bottle of beer. "So, you're Che?"

"Some people call me that."

"Motorcycle out front, black hair, big arms. Jersey told me 'bout you."

He leans back on the couch. "Pillow talk?"

"She my sister, asshole."

He chuckles and holds up his beer. Their bottles clink together. "Your face is clean, not messed up like Jersey's."

Rosie waves her hand around her face. "She the only one in the family with that shit."

"What are you doing here, Rosie, besides breaking parole and hiding in a murderer's house?"

Rosie takes a long swig from the bottle. "Visitation."

"You say that like someone who's recently been in prison." Che matches her long swig.

"Don't worry 'bout where I been," Rosie says. "Why you here?"

"Came by to see Jersey. Got some work for her."

"Work? Like killin'?"

Che takes another swig from the bottle. "Don't know what you're talking about."

"My sister told me what you and those other rejects doin'. I want in."

"You tell me where Jersey is." He finishes his beer and drops the bottle on the floor. "What's she up to now? I mean, she working a hit?"

"You seen them idiots at the door. I need ten big by next week."

"Ten? I can get you ten. Where's your sister?"

Chapter 34

It's 12:18 in the morning, and Jersey stands at an intersection with no car in sight. A street sweeper rolls down the street, cleaning curbs and gutters. Her thumbs tap on Euro's phone. *Still want contract filled?*

Two minutes pass. *Who r u?*

Jersey replies. *Someone close to the owner of this phone. I know about it.*

A stoplight changes from red to green. The 'L' train clacks above her head. Two teen boys in oversized jackets step to the intersection across the street from her. The smaller one pings open a switchblade knife in his right hand. He smiles as he says, "Look what I have for you."

Jersey slips the phone into her back pocket and glares at him. She pushes her sleeves up to her elbows and raises her right fist into the air.

Four young eyes focus on her right fist, the size of an Acme brick. Her eyes brighten, her smile widens as she crosses the street. The kid closes the switchblade, unaware of Jersey's left hook charging at his temple until it is too late. Her backhand slams across the other boy's nose. Blood splatters across the cement.

Jersey grabs a handful of coat and pitches the kid against the building like a worn pillow. When she steps away, only their painful groans follow her.

A half a block down the street, her phone dings a reply. *Same place in twenty min.*

Jersey answers. *Bring money.*

Three blocks away from the destination, she passes a busy vaping store. There are plenty of people inside and out: drunk pedestrians, squawking rappers, stoic recreants and psycho renegades. They see a woman, alone, an easy target.

A few feet ahead, two more idiots stand in the center of the sidewalk. Their arms crossed like gangstas in a hip-hop movie. They look a little older, a little more significant this time. She slips the hunting knife from the neck sheath under the front of her shirt as she crosses the street. The traffic light turns yellow. The chrome blade flickers from the streetlight. Jersey stares at the one she needs to take out first. She watches naïve eyes glance down at her hands. One boy taps his cheek. They separate as she passes between without a sound. Jersey's knife slides back into its sheath.

Fifteen minutes later, Jersey is the only customer inside the Black Raven Tavern. Almost as large as a Hollywood actress's closet, the small bar consists of three tables with well-worn vinyl booths and a bar with four high-rise stools.

A brass bell above the glass front door announces someone's presence. Fedora enters wearing a wool overcoat, gloves, and a black hat.

Jersey's eyes look up from four empty shot glasses. "Sit down, let's talk," Jersey says as her finger spins a hunting knife around on the tabletop.

"What do you know? Interesting."

"Not expecting me?" Jersey asks.

"You told me you wanted out after Euro's death."

"Changed my mind."

The stone-faced bartender slides two more shots of whiskey on Jersey's table as Fedora slides in on the other side of the booth.

The bartender asks, "You want a shot?"

Fedora watches the knife spin, reaches across the table, and stops it turning. "No, nothing. Leave us alone."

"I'm back in. You deal with me and only me from now on," Jersey says. She downs both shot glasses. "Did you send two contracts on Maggie McCall?"

"No, of course not." Fedora's hands drop below the table. "I expected Euro to be quick and clean. He was sloppy, too full of himself. He didn't follow the rules."

"Shut up. He's dead. Drop it, or this knife will slice your throat open."

Fedora leans across the table toward Jersey. The revolver barrel taps Jersey's inner thigh. "Think you can do that before I put two bullets in your gut?"

Jersey jams the tip of the knife into the tabletop. "I'm here to finish the job."

Fedora's eyes shift to the bartender behind the bar. He flips a towel over his shoulder, then lines up the wine glasses for tomorrow's crowd.

Fedora speaks low to avoid the bartender's ears. "The deal's off. He got stupid and died. He was supposed to do a quick, clean hit. The only one dead is Euro. Do you know who came to help her?"

The bartender wipes the corner countertop near them.

"You." Fedora flashes the chrome revolver at him. "Go check on something in the alley and don't come back 'til I say so."

"Not supposed to have that in here," the bartender says.

"That right? You going to call someone about it?"

He shakes his head. "No." He turns toward the back door.

"Before you go," Jersey says, "I need two more shots."

The bartender pauses for a reply. "I got work to do before closing."

Jersey slaps a Ben Franklin on the table. "Put the bottle on the table and get out."

The metal back door slams shut.

The brim of the black hat slides lower over the forehead. "Deal's off. Someone helped her. Maggie McCall is still alive with round-the-clock protection. I got another plan to take out both. Don't need you."

"Both? You got two hits?"

"Yeah. Did Euro forget to tell you there were two? Maybe you're not the right person. I should find someone else."

"You got me and you're gonna pay me." The tip of her knife scrapes a large dollar sign on the tabletop. "You're a piece of shit and I would kill you in a second, but as long as you supply me with money, you can live."

Fedora slides to the end of the booth and stands an arm's length away from the knife while holding the chrome revolver. "I got my own plan."

"You don't have shit, otherwise why'd you come here? McCall don't like you, do she, because maybe you got something to hide?" Jersey leans back in the booth. "I'm guessing once she's voted in as the new State's Attorney, you are shit out of luck."

With pupils wide open, Fedora stares too long at Jersey. The gun barrel taps the tabletop as the finger moves to the trigger.

Jersey glances at the revolver, then back to Fedora. Jersey's fingers wrap around the knife handle, the tip scrapes across the table.

Fedora's lips relax, eyes blink. The revolver slips back in the coat pocket as Fedora sits back down. "Same deal, same price. Ten before, ten when done."

"Twenty," Jersey says. She thought to herself, twenty thousand? Euro told me we were going to split ten thousand, fifty-fifty. That slimy bastard was going to keep the second ten for himself and not tell me. "You said two hits? McCall and someone else for ten apiece." She twists the knifepoint into the wood. "Everyone is on edge, watching. It will be much harder now. Forty sounds good for two. Twenty now and twenty when I finish. You bring the twenty with you?"

"You already have Euro's cash."

"You gave that to Euro, and he's in hell. You want it back? Go get it from him. Now I want sixty."

"Thirty."

"Let's take a look at the picture of the second hit."

A gloved finger slides nervously across the red pin on the hat. A picture is pulled from the inside coat pocket. "But you do this guy first, and then McCall second. This guy is her head of security and a police captain. He's too dangerous to keep alive."

Jersey holds the picture and leans back on the cracked vinyl booth. "Captain Kurt Maxwell? You want me to kill Truk...in Chicago?"

"He has his boys around McCall all day and all night. With him dead, those dumbass cops won't know what to do. McCall will be easy pickings."

"Truk is a Chicago icon. Everybody knows this man. Everybody loves this man, except you." Jersey flips the photo back across the table. "I'd be dead the next morning if I killed him here." Jersey grabs the bottle and pours two more shots. "I need more than forty for him in the mix. It's going to take sixty, thirty upfront and thirty more to take him out."

"Didn't say where you had to do it. Take him out of town. Fuck his brains out and shoot him in the head."

Jersey ponders the thought. "Maybe." She drains one shot glass in a single gulp. "Rumor on the street is he's been talking about me since I saw him at the police station."

"Fifty. For that, you make it clean. No collateral damages."

"Need more," Jersey says, "not enough for the two."

Fedora reaches inside the left coat pocket.

Jersey's fingers wrap around the knife handle again. "Slowly," she warns.

A thick white envelope from the inside pocket is placed between them.

"This is twenty, thirty more later. Take it or leave."

"No, thirty now, thirty when done. I'll take that white envelope on the other side of the coat."

Fingers slide the other envelope out. "That is ten and twenty. Thirty more when they're both dead. Where are you taking him?"

Jersey stacks the two envelopes on the table. "Okay. Deal. You don't want to know where I'm going?" She drinks the last shot and pushes the glass to the other side of the table. "I got a spot in mind."

A matchbook with SECOND CITY scripted on the front cover sits in the battered copper ashtray. Fedora pulls out a match and strikes it. The phosphorus tip burns bright yellow. The match burns halfway and placed on top of the envelope. A black circle grows on the burning paper. "Finish the job before the election." The gloved hand smothers the flame. "Or you're as dead as this match."

Chapter 35

"It's 2:15 in the morning, still early," Jersey says as her hand pulls on Truk's arm. "Let's go downstairs with the crowd."

Truk stands halfway up a narrow one-floor stairwell in the French Quarter of New Orleans. A twinge creeps up the back of his brain. It's a feeling when something is getting ready to go down. It's what's kept him alive in Chicago, but he's not there now. He knows every inch of Chicago and nothing about New Orleans.

This is risky. Truk knows she's a killer, but he promised Maggie he would take Jersey out of town and stay close to her. Maybe this is too close. He should have blown that baseball-size hole in Jersey at the police station when he had the chance, but this woman makes him drool.

Black fleur-de-lis logos over gold paper horns with white plastic mouthpieces blare outside. Firecrackers pop, sparklers spray feverish glitter in the air.

"This is N'awlins, baby," Jersey sings out. "And a rockin' party crowd on a Sunday night. Ain't nuthin' gonna stop these people after the Saints beat Chicago 39-33 in overtime."

Truk looks down the stairs to the street at people walking by with their twenty-four-ounce clear beer cups in hand. "Don't know, Jersey." He wiggles his arm as the platinum watch slides to his wrist. His thumb spins his Super Bowl diamond ring around his right index finger. "You know I got someone looking for me to collect their money after the game. I can't believe the Bears lost. Maybe it wasn't such a good idea to come here. The bastard already called me and said I owe him tonight, or I'm dead. Could be out there waiting for his money."

"Good God, Truk. That shit happens in Chicago, not here. Ain't nobody going to take you out for a lousy bad gambling debt in N'awlins."

"Bad debt? This ain't some little bad debt. I owe fifty big ones." Truk checks his pocket like he has the money. "Damn Bears. That front line should have held the Saints at the goal line. They ran the same play nine years ago, and I stopped that running back jumping over the line. All Chicago got now is a bunch of pansies. Maybe I should come out of retirement and teach those Bears how to tackle."

"We came here for some fun." Her arms wrap around his neck, a wet tongue flicks against the tip of his nose. "I will protect your sweet, retired linebacker ass." The heel of her knee-high platform boot pierces his thin boat shoe, twisting between his toes like an ice pick. "These boots will save you."

His hands slide down her back and over her ass. Truk feels nothing underneath. A smile crosses his lips. "*Sure* you can do that? Where's that knife you always carry? It's damn sure not under this dress."

"This dress?" She pushes him away and holds her arms out straight. "I bought it yesterday just for you. Do you like these arm-length black gloves? I think they make me look sophisticated."

His eyes scan the low-cut, knee-length yellow dress with a colorful New Orleans jester painted across the left breast and abdomen.

She spins fast enough to prove there is nothing underneath. "You like it?"

His brain devours this six-foot, Southern girl born a hundred and fifty miles from the Crescent City itself. He likes big women, meaning big muscles and a bigger ego. "Yeah, I like."

Truk trudges down the steps.

"Don't feel good about roaming the streets. I'm too easy of a target."

"That's why I brought these masks," Jersey says. "This gold one for you and the black one for me."

"You think this will make me disappear in the crowd? A gold mask on a six-foot-five man?"

Jersey intertwines her fingers into his and pulls him through the thick mass of a crowd down Bourbon Street. The adrenaline tingles in his head with a bad feeling. Fireworks crackle like popcorn in a pan. His eyes sweep back and forth. Drunk noise flows around his ears. In the center of the street, people rush from every direction around him.

A hand grabs the back of his head. Jersey's big wet lips shove onto his. Her tongue sticks down his mouth like a snake sliding down a gopher hole. His hands push back, lungs gasp for air.

"Come on, Truk. I got plans for you tonight. I'm gonna do something to you, you ain't never had done to you before." Her hand wraps around his scrotum. "But not yet. It's not even three o'clock. You got to promise me, baby. You go where I go, and you do what I do."

His arm almost pulls out of the socket as she runs, holding his hand. He can barely keep up with her spiked heels. Five minutes away from the mass of drunks, she still has his hand like a vice grip. Her plastic card swipes through the metal stripe reader on an abandoned three-story hotel. Magnets release, the metal door unlocks. Her gloved hand pulls the door open. She rushes by the small hotel's dusty, empty front desk and releases his hand.

"Come on, Truk. Race you up the stairs to the top floor."

Seconds later and four floors up, the door bangs open. Blackness surrounds them with the moon and stars hiding behind clouds. Truk pants hard and grabs his knees. "Damn, girl. I'm out of shape."

A few blocks away, a local news helicopter hovers over the French Quarter. A spotlight swings back and forth over the crazed crowd while the camerawoman gathers footage for tomorrow's news report.

A one-foot-tall, galvanized metal pail sits alone in the middle of the rooftop. Jersey walks over, inspects the contents, then grabs a small remote. Three one-thousand-watt halogen portable tripod work lights stand in a half circle, waiting in the dark.

Her hands play with Truk's hair. "I promised you I was doing something special."

Truk's bright teeth shine through his enormous smile. "I'm ready and waiting for what you got, Jersey."

The small remote in Jersey's hand clicks. Night turns to daytime on the roof as lights from all three metal tripod stands explode with brightness. "We are going to make a film tonight, and it will be the rage of the internet."

She pulls the dress off over her head. Truk's eyes burn a permanent image in his brain of her large, firm breasts. Legs separated, she stands in her black knee-high boots and arm-length gloves and points her finger toward him. "Your turn."

He gladly pulls his Crescent City Blues Festival shirt over his head, drops his pants, and kicks them away. Hands in the air, Truk calls out, "I'm ready."

"Oh, baby, not yet. You still got stuff on."

He looks down. "All I got on is this stupid mask. You still got boots, gloves, and mask on."

"You got your watch and ring on. You gotta take everything off."

Angst captures him. "You gonna try to rob me? I never take my Super Bowl ring off."

Her boot kicks the pail on its side; a .40 caliber pistol, a one-pint plastic rum bottle full of gasoline, a throwaway lighter, and two roman candles fall out. She lights the two roman candles and aims them at the local news helicopter a block away. "Watch this." She needs confirmation of the kill.

◆

Flaming colored balls fly by the aircraft. "What the hell is that?" The pilot turns the helicopter around. "Look, the rooftop is lit up like Monday Night Football." He scans the roof with his search-light. "Aim the camera back that way." He watches a woman shoot red and green flares toward them like heat-seeking missiles. Iraq flashes in the pilot's mind. "Look out, incoming." His finger reaches for the missing trigger on the cyclic stick—his army pistol tight under his left armpit.

The spotlight scans the roof, and the camerawoman points at the building. "Look, there are two on the roof."

The pilot rolls the stick right and dodges the fireballs.

"They're both...naked?" the camerawoman asks. "Contact the station and tell them we have two naked people on a rooftop."

Truk watches the copter coming closer and then switches back to her. "I'm naked here. I'm a cop. I can't be here." He reaches for his pants.

The toe of her boot flips the pail upright. She drops the smol-dering candles in the metal pail and pours gasoline on top, shoot-ing flames head-high.

Truk's hands dodge the heat. Distracted from Jersey for only a few seconds, he turns back with his pants in his hand. A pistol barrel points at him.

"Told you I was going to do something you have never done before," Jersey says.

"What the hell are you doing, Jersey? Put that…"

With a flash from her gun, a bullet slams into his chest. Truk falls backward.

"Hope you got that on video," the pilot says.

"It's running. You keep the spotlight on them. It's like they want to be on television, and they're naked. We can't show this on TV."

"Pan down on their faces."

"The man's face is covered with a gold mask," the camerawoman says. "Is he dead? I can't see the woman's face because of her hair and mask. Is he dead?"

Sirens wail closer.

"Truk, you still plan on being the lead security for Maggie McCall during her campaign in Chicago?" Jersey asks.

He groans. "What?"

"Truk, you're my hit tonight." A serrated hunting knife slips from the inside of her boot as she straddles over his chest. "Nobody will take you out in Chicago. You're too well known, too connected, too loved. You got a Chicago Super Bowl win under your belt and a ring on your finger. But I got you to come down to N'awlins, and you are bird-naked on a rooftop." Jersey sits her bare ass on his limp groin. "Can't have you going back to Chicago." Her head leans back. "Truk, baby. Ooh, you're not dead yet."

"What the hell is she doing? They've got bright lights shining on them," the pilot says. "She not…"

"Yes, she looks like she's… I'm getting the Pulitzer or fired, but I am not turning this camera away."

"That was so much fun earlier up in our room, Truk. I think the third time was the best. You think so?"

His lungs struggle for a breath.

"Time for the collection plate. I think you got something I need." She holds Truk's wrist against the roof and slams the blade across his fingers. Blood showers the rooftop. He screams while the fingers roll away from his hand.

Jersey pulls his Super Bowl ring off the dead finger. "I have to have something to remember you by. This should be sufficient."

Blood pumps out of Truk's chest wounds as deep breaths struggle to capture oxygen.

"Funny, with all this going on, the helicopter, the lights, the camera, I hope we'll make it on television tonight. You think we'll be the big breaking news story? Don't get no big head now, Truk. You ain't my biggest mark. McCall is more money than you, but you do have the biggest—"

"Are you getting all this?" the pilot asks. "What the hell is she doing?"

"I sure hope this gets on national news tomorrow," Jersey says. "I need proof you're dead." Jersey stands again and waves her gun in the air and fires once. "Come on. Shine that spotlight right on both of us." Jersey turns the gun toward Truk's chest. "Let's do one more, just to make sure." She fires again.

Blood gurgles from Truk's throat, shallow breaths stop.

A police helicopter with a large searchlight charges in from the other side of the building. A voice calls out from the police helicopter, "This is the police. Put your hands up."

Jersey looks down at her victim. "Oh, this is fantastic, Truk. I got more cops to shoot." The remote in her hand clicks, and the lights on the tripods blacken. She swings around and fires three times at the police helicopter. Bullets ping through the shell and hit the engine. Oily smoke billows outward as the pilot struggles to land on the street.

She releases the magazine from the handle and drops both into the burning pail. Jersey sprints to the back edge of the building where a folded black sundress waits for her and a forty-foot rope hangs over the edge of the building. Other police helicopter searchlights scan the rooftop for her as she snaps open the black sundress and slides it over her head.

Jersey grabs the rope and slides over the side. One shove with her feet, and she rappels down the side of the building.

A half block away, Jersey turns back, pulls the mask and gloves off, and drops them in a public wastebasket. Police cars have surrounded the hotel. She puts the phone to her ear while she glances back at the battering ram slamming against the front door. Her thumb spins the oversized Super Bowl diamond ring around her index finger as the phone rings twice.

Fedora answers, "Yeah."

"He's out."

"Dead?"

"I said, he's out!" Jersey mixes into the drunk crowd on Bourbon Street.

"You're as dead as the match if he's not."

Jersey breaks the phone, pitches the two pieces in the trash, and turns into a noisy bar.

Chapter 36

Four hours later, white cumulus puffs hang in the blue sky. Reflected sunbeams bounce off high-rise glass and chrome buildings. Inside Maggie's new apartment, she punishes the heavy bag that hangs from the ceiling. Neon orange and black gloves pound the bag harder than she ever has done before. She exhales with each punch. "Damn you, Remo Wolf. Why did you tell me about the Killing Club?" After a flurry of six into the bag, she shoves it backward.

Her phone buzzes on the countertop. UNKNOWN is on the screen. She knows who's calling and pushes the phone away from her. "Don't call me, you bastard. I don't want to know any more about your vigilante killers." Her left jab connects. "Damn you." Another flurry hits the bag. Her breaths shorten. She clutches the bag. "What the hell am I going to do with you?" She shoves the bag away and delivers a left, right upon its return. "Damn you, Remo Wolf."

Her phone buzzes again. The boxing glove spins the phone around. It's the Chicago Police Department's main number.

She slides a glove off and taps the speaker. "Hello?"

"Miss McCall, this is Captain Mayfield."

"Are you calling me to tell me Detective Wolf is in jail?"

"No, ma'am. I have some information you need to know."

Maggie pants while she slips the other glove off and sits on a barstool. "What information?" She takes a drink from her sports bottle.

"I just read a report from the parole board. Gerardo Hernandez is being released."

She stands. "When?"

"Today."

"No. He can't. They sentenced him for twenty-five to life." She drops back to the chair. "It's only been...sixteen years."

"Yes, ma'am, I know. Illinois is trying to clean out the prisons. Something about decreasing the cost."

"Empty the prisons? Start with druggies and non-violent. Hernandez is a rapist, my sister's rapist."

"Just wanted to give you a heads up. Not sure what time. But remember, he will continue as a parolee for the rest of his sentence."

"Oh, great. We all know parolees are clean-cut Americans. Church, school, charity work. The rapist needs to be in prison."

"I suggest you try to stay clear of him. He's nothing but trouble for you."

"Right." She disconnects the call and throws the gloves in the corner of the room. The back of her hands wipe tears away. The phone buzzes again. "What? You got some more bad news for me?"

"It's Remo. I just needed to hear from you. Are you expecting someone else?"

Maggie wipes her nose and eyes. She drops the phone on the counter in disgust and pushes speakerphone. "Captain Mayfield called. He told me Gerardo Hernandez is being released today."

"No, too early. The bastard has another ten or more to go before parole consideration."

"Remo, he can't come back to Chicago." She pulls a strand of hair behind her ear. "I can't have him here. My beautiful sister couldn't take the shame and committed suicide because of him. She's dead, and that bastard's alive."

"I can watch for him," Remo says on the phone. "I will tell you when he gets back."

Maggie paces the floor with her phone in one hand and her hair held back by the other. Her stomach burns with acid rolling up her esophagus. She bends down on her knees and curls to the floor. "I don't want to know." She sits up, her stomach tightens. "No, wait, yes, I need to know where he is. Maybe I can have Truk arrest him. Or you, you can do that. Right? Arrest him on some bullshit charge and put him back in jail as soon as he gets back to Chicago. You can do that for me. Would you do that?"

"Maggie, I will do whatever you want."

She stands straight and turns to gaze out her high-rise apartment window. Sunlight sparkles on blue water as boats linger on the lake. She presses her hand against the cool window. "No, my sister deserves more." She wipes her eyes and nose again. "She's dead because that...that scum raped her." She drops onto the couch and raises her knees to her chest.

Remo hears her sob heavily on the other side of the call. "Maggie...I can help."

Maggie rises and returns to the window again and stares at a single white contrail in the sky. "I bet he thinks he beat the system. He'll be back to do the same thing again and again. I can't let him do that."

She faces the adjacent wall where a five-by-seven selfie of Remo and her at Millennium Park last summer hangs. Her finger brushes across his image. Tears spill down her cheeks. "You can come back to me if..." The back of her hand wipes tears away. "You're part of that group that kills people. You can come back to me if you...if you kill him."

"Shut up, Maggie. Don't say that."

Holding back more tears, she kicks the bag. Her voice quivers. "I want you to kill that son of a bitch. Kill Hernandez before he gets to Chicago."

"No, Maggie. Get that out of your head."

Her feet shift back and forth on the floor. "God damn it, what the hell should I do?"

"Maggie, you can never come back from that once it's done. I can have him breaking parole. Run a red light, speeding, drinking, smoking pot, I can do that, but you don't want me to kill him. You don't."

"I never want to see him in Chicago. Do you understand me? Call me when you're done." She hangs up.

Chapter 37

Remo returns to Davy's basement. "What time is he being released?" Remo asks.

Davy hacks into the Illinois Parole Board website to the prisoners list. "Gerardo Hernandez's hearing was three weeks ago at Pontiac Correctional Center. His out-processing is at noon, you know."

"I was at that prison about two years ago. Do you remember that kid that killed his mother and all her cats?"

"Yeah, gruesome, you know."

"He and another inmate were cleaning the lobby. He stepped in front of me and whispered to me an inmate told him about a murder. The warden investigated it and was total bullshit. Anyway, Pontiac is small. My guess is Hernandez will head for the closest bar when released." He flips his watch on his wrist. "That's three hours from now, and it's a ninety-minute ride. Better get on the move."

"Don't do anything stupid by yourself, you know."

Remo smirks. "I haven't done that since I discovered girls."

❖

Remo glances at his watch, a little after eleven. He sits on the Indian in a parking lot. Across the street, a red neon sign announces Tony's Bar is open. He finishes the last of his coffee and stares at Gerardo crossing the street. Like the siren's call from a neon sign, Gerardo steps inside.

Gerardo Hernandez pushes open the door to the bar and steps inside. Ceiling fans spin slowly with lights dim. A jukebox plays eighties music. Three men sit at the bar with a few couples at tables.

Gerardo straddles a stool and tells the bartender, "Shot of whiskey and a beer."

The bartender empties the small dishwasher and places the steamy glasses on a towel. "Sure. Got a preference?"

"What do you mean?" Gerardo asks.

"Preference, you know, a brand of whiskey and beer."

"No, whatever you got."

"We have Wednesday Happy Hour until six. A dollar for PBR."

"What's PBR?"

"PBR, Pabst Blue Ribbon. Where have you been the last fifty years?"

"Don't worry about where I've been." He digs into his front pocket for the five dollars left in his prison account. "A buck? Yeah, give me that."

The bartender opens the can and slides it across the bar. "If you don't mind me asking, your name Gerardo?"

His eyes shift around the room, then back to the bartender. "What of it? You got a problem with my name?"

"No, someone came in, dropped a hundred-dollar bill down and said your drinks are paid." The bartender leans toward Gerardo and, in a low voice, says, "Just out of prison? You should skip town before you get thrown back in."

"Yeah? Then give me two shots and two beers."

A few hours later, Gerardo stumbles outside. An intersection light turns red. He presses his hand along the wall to balance as he walks. He steps off the sidewalk, turns into the alley, drops to his knees and vomits.

Remo's arms are crossed as he stands by the dumpster in the alley. "You are one dumb shit."

Gerardo climbs his way back up the wall to an unsteady stance. He tries to shove Remo away, who doesn't budge. Instead, Gerardo's shoes slide as he stumbles backward.

"Breaking parole a few hours after your release, not smart, Gerardo." A siren wails in the distance. "Turn around and put your hands behind your back."

"I'm not doin' nothing."

Remo slams Gerardo against the brick wall. In two seconds, Gerardo's legs are swept away. He falls to the ground, face-first, and his hands are zip-tied behind his back. "Sheriff is on his way." The siren comes closer as Remo walks away.

Maggie's phone rings. 'UNKNOWN' pops up on the screen. "Hello," Maggie says.

"It's done. I'll be by later tonight."

Chapter 38

It's Tuesday night at the Killing Club. The unlocked front door of the dark house swings hard and wide as Solido kicks it open. He lights a kerosene lantern. Sitting on a weather-worn end table, it hisses as a yellow flame glows inside the mantle.

He has a bucket of fried chicken under one arm and a sixty-four-ounce green plastic cup with a long red straw in the other hand. He calls the half-gallon cup filled with a mix of Dr. Pepper, Diet Sprite, and Tab a DDT. Five minutes later, the last chicken bone drops into the bucket, and the straw slurps the DDT concoction.

Through the half-open front door, a voice from outside yells out, "Come out, asshole." A grenade crashes through the window and rolls across the floor. Red lasers bounce off walls looking for a target. Heavy footsteps rush the porch, the door flies open. "You're busted, mother f—"

Jersey charges inside and collides with a four-hundred-pound wall of fat and muscle. She bounces to the floor. Solido laughs. "Ha, you dumbass. I was gonna knock the shit out of you 'til I saw that polka dot face of yours." He still holds the cup and, through the straw, sucks the last drop of DDT. The empty cup bounces on the floor.

Jersey's vitiligo is worse than ever. More than half of her face has scattered white hypopigmented patches over her once-perfect olive skin. She picks up the bogus grenade.

A voice comes from outside. "Okay to come in?"

Solido recognizes the voice. "Yeah, sure, li'l bro, come on in."

The late Euro's little brother, 3Fingers, gained his name five years ago after a bullet shot his fourth and fifth finger off. Those fingers are missing, but the grip with his other three crushes bricks like dry dirt clods.

Solido high-fives him and feels the strange sensation of the right hand. In a flash, he grabs 3Fingers and slams him against the table, straddling the kid. Solido's massive hand pushes on 3Fingers's chest like an anvil, making it hard for him to breathe. Inches apart, face to face, Solido says, "Never liked them fingers of yours. They creepy the way you use 'em. Maybe I should shoot the rest off. They no good anyway, right?"

3Fingers's eyes roll from Solido and look toward Jersey. "You gonna stop this shit?"

Jersey watches the sideshow with a smile. "Nope, gonna see how you get out of this. If you can't, I guess you don't deserve to be here."

"Yeah?" 3Fingers clamps his teeth down onto Solido's nose.

Solido screams, "You son of a bitch!" He shoves 3Fingers over the table.

A six-inch blade flies out from 3Fingers' waistband with the point under Solido's chin. His vice grip-like three-finger hold around Solido's neck makes him gasp for air. "How 'bout I gut you now and throw that fat liver of yours to the rats outside?"

Jersey jumps between them like a referee at an NFL game. "Okay, you both made your point. He can stay."

As they part, 3Fingers' blade swings wide near Solido's face just far enough not to cut him. His boot kicks hard into Solido's groin.

Solido laughs. "You gonna have to kick somewhere else, little bro. Too much fat around my balls for you to get to 'em. I've been kicked a hundred times, and nobody got to 'em yet."

The racking sound of a shotgun stops everyone. Jersey recognizes the same sound from a few weeks before when Truk pointed a shotgun at her in the detectives' bathroom. All eyes turn to see Che behind them. "Are you children fighting about lunch money?" Che asks.

Solido backs off and smiles. He stomach-bumps Che, almost knocking him to the floor.

"Who brought the beer?" Che asks.

The three look at each other, empty-handed, as Che steps away from the front door and reveals a case of Goose Island IPA on the floor.

Jersey's eyes pop wide. "Che, I love you, honey. My favorite."

Che glances at 3Fingers and wonders why Jersey invited Euro's little brother here? The CPD has been looking for him since he supposedly killed the school principal and disappeared from school.

The four stand together, beers in hand. Che says, "To Euro. Too bad he got sloppy." The four bottles clink together. They slam the brews down in five seconds—one after another, the bottles crash into the corner.

Che watches Jersey close to see if she acts suspicious about him. Her voice is normal, no extra swallows, no glances at him or playing with her knife. He wants to know if she is going after Maggie again. Has she seen Fedora?

"Damn, that's good," 3Fingers says. "Never had one of them. What's it called?"

Solido spits on the floor. "That shit is nothing but skunk piss. You can have the rest of mine." He shoves the bottles toward the new kid in the house.

Jersey grabs another and empties it as fast as the first. "Best damn beer ever made."

Che points toward the floor near the door. "That's okay, Solido. Got you a DDT."

"Now that's what I call a damn good drink."

Che looks at 3Fingers. "You don't sound English like Euro."

"Nah, born here in Chicago. We not real brothers, just stayed together in foster homes. When I was a little kid, always thought he was an alien or something with that accent."

"I've known this little piece of shit since he was sucking on his momma's tit," Jersey says. "After she died, he started conning people in Head Start." She reaches for another bottle. "Sounds like he's ready for KC. What do you guys think?"

Solido rubs his nose and says, "I already tested him. Seems okay to me."

Remo points his finger at the kid. "I know you. You're the one that killed the high school principal about a year or two ago. True?"

"Hell, yeah. I killed that bastard."

"Why did you do it?"

"He pissed me off, wanted to put me in ISS."

"What's that?"

"ISS, in school suspension. I told him no way am I doing that again. Kept me from dealin' my drugs. I couldn't stay for an hour after school. Too much shit to sell that day."

"And what did you do?" Che asks.

His fingers point like a gun. "Shot that bastard in the head three times. Then left to finish my deliveries."

As an undercover cop, Remo gets his confession in less than five minutes on a cold case from last year. Truk will like this. "Everybody, sit down."

3Fingers sits between Jersey and Che.

"You comfortable?" Che asks.

"Yeah, sure," 3Fingers quips back as he tries to sit tall but can only reach to shoulder-high to each person next to him.

Che taps the shotgun barrel on 3Fingers' head and looks him over. "Think you can kill somebody once a month? One thing to kill when you're mad, another when you're not."

"I love this idea. Kill somebody, cut something off, and do a little show-and-tell like Euro told me when I was in high school."

Che eyes Jersey, then nods to her. They squeeze closer together with 3Fingers squished in the center.

"It's entertainment time," Che says. "Who's first?"

Solido stands up. "That would be me. I got a sweet kill this month, Vincent Sepulveda. Yeah, it was fun. Caught him and a girl at the docks. Arrogance makes it easy. All these cop killings and he's out late at night. Too easy, man. Sit down, boys, and let me tell you all about that surprised look when I stepped in front of them."

Half an hour later, Jersey steps behind the podium. She holds her prize up high in the air. "I got a ring, a Super Bowl ring."

Heat rolls over Remo. His pupils dilate, and a sour taste rolls in his mouth. What he can't do is stand up and shoot Jersey. He wouldn't have time enough to turn around and kill Solido and the little shit that came in tonight. She and the others can't know Truk was his friend, his boss. Shaking inside, his hand grabs the edge of the seat. His ears roar as Jersey's words turn into an imperceptible mess. All he hears is 3Fingers laughing.

Che swings the shotgun butt against 3Fingers' head. He flops to the floor like a half-filled basketball. In a second, 3Fingers feels the barrel shoved against his throat.

Che's eyes glare into 3Fingers. "Shut the fuck up," Che yells as he pushes the barrel harder into 3Fingers' neck. "I don't like fucking uninvited intruders or fucking assholes that laugh like a fucking hyena."

"Che, I invited him," Jersey says.

3Fingers shoves the barrel away from his throat. Che's boot heel slams into 3Fingers's sternum, knocking his breath away. Che pushes the barrel back against his throat. "Ever seen a man decapitated by a shotgun blast at his neck? I have. The bloody head rolls down the floor."

"Che, put that shotgun down," Jersey demands. Her hand slides across Che's injured shoulder. He flinches from the pain as he watches her nervous smile. Jersey quickly changes the subject. "I want to hear about your kill. Who did you take out?"

Che's eyes laser into the kid on the floor. The shotgun is snug into 3Fingers' neck. Truk flashes across Remo's mind. Why the hell did I bring Jersey into the station and let Truk see her? It's my fault another friend is dead. Afghanistan, Bobby, and now Truk. They're all dead because of me. And Maggie...my God, she almost died because of my stupidity. This whole thing is dive-bombing. I want control of who dies. Goddamn fucking killers and perverts and rapists. That's who needs to be dead, not people I know, not people I love. He feels his fingertip press against the trigger. Shit, just do it. Kill them all right now. Do it! Goddamn. Do it!

Solido taps Che's back. "Come on, man. Back up."

Che swings the shotgun barrel and slams it against Solido's arm. Buckshot splatters the wall. Solido grabs the barrel and slams his elbow against Che's head. He falls.

Solido hands the shotgun to Jersey. "Che, man. You all right? That was bad shit, man."

Che wipes the tear off his face and stands. "Sorry. I got caught up. Rage, bullshit stuff." He turns to 3Fingers and holds his hand out to shake. "Sorry about all that. It won't happen again."

Nervously, 3Fingers holds out a fist to bump rather than a handshake. "Okay, man." He nods. "All good."

Jersey racks the shotgun until it is empty. "You can have it back now."

Remo must keep his cool as Che. He grabs the barrel. "Thanks, won't happen again."

Jersey smiles. "Damn right. I'll cut your throat before you do that again. You scared the shit out of me."

Che turns to 3Fingers as if nothing happened. "Think you're up to this?"

"Yeah, I can do this stuff."

"Good. Got a test run for you. I work solo, but I need a little help tomorrow. Do this clean, and I'll get Jersey to find an easy mark for you next time. You like boats and water?"

Remo has the evidence. Jersey admitted she killed Truk, but did she kill Bobby? He has to find out before he drags her to the police station. He'll ask Captain "Ton" Kimball tomorrow what to do.

Chapter 39

Remo taps 'M' on his phone. It rings.

"Hello," Maggie answers.

"Are you sure you want to help me with this?" Remo asks Maggie.

"I told you I would. I owe you for what you did to Gerardo Hernandez."

"Maggie, you don't owe me anything. I would do anything for you. 3Fingers will help me with this. Going to let him take the fall if things don't go well."

"I said I'd help."

✦

Chicago Union Station, or CUS, is packed late Wednesday afternoon. Police officers scan the crowded lobby. A dog wears a bright yellow security jacket and meanders through the crowd as it sniffs shoes and pant legs.

A flabby, pale man tries to blend, but his half-inch, red, short-cropped Mohawk says otherwise. Five-day-old hair on the sides of his scalp prickles through the Russian hammer and sickle tattoos. A scruffy beard with patches that looks like mange on a homeless dog.

Blending in a crowd would not be possible, except he's in Chicago, and half the weirdos wander inside CUS looking for loose change and suitcases to steal. He wears an unbuttoned, long sleeve plaid shirt. His fingers brush the pistol stuck down the butt crack of his baggy pants.

His earbud is tuned to the police scanner broadcasting a BOLO, be on the lookout, for a man with a red Mohawk near Midtown. There's a lot of Mohawks in Chicago, but only one red in CUS. He listens to the police scanner on the Bluetooth when a voice breaks through. "See a red Mohawk, southbound, first floor."

The man carries a workout bag in each hand, one with a package of marijuana, the other with crumpled newspaper and a two-ounce bottle of glycerol next to an open baggie of potassium permanganate. He watches the dog closing in. His fingers drop the first bag, and the pot falls out the side. As he expects, the dog sniffs and sits next to the bag. Good drug doggie.

The second bag is half unzipped. While walking, he pours the glycerol on the purplish-black glistening crystals and drops the bag next to the wall. Purple smoke seeps past the zipper, and then yellow and red flames spit out the open bag, igniting the paper. In seconds, smoke and flames spew in the air. Cameras record people running and a red Mohawk walking to an exit.

He pushes the glass door open where a cab line has twenty people long and steps in the front of the line. He hands the waiting passenger a crisp Benjamin Franklin bill. Without a sound, he steps inside the back of the cab. The young cabbie asks where to. No reply, just a finger pointing straight ahead.

The cabbie looks in the rearview mirror. "Nice Mohawk, sir. Red, don't see many of those."

The cab's tires roar across the metal sections of the Chicago River bridge. The man points at the corner of Harrison and Federal. He taps the cabbie's shoulder. "Here." The car stops.

He steps out, looks over his shoulder as the cab leaves and enters a Pakistani restaurant. A thick cloud of turmeric hovers inside as he walks to the kitchen. Dead fish and week-old spoiled milk infiltrate his nostrils as he opens the back door to the alley. Next to the garbage bin, a homeless man lies on his side, smelling as bad as the dead fish.

A filthy hand reaches for the man's pant leg. "Got a dollar, mister?" the homeless man asks. He looks up and sees a pistol aimed at his head. "Sorry, mister." He covers his head with his hands.

"Hey, old man. Look at me," the Mohawk's gruff voice calls.

After a quick glance at the red hair and the plaid shirt, the bum curls up in a ball. "Go ahead, mister. I don't need your dollar. Just go on, leave me alone."

Two bullets fire into the overstuffed shopping cart.

"You didn't need to do that. I got food in there."

The Mohawk man sprints to the sidewalk and jumps in front of an oncoming cab. Brakes squeal, the taxi stops inches in front of him. His hand slams a fifty-dollar bill on the windshield. The driver motions for him to enter.

The back door creaks open. He climbs in and slams the door shut. "Monroe and Lake Shore Drive, near the Chicago Yacht Club."

Blood orange sunlight bounces off the fire-bitten skyscraper walls. He turns to watch behind him to make sure no one follows. The bum won't forget the red Mohawk when the police question him.

Spread out across the back seat, he pulls the plaid shirt off. Skin-colored foam padding covers the chest and stomach. He peels the foam away, revealing a black skintight t-shirt covering chest and arm muscles. The Mohawk skullcap slides off Remo's jet-black shoulder-length hair; his fingers peel the beard off his face in one motion. He drops it all inside the plaid shirt and ties the arms together.

As a favor to a close friend, Remo has agreed to drag an asshole off a boat and have uniformed police arrest him. Captain Kimball, who brought Remo back as an undercover police officer, knows Semion Tyruinov raped his niece, but he needs help to get the perp off a boat in Lake Michigan. But if this goes bad, it could expose Remo's cover.

Remo tells the cabbie to take his time before pushing 'redial' on his phone.

Captain Kimball answers. "Hello."

"Back from the station," Remo replies.

"Smooth?"

"Yes. Heading to the yacht club."

Remo stares at the rearview mirror. The cabbie glances every few seconds back at his passenger.

"Word on the street has Tyruinov connected to the Wrigley Field robbery. Maybe we can slap two convictions on him tonight. Nobody else knows about you doing this, right?" Kimball asks.

Remo doesn't want to answer the question.

Chapter 40

Captain Kimball says, "The mayor's party is tonight. Be at his house at ten o'clock. A lieutenant I trust will be at the front door letting people in with their invitations. He has your academy picture. You need to convince him that it's you. I'll have a tux waiting for you to change downstairs in the library. Come up to the second floor, and I will introduce you to my two suspects protecting Tyruinov. Ten o'clock sharp upstairs. I need you to figure out which is the bad one and then do your thing."

Remo's lips tighten, and he nods to himself. "Yes, sir." He clears his throat and says, "I have information about Truk I need to talk to you about."

"You know something?" Ton asks.

"I know who did it. Told me face-to-face."

"Come to my office tomorrow morning." Captain Kimball needs help, and this is very personal. He knows who raped his niece, but he needs help to get the perp off a boat in Lake Michigan. The mayor's party/fundraiser is a perfect place to start.

Semion Tyruinov, a Russian mafia man, soaks in sunlight on his yacht at the Chicago Yacht Club. He raped the sixteen-year-old niece of Captain Kimball last month. It would be an easy arrest, but someone higher in the police food chain protects Tyruinov as long as he stays on the Russian-registered boat. Kimball thinks the high-ranking cop will be at the party tonight. Remo asks 3Fingers to help and knows he must be careful with this shakedown. Neither Semion nor 3Fingers can see Remo as a cop.

Remo calls Maggie. "You sure you want to help me?"

"He's a rapist, right?" Maggie asks.

"Yes."

"No one dies, right?" Maggie asks.

"No," Remo says. "No one dies. I'm only supposed to find his informant." It's like the weather, hoping your prediction is over fifty-one percent correct.

A long pause on the phone. "All right, I'll help."

The cabbie's eyes peer in the rearview mirror and try to listen to the phone call. "Almost at the yacht club," the cabbie says.

Remo ends the call and glances up to ensure the cabbie sees his face. Remo looks out the window. Tall white masts metronome to the waves.

"Turn left on Lake Shore and stop at the club entrance."

The cab turns into the club entrance and stops at the curb. "Twenty-two dollars. You want change from that fifty you slapped on my windshield?"

Remo flips a Ben Franklin bill to the driver and opens the back door. He points to the dashboard. "Cab 8X99, be here at six tomorrow afternoon, sit for me, and you get three more just like it. I don't like waiting. Got it? If you don't show up, I can find you and your family in a few hours. And you've never seen me before, right?"

The cabbie's thumb and finger rub the new bill and confirm it's real. A single nod seals the deal. "Okay, six tomorrow."

Remo's watch shows 7:15 PM. His flip-top Zippo lights the clothes bag and he drops it in the metal wastebasket. The night engulfs him as the cab speeds off. As he walks toward the shoreline, his silhouette glimmers behind the burning clothes. It's time for Remo to check out his target for tomorrow and then head to the mayor's home.

Chapter 41

I t's ten o'clock and Remo's tux fits GQ perfect. He steps onto the top stair of the second floor. Chief Clifton "Ton" Kimball waves toward Remo. The nickname Ton comes from a disorder called acromegaly. His pituitary gland pumped too much growth hormone in him as a teenager, giving him massive-sized hands. As a young boxer, he was 27-0, hitting his opponents with 'a ton of bricks.' He won every match by first round knockouts. The mayor, Ton and two high-ranking officers circle tight and talk aloud.

"Remo, how are you, my friend?" Ton's massive hand presses against Remo's back, almost covering both scapulas. Remo is tall and robust, but Ton towers over him. "I want to introduce you to Mayor Bill Bratton." He turns to the mayor. "This is Detective Remo Wolf."

"I've heard a lot about you, detective. Your ups and downs and your ups again," the mayor declares. "Congratulations on your successes."

Remo pushes the earpiece farther into his canal, then says, "Thank you for inviting me to your beautiful home, Mayor Bratton."

"You're welcome. Now, if you will excuse me," the mayor says. "I must mingle. An election is near."

"Remo, have you met Deputy Inspector James Makim and Inspector Charles Krupin?" Ton asks.

Makim's eyebrows wrinkle at Remo. "Still think IA should have questioned you more about your alleged ambush and the death of your partner."

Krupin laughs. "Alleged? Makim, you are such an ass." He laughs again and slaps Makim's back.

Remo laughs, then pushes his finger on Makim's chest, covered with almost every salutary ribbon the Chicago Police Department makes. "I'm cleared of that bullshit. I'm still looking for that man in the black fedora." His eyes scan Makim from head to feet. "About your height and weight with the same color eyes, sir." He turns to face Krupin, Remo's biceps stretching the tux stitches. "I'm just a lowly detective, but there is a mendacious smell coming from the two of you."

"Big words coming from a drunk," Makim says. "Excuse me, an alcoholic."

"Gentlemen," Kimball says. "We should welcome our guest."

Makim smiles. "Of course, my apologies. I'm sure IA was thorough."

Remo grabs a champagne flute off a silver tray passing by. "I'm sure you have your own story to tell, Makim." Remo adjusts his earpiece. "Tell me how you conned your way to be the deputy inspector." One of them keeps Semion Tyruinov safe. Remo feels it.

Chapter 42

Thirty minutes after midnight, Remo strips off the tux and into his regular clothes as he slips out the back of the mayor's house. He flips his burner phone open and pushes a button.

Before the first ring ends, Davy answers, "Working on it, you know." Davy's computers network through the CPD personnel files of James Makim and Charles Krupin.

Remo says, "Hope you heard all that tonight, Davy. What have you got for me?"

Davy spins his chair in circles while he looks at two screens. "Krupin is half Albanian and half Greek. His parents came to America in 1946 after WW2 ended. Not any connection to the Russian Mafia, you know."

It's irritatingly good to hear the 'you know' again. Remo hasn't talked to Davy in weeks. Never know week to week or even day to day if the psychotropics are still circulating well in Davy's brain. Today, they are.

"James Makim, on the other hand, is all Russian, you know." Davy looks at the immigration logs from Ellis Island on the left screen, with the right of New York census reports from 1920 through 1950. "His grandparents fled to America in 1917 when the communist revolution started. Ellis Island inspectors changed the last name from Maksimov to Makim. James Makim, aka Maksimov, lived his entire childhood in the Russian section of Brooklyn's Brighton Beach, you know."

"Was there any mafia near him?"

"Plenty. Half a dozen convicted felons within two blocks of his parents' house, you know."

"Why is he here in Chicago?"

"The Irish had squeezed the Russian Mafia space here in Chicago. They needed someone inside the Chicago Police Department to put the squeeze back on the Irish. Makim transferred eight years ago. I called my buddy in New York, and he told me Makim was under investigation from the NYPD when transferred. He knows his business; six of the high-ranking Irish died in the first three months he was in Chicago, you know."

Chapter 43

The next day, Semion Tyruinov marvels at his short red hair in the specialty designed six-foot-tall floor mirror, which concaves just enough to make the five-foot-six-inch man look three inches taller. With a half-smoked cigar in his mouth, his low-slung swim trunks let his belly hang out farther than his flabby man breasts. He thinks the black hair covering his shirtless back and chest is sexy.

He likes women, the younger, the better. Two teenage girls lie over wicker chaise lounges on a yacht, wearing bikinis with less cloth than a handkerchief. They soak up the last few minutes of the sun.

At the end of a three-hour fishing trip, the *Solstitial Points*, a Black Swan-class sloop registered in Russia with a length of three hundred feet and thirteen hundred fifteen tons displacement, creeps toward pier sixty-two from a day of fishing. Converted to a private yacht in 1988, it is now worth thirty million.

The engines rev as the captain shifts to reverse. He closes in on the dock. The boat slips in like parallel parking on the street.

Semion despises the old Soviet Union and its stupid communism. His scalp hammer and sickle tattoos were from his days as a naïve kid who believed in his country. Things changed. His money is now his, not some thief in the politburo's. In defiance, the girls lie on top of old communist red flags—tight asses smearing lotion into the yellow hammer and sickle.

With his small glass in hand, half-filled with Macallan 1947 scotch, he walks down the starboard side of his yacht in front of two slicked-haired men in black t-shirts and gold chains. Both men behind Tyruinov carry an AK-47 with an extra-long forty-round magazine. They are never more than a few feet away from their boss.

A skinny man runs to Tyruinov and pulls him inside the cabin with a large-screen TV. The news reported a terrorist attack yesterday. The chief of police speaks from a microphone promising to find the perpetrator. Inside the Chicago Union Station, a surveillance camera shows a man with short red hair, like Semion, dropping a bag with purple smoke. This is a setup. He's been on his yacht, fishing and watching his sunbaked teenage prizes for days. But why would someone imitate him for a terrorist attack?

He puffs on the cigar, and smoke billows around his head. Semion is no fool. He has his own Chicago cops on the take watching over him. A high-ranking cop is expensive, but so is safety, and he is safe on the *Solstitial Points.*

◆

Maggie sits on a bench near the yacht club while she calls Remo. "You put the prize on the boat?"

"Almost." Remo lies prone two hundred yards away, wearing a neck gaiter over his mouth and nose. He tightens the suppressor on his M24 rifle.

"Remember? I'm helping with arrests only. No killing."

"Right, I'll arrest him, and you prosecute him. Another notch for you. Stay on the line with me."

Remo looks through the rifle scope. The crosshairs follow along the waterline as 3Fingers dog paddles to the port-aft corner. He holds a watertight container, the size of a cigar box, filled with magnesium and a remote control lighter.

Clicking his waterproof two-way radio, 3Fingers asks, "You want it here?"

Remo clicks his radio back to 3Fingers. "Right there, three feet under the waterline."

3Fingers dives and sticks the explosive to the hull.

Remo tells Maggie on the phone, "Prize on boat. You're up."

"I'm freezing my ass off over here. This dress better work."

Cool air swirls as darkness consumes the city. Maggie carries a brown leather pouch as she cat-walks past several million-dollar boats. The sun's yellow apex disappeared below the waterline minutes after her arrival. She stops at the gangplank of the *Solstitial Points* and sees a blunted fat man smiling.

"Semion Tyruinov?" Maggie asks.

He leans against the railing. "Are you ready to talk about my immunity?"

"Are you ready to talk about the Wrigley Field robbery and hand over the one and a half million dollars you're hiding?" Maggie asks.

"If the deal is as lovely as you, then I will sign it." Semion Tyruinov motions his hand for her to walk up the gangplank.

At the top, when she steps down onto the deck, her red and yellow floral dress flutters enough to draw Semion's eyes to her firm legs. Her shoulder-length red hair beams as bright as the hemline flowing across her upper thighs.

One guard scans her with a handheld metal detector and nods she's clear.

"You think I can hide something here?" she growls at the guard. Afterward, Maggie sweeps her finger around her ear and touches a button similar to a hearing aid. Remo can hear the conversation in his earpiece. "Let's get this over with."

Semion's hand strokes the back of her silky dress. She feels violated, she feels his cruelty. Remo and Captain Kimball need to throw this hairy, fat bastard rapist in jail.

A full head and shoulders above him, Maggie exaggerates for sex's sake, stepping like a model on a catwalk. With each high-heeled step, Semion's eyes never leave her.

Two hundred yards away, the crosshairs in Remo's scope, level at the Russian's head, follow his movement. Remo shifts to Maggie, scanning her not-enough dress and too-revealing thighs. "Damn dress should work on anybody," Remo says. Maggie and Semion step around the chaise lounges of more teenage bronze skin. She thinks the poor girls must be cold.

They disappear inside the bridge, and Remo switches the scope to infrared. Four bodies appear, Tyruinov and Maggie standing at the bar and the two bodyguards. Each AK-47 lights up red, still warm from shooting fish in the water. Cool liquid flows down her throat. Her cold glass is placed on the bar as her hand delves into the briefcase. His scope moves to Tyruinov waving his red arms and shaking his head no to her. Her long slender fingers point down on the bar. She throws a cold glass across the room. Semion holds his hand out to stop the man when a bodyguard steps toward her.

"Better not raise that barrel, idiot," Remo says. "I'll take you out in a second."

Chapter 44

"You damn well better sign these papers, Tyruinov," Maggie demands. "Or I will shove your head up your ass so far nobody will find it for days."

He places his empty scotch glass on the coaster. "Someone on the news imitated me. It looks like a setup. You involved with that?"

"I don't know what you're talking about. I'm trading your worthless fat ass for the Wrigley Field robbers, and I want *all* the money they stole back in my office tomorrow. Sign these, and let's move on."

"No. That is not a good idea. You call your boss, *the CCSA*, Richard Watters, and I want immunity from this so-called terrorist attack added to the list before I sign it."

Remo watches Maggie pull her phone out from the pouch. His phone vibrates.

Before he can say anything, she blurts out, "This is McCall. Put Richard Watters on the phone, now. We need to add something to this deal we made." She waits ten seconds as Remo says nothing. She speaks again. "He says he wasn't at the Union Station yesterday... I know." She glances at him. "Looks just like him. Says he hasn't been off the yacht for several days." She turns toward Tyruinov and shakes her head. "Says he has witnesses." Scanning the deck. "Most look under eighteen."

Remo says, "Looks like my Union Station setup worked."

"Never mind that. You'll have the extra paperwork tonight. W here?... Why there?... All right." She puts the phone down on the countertop.

Through the scope, Remo watches Semion hold his hands up like a surrender, then nods his head yes. He pours another drink for both and motions to walk outside to the deck. Maggie lifts the edge of her dress as she steps over the tall trestle. Side-by-side, he watches as she steps a little extra on the high heels and her breasts bounce in the low décolletage.

"Sell it, girl," Remo says as he smiles. "You know, on a man, only one head works at a time."

A floodlight beams down on the smooth teak deck. "Here, stop here," Semion says. "The light is perfect on you." They stop at the brass railing. He leans next to her right side.

Too close for Maggie's comfort, her right hand pulls out a page from a folder.

Tyruinov laughs out loud and pats her on the ass. He obliges his ego by giving minute-by-minute details of his conquest of Captain Kimball's niece's rape.

Maggie's teeth grind with hate.

A skinny man approaches and says, "Boss, a question for you."

"Excuse me." Tyruinov steps away.

Her fingertip holds the button down behind her ear. "Shoot the bastard. Don't kill him, just shoot his dick off." She smiles and says, "Shoot him, and I'll make you happy tonight."

Semion steps back, his hand pats her butt again. "You say something?"

She shakes her head. "No, just looking at the water."

"You are a beautiful woman, Maggie McCall." Tyruinov's smile crosses over to evil. "For you, I will break my rule of sex only with women younger than me."

"What do you mean, younger? I *am* younger than you, you ass."

"Before I sign, you must agree to spend the night with me. I don't take no when I want sex."

"The CCSA office is downtown," Maggie says. "Mr. Watters will meet with you in his office with the additional paper about your Wrigley Field immunity."

"The CCSA office? Ludicrous. I will meet him and you at my hotel bar. No place else."

"Perfect," Remo says. "Couldn't be better."

Before Maggie replies, Semion signs the first immunity page, then puts his hand on her ass again. She spins away, grabs the page from his hand while forcing a smile and points her finger at him. "Not yet, little man." The page slips back inside her pouch. "We can talk about tonight when we meet in your hotel lounge *after* you sign the other immunity papers you claim you didn't commit yesterday." With a flirtatious smile, Maggie says, "Excuse me, but I must go."

Remo waits for Semion to step down the gangplank and enter his car. As the taillights disappear, Remo pushes the remote. The lighter ignites the magnesium, and the underwater box burns a hole in the hull. The boat is not going anywhere tonight.

Remo runs to the waiting taxi, dropping two Franklin bills on the front seat. "LaSalle and Huron, fast."

The cabbie's eyes pop up in the rearview mirror. "You said three."

Remo flaps the extra bill in the air. "You get the third when we get there."

Six minutes pass as Remo follows the plan in his head again.

◆

Two officers Captain Kimball has picked to help wait in the alley. The cabbie swings the steering wheel right and stops in front of the building. The seventy-year-old Harrison Hotel has extinct external fire escapes and a thirty-foot protruding neon sign buzzing like a hundred beehives. The bar is busy. Large plate-glass windows show it's packed with whiskey men and martini women. Tyruinov's office is on the fifth floor.

Remo pulls out the badge on a chain from under his shirt, revealing his Chicago shield. The cabbie's eyes glance back to the rearview mirror. Remo drops the third bill on the front seat and says, "Don't come within a mile of this place until tomorrow morning, and remember, you have never seen me before. You don't want the police visiting your wife and two daughters." The back door of the cab closes. Remo slides the gun case down the alley toward waiting cops. He runs up the fire stairs to the fifth floor, boots clicking on every other metal step, and then climbs through a hallway window. Remo steps inside the cleaning closet next to Tyruinov's office and waits.

Chapter 45

The Harrison Hotel bar booms a heavy bass. Every stool and every chair are taken. A local blues band rocks hard in the corner with jet engine decibels. The bartenders can't keep up.

Maggie's skintight black dress exudes perfect legs sitting on a tall swivel chair inside the bar. Her knees cross as the hemline creeps across her thighs. Every man's attention focuses on the red stilettos in slow motion. Her martini glass is half full, and three men have hit on her the last fifteen minutes to fill it. She glances side-to-side for 3Fingers in the bar. She texts Remo the bad news: the boy is missing.

Semion Tyruinov enters the bar with a large man following. Tyruinov waves to the bartender, who nods and pushes a button under the countertop. Part of the wall pops open to a hidden elevator. Semion smiles at Maggie and grabs her arm, pulling her toward the elevator. The martini glass drops to the floor as her fingers grasp the manila envelope with the fake immunity papers.

"You look lovely, Maggie. We will have some fun tonight."

"Yeah? I got a few tricks I want to try on you as well."

The elevator closes. A minute later, five floors up, the elevator doors open.

Inside the closet, Remo racks the slide of his gun. He finishes the last of a pint bottle of Bulleit Bourbon, drops it on the floor and pulls the neck gaiter over his mouth and nose. Remo hears Russian voices and footfalls. Not good. Maggie was supposed to tell him through the earpiece if someone came with Tyruinov. Shadows cross under the closet door space in front of him. Remo turns the doorknob and cracks open the closet door. A man wearing a shoulder harness strapped across his back stands next to Tyruinov, with Maggie in front.

It was supposed to be quick and easy, five minutes, ten at the most. Hit Tyruinov in the back of the head and handcuff him. A big gold star for Kimball arresting his niece's rapist. Where the hell is 3Fingers and why did he not take out Tyruinov's bodyguard downstairs?

When the office door opens, Remo steps out from the closet and gun butts Tyruinov's bodyguard, dropping him to his hands and knees.

Semion turns around with his pistol pointed at Maggie's head, her hands tied in front and a gag in her mouth.

This was not the plan. With all Remo's contingencies, Maggie, with a gun to her head, was not on the list.

"Tyruinov, let her go and I won't kill you."

Semion's crooked smile grows. "Look what you did. The man you assaulted is Deputy Inspector Makim."

Shit happens fast. Remo hit a CPD deputy inspector. Grounds for dismissal. "You mean James Maksimov," Remo says. "Part of your Russian mafia? The CPD will stick a medal on my chest for revealing your man on the take."

Tyruinov pulls Maggie's hair. Her head snaps back, exposing a red slap on her right cheek. Semion Tyruinov did the wrong thing; he hit Maggie.

"What are you going to do now, Detective Remo Wolf? Yes, I know who you are, and I know who this pretty little thing is to you. And because of that, you will put your pistol on the floor."

"All right, don't go Crazy Ivan on me." Remo bends down and drops the gun on the floor, but the .32 caliber holstered on his right ankle stays put. Semion's foot kicks the weapon away.

"Maggie McCall, you didn't fool me one bit. You think I don't know you have the Wrigley Field robbers in custody? Makim told me before you came on the yacht." His fingers pull hard on her hair, rubbing his bristle-haired face into hers. "The news media will have a heyday reporting an undercover cop and a prosecutor found naked in an alley."

Makim shakes the cobwebs out of his head and stands. He grabs Remo's shirt. "I'll enjoy killing you, Wolf."

Semion's eyes turn toward a motion behind Remo. A gun barrel swings past Remo's ear. Maggie covers her head. Remo spins to see gun flashes in front of him and then a Mack truck hitting his head. Tyruinov lies facedown with a bullet hole in his back. Blood pours out of Makim's skull. Remo falls as he swipes at the boot of the assassin.

Chapter 46

Remo's head spins like a top. Screeching, rambling words come from behind him. He turns toward the noise, and something slaps him. An out-of-focus face with bright red lips yells muffled words. A hand slaps his face again, his focus returns.

Maggie yells, "Remo. I said, go get that bastard."

He hears footsteps bounding down the stairs. Shaking his head clear, he jumps up and charges toward the stairs. Somebody is jumping two steps at a time, now an entire floor ahead of him.

Remo fires three quick shots; two bullets splinter the railing, and the third hits the target. Remo jumps across the railing to the floor below. His boots pound the wood stairs.

An Uzi bursts a line of holes across the wall above Remo's head. Another jump over the railing gets Remo one floor closer. He sees a bloody handprint on the third-floor door with two fingers missing.

Remo says, "It has to be 3Fingers." He pulls the door open and follows a trail of blood down the hallway. It turns into the men's bathroom. Remo kicks the door open and yells, "Come out, kid." Water runs from the faucet, and paper towels spread over the floor

Behind Remo, 3Fingers has his arm wrapped in paper towels. The Uzi gun butts Remo in the back of the head. He drops to his knees and hears the kid run away.

"Damn it." Remo runs to the stairwell door and opens it. Bullets rip into the top of the door as it slowly closes. Remo pushes the door open again with the same result. He looks both ways down the hallway and runs toward the window at the end of the hall. He shatters the window and hurries down the fire escape stairs.

3Fingers runs outside the hotel, shoving trash cans and people out of his way. He turns into the alley.

Remo chases after the noise. He stops at the alley entrance and glances around the corner of the building. A barefoot man wrapped in a filthy blanket lies on his side next to a dumpster, swatting flies from his face. Decomposing rats and rancid milk odors fill the air.

"Come on out, kid."

"Get out of here, Che. He was my hit."

Remo realizes 3Fingers doesn't know he is a cop. He slips the badge under his shirt and calls out, "Come on. We need to get out of here before the cops come."

A voice comes from behind Remo. "Hi. What's goin' on?"

He looks behind him. A trashed-out girl with rotten teeth and tattered clothes smiles at Remo. She looks around the corner, and Remo pushes her behind him. "Get back, idiot. He has a gun."

She points down the alley and says, "I sleep down there. Don't you be tryin' to jack my place."

Remo grasps her dirty sweater, and she falls on her butt. He turns back toward the alley and yells, "Come on, kid. You got a dead end behind you."

3Fingers steps out from the dumpster and fires the Uzi. Bullets bounce off the brick building as the barrel flash spews fire into the air.

"Remember when I asked you if you can kill without being mad?" Remo turns the corner and fires twice into the dumpster. "You mad now or just a scared shitless little boy?" Remo's head spins. Is it the booze or the gun butt to his head?

"Let me out, Che. You took my hit from me. You said I could have it."

"You should have done what I told you. Busboy kills the bad man in the bar and runs away. No one would have picked you out. Tyruinov may be dead, but you got witnesses. Lots of them. People in the street and inside the hotel lobby, they'll be on the news talking about you."

"No. You took my hit."

"I'm willing to let you have Tyruinov."

"Jersey will take care of it. She's waiting on me."

"Jersey? What has she got to do with you? Besides, you forgot something. You need a piece of him to show off. Nothing to show off means you didn't do it. I think I'm going back and cutting me a couple of fingers off. When I show up next week at our funhouse with two fingers, I'll give them to you for that mangled mess of a hand you got."

"I wasn't trying to kill Tyruinov."

Remo tilts his head sideways. There was only one other cop there. The Killing Club kills cops. "You were after Makim? A deputy inspector?"

The girl steps around Remo and staggers down the alley.

"Get down," Remo yells.

She waves her hand in defiance.

Sirens wail in the distant air. 3Fingers snaps a new clip into the Uzi, steps out and fires a burst. Brick shatters across the building wall. The girl steps down the alley as if nothing happened. 3Fingers grabs her and holds her in front of him. She screams at him to let her go. He fires the Uzi again and then rushes toward the street.

A horn blares, tires screech. The girl's scream ends with a thud on a car hood.

Chapter 47

The girl looks like a broken mannequin on the pavement. 3Fingers' trail of blood returns, and Remo follows it across the street into an abandoned apartment building. Inside the small lobby, ribbons of drywall tape hang from the ceiling and the walls are carved with holes large enough for people to walk through. The stairs to the room have crumbs, used matches and wadded newspapers piled in the corners. He hears footsteps run up the stairs.

Remo steps up the dark stairwell. If the Uzi pops out, he has no place to hide. He's a dead man. "Come on, man. Let's put the guns down, go have a beer and laugh about tonight." He waits for a response. Nothing. "How about another one of those IPAs? You like them, didn't you?"

Remo hears a burst from the Uzi two floors up. "Shut up, Che. Leave me alone."

Distant footsteps run across an upstairs hallway. Remo's boots pound up the stairs two steps at a time, following a blood trail. People scream as he reaches the hallway. He hears glass breaking. Remo pops his head around the corner and looks down the hallway. Two apartments on the left have missing doors, and 3Fingers is trying to escape out a window. Remo fires, hitting the kid in the thigh. 3Fingers drops and rolls inside the apartment.

"What are you running away from? You don't need to run from Che."

"Fuck you, Che." He fires a quick burst into the hallway wall.

Remo calls out, "Come on, let's go celebrate your first kill." Nothing. "Listen, I got me another nice kill I can talk about at our next meeting. You can have this one. It's clean, all yours. Let's go back, and you can take whatever you want from Makim."

The apartment is forty feet away. If Remo runs down the hallway, he'll need a surprise, a diversion. He'll need a drink. Pulling out his last pint bottle from his inside jacket, he downs half.

Always loaded to the max, Remo pulls out a flash grenade from his cargo pants pocket. He pulls the pin and lets the handle pop in the air. Rushing down the hall, he stops next to the apartment entrance, pitches it inside, and covers his ears. Seconds later, the grenade explodes. Smoke and dust swirl in the air.

3Fingers squirms on the floor. Blood pours between his fingers with his hands over his ears.

Remo steps inside and kicks 3Fingers in the shoulder, rolling him on his back. He jams the pistol into 3Fingers' neck. "Can't let you out of here, kid."

3Fingers grabs a broken piece of mirror on the floor and swings a wide swath. An electric shock shoots up Remo's right arm, and he drops his gun.

The Chicago Police shield on the chain pops out of Remo's shirt. "You're a cop?"

3Fingers punches Remo's bleeding arm. 3Fingers jumps up when Remo rolls away.

"I should've listened to Jersey. She thinks you're dirty." 3Fingers grabs a metal folding chair and hits Remo across the chest.

Flat on his back, Remo kicks 3Fingers in the ankle, dropping him to the floor again.

He jumps on top of Remo, wrapping his mangled hand around Remo's neck. "Did you kill Euro? It was you! You killed my brother."

The grip is more than Remo ever expected. Bending down, he reaches inside his boot for a knife. Six inches of steel stab into 3Fingers' left flank. He howls and releases the death grip.

From outside, a man hanging on a rope crashes through the window. Captain Ton Kimball's military boots land on the floor. He pulls out two handguns. 3Fingers rolls on the floor and grabs the Uzi and pulls the trigger. It clicks again and again.

Gasping for breath, Remo says, "What the hell are you doing here, Ton?"

"I told my niece I would find who did that to her and kill him myself. I couldn't take him off that boat. As long as Makim or Krupin were around, Tyruinov was protected, and I needed you to pull him off the boat."

"It was Makim. He's dirty," Remo says. "The kid shot has nothing to do with your niece's rape. He shot Makim inside the Harrison."

3Fingers rolls to his hands and knees. "Wait a minute. I recognize that voice. It's you. You, you're the one on the phone. You paid me to kill Tyruinov."

Remo looks at his friend. "Ton, is that true?"

"Yes. I needed a backup plan but can't have a hitman I paid on the loose. Not good for my pension plan." Ton motions to 3Fingers. "Up."

The kid struggles to his feet. Blood drains down his side from the stab wound and a bullet in his leg.

Remo looks confused. "Wait. Makim was your hit? He was your target, not Tyruinov?"

His hand covers the stab wound. "Yeah, he was."

Remo points to Ton. "And he paid you to kill Tyruinov? You had two hits tonight?"

3Fingers struggles to keep his balance. "Yeah, two. I was making beaucoup money tonight."

Ton puts the pistol in his right hand down the front of his pants and steps to the kid. "Pigs get fed, hogs get slaughtered."

Ton's massive fist hits the kid across the face. Flying across the room, he slides to the wall with a broken jaw. Ton reaches for his pistol. It's gone. Leaning against the wall, 3Fingers points the gun straight ahead.

"That was the wrong thing to do," Ton says. "Now you're going to die." Ton raises the pistol in his left hand at his paid assassin. Both guns fire. A bullet buries into 3Fingers' chest, exploding his heart.

Ton falls to the ground and rolls. "Son of a bitch, that hurts."

Remo crawls to him. "Ton, come on, man, roll over. Let me see." There is no blood on the floor or on Ton. A bullet hole burned through his shirt. Buttons fly off as Remo rips the shirt open, revealing a round piece of lead stuck in Ton's armored vest.

"That hurts like a mother." With eyes squinted tight, he rubs his vest.

"That will be a bruise the size of a softball," Remo says.

"Help me up."

"Listen," Remo says. "I can take care of this mess. You get out of here."

"Check him first. Make sure he's dead."

With the boy's back is against the wall, arms next to his sides, and no breaths, Remo checks for a pulse—nothing.

"He's dead." While helping Ton stand, Remo says, "You are a lucky cop."

"Lucky, shit. Wearing a vest is not luck. You should try it some-time."

"I get this rash from it. It doesn't fit me right. Can't pull my Cubs t-shirt over it."

"I owe you one," Ton says. "A big one."

"No need to wait on that," Remo says. "I can't be the cop chasing the kid. It would blow my cover."

"Say no more." Ton points to Remo. "Tomorrow morning, in my office, and we talk about Truk."

Semion Tyruinov lies on an ambulance gurney, lethargic. His blood splattered across Maggie's new little black dress.

"Miss McCall," an EMT says. "His BP is low. He's going into shock. We need to take him downstairs and to the hospital."

Maggie's red spiked high heel spins back and forth in the little Russian's groin. He moans. "See this amnesty form?" She rips it in front of his face. "You will die in jail, Semion Tyruinov. I will make sure of that." She kicks the gurney; he groans in pain. "This blood-stained Armani dress cost me almost a week's pay, you son of a bitch. This dress was not for you. I bought this for Remo Wolf." She opens Semion's wallet and pulls out a wad of hundred-dollar bills, then drops the empty wallet on his chest. "You piece of shit, this should pay the bill to clean my dress." She shoves the money into her cleavage. "Get this bastard out of my sight."

The heart monitor shrieks a single note. "Cardiac arrest," the EMT says.

At the same time, Remo stands at the top of the stairs, arms across the banister. Makim is dead on the floor and the carpet is stained red by the open door. Her voice is music. The dress, snug against her body. The ceiling lights glisten in her red hair.

"Hey, beautiful," Remo says.

She turns toward Remo. Blood drips onto the floor from his arm. A wall of fright pounds into her like a tidal wave. She sprints in high heels, plants a kiss on him, and squeezes his bruised neck tight. "Please tell me you're okay."

Remo nods. "Yeah, sure."

"My God." Her hand waves in front of her face. "This whole thing made me hot," Maggie says.

"Blood on your dress? Are *you* all right?" he asks.

Her fingers jostle her hair. "Oh, hell yes. It's only Russian blood. You scared the shit out of me, Detective Wolf. I need a drink, and not downstairs."

"Me too."

"You're bleeding," Maggie says. "Let me look."

"Just a cut from a broken mirror."

She pulls his shirt sleeve up over his deltoid. She stops and looks. "How did this happen?" Her hand wipes the blood off the tattoo. "No one could have done this in a million years." The eagle tattoo had been cut just under the neck. She wipes a single tear off her face and smiles. "This doesn't count. Cutting the neck doesn't count. You still have an eagle head. You have one tattoo left."

Chapter 48

A lakefront freeze envelops the city the following morning. Maggie McCall sits at a small round table for two in a cozy Chicago Chinatown tea shop near West Thirty-Fourth and South Princeton Avenue. Both of her hands wrap around a porcelain cup full of hot liquid, trying to stay warm. The table is sticky from sugary pastries. A blackboard on the wall lists several teas in Chinese yuan prices, not dollars.

A black hoodie, black baseball cap and oversized sunglasses conceal her face. There is no good reason for a prosecutor to be here meeting a convicted felon who, again, is out on bail.

Dust bunnies swirl across the floor when the front door opens. A petite Chinese man with raven hair combed perfectly enters. Crossing the room, he slides a chair out and sits across the table from Maggie. With a mixed Ivy League/Chinese accent, he says, "Okay, I'm here. What do you want?"

"Johnny Quan, glad you decided to come," Maggie says. "You know what I want. I told you this morning. That's why I'm here."

He slips his black leather gloves off. "Do I?" The waitress passes by, and he points toward the blackboard and rattles an order of tea in Chinese.

She takes a sip from her cup. "You know the deal. Do this, and I will ignore your import business."

"My business is legit. I graduated from Cornell University. Which Chicago Community College did you attend?"

"Legit?" She scoffs. "I could annihilate your business tomorrow."

"If I do this for you and others find out, there is no telling what someone might do to me. Don't get me killed, lady. I have no problems with you."

"You do this one thing for me, and no one will find out about it. When you finish, I will make sure the CCSA goes easy on you at your trial next month."

Leaning back with arms folded over the long black wool coat, he says, "Maybe I want more."

"Maybe I should have you locked up when you walk out the front door," she snaps back.

He grabs the table edge in front of her and leans across until his face is inches from hers. His Ivy League accent is gone and replaced by his childhood street talk. "I slice pigs down the gut. Maybe you next one?"

The waitress slides a porcelain teacup in front of him while ignoring the conversation.

His fingers spin his teacup in slow motion as steam rises. "You don't know what I do," Johnny says. "You not smart enough to catch me. I got alibis for that murder." He grabs his gloves and smacks them on the edge of the table as he leans back against the chair. "If what you want gets out, I have to disappear. I got to watch my back for the rest of my life." He stands. "All for you and your *I'll-go-easy-on-you* attitude. Who else can do this favor for you? Any others? No, no one can."

The warmth is diminishing from her cup. "Sit down, asshole," Maggie says. "You want me to count the convictions when I was in Ohio? I've watched nine convicts strapped to a table as poison is shoved in their veins. In Chicago, over five hundred years in the pen between twelve convictions. And I've got a special place waiting for you, Quan."

He stands ready to leave. "You can go to hell, little Miss Assistant DA."

"You'll be there with me when I shove poison in Satan's vein, too. Sit down!"

Hands still on the table, he leans even closer and whispers, "All right, but I want ten thousand."

"No, one thousand is all you get."

His fingers grab the top of his teacup. "Ten." He drinks the rest of his tea. "And tonight, or not at all. You know where the place is, and then after that, don't come back to Chinatown. I don't want you near my family or my business. Chinatown bad for you. You bad for Chinatown."

"I know the place. I'll be there tonight." Head down, covering her face, she drinks the last of her tea. "You want ten? I'll give you ten. If I walk out and push the hood off my head, the cops will be in here in a second, and I will make sure you get ten. Ten years in the penitentiary at next month's trial." She stands, hoping the bluff holds.

His motionless stare is long. "Tonight."

"The deal's on, but you kill anybody else in this town, and I will personally send you to Cincinnati, Ohio and shove that poison in your vein myself."

He watches as she leaves with her hoodie still covering her head.

Chapter 49

That evening, Maggie's two fingers pinch the stem of a full martini glass while sitting at the table in the back of her favorite dive, gorgeous as usual. Her fuchsia overcoat hangs on the coat rack behind her. Wood crackles in the fireplace across the room. The nineteenth-century New Gate London wall clock shows 8:45. The usual crowd trickles in after ten. There are five empty tables with only one other couple in the restaurant; young and in love, they pay no attention to the world around them.

Remo walks in without a coat, wearing his Cubs t-shirt and jeans. She waves. He smiles back. His scotch with one cube is waiting for him at the table. Reaching over, he lightly kisses her creamy red lips. His eyes scan her baby blue dress with perfect décolletage.

The waiter steps to their table. "Mr. Remo, welcome back. Miss Maggie ordered your normal scotch. Is there anything else for now?"

"One more for me, please," Remo says.

Maggie waves her hand at the waiter. "Not right now, Sean. This will be fine."

A young waitress stands against the empty bar eating ice cream from a glass with unblinking eyes fixed on Remo. Maggie glances toward her and leans back. The corners of her lips slightly lift as she turns toward Remo. "I think you need a bigger shirt."

He nods. "Yeah, working out pretty hard lately. The bad guys are getting tougher. Got to keep up with them."

"Except a girl can take you down any day she wants," she mumbles.

Remo sips his scotch. "What?"

"Nothing, darling." Her fingers spin the red plastic pick holding two green olives lazily inside her martini.

Remo watches her red lips suck an olive off the plastic pick. He puts his scotch glass down and shakes his head. "How in the hell do these guys know where to shoot me? They shoot every one of my tattoos in the head, always the head."

The owner approaches the young couple and whispers. They stand, the young man shakes the owner's hand as the woman hugs him and they leave.

The waitress at the bar still fixates on Remo. Her full lips slide around a spoonful of ice cream. Maggie looks up and raises her eyebrows at the waitress, who waves the spoon in response.

Maggie turns back to Remo. "How many eagles do you have left?"

He drinks half of the scotch. "One. My first one. You know that. I think another scotch would be good. Why do you want to know?"

"You mean the one that 3Fingers guillotined?"

"Yeah."

"Thought so."

"Why are you asking about the tattoos?"

Ignoring his question while she holds her martini in the air, Maggie says, "To the original eagle and the 101st Airborne. Cheers."

The owner returns to their table, clasps his hands in front of them and smiles. "Mr. Remo, Miss Maggie has told me this is a special night. May I take a picture of the two of you?"

Remo's eyes shift toward her as she hands her phone to the owner. Remo's glabella bunches between his eyes in curiosity.

"Smile, Mr. Remo."

He looks at her as she raises her martini glass to him. Courtesy overcomes Remo's reluctance as his scotch glass clinks hers in waiting. The phone camera light flashes.

"Special night?" He swallows the other half of the scotch. "Am I forgetting something? Are we winging it, or do you have a specific plan?"

With a flirtatious but mischievous smile, she answers, "Oh, I have plans. Something new. Something extravagant." She sips her martini.

Fog rolls over Remo's eyes like binoculars turning out of focus. "I don't feel good."

"You shouldn't. Not after that Mickey I put in your drink."

His thick tongue slurs, "Maggie...what...are you...?"

"What am *I* doing? I'm going to help you, darling. We will take a brief ride because I made a deal with Johnny Quan. He said he would help me in return for giving you to him."

Remo's left arm drops toward his ankle holster, but his fingers feel like cream cheese. His eyes watch her turn sideways as he rolls to the floor.

Maggie raises her hand high in the air. Two EMTs waiting outside push a gurney through the front door and next to the unconscious Remo. Maggie's eyes shift toward the waitress still standing at the bar with her spoon in hand. Maggie steps to her as the EMTs lift Remo on the gurney. With a half-smile, Maggie asks the waitress, "Any problems?"

The spoon clinks inside of the empty glass. "No, but when you tire of him, I'll take him off your hands."

"Thanks, but I'll keep him for now." Maggie follows the gurney as it rolls outside to a waiting ambulance with lights flashing. With her prize loaded in the back, Maggie climbs in and the doors shut behind her. The emergency lights go dark, and the ambulance turns the corner slowly.

The driver asks, "Where we are going, Miss McCall?"

"South Keeler and Sixteenth."

"Keeler? Hell no. That's K-Town. I don't *ever* go to K-Town. They'll strip this ambulance and kill everyone inside at a stoplight. Nope, not there."

"Listen, you little pissant," Maggie barks back. "I paid you two hundred bucks to take me anywhere I want. Nobody there will hurt you where we're going."

"Listen, lady. I got no desire to die today."

"If you don't take me there, I will pull the license of this ambulance company, and you can piss your certification goodbye. Man up and get me there fast."

"All right, but if I get shot, you will be in a lot of trouble."

She whispers in Remo's ear, "Not as much trouble as he will for driving around with a drugged man in the middle of K-Town." She releases the straps around him on the cot. "Time to strip down for me, darling. Ankle holster first, no guns allowed where we are going." She pulls his shirt over his head, unbuckles the belt, and pulls the pants down. "Really? Do you not own any underwear?"

After ten minutes, Remo's eyelids flicker. The ambulance driver watches the street for trouble while he unloads his passenger. Remo gazes at blurred stars as the gurney passes through a dilapidated storefront. Maggie follows behind them.

Johnny Quan stands outside. "Look, I told you that drink wouldn't last long. He's moving. This could be disastrous if he wakes."

Maggie pushes the gurney faster. "Hurry up." She points to the table. "You got the gas ready?"

The two EMTs shove Remo to the stainless steel table as Quan places the mask over Remo's mouth. He sleeps again.

Maggie glares at the two EMTs and squeezes her hand on the driver's shoulder. "You be back here in two hours, on the dot. Don't give me any lip about you're out on a pickup. Be here or lose your jobs."

The roar of the ambulance engine fades away in the distance. Maggie holds the mask over Remo's face as Johnny checks his medical equipment before grasping the overhead light and shining it on Remo's face and neck. Looking at Maggie once more, he asks, "You sure about this?"

She pulls the sheet down to Remo's waist. "Do it."

❖

Remo lies in bed at his home. A white sheet covers him. Maggie pulls the blinds, and bright sunlight slaps his face. The anesthesia pounds his head worse than his last hangover. His body feels a hundred pounds heavier. Maggie, still out of focus, stands next to the window. A big yellow ball in the sky screams its brightness at him. His vision widens, his focus returns. Her oversize Chicago Bears jersey covers her from mid-thigh up. She has bare legs crossed at the ankles and holds a coffee cup in hand. "Good morning," she says.

Surprised by her presence, he fumbles under the pillow. His pistol is not there.

She pulls the long metal hair stick from behind her head. Her red hair falls perfectly around her shoulders. "Silly boy." She points to the desk across the room. "I put it over there for safekeeping."

After a half-assed attempt to reach for the gun, his head pounds and drops to the pillow again. "What did you do to me last night?"

"I saved your life."

"Saved me? From whom? Didn't know anyone was after me last night."

Maggie puts the cup on the dresser and sits on the edge of the bed. "Listen, Remo. I took things into my own hands. Destiny bullshit sort of stuff."

"Let me get this straight. You drugged me and gave me this massive headache to save me?"

"Well, yes. I don't know if you would have done what I wanted, so I did it anyway. You know that forgiveness versus permission crap."

His head feeling less heavy and blurry, he sits halfway up, stuffing his pillow against the headboard. "Coffee, please."

She steps to the dresser and grabs the cup. "It's hot, be careful."

After taking a sip, he stops and looks at her. "You didn't, ah..." pointing to the cup.

"Oh, no. Like you want it, half teaspoon of honey, nothing extra."

An image pops in Remo's head. "What about Johnny Quan? What was he doing with you?"

"Not me, darling, you. It's what he did to you. You must promise no retribution against Johnny. After this, you can take on Jersey and that Fedora person."

"What? What are you talking about?"

She stands, her naked legs wide apart, with her hands on her hips below the number 54 on her jersey. Her eyes glare into his. "Promise me."

His hand waves in front of her. "All right. No retribution. What did he do?"

She flips the bedsheet back, revealing a naked Remo with five fresh eagle tattoos. One on each arm and leg and the left chest.

With a commanding voice, she says, "You had one tattoo left for someone to shoot, and then I know you would probably die. I'm not going to let you die. Johnny Quan was the only tattoo artist willing to do what I wanted. You should be proud of him. His work is fantastic."

Remo views the tattoos. He points to the one on the chest. "This is not the logo for the 101st. It's not a profile. Why is it so large and with eyes?"

"He can see me when I'm with you."

Chapter 50

A local television station announces a breaking news flash on the five o'clock broadcast. Annalisa Moreman, a news anchor, reads from the teleprompter. "Good evening, Chicago. Miss Maggie McCall, Assistant Cook County State's Attorney, is giving a press conference on the Cook County Criminal Division Courthouse's steps. Let's go to Brenda Nielsen now."

Maggie stands behind a tall podium with five microphones taped together. She counts twelve reporters, each with their cameraman next to them, eighteen more reporters with their audio recorders held up high in their hands. Each is hoping for something interesting. Suspicion and questions sell papers and get more people to watch the television.

A scattering of people on the sidewalk watch the spectacle unfold on the courthouse steps. She glances at a young man to her left as he points to her to talk.

"As a candidate for Cook County State's Attorney, I am releasing my six-point plan to clean up the CCSA office. Richard Watters has lost millions of dollars of uncollected fines and judgments because of the CCSA's office incompetency. There is a backlog of months, if not years, in cases. The personnel turnover in the office is unprecedented."

A camera spins back to Brenda Nielsen. "Annalisa, Miss McCall has agreed to give us an exclusive interview immediately following her announcement. We will have that available tonight at ten o'clock."

Outside at the courthouse plaza, there is a small pergola. Maggie sits on a stool with a bright light shining on her face. She winces at the thought of talking to Brenda Nielsen, the reporter who questions every conviction as an injustice to the poor Chicago downtrodden. She sits across from Maggie.

The cameraman aims his lens at Brenda. With a flip of her hair and a plastic smile, she asks, "We have Miss Maggie McCall with us today." Brenda turns her left shoulder a few inches to reveal her better side. "Miss McCall, what made you decide to run for the Cook County State's Attorney's position?"

Maggie smiles back. "Thank you, Brenda. After over forty felony convictions and sending dozens of criminals to hundreds of years in jails, I know I can do more for this great city and county. The people of Cook County and the City of Chicago deserve to be safe. Being the CCSA, I can do much more to help."

"Who helped you with your six-point plan?"

"Each of these six items is within the core of our county's problems. I hold each very dear to my heart and will do everything I can to implement each and every one."

"After you announced your candidacy, you have continuously charged Mr. Watters as incompetent. Do you think Mr. Richard Watters, the present State's Attorney, feels slighted? He invited you into his office five years ago, and now you want to take his job."

With an equally plastic smile, Maggie replies, "I feel there is a need for new directions for our city and Cook County. I have pondered this move for months. The encouragement from many business leaders has been enormous. As far as Mr. Watters is concerned, we have been in discussions."

"Has Mr. Watters agreed with you?" Brenda asks with arched eyebrows. "Is he going to announce he is stepping down?"

She feels like someone poured cement powder on her tongue as she clears her throat. This is not her comfort zone of charging into an accused within the courtroom. Politics is a firm slap on the face. "I expect Mr. Watters to continue pursuing this illustrious position. I let him know of my plan ahead of this announcement, and he wished me luck."

"So, he is not endorsing you on the ballot. He is not even supporting you on the ballot." Brenda's smirk says it all. "Do you think he meant good luck with that?"

So much for being polite. Maggie takes a breath and says, "I believe the great city of Chicago needs a new direction, and my six-point plan, which is being released to the public, as we speak, will improve safety, health and public relations with the populous of Chicago. It will bring safety to women and children under constant threat. As we hear on the news every day, young teenage boys and girls are being gunned down. I wholeheartedly believe my plan will help reduce that terrible statistic."

Brenda Nielsen looks directly into the camera and says, "There you have it. Maggie McCall is running for Cook County State's Attorney and promises things will be better for you if you vote for her."

❖

The following week, USPS delivers boxes of letters on a wheeled dolly to her office. Halsey, Mr. Watters's secretary, knocks on Maggie's half-open office door. "Miss McCall," she says. "The asshole wants me to remind you, you cannot use government time for your campaign."

A quick nod, both agree he *is* an asshole. "These letters are from fans of the community. I can't regulate where they're sent." Maggie smiles and looks at the clock on the wall. "It's 12:02. It is officially lunchtime, my time. I don't see any political property. Do you?"

Halsey turns to make sure her boss is not near and whispers back to Maggie, "See you after lunch...and good luck."

"Maggie," Danny Williams, her executive assistant and unofficial campaign manager, steps behind Halsey. "I have some news we need to talk about—in private."

Halsey wiggles her fingers goodbye and leaves.

Danny presses play on his phone. Maggie watches a video of Remo aiming his pistol toward Rolly Chang and Johnny Rivera's backs. The building beside Remo is on fire. The video seesaws in and out of focus. Mouths are moving, but the sounds of the voices are mumbled. Remo, holding his pistol, steps back. The Cadillac SUV blocks the view.

Two seconds later, clarity fades as the sound of a gunshot erupts. Johnny falls forward to the ground. It looks like Remo shot Johnny Rivera in the back.

The video lasts four seconds. Four seconds is a long time in a campaign.

"Okay, not good. Here's what I saw," Maggie says. "Remo had two suspects in custody, but there were no arms up. Why? Inaudible words were spoken. Why poor sound? I didn't see either of the two turn toward Remo. That's not good either. This video is not coincidental to my campaign. Who was the person videoing it?" She steps to the side of her desk. "This is a setup. Somebody must want something. Otherwise, it would have been released to the news by now."

Danny's phone dings a new message. "Oh, shit. It says to watch the news."

Halsey knocks on her door. "Maggie, you need to turn on the local news."

Danny grabs the remote and turns on the television. The words 'BREAKING NEWS' in bright, bold, red letters splash across the screen. Brenda Nielsen comes on with a smirk she can't hide. She holds a large envelope in her hand, stating an anonymous person dropped it off at the station desk a few minutes ago. The camera slowly zooms in while she looks directly into the lens and announces, without specific words, a coming shitstorm. The screen changes to the video Maggie watched a few seconds ago. "We have received this video clip within the last hour of what looks like Detective Remo Wolf shooting a man in the back." After the video plays twice, a picture of Remo before he went undercover is on the screen. "We have been told there seems to be a connection between Miss McCall and this detective." Another recent picture flashes on the screen of Remo and her standing and smiling together.

"She killed his cover," Maggie says. "The Club will be coming after him. How did she find that picture? Turn it off."

"What club?" Danny asks.

Maggie shakes her head. "Nothing. Forget what I said."

"You want me to call the detectives' office and see if he's there?" Danny asks.

"No, he's gone deep undercover by now."

A yellow sun pierces a ceiling-to-floor window in Maggie's office. Glare bounces off the silver picture frame on her desk. It's her favorite hole-in-the-wall with Remo and her sitting at a table. They're holding their drink glasses next to each other, and he's wearing a Cubs t-shirt and his perfect smile. It's the night she kidnapped him and put five more tattoos on him to save his life.

"We will never find that man. He's a gopher with too many holes in the city. It would take us weeks if not months to find him—if ever."

She shakes her head. "It will take more than eagle tattoos to save him this time."

"Ma'am?"

She waves her hand. "Nothing."

"What are you going to do?"

Stuffing papers in her briefcase, she says, "Call forensics and have them review the video. Make sure it's legit. Have to make sure there is nothing edited, spliced, or photoshopped."

Chapter 51

Jersey leans back into her chair, holding the television remote, and keeps pushing replay. The video restarts again and again. "You damn dirty son of a bitch, Che." She straightens up in the chair. "That was you in the ambush. I never saw your face. I can see you now, a big man in a police uniform standing next to the police car. I should have killed you in the garage. If you were dead, then Euro would still be alive. You killed him at that prosecutor's house. It was you." She stands and pitches a knife. It stabs the center of the target on the wall. "I'm going to kill you."

Rosie stands from her chair. "How good you know this guy?" She remembers she gave out info to him about Jersey. "He's a cop?" Remo was sitting in their front room and promised her a hit for ten thousand in the next few days. She needed the money, so she believed him.

Jersey turns back. "Shut up. I have to think." She finishes her Goose Island beer and slams it on the table. "At least he doesn't know where we are. Otherwise, he's going to try to kill Solido and me. We all killed cops and talked about them." She steps to the window and pulls the blinds down a little. "It will leak back that I killed Chicago cops. The entire force will come after me."

Rosie walks toward her bedroom. "I gosta get out a here. I ain't goin' back ta the slammer."

"We'll be okay for a little while," Jersey says. "We don't need to leave just yet."

Rosie comes out of her room with clothes sticking out of her backpack and turns toward Jersey's bedroom.

"Whoa, girl. Where the hell do you think you're going?"

"I need knives. I don't need none of them big ones. That'll put me in jail." She spreads a pile of knives across the dresser. "Smaller than four inches. Can't get stopped with a knife longer than four." She spins the backpack around, shoves several knives inside and turns toward the closet. "I need money. Where is it?"

Jersey shoves Rosie back. "You ain't getting shit. I know you already stole from me."

Rosie stares at Jersey. "What you talkin' 'bout?"

"I know you stole money from me. Almost the first day you were here."

"That's bullshit. I ain't takin' nuthin from you."

Jersey glares at Rosie. "The cops searched this house, and you know what they found? My box of money, except some of it was gone. You took it."

"You wrong, Jersey. Bet them cops took it. Not me. I didn't take nuthin."

"How'd you know to go to the closet for money?"

"All right, fine. I took some. I didn't take it all. I could have and run, but I didn't."

"Why are you in such a hurry to leave? You know something?" Jersey's eyes widen. "Shit. Wolf is a cop, and I'll bet he knows about my house getting searched. He knows where I live."

Rosie glances at the knives spread across the dresser. She grabs a large one and points it at Jersey. "I need money."

"Little sister, you've never been fast enough to beat me at anything. Think you're going to now? I can take you with my bare hands."

Rosie points the knife at Jersey and takes a step forward.

Jersey takes a defensive stance. "This would be the first time."

Rosie's knife clatters to the floor. "I'm gone. Get out of my way." She hastens to the back door and glances out the window. Opening the door, she says, "Good luck, sis. You need it." The door slams behind her.

Chapter 52

On the south side of the Chicago River, a five-story, gray stone building stands with 'CFSSC' painted across the top in black three-foot-tall block letters. The Chicago Forensics and Strategic Storage Center is where police evidence is collected and stored. Razor wire crowns atop a ten-foot chain-link fence surrounding the building. A guard tower stands next to a narrow driveway with an industrial sliding chain-link gate allowing one vehicle in or out at a time. A police officer pretends to read his clipboard, then looks above his dark glasses. Maggie's car slows to a stop next to him. With a flash of her department badge, he lets her through.

Inside the building, staccato clicks of her high heels echo down the white-tiled floor. She stops at a dark stained door, turns the knob and pushes the door open. A conglomeration of keyboards clacking, people talking and computers beeping fills the air.

A man in a white lab coat cuddles a wireless mouse in his right hand, his eyes glued to a computer monitor. 'Antonio Souza, PhD, University of Chicago' is embroidered in blue above his left chest pocket. A lanyard holds his City of Chicago identification card around his neck.

"Tell me what you have," Maggie says.

He pulls the wire-rim glasses from his face and places them on the desk. He shakes his head at her. "I told you on the phone, Miss McCall. It's too early."

"I need something now," Maggie insists.

"Miss McCall, this will take days, if not weeks, to confirm if that video is real. If Detective Wolf shot that prisoner."

Maggie reaches for the ID card. "Listen to me, Professor Souza." Maggie releases the card and leans forward with her palms flat on his desk. Souza glances at her cleavage. Sex sells. "It's Tony, isn't it? I'm confident you can find how this was manipulated. I don't believe for a second this is real. Detective Wolf did not shoot *anyone* in the back. Got it?"

Her elbows tighten closer. Souza glances again at her cleavage and then back to her face.

"Didn't you bring your wife and two children from Argentina to Chicago recently? Listen, Tony." Maggie turns and leans against the desk. She slides Souza's glasses back on his face. With a perfect smile, she says, "If I need to come here more often, I will. I need you to get this info ASAP. Understand? I know you can do this for me." Her index finger wraps around his lanyard, jerking him closer to her. "Don't get me wrong, I can be as nice as the next girl." Her smile disappears as she pulls hard on the lanyard. "Or I can find a way to put half your family on trumped-up charges and deport them next month. Tomorrow morning, I want some evidence. Got it?"

"Yes, ma'am, I'll start right away."

Souza waits for the door to close behind her. He touches a favorite on his phone.

"You told me nobody would find me... I fixed it for you as you wanted. I trimmed the edges, added muzzle flare, everything... I understand what you are saying... No. I am saying she told me if I don't find the original, she will send my family back to Argentina... I gave you both videos. I want out."

Chapter 53

The sun gives way to the end of the day. From her office window, a cloudless sky turns indigo. Maggie's ups and downs feel like a seismic graph of a volcano erupting for the last twenty-four hours. Her eyes water. She knows she won't see Remo tonight. She won't see Remo for a long time, if ever again.

Danny is sitting at his small desk in her office. She turns toward him. "Danny, I got to get this figured out."

"Chicago people are fickle," Danny says. "They will flip to Watters quickly if we don't fix this."

"Right," she sighs. "I know."

"Don't forget the fundraiser tonight." Danny swings his laptop around the desk. "You lead by eighteen points after your announcement. Since Detective Wolf's television debut, you dropped nineteen points. I need to stay another thirty minutes or so. I'll catch up to you when I'm finished."

"Right, got to go." She stuffs papers in her shoulder bag and heads for the door. Maggie's high heels click like quarter notes down the abandoned hall.

The elevator door opens. Two hands shove Maggie back. "Maggie McCall," Jersey says with a smile. She looks down both sides of the hallway. "You alone up here?"

Maggie's shoulder bag, holding a Glock and two full magazines, slides down her arm. She wraps the shoulder strap around her left hand twice. "What do you want, Jersey?"

"You know who I am?"

"Pretty damn obvious, don't you think? A blind man would cringe at that face."

"That's not very nice." Jersey reaches for Maggie's face. "You hurt my feelings."

Maggie slaps Jersey's hand away. "Back off, bitch."

"Let's go to your office and talk."

"I'm not going anywhere with you," Maggie says. "What do you want?"

"Since the moment Che was on television, *excuse me,* Detective Wolf, I knew what was going on. You know about all the bad shit that needs to be hidden."

"I don't know what you're talking about, and you're in my way. Move your ass!"

"Don't sling that shit on me." Jersey points her finger near Maggie's face. "You know exactly what I'm talking about, and you know about the killings, and you did nothing but hide the facts."

Maggie slaps Jersey's hand away again. "Get that finger out of my face."

Jersey points toward herself. "You need to bring Che to me."

"Why should I do that?"

Jersey's finger pushes against Maggie's chest. "I got this figured out. That piece of shit killed cops just like the rest of us."

"Every person he talked about was fake. He killed no one."

Jersey's finger taps Maggie's chest. "Wrong."

Maggie's palm shoves Jersey's forehead, pushing her head back. "I'm going to snap that finger off."

"I think your boss would love to hear about it, don't you? A cop killing cops while his girlfriend-prosecutor knows all about it?"

"So, you're going to tell Richard Watters you're killing the police and then say you paid a police officer to do the same thing? Did you get a check or a credit card receipt? Which part of that do you think *nobody* will believe?" Her hand tightens around the purse strap.

Jersey's smile disappears, eyes widen, her nostrils flare open. "Because I know where your little brother lives. Seattle, right?" Jersey turns her phone toward Maggie. A picture of David, her brother, standing in a checkout line. "Give me the cop."

Maggie's pointed fingernails jab into Jersey's throat. A left roundhouse of Maggie's heavy purse hurls against Jersey's ear as her head slams back against the elevator door.

"You touch David and I'll kill you myself."

Jersey shakes her head, clearing the fog. She stares at a gun barrel pointed at her face.

"You need to leave. Now!" Maggie says. "I have no problem pulling the trigger."

"Bring Remo to me, or bad things *will* happen to David."

"I don't even know where Remo is. He's on the run, gone. Who the hell knows where he could be?" Maggie's gun motions to the side. "Back away from the elevator."

"There is still a contract out on you," Jersey says coyly. "Let's play a little while." A knife slides out from the inside of Jersey's thigh-high boot. "Come on, pretty girl," Jersey leers. "Tell me, how fast are you with that gun? Fast enough?"

Jersey grabs Maggie's breast. She flinches as Jersey swings the knife, hitting against the barrel. A gunshot echoes down the hallway. The bullet thuds into the wall.

Maggie drives her high heel into Jersey's foot. A red circle grows on the floor around Jersey's boot.

"Damn, girl," Jersey laughs. "You got those heels shaved to a point?"

"Get out of here." Maggie pushes the elevator button while pointing the barrel between Jersey's eyes. "I won't miss again."

Maggie's office door opens.

Without turning around, Maggie yells out, "Shut the door, Danny."

The elevator dings. Aiming her knife at Maggie, Jersey steps backward as a line of red drops follows inside the elevator. Jersey blows her a kiss and says, "See you later, girlfriend."

Their eyes lock on each other as the elevator doors close. Maggie takes a deep breath; her arm goes limp as she holds the pistol to her side.

Danny rushes to her side. "You okay? Who was that?"

Out of breath, Maggie slips the gun back into her bag. She sends a message to Remo on his pager. *Be careful. Jersey knows everything.*

She steps to the hallway windows. Jersey is limping down the street.

"Back inside the office," Maggie says. "We need to cancel the fundraiser. We're going to be busy tonight."

"Who was that?"

"Someone who is not planning to vote for me."

Chapter 54

An hour later, Danny plugs a white cord into Maggie's phone. He says, "I'm ready."

Maggie hands Danny a pair of noise-canceling headphones. "Put these on, and don't say a word. You don't want to hear anything I am going to say." She presses a recent number on her phone and types a message.

Remo's pager buzzes. *Call me.* He flips his phone open. While sitting on a bench inside Mount Carmel Cemetery, he speed-dials Maggie's number.

Her phone rings. 'UNKNOWN' is across the screen. "Remo, darling," she answers.

"You know I didn't do that," Remo says.

Inside Maggie's office, she stands in front of the large windows. The sky is as black as death. Red warning lights flash on top of tall buildings. She sighs deeply. "Yes, I know that, but nobody else does. Professor Souza at the CFFSA said the video was unaltered."

"That's bullshit."

She turns to see if Danny is still wearing his headphones. "You on a burner?" Maggie asks.

"Burner, yes. Why?"

"Jersey knows."

"Knows what?"

"About us, your plan, the club. I can't say much over the phone. Jersey wants me to turn you over to her, or she'll reveal the plan."

"Obviously she has no witnesses. They are indisposed. Who would believe her?"

"Doesn't matter who believes her. An accusation this close to the election would kill both our futures." Maggie strokes her fingers through her hair. She adjusts Danny's headphones on his ears. Her toes squirm inside the high heel shoe. "You need to come in. I can put you in protective custody or a separate cell with no one else around. Hiding makes you look guilty."

She moves the cord away from her elbow that connects her phone to Danny's laptop. Four large letters blend into the screen background, ON IT, Online Illinois Tracker. Danny is deaf to the call, but he watches his screen display random horizontal lines crossing vertical lines over a Chicago map.

"Protective custody? Solitary confinement in a prison cell," Remo says. "I prefer not to. It seems prisons have not been the safest place to be. There are too many accidental suicides in prison."

"We can work this out," Maggie says.

"No thanks," Remo says. "This is a setup, and I *will* find who took the video and...well, he will tell the truth."

"Do you have the video from the news?" Maggie asks. "I can send it to you. May take a few seconds to transfer it from my computer to your phone."

"Send it after I hang up."

"No, no. I'm sending it while you're on the phone. I want to make sure you see it. It'll take just a moment or two." The horizontal line on the ON IT screen slows down. "Darling, tell me where you are, and I can come see you."

Danny motions to stretch the call out. The horizontal line stops. The vertical line rolls left to right.

"Meet me somewhere and let me bring you in. Voluntary surrender. This will help both of us."

"Both of us? Are you trying to make this a campaign issue? Bringing me in for a few more votes?"

"No, no, not at all." Her throat tightens, a quick cough loosens it. "When I'm the new Cook County State's Attorney, I won't prosecute you. I'll say there is not enough evidence." The ON IT vertical line stops. It crosses the horizontal line at highways I-294 and I-290, or the "Ike," as Chicagoans call it.

"What the hell are you talking about? You want to prosecute me. I told you this was a setup. Maybe...maybe you think this is a good thing. But only for you." His phone snaps closed.

Maggie motions to Danny to take his headphones off. "Did you locate him?"

"He is somewhere near I-294 and the Ike. A big cemetery is near there," Danny says. "Are you going to call Chief Maxwell and have him send out a squad for Wolf?"

Maggie shakes her head no. "Of course that's where he is, Mount Carmel Cemetery. That is where his partner, Bobby Lynch, is buried."

"Then you got him. Send out a squad for him."

"No. He's gone by now. It's dark and too many places to hide and escape." Maggie folds the laptop and holds it under her arm. "I'll carry this with me. I have his phone number, and I'll call him in the morning with the ON IT already running. Maybe it will locate him quicker."

"You need to bring him in," Danny says. "The polls are turning against you. You bring him in, and you win this election."

"Listen, we canceled the fundraiser tonight," Maggie says. "I need to go to the one full of bankers tomorrow morning."

Danny hands her two manila folders. "Right, you need to focus on two whales, Jacksboro and Wilcox. Both have a ton of money, and both hate Richard."

She drops the folders into her pouch. "Meet me there at nine and don't be late."

❖

A single headlight turns down a side street next to Mount Carmel Cemetery. The Indian rumbles slowly while Remo looks for a specific elm tree, wide, tall, a century old. He stops next to the metal fence, cuts the engine, and snaps the kickstand out. Rolling over the fence like a high jumper, he lands on the other side. Bobby's gravesite is fifty feet away with his name, dates, and Protect and Serve etched on the tombstone. On his grave sits a burning three-wick candle, a folded note, and a handful of fresh mixed flowers. A mass of wilted flowers lies at the corner of the headstone. He looks around. Remo aims his pistol at a shadow next to a tree trunk.

"Come out with your hands up."

Becky Lynch steps forward with her hands in the air. "I don't have a gun."

Remo lowers his weapon. "Just cautious." He decides to continue to hold it and not holster it. "All these flowers from you?"

"Come most nights when everyone is gone."

"My first. Couldn't make myself come."

"Your fault he's dead."

Remo nods. "Maybe."

"Watched the news, and you're in trouble. If Bobby were alive, he would have helped you."

"If he was alive, I wouldn't be in this mess."

She gathers the elongated utility lighter and the folded note from the ground. "I miss him. I'm leaving."

"Where's your car?"

She stabs the night air with the elongated lighter. "Front gate. I like the walk."

"You can leave the note."

"It's private, just him and me." She trudges off.

Remo glances at the flowers and notepad next to it. "You left your…" She's too far down the path to hear.

Picking up the notepad, he sees imprints on the top page. He tears it off, shines it at an angle from the candlelight and reads, 'I'M SORRY.'

"I'm sorry too, Bobby."

Chapter 55

An hour later, inside one of Remo's apartments, he shoves t-shirts, an extra pair of jeans, his laptop and a charger into a backpack. He checks the window every few seconds. He slings his bag over his left shoulder. The picture of Maggie and him at the hole-in-the-wall restaurant hangs on the wall next to his bed. Smashing the glass, he pulls out the photo and shoves it inside his leather jacket. A single gray smoke trail climbs above his incense holder. His thumb and finger press it out.

Remo checks the saddlebags while the engine idles in the back alley. "Damn, not enough ammo." Snapping the top of the saddlebag back down. "Can't buy ammo at the store, probably has my face and name already listed as 'call the cops.' The warehouse on the west side has what I need." His leg swings wide over the seat. Kickstand up, Remo revs the engine twice and pops the clutch lever as the back tire laces a rubber track on the concrete. He's on the run.

◆

A narrow abandoned bridge built in the 1920s hovers over a flowing creek. The engine rumbles as tires roll slowly across the bridge. An empty warehouse stands on the other side with faded paint across the top declaring Jackson and Pitchman once owned it before the last World War. It has been vacant for decades. Remo's bike coasts to the back door.

His prepaid phone is three days old, too old for a man on the run. Traceable. Minutes later, he leans back in an overstuffed leather chair inside the building, feet propped up on a well-worn desk inside the glass-enclosed office. His plastic fork pierces diced beef from an MRE, meal-ready-to-eat. A short glass with a double shot of scotch sits next to a half-full bottle. On the phone, he watches the video Maggie sent him.

Behind him, a safe is embedded in the concrete floor. He spins the combination lock and snaps the lever open. Grenades and boxes of ammo sit inside. He needs to keep the SIM card containing the video, so he pulls it out of the phone and drops it in the safe. He reaches for a new burner phone. The safe door slams shut, and the dial spins. "All right, I need a real meal." The motorcycle crosses the bridge and turns right toward Stevenson Expressway. The engine sound fades down the street.

Chapter 56

Davy's mobile phone rings next to his bed. The screen reads, 'UNKNOWN.' "Hello," he mumbles.

"You alone?" Remo asks.

"Yeah, it's after midnight. What happened? Can't see you shooting someone in the back, especially with witnesses, you know."

Remo raises an off-white ceramic coffee mug to his lips. The last of the coffee slides down his throat. He is the last customer inside a small diner with black and white squares covering the pre-seventies floor. Red and black vinyl booths and Formica-covered tables align against the walls. Out past the plate-glass window, yellow lights wheel through the air, warning no one that a street sweeper cleans trash off the road.

"No, it didn't happen that way. Jiang was behind me, lying down with a bullet in his leg and half his face gone. He tried to shoot me but missed and hit Rivera in the back. Bullet went clean through, so there is no bullet for ballistics."

"Had to be a cell phone video, you know," Davy says.

"Yeah, had to be," Remo says. "Along with the video, someone sent several stills to Maggie and the press. Bet he downloaded it to a computer and sent it out."

"Did she send those pics to you from her phone, you know?"

"Pretty sure it was from her laptop to my phone."

A waitress dangles a half-burnt cigarette in her mouth and strides to Remo with a clear carafe full of black liquid. She taps the ash onto his empty pie plate and fills his mug again. Remo points to the pie plate on the metal counter for another slice. "Thanks, Betty." She takes the fifty-dollar bill folded between his fingers to keep her quiet.

"I can track the IP address, you know."

"How?"

"She sent the video from her laptop to your phone? Bring your phone to me, you know."

"That's evidence. Some lawyer could figure out how to use it against you. You don't want that."

"But you got it, right?"

"Still got the SIM card, but I don't hand anything over to anyone."

Davy chuckles. "All the stuff I have in the basement is enough to put you and me away for a long time, you know."

"It's hidden in a safe place."

"Bring that SIM card to me in the morning, and I can plug it into my computer. I can hack into her laptop through the card and download the video and everything else on her laptop. I have a way to pull that IP address, you know."

Remo's pager beeps. It is the phone number to the camera above the front door of his central apartment. "Hold on. I need to call another number on a separate phone."

Remo pulls another phone from his pocket and calls the camera's phone number; the phone screen shows police with SWAT gear walking up the steps to his second-floor apartment. He scrolls left and right with the camera, revealing five officers at the door and two at the bottom of the stairs.

"I got company, Davy. One of my apartments has been compromised. Got to go," Remo says. "Can I stay at your place for a while in that extra room in the garage?"

"No." With a click, the phone goes dead.

Chapter 57

Remo taps T** on the phone, then watches the scene.

Detective Belly Lynch hears talking behind the front door. He steps to the side of the door and lets the four police officers in black Kevlar gear and riot helmets stand at the door. One officer holds a tactical breaching tool, a battering ram. It's the master key to all entries.

"Ready?" Belly whispers for confirmation. Each officer motions, thumbs-up.

"I've got this place rigged to explode. Don't come in here." When Remo pushes H** on the phone, an air horn blares inside the apartment. He laughs and pushes FL**. Flood lamps from the corners of the outside overhang snap bright toward the front door.

Betty slides another slice of apple pie across the table. "Playing a game on your phone?"

Remo holds his phone against his chest. "Thanks, Betty. You're a doll."

Remo taps S** on his phone. White smoke fills the apartment and rolls out from the front door threshold across the officers' black boots. The lead officer holds his arm up in a stop position. Belly sweeps his hand in the air. "No, he doesn't." He yells above the air horn, "Go on, bust through the door."

The battering ram pounds against the deadbolt lock and shatters the flimsy door. Men charge inside and within minutes call out the front room and kitchen are clear. Belly steps into the apartment while fog as thick as a San Francisco morning blocks his vision. Bright lights snap on from the ceiling. The air horn still blares.

Remo taps G** on his phone. The sound of gunfire bursts from the bedroom. Belly drops to the floor. Remo switches to another camera inside the apartment above the front door.

A neighbor's voice from the other side of the wall yells, "I'm calling the cops."

Belly yells out toward the broken front door, "We are the cops, you idiot."

Remo laughs as he watches bodies step through the fog. He takes another bite of the pie.

"Remo Wolf, you are under arrest for the murder of Johnny Rivera. Come out with your hands up." Belly's pistol scans the fog. He taps the back shoulder of the last officer in line and yells above the horn, "Go back to the kitchen and break that window. Get this smoke out."

Remo's voice yells from the bedroom, "Get out while you can. I'm going to blow this place." He switches to the camera in the hallway toward the bedroom and sees three officers lined up behind each other. Remo pushes G** on his phone again, and the sound of gunfire erupts from the bedroom.

An officer swings around the open door and fires twice. A lampshade explodes, and the window shatters.

Remo calls out, "All right. I give up. Stop shooting."

Smoke thins as officers rush in, only to see Remo is not in the bedroom. The horn silences as Remo forks the last bite of apple pie into his mouth. Belly's police radio on his belt calls out, "Gunshots reported near the corner of North Peoria and West Ancona Street."

"On our way," a police unit replies.

A bullhorn hangs from the ceiling, and a speaker sits on the night-stand. Remo's voice comes across the speaker. "Missed me, Belly. Missed me by about five miles."

Belly slaps the speaker across the room. "Think you're a smartass, don't you, Wolf?"

Chapter 58

L ater that night, at a neighborhood bar on the West Side, the bartender asks, "Che, what's going on? You are usually out of here by midnight."

Remo may be on the run, but he's still undercover to people who don't watch the local news. As Che, he sits alone on a stool. Dim lights shine from a recessed false ceiling. At the other end of the bar, two gentlemen debate Chicago sports, then one raises his beer glass toward Che and nods hello. He wonders if it's because they recognize him.

He taps the shot glass on the counter. "Another one."

"Are you sure about that, Che?" the bartender asks as he wipes down glasses with a towel. "Looks like you've had enough. Time to head home."

"Not yet. Need to avoid the home scene for tonight. Besides, that C note is still talking." The heel of his hand rubs the top of his thigh. So's the shrapnel in my leg. He flips his wrist to look at his watch; it's almost two o'clock. "We got time for a few more." His elbows rest on the bar as his head droops. "Load me up."

The bartender pours another shot of Bulleit. "Bad day at the ranch?"

"Lately, every day is a bad day. Chicago, Marjah, the North Pole, every place." He throws the shot to the back of his throat and slams the glass on the bar. "Another."

"Marjah? Were you in Afghanistan? I was in the 82nd." The bartender pours another.

Remo realizes he never said Che was in the military. "No. I said Marshall."

Two young skinheads with matching neck tattoos step into the establishment. The one with a long Fu Manchu mustache hanging below his chin looks predatory. His hand shoves his buddy. "Bullshit, I told you she was screwing everyone."

They step to the bar, one on each side of Che. Che taps his shoulder holster. Empty, because he's in a bar and drinking heavily.

"No way," the other skinhead says. "I know her family. She's a nice girl."

"Two 312s, buddy," says the one with a Fu Manchu. "Nice? Nice to everyone in her bed." A slap on Che's back. "I mean everyone. Ain't that right, bro?"

Che takes his shot of Bulleit. "I'm just sitting here drinking my bourbon, minding my own business." He holds the glass in the air. "One more."

"Whoa, buddy. Who do you think you are? I asked you a question. You're supposed to be on my side."

"Can't be on your side, don't know you."

"Last one, Che," the bartender says. He fills the shot glass.

The skinhead slaps it across the bar. "You don't drink until I say you can."

Che's snitch walks in. He has more information about Rolly Chang, but instead, he turns around and leaves.

"Now you did something bad," Che says. "You hurt my business."

"Listen, asshole. I think I'm gonna shave off that pretty black hair you got." A switchblade snaps open. "You need to look like me."

"Then I'd need a busted nose and broken teeth."

"What?"

Che grabs the skinhead's wrist holding the knife and snaps it across the edge of the bar. A fist slams into the skinhead's nose, Che bashes the face against the bar counter. The battered man drops to the floor and moans. The fight was over in a few seconds.

The second guy's eyes are frozen on the man who pulverized his friend. He holds his hands up, chest-high. "I got no problems with you. Mind if I take him out of here?"

"Pay the bartender for the two beers." After the two leave, Remo rubs his eyelids. "Okay, one more."

"That last one was the end of your C note."

"Max, come on. I saved you from those idiots tearing this place up."

"Che, I can take care of myself. The sawed-off shotgun in my hands behind the counter would have worked just as well."

"Are you a bad man?" asks one of the two men at the other end of the bar.

"No, just don't like long fights."

"Wasn't much entertainment for us, but enough that I got your next shot covered."

"And I'll get the next one after that," the other man says.

A few minutes later, Remo opens the front door to a black silence with no cars, people or noise. He pushes a button on his phone.

Liza answers. "Hello."

He pulls the phone away from his ear and drops his hand to his side. He hears her say hello again.

"Remo?" He hears the siren voice of a woman from the past. "Is this you?"

His hand rubs his face. "Yeah, it's me."

"It's late. What are you doing?"

"I'm down. Hit bottom. Nowhere to go."

"Not true. I'm here. Come to my house."

"I don't want to get you in trouble."

"Tea will be ready when you get here."

His fingers slide through his hair. "All right." He snaps his phone closed.

Across the street, Remo's eyes focus on a person standing next to a small motorcycle. The kickstarter rat-a-tats the two-stroke engine. It sounds like the same engine Bobby and he chased. Remo tries to focus as he swings a leg over his seat and shoves the kickstarter down. The engine revs. A horn beeps twice as a garbage truck rolls by in front of him. It passes, and the bike across the street is gone.

Chapter 59

At the crest of a hill, twenty miles from Chicago, a razor wire roll crowns the fifteen-foot-high chain-link fence and surrounds Liza's five-acre homestead. Bright lights shine down on her home with a modern high-pitched green metal roof and sandstone walls. The front gate is open for her visitor.

Her twenty-year-old camo-patterned Jeep sits in front of the single metal garage door with dried mud spattered across its oversized black wheel wells. A bumper sticker on the back window says, 'SAVE OUR TOWN.' Two snakes and a doeskin hang on a clothesline at the side of the house. Her hand holds the barrel of an AR-15 resting against her leg with a full magazine.

A low rumble creeps toward her as the wind shifts in her face. She steps inside as the motorcycle rumbles past the open gate.

Remo pulls the bike close to the front porch steps and kills the engine. She left her door open.

The front room is immaculate, with a white leather couch and high-back chairs. A baby grand piano stands in the corner and crossed logs burn in the fireplace.

He instinctively taps the pistol in the shoulder holster as a tea kettle whistle blows in the kitchen.

Remo steps into the kitchen, but she's not there. Steam billows from the spout. He slides the kettle off the burner, then steps back to the open front door. The gate is closed with a large padlock on it.

"I could kill you right now, shoot you in the back. Detective Wolf in my house, no one would doubt it was self-defense."

He raises his hands, head high. "I'm in trouble and thought I could stay for a day or two." He turns around toward her. His eyes focus on the black hole of an AR-15 barrel pointed at his chest.

"You left me after you promised me you never would."

"I was wrong. I thought the army wanted me."

She points the gun barrel down. "I wanted you!"

Remo steps to the mantle and picks up the picture of the two of them before he joined the army.

"Put that down, you bastard." She aims the gun at his head. "Put it back."

"Okay, only if you promise not to shoot me."

She points the barrel toward the couch. "Sit down."

A minute later, she returns with a serving tray. Remo's jacket lies next to him across the back of the couch. His black t-shirt is tight against his chest and arms. She tries not to look while she pours black tea into two dark blue ceramic teacups without handles. Her fingers hold the cup in front of him. Taking it, the ceramic is hotter than expected and he quickly puts it on the coffee table.

Her two fingers hold her small cup. She sips while her unblinking black eyes stare at Remo. "Too hot for your delicate fingers?"

"No." He reaches inside his jacket for a bottle and pours bourbon into the cup. "You live alone?"

Her fingers touch Remo's hand and the bottle. "What happened to you?"

Remo sets the bottle on the table. He clears his throat. "Not sure. Friends killed...murdered in Afghanistan. Kids were ambushing us in a deadly city. IEDs killing innocent people."

"How do you manage it?"

He points to the bottle. "This," then pulls his sleeve up to reveal his tattoos, "and these."

Remo gazes at her light brown skin, eloquent cheekbones, and lips as smooth and full as when he left her to join the army. Right now, he's trying to remember why he told her no when she wanted marriage. Idiot.

"You didn't answer my question. You live alone?"

She drank the rest of her tea. "The only male that comes here is Moog."

"Moog? How often does he come by?"

"Moog? You forgot my dog's name?"

"Right, the Pointer. I forgot. Did you ever marry?" Remo asks.

"No."

"Want to ask if I ever married?"

She looks at the rifle resting against the cabinet door, then at him. "No." She steps outside.

He follows. "Why did you ask me to come here?"

She turns back. "What happened in Chicago?"

Chapter 60

After twenty minutes, Liza hears more than she wants. "This girl, the attorney, you love her?"

"I'm not here to talk about her. It's a...a Byzantine relation."

"Byzantine. Have you ever had any other type of relationship with a woman?" Her finger blots away a small tear. She hides a quick sniffle.

Slipping a second bottle from the inside pocket, Remo takes another drink.

"Don't remember you drinking this way."

"What way?"

"Out of your pocket. When did that start?"

"The army, no more letters from you, loneliness, and bullets flying by my head. It's the only thing that lets me sleep." He takes another drink. "Still can't sleep well with or without it."

Thunder rumbles overhead.

"I need to get Moog in the house before it rains, and you need to get back to Chicago." She steps off the porch toward the fence and yells, "Moog, come on, boy. Where are you?" She steps to the gate and rolls the combination on the lock the size of her hand. It snaps open. She pulls the gate open. "I changed my mind. You. Out. Back to Chicago." She turns around. "Moog, come, boy. Rain is coming."

Like flipping the faucet handle full blast, the rain hits with heavy sheets of ice water. Rain slaps her face.

"Is there a place he usually goes?" Remo asks.

Her long raisin-black hair is plastered to her head and clothes. "He has a hole he dug behind those two boulders on the left. He thinks he hides from me there."

Remo zips up his jacket and steps down the trail. His boots slide over the mud with each step. Moog is curled in the hole. "Come on, Moog. Got to get inside." He slips his hands under the dog as it whimpers. "You okay, boy?" He carries the big dog in his arms past the gate. Liza closes it and spins the combination. Once inside, Remo places the dog near the fire. All three are soaked.

"Is he hurt?" Liza asks.

"Not sure yet." His palm rubs across the dog's body and head, no whimpers. "Tell me, boy, what's wrong." He checks the legs, and the front paw jerks back. "There it is, looks like a thorn in the paw."

"Moog, baby. I'm sorry."

"You hold his head, and I'll pull it out," Remo says. A quick pull and a whimper end the dilemma.

"I'll get a few towels. He's old, not good for him to be cold and wet."

"How about one for me too?" Remo says as she disappears around the corner.

She returns with folded towels in hand. Remo's shirt is off. All she sees are muscles and tattoos. She flips a towel at him and bends down on her knees to gently rub Moog's wet fur.

"Thanks, I was getting cold."

Her eyes wander from Moog to Remo's boots. She dares not look up. "Take your muddy boots off and put them on the porch. I'll make more tea."

After fifteen minutes, she returns with a teapot and two cups on a serving tray. Remo and Moog are lying down, curled up in front of the fire like a boy and his dog. Moog's head lies on Remo's arm.

Liza watches them, seeing what could have been. She places the tray on the coffee table. "Looks like you two are best friends." She pours the tea.

"He's happy to be warm and without a thorn."

Moog licks his face. Remo turns to look at her to see she changed clothes to a way-too-low V-neck sweater and jeans too tight for him to be alone in a room with her.

"I thought I should head back to the city." He sits and faces her. With his legs crossed, Moog rests his neck on Remo's thigh.

"When did you get tattoos?"

He points to his deltoid. "Got these five eagles in the 101st Airborne when I was a naïve kid. Four hit with bullets. This is the last of the originals."

"The others look newer." Her finger touches the one on his chest. Her eyes rise up to his.

"Yeah. Got that one when I was unconscious."

"Unconscious? You mean drunk?"

"No. Drugged, by Maggie."

"Maggie." The nail on her finger scratches a line across his chest. "You *must* love this woman. You're sitting in front of me with your shirt off, I'm wearing a sweater with nothing underneath, and you bring up *Maggie*." She hops up. "Come on, Moog, time for bed, alone. Good night."

Moog's eyes follow her as she steps away. His neck stays on Remo's thigh.

"Really? You come to my house and steal my dog?"

"Liza, he's right here, just tired." Remo stands as Moog rolls on his side. She tries to slow her breathing. Two steps and he's inches from her.

"You love her?" Her fingers wipe away the damp strands of hair on her cheek.

He breaks eye contact. A deep sigh releases a weight in his chest. "No, just close friends."

Her lips twist, nostrils widen. "As close as we were?"

"No." I might be lying about that one. But then again, she is trying to arrest me.

She glances at the window while thunder rolls like rocks in a barrel. Her eyes return to Remo. "Shouldn't be here. You should stay far away from me."

"You mean like twelve inches this far?"

"Shut up." Her fingers grasp his hair. "Damn you, Remo." She pulls him to her lips. "You're going to break my heart again."

Chapter 61

Remo's dry leather jacket and boots lie next to the fireplace. A tapestry lies over him. He buries his face in the corner of the couch, trying to avoid sunlight. A sledgehammer pounds his temples with each heartbeat. The inside of his mouth tastes like a four-day-old biscuit. The phone rings loud, Notre Dame bells loud. His thumb flicks it open. "What do you want?"

"It's past noon," his snitch says. "I called you several times. You didn't answer."

Remo slides his hand across his hair. "Busy last night and this morning."

"Last night, you said no one would be there. You lied to me."

"Shit happens sometimes. I didn't know those assholes were coming in. What you got?"

"Rolly Chang. I knew where he was. He had more heroin to sell. He sold it all last night, but you wouldn't answer your pager. I had him last night. Maybe that would have cleared you."

Remo grimaces from the missed opportunity and excessive alcohol. "Okay. Where's he next?"

"He's gone. He won't be back for weeks, not sure if I can find him again. I'm doing my part to get my brother out of jail. You need to do yours."

"Your deal with me is still good." Remo rakes his hair back. "Find Chang. When I cuff him, you can have your brother out."

The smell of bacon and blueberry pancakes penetrates the house. Moog jumps up on the couch and lays its head on Remo's lap.

He rubs the dog's head. It licks Remo's hand. "I might have messed up a few years ago."

Liza steps from the kitchen to the living room and wipes her hands on a towel. "Thought the smell would get you up. Come, eat with me."

Moog jumps off the couch and heads to the kitchen. Remo straightens his wrinkled t-shirt and follows the dog. He steps by the frying pan and smells the bacon, except it's not flat, but instead, long and round. He looks out the back window at another snakeskin hanging on the fence.

"You always liked snake. Still do?"

Remo snaps the cap of another pint bottle.

"You can stop that now," she says.

"Stop what?"

"Before the army, you were vibrant, smiling every day." She points to the bottle. "Now, awful stuff happens to you. Promise me you'll stop."

He tightens the cap on the bottle and slips it back into the pocket of his jacket.

She shakes her head and holds her hand out. "Give it to me, please."

He hands it to her as she slides his plate on the table and takes the bottle.

"Time to eat."

After he takes the last bite of his pancake, he looks at the walls. "You still crocheting and making blankets and tapestries?"

"Nothing else for me to do while I wait."

"Wait for what?"

Liza sips her coffee, then turns her head slightly. She lifts one eyebrow and asks, "Why are men so stupid?"

*

The Indian rumbles outside the front door. Liza holds the gate open. He pulls up to her and stops. "I shouldn't have come here."

Her finger wipes a tear from her cheek. Her lips struggle into a forced smile. "No. I'm glad you came. It's been years since I've had a happy heart, even if it was for a few hours." She looks down while the back of her hand wipes her eyes.

"I need to get back and..."

She nods. "Right. Fix this problem of yours. You should stop by the cemetery before heading back to the city."

"Yeah. I need to see them."

The bike heads down the narrow trail toward the main road. Liza locks the gate as the engine sounds disappear.

Remo turns off the two-lane asphalt several miles down the road, crosses under a stone archway, and stops next to his parents' plot. They lie next to each other for eternity. He opens the door to the small shack he built after burying them and grabs the broom. "Looks a little unkept. I'll come back more often and keep everything clean."

He sweeps the dirt off the tombstones.

"It's been rough, guys. Hope you understand. I've had too many friends die, and the bourbon helps me forget—sometimes." Remo has always felt they still talk to him, and he still listens. His hand brushes loose dirt off the tops of their tombstones. "Okay, okay. Don't yell at me. I know Liza's right. She's always right." He raises a bottle next to his lips and stops while looking at the tombstones. "I'll try. That's the best I can do, try." He pours the bourbon on the ground.

A cold wind shifts directions with dark clouds rolling in. Remo feels water sprinkling on his head and jeans, so he flips the collar on the leather jacket up. The rain increases. There is no place to go except inside the small shack. He steps in and pushes the door closed. Through the window, he watches the rain lash the tombstones clean. Zipping up his jacket, he huddles in the corner and falls asleep.

Fireflies flicker around tree leaves. Fingers grow from branches. Trails of green and white light shoot across the dark horizon. Like a heavy weight, black clouds flatten the moon. Colors swirl around him like a funnel cloud. His father's face fills the sky. He says, "Reconcile. Remorse."

The dead girl in the alley runs toward him with dark eyes and a pale face. She cries out for his help before evaporating into smoke.

Maggie floats across the tops of the trees. In her Chicago Bears jersey holding a coffee mug, she whispers, "No one loves you like I do."

Can he trust her? She makes him happy. Her red hair turns black, swirling and covering her face. She stands on an iceberg as fire surrounds her feet. Her hands melt as steam pours out her wrists. The iceberg turns into a fiery cloud, engulfing her, and floats away. She's gone.

Thunder rumbles deep, filling the moon with streams of water. Lightning bolts sear jagged lines through the moon. The sky explodes into daylight.

Remo jerks as lightning strikes a tree nearby. Moments later, the rain stops. He steps out of the shack to see a tree trunk split down the middle fifty feet away.

Remo grabs a towel from a shelf, sweeps the water off his bike, and then wipes the face of the tombstones dry.

After closing the shack, he sits back on the bike. He must fix these lies. If Maggie gave Chang immunity, he could clear Remo. Tapping favorites on his phone and then CPD-DOC, Department of Organized Crime, he hears the phone ring twice.

"Kimball here."

"I can bring in Rolly Chang, but I need backup."

Captain Ton Kimball turns around to make sure no one is behind him in the building. "What in the hell are you doing, Remo?" Ton straightens his back as his leather soles quickly slap the highly polished floor. "We have a BOLO out for you." He steps outside as cold wind swirls around his head. "You can't waltz in here with a criminal and expect everything to be good, even if it is Chang. Besides, Chang is narcotics. That's the Bureau of Organized Crime, not you. After Truk died, Chief told me to come in and clean up his mess, so I gave Belly Lynch all your crap."

"Belly? He can't find shit if it's burning in a sack."

"You should be grateful. I gave that Irishman the assignment to get him off your ass. He wants you pretty bad."

"Thanks, Ton. You're one of the few I still trust."

"You're wrong about that. I'm the only one left. Everybody else wants you in jail. Be careful. Belly has the addresses of some of your hideouts."

"I know. He hit one of them last night."

"His last report requests for more men to find you. You need to find this video."

Remo snaps his phone closed and asks himself, "What was the name Maggie said at forensics?" He types in CFSSC on his phone and finds Antonio Souza, PhD.

Remo pushes D*, and the phone rings.

"Hello," Davy says.

"Need some info. House number of Dr. Antonio Souza who works at CFSSC."

Chapter 62

Professor Souza awakens in his bed from television noise in the den. He thought he turned it off before bed. Through sleepy eyes, he reaches for his robe and ties it across his waist, then tiptoes out of the bedroom. The porch light shines outside the front door's etched glass. It shouldn't be on at night. Souza stops halfway down the hall next to the partially open basement door, looks down into the blackened room and closes the door. The television channel changes in the den.

"Who's there?" Souza asks as he turns the porch light off.

The channel changes again. Souza grabs the glass vase on a small table in the hall.

"Who's there?"

He steps to the entrance of the den. An old James Stewart and Doris Day film is playing, *The Man Who Knew Too Much.*

"I have always loved these old movies. Don't you?" Fedora asks.

Souza turns toward the back corner of the den. Fedora sits in an overstuffed chair.

❖

Remo runs past sleeping houses until he reaches Dr. Souza's place. The porch light shines above the front door, with a row of waist-high hedges lining the front of the house. Through the plate-glass window, a single light flickers. He steps over the hedge and leans near the window. The porch light turns off.

◆

"Jesus, you scared me," Souza says. He puts the vase on a table. "What are you doing here?"

"I'm confused and thought you could help me."

"Confused? About what?"

"Your last call, you said you couldn't help me anymore." Fedora's foot shoves the coffee table. It scratches across the hardwood floor. "After all the money I gave you. It seems you forgot about that." Fedora stands with arms out and yells, "Once you take the money, you're in for life."

Remo leans in closer to the window. The television is on, but he hears more voices.

"I told you, I want out. All this is too much. McCall said she would deport my family, and now there are people from the attorney's office in my lab all day."

"Why the sudden good morals? You took my money, and you knew it wasn't legal what you did." Fedora steps closer. "Are you by yourself? Where's the wife and kids?"

"They are out of town visiting family." He waves his hands. "This is too big. I want out. I promise I won't tell anyone."

"How do I know you will stay quiet?" Fedora says, and a chrome revolver slips out from the overcoat.

"Whoa, no need for that," Souza says as he backs up to the hallway.

Fedora steps to the hallway inches from Souza. "What's the door lead to?"

"The basement, why?"

"What's down there?"

"Books, storage, old furniture," Souza says. "Okay, listen, I can keep this up a little longer. No problem."

"Open the basement door." Fedora points the gun barrel down the hallway.

Souza steps to the door, opens it then turns around. Fedora surprises him by being so close. Souza feels the gun barrel against his chest. "Wait. What are you doing? Stop," Souza begs.

Two quick flashes from the revolver and Souza's body bounces down the basement stairs. Fedora aims at Souza and fires again.

Remo pounds on the front door. "Police. Open up." Two bullets fly through the door near him.

Fedora snaps the cylinder out of the revolver and ejects the shell casings attached to a moon clip. Another clip of six cartridges slides in the cylinder. Two more bullets pierce the front door.

Remo kicks the door in and rushes into the living room. "Police. Everybody down. Hands on your head."

The television changes scenes with Jimmy Stewart talking. Remo scrambles down the hall to the kitchen. The back door is wide open.

After finding Souza downstairs, he finds the moon clip of shell casings with FEDERAL .38 SPECIAL printed on the back. He remembers a chrome .38 Special revolver pointed at him in the alley.

Chapter 63

Captain Ton Kimball has bitten off more than he can chew as he rummages through a pile of papers on Truk's desk while talking to a person from the office of the Deputy Chief of Internal Affairs on speakerphone. "Damn it, Dan," Ton says. "It's after midnight. Do you ever go home? I don't have time for this crap now. You know I'm just the cleanup man."

"Ton, this is not a request," Dan says. "This is a direct order from the chief. He needs all activity, all reports from Detective Wolf from the last hundred days, on his desk by tomorrow morning. And by the way, why are you in Truk's office this late? You should go home and rest after you get the paperwork sent."

"Rest? You said you want this tomorrow?" Ton pulls last week's reports from a third of the way down the pile on Truk's desk. "I can't find my ass by tomorrow." His personal cell phone lights up an unknown number. I got enough trouble right now, Remo. Don't call me.

Dan says, "You better, or I'll demote your ass to a pavement-pounding police officer."

"Right, I got to go."

"Do not make the chief wait. You got that?" The phone goes dead. Ton answers his personal phone. "Hello?" Please don't be Wolf.

"You got a minute?" Remo asks.

Ton inhales deep. "Sure."

"I feel bad. I had Jersey sent into the station to be interviewed. I wanted her out of the way while I checked out where she and Euro talked at the bar. I should have figured out a way to send her somewhere else."

"Not your fault, man. How did you know Truk was going to hook up with Jersey?"

Truk's laptop dings. A text from Belly pops up. I'm going to three places. 24377 Magellan and 1426 Detroit and 624 E Ball. More to come.

"Belly's hitting three more of your places. You need to leave town."

Chapter 64

Monday morning light sparkles across glass buildings. The air is clean and brisk as it flows in from Lake Michigan. Danny slips Maggie the campaign contribution list with the amounts given to date. She is twenty-three percent ahead of Watters in money, but dead even in the polls.

Maggie unfolds the morning paper. *The Chicago Tribune* front page blares out, 'WHERE IS DETECTIVE WOLF? CHECK WITH GIRLFRIEND.'

"Danny, get me Williams at the *Tribune*."

Seconds later, his phone rings. "Hello," Williams says.

"Listen, jerk. What's with the headline? Don't I pay you enough?" She cuts off the apologizing chatter back to her and pounds her desktop. "What is this crap about me on the front page? Is that your doing? Maybe you should go into politics, your excuses are worthless." Williams replies, but she cuts him off. "Well, you're the assistant editor, Robert. You can stop anything you want. I'm running for the Cook County State's Attorney office, and nothing will stop me. You say that again, and you're off my payroll and on my shit list."

She pitches her phone on her desk and then turns toward her open door.

"Danny!"

He sticks his head in the doorway. "Yes, ma'am."

"Get me that bastard, Captain Kimball, on the phone."

Ton sits in Truk's office and cringes as the phone rings for the seventeenth time in the last twenty minutes. Maggie's name pops up again; he finally answers. "Maggie, I got nothing else to say to you. I'm doing the best I can."

"Bullshit, we have to help Remo. You owe him. Remember Semion Tyruinov?"

A deep sigh releases as Ton plops into his chair. He touches his chest where 3Fingers's bullet hit his armored vest. There seems to be a permanent bruise. "Maggie, I can't tell you anything. Internal Affairs is still investigating this, and they are all over my ass about it. No one knows where Remo is."

"I know that. You won't find him until he wants to be found. Is the video legit?"

"Listen, Maggie, I promise you, I don't know."

"I'm the Cook County Assistant State's Attorney, and I'm asking you to confirm this. Is this real?"

"Call me back on my cell."

"Don't hang up on me, Ton." Her phone goes dead. She slides it across her desktop again. In a second, the phone is back in her hand. She flips through her address book and pushes TON.

Ton's phone rings. He pushes decline when Maggie's name pops up. The ringing stops.

She looks at her phone. "Oh, you son of a bitch."

Ton leans back in his chair and looks at the news website. He pushes the hyperlink on the laptop and watches two men stand ten feet in front of Remo. Johnny Rivera has his arm hanging around Rolly Chang's neck at Garfield Park. Remo was right all along, he had Rolly Chang. The video goes a little out of focus as Remo's pistol aims straight ahead at their backs. Indistinct words are said. He can't tell who said what. Remo steps back behind the Escalade. The focus returns as one shot is fired and Johnny falls.

Ton pushes the link again. "This is going to bite me in the ass." He knew about a leak in the department, but he didn't want Chief Moreland to know Remo was dogging Chang. If Moreland knew more, that might have led to information about the Killing Club.

Chapter 65

The Indian engine rumbles down the East Eisenhower Expressway, the Ike, as stratus clouds surround a silver moon. Miles in front of him, red lights flash at the tops of vertical masterpieces of concrete, glass and steel. Random, white, square lights shine through windows from empty offices. At near three in the morning, a few headlights travel westbound. Forecasters predicted patchy fog; nothing was said about the ice crystals in the air slapping his face. The fringe on his jacket sleeves waves wildly behind his arms. He throws an empty pint bottle onto the grassy median. He's tired of today, and tomorrow needs to hurry.

The ice crystals on his cheeks feel like his last days in Afghanistan. A fresh recruit's second night jumped in front of Remo as the Humvee rolled over an IED. The kid saved Remo. Bobby also saved him. Two kids died saving Remo Wolf. Why do people think he is worth saving?

His tachometer needle sits at 2600 RPMs as the bike's engine bellows down the Ike. The engine echoes as it passes under a cold concrete bridge. Remo watches from his rearview mirror a set of headlights change lanes each time he has. He wonders if he's paranoid or correct and decides to test his thoughts. The RPMs slow as he veers off the expressway.

Remo glances at his mirror again. The vehicle exits as well. He recognizes it as an unmarked black Ford Taurus. The road veers right away from the expressway toward warehouses. He slows toward the intersection despite the green light. The Taurus slow too, staying at least ten car lengths back. The light turns red for Remo, and a tractor-trailer bangs across poorly repaired potholes and crosses through the intersection from left to right. The headlights behind him creep closer while Remo listens to the police radio through his Bluetooth. "Possible motorcycle located."

Another tractor-trailer comes toward the intersection from his left. The light stays red for Remo. He accelerates and turns right in front of the truck. It slams on its brakes with its tires squealing and sliding to a stop in the middle of the intersection.

Remo turns the motorcycle lights off. The headlights behind him round the corner with blue flashing lights on the roof and a siren wailing alone in the night. Remo downshifts, turns at every corner, winds his way through streets to an alleyway and pulls behind a large garbage bin and waits. The siren is a block away and then silences. With his headlight and taillight still off, Remo's Indian rumbles between his legs. Emergency lights swirl past the alley. Remo quietly rolls down the alley back to the expressway.

Chapter 66

Davy awakens at 3:32 AM to noise from inside his house. Someone yells, "Damn it." Davy flips on the kitchen light, revealing a fishing net covering a man on his hands and knees. Davy swings his metal baseball bat like he is going for a home run.

Remo ducks, feeling the air whip past his shoulder.

"Davy, stop. It's me, Remo."

The bat clangs on the floor. "What are you doing here? How did you get in?"

"My key, remember? You gave it to me." Remo struggles to pull the netting away. "Totally forgot about the net. It definitely will hold an intruder." Remo stands. "I need to crash for a few..."

"No, you can't stay here. You said the garage, not the house, you know." Davy waves his arms wide. "Who else is coming? Phantoms, night riders, they're out there. They're waiting for me."

Remo's police radio crackles on his belt.

Davy looks toward the noise. "It's coming through the radio. It knows where I am. Why did you come?"

Remo turns toward a sound outside, steps to the living room window and clicks one metal blind down. A car drives down the street with its taillights shining on the blinds.

Davy pushes on the back of Remo's shoulder. "Get out. Get out. Get out of my house."

Remo lets the blind pop back up.

"I saw it. Red eyes outside. Predators," Davy says. He turns away from the living room and hears a snap like a hammer cocking. "A gun."

♦

Detective Belly Lynch sits on the edge of his desk, his phone to his ear. "Got it." The detectives' office is empty except for him. He slams the landline phone receiver down, then raises it back to his ear and punches new numbers. "Got an address. I need a SWAT team ASAP." He waits for the gibberish on the other side of the phone to end. "Okay, okay. Then, at least get me four officers and a battering ram. I'm talking about that killer, Remo Wolf. I know where he is. I got this bastard, and we don't need to wait for the sun to come up."

♦

"Davy, not a gun." Remo touches the metal blind again. It clicks and clacks as he pushes it down and releases it. He rolls the backpack off his shoulder and drops it on the couch. "I'm in trouble."

"No! How do I know the cops aren't busting through the front door any minute? I can hear them. The guns, I hear them. They're coming in, you know."

"I was careful. Rode nice and slow, and quiet. I promise I have never told anyone about you. No one."

♦

Three cars with flashing blue lights and sirens scream for everything to get out of their way. Belly's team rolls down the street, past shot-gun houses and convenience stores. His hand pats the pistol in his shoulder holster and then reaches for the radio microphone. "One block west, turn right, then one more block." A bass drum pounds in his chest. He will be the Hero of Chicago.

Blue lights shatter the midnight's darkness. Belly's car slides sideways and blocks the intersection while a second car cuts off the other end of the road. A third vehicle stops across the street from the house. The team pours out of their vehicles and charges toward the house.

The entire house is dark, with curtains closed and no outside lights. Belly motions for the team to follow. His heart pumps double time. A hand latches on Belly's shoulder. The vest itches, straight jacket tight. He hears voices inside the dark house as he checks the doorknob—locked. Belly holds three fingers up, two, one. The officers line up behind Belly, with a hand on the shoulder in front of them. He motions for the battering ram. It pounds against the front door lock.

✦

Davy walks to the sink and grabs his faded blue plastic Chicago Cubs twelve-ounce beer cup. He fills it with water and drinks half. Shaking his head, Davy tells Remo, "You can't stay. Nobody can stay. Nobody has ever spent the night here. Not once, you know."

Remo follows Davy into the kitchen. "Listen, Davy. I parked in the back." Remo waves his hands. "Nobody will see the bike."

Davy raises the blinds over the sink. "Where? Where is it? It's not out there, you know."

"It's in the garage." Remo moves the cup over a few inches and steps next to Davy. "Nobody will find it."

"Don't! No!" Davy grabs the cup. "Don't touch my cup. Only me. Only me, you know."

"Listen, Davy. I can tell when you miss your meds. How many days have you been off?"

"I'm fine, you know. I'm good, I'm fine, you know."

"No. No, you're not." Remo removes the daily pill container from the cupboard. Davy lunges and tries to pull Remo's fingers off the plastic box.

"No, that's mine, you know. That's mine, no, no." Davy punches Remo in the chest several times. "I want my pills back!"

Remo gently pushes Davy back. "Today is Thursday, and there are pills still in the Monday, Tuesday, and Wednesday slots."

"No, not true. Those are not my pills. I took my pills." Davy grabs the cup and pours water into it. He holds it tight to his chest. His eyes protrude, nostrils flare. He falls to his knees and begs. "I want them. They're mine. Not yours, not yours." The cup falls from his grip and drops to the floor. Davy kneels in a puddle of water. "My cup, it's dirty. Bugs and spiders inside." Davy stands and turns on the kitchen faucet. He fills the cup half-full of liquid dishwasher soap and scrubs the inside with his fist.

"Davy, I will let you sit on the Indian all day long if you take yesterday and today's pills right now."

Davy stops with soap bubbles over his hand inside the cup. "I can sit on it?" Davy smiles, but just as suddenly, his smile disappears. "But you aren't staying here, you know."

"No, of course not." Can't argue with a man when he is off his meds. "Take these, and let's talk about the video and the IP address."

Remo's pager buzzes.

"Oh shit. I don't have time for you, Belly. Damn it, get away from the door."

Chapter 67

The fourth man swings the battering ram, shattering the lock and knob and banging the door against the wall. Belly and three officers charge inside. An officer calls out, "Police." A motion sensor lights the living room. Belly swings his pistol at the lamp. No one there. He turns back to the center. "Left clear," he says.

The second man sweeps right. "Right clear."

The brown leather couch sits empty, with a matching ottoman in the center of the room. Classic Indian motorcycle racing photographs hang on the wall. The third man charges through the living room, and he leans against the wall to the kitchen. "Room clear." A clank comes from the bedroom.

Belly steps to the side of the doorframe. "Wolf, come out. If I come in, we shoot first." He motions to the man with the battering ram. Belly counts down with his fingers, four, three, two...

A cell phone rings, and Belly freezes. A phone sitting on the ottoman rings again. He touches the speaker button.

"No need to destroy my house," Remo says. "Walk in the bedroom. I have something there for you."

The men scan the room for cameras in the corners. "Where are you?" Belly looks at the ceiling. "I will get you, and you are going down, you son of a bitch."

"Enter the bedroom. No one will get hurt. I'm not a killer." The phone clicks dead.

One man turns the knob and pushes the door open. "Sir, this was on the bed. He must have known we were coming."

'Strike two. You call yourself a detective? I got lots of places in Chicago.'

Belly turns back toward the broken front door. "We're done."

♦

At seven in the morning, the upstairs detectives' office door opens. Belly walks in. "Anybody know where Remo Wolf is?" His hand jerks the captain's office doorknob open. "Wolf is gone. Checked several places."

"Figured that." Ton closes the laptop. "Didn't think it was going to be that easy, did you? Wrists together, waiting for your handcuffs."

"I'm going to get that asshole because he killed my brother," Belly says.

"All right, enough of that." Ton steps around the desk and points his finger at Belly. "He did not kill your brother. They were both ambushed and shot. Bobby Lynch died in the line of duty. Remo didn't pull the trigger. Someone else did."

Chapter 68

At eight in the morning, Davy's meds latch on to neurons screaming for help. Down in the basement, Remo watches Davy's fingers type like a video in fast forward with gibberish flashing across the screen in front of him.

"Don't know how good this guy is, you know. If he tried to photoshop, you know, cut it down, splice, add a flash from your gun on his own, won't be able to find it. If he went to a website or a social media site to get it done, much of what they do is on the cloud. I can find that, you know."

The PC scrolls twenty videos per second, hunting for a visual of Rolly and Johnny together. It stops.

"What's that?" Remo asks.

"It ran out of pics, you know."

"What? This is the internet. It can't run out of pictures. There are billions."

"No, pics of both together. Found pics of each but nothing together, you know."

Two hard knocks on the front door startle them. Davy spins his chair toward another big screen. A camera hangs from the front porch eaves and slowly turns. His neighbor is on his porch, standing alone, with a half-sawed-off baseball bat in hand.

The hour hand on the wall clock has moved eleven hours. They have been downstairs all day long.

Davy pushes a button. The speaker above the door blares out, "Donald, isn't it? What do you want?"

He looks at the speaker. "Need you to open this door."

Davy sees car lights move past the house behind Donald. "Why?"

"You got something of mine, and I want it back."

Davy looks bewildered at Remo. "I got nothing of his, you know." A drawer slides open, and he pulls out a Smith & Wesson .460 Magnum revolver with an eight-inch barrel. "Be back in a minute."

"Crap, Davy. Are you expecting grizzly bears on your street?"

"No, but never want to shoot a man more than once, you know." He flips the light switch up as his feet clunk up the wood steps. Several flood lamps on the porch turn night into day. With the right hand behind his back holding the revolver, Davy pulls the hammer back and opens the door with his left hand. "What's up, Donald?"

"Don, not Donald. I'm not a duck."

"What do you think I have of yours, and why did you come here with a bat in your hand?"

He glances at the bat. "Oh, sorry." He pitches it in Davy's front yard. "Forgot I had it. The kids and I play Wiffle ball, and one of the kids hit it over your fence."

Davy slips the barrel down the back of his pants and flips the baggy sweater over it. "I can go to the backyard and pitch it back over, you know." He tries not to say 'you know' out loud. Maybe whisper it to himself, instead.

"Yeah, that would be okay, but I thought I would get it myself."

Davy looks at Don's face and waits for him to say why he is there. Why does he want to go into the backyard? Not much there, no plants, no trees, only two metal chairs and dirt. Or does he want to walk through the house? Is he looking for Remo? Is he a cop? "Sure, come on in. You can go with me to the backyard, you know."

The door opens wide. Don steps across the threshold. He wipes his dry feet a little too long on the mat as he looks left and right.

"That's good. I think your shoes are clean enough, you know."

"Sorry, didn't want to bring in dirt." He raises his arms in a big Y shape for a second. "Wow, this is a nice house. Kind of messy, but nice. Live here alone?"

The front door closes and snaps with an automatic lock. "Why are your hands up, you know?"

"Sorry." Don drops his hands and starts walking toward the back door. "This way, right?"

Davy touches four digits on the wall switch next to the back door. Three magnetic locks snap open.

Don opens the door. "No dogs?"

"No dogs. Go right ahead and get your ball, you know." Damn it, meant to whisper it.

Charcoal smoke rises on the other side of the fence. Barbecue sauce lingers in the air. A quick pitch up, and the ball flies across the fence.

"Lots of smoke, you know."

"It's a large smoker. Should be ready for dinner tomorrow."

Davy hears nothing on the other side. "The kids are not over there? Thought they would make some noise when the ball came back, you know."

"Hmm, I don't know. Maybe the kids went back inside. Want some brisket? Got two large slabs just about ready."

"No. Come on, I will let you back through the front door, you know."

Don rushes through the house and turns the front doorknob. It doesn't move.

"Automatically locks every time it closes, you know." Davy touches a four-digit passcode on the wall and unlocks the door.

Don rushes down the front porch around to his house. The bat still lies in the middle of Davy's yard.

"Don, your bat." Why did he leave the bat? "You forgot your bat, you know."

Remo watches every step both men make outside the house. Davy steps to the bat in his yard, picks it up and flips it several times like a short baton. Davy tiptoes to Don's porch. He hears laughter from the inside, not of children but grown men.

"You did it," says one man.

"This is awesome," says another. "Did your neighbor suspect anything?"

"Nah, I'm too good for that. No clue, not a thing."

"This video is unbelievable. We can see your hands and arms up and everything."

"Told you this camera could see through a house."

"Looking through two houses? This camera really is special."

Davy steps on the porch and looks through a broken window shade blind to reveal a TV with infrared pictures of two men, Davy and Don. Don replays holding his arms up in the air inside Davy's house. They laugh.

An eight-by-eight-inch black box on a tripod sits behind the couch, looking like a 1950s Kodak box camera. An infrared camera like no other.

All infrared cameras show heat, like hot air escaping through a vent or a hot water pipe leaking, but only a depth of a few inches. This one shows Don's and Davy's body heat through two houses.

"What are you going to do with it?" one man asks.

"Patent it, make a billion dollars."

"Yeah, what about us? We helped."

"Sure, guys. All three of us will be rich."

Wood creaks outside on the porch, the three turn. Don opens the door, but no one is outside.

Down in the basement, Remo types in a website on a keyboard. His phone is trapped between his ear and shoulder. "Yeah, man. That's it. Owe you one."

On the website jugeum.org, Remo finds a video of Rolly, Johnny and himself at Garfield Park. Just above the ground and behind Remo, a small red flame is visible for a second. The gunshot from behind.

The door opens, and Davy steps down while missing his staircase traps.

"Think I got something," Remo says. "Look, this is the last frame of the video."

"Sure is. How'd you find it, you know?"

"Took your lead on the video search. Rolly is an alias. I called a Chinese buddy, and he texted me Rolly's real name in Chinese. A bunch of squiggly lines. Copied that and sent the search again with my name." Remo points at the website address. "What is jugeum.o rg?"

"North Korean website, you know."

"Korean? This a Korean website?"

Davy's fingers type furiously to reveal a Chicago map on the monitor. "No, it's from a private server here in Chicago made to look like a North Korean site, you know."

"Can you track where this came from?"

"Oh, sure. It will take a while, you know. Hey, what do you know about infrared pictures and cameras, you know?"

"Not much. They're used to see inside drywall, inside a box, short distances. Plumbers use them to look for water leaks in pipes."

"My neighbor has a homemade camera that can see through two houses, you know."

"How big?"

"Hmm, maybe six by six inches, you know."

"I could use that," Remo says.

"I'll borrow it tomorrow when he is at work, you know."

Chapter 69

Maggie leans against the windowsill in her office. She looks at her reflection. Twelve- to eighteen-hour days can make a girl age quickly. Her day-spas and Botox haven't kept up with the stress of the last few months between Remo and the election. She used to feel invigorated after two hours on the treadmill and the heavy bag. Coffee and rice cakes are not enough. Her finger tugs on a new laugh line. She didn't laugh.

Outside Maggie's office, Danny opens the door. "Not good news."

"What?" Maggie asks.

"The polls have you slipping. Your three-point lead is back down to one—basically, a dead heat. You got to do something, Maggie. Now. You need to go after Detective Wolf."

"I know the man. Remo did not shoot down a suspect without cause."

"The video says otherwise."

"I don't give a rat's ass about what the video shows." She opens the top drawer of her desk and picks up the picture frame of the two of them at the restaurant. "It has to be manipulated, somehow."

"You heard the analyzer. There were no breaks in the video, and the guy's credentials are exceptional. If he said there are no breaks, no manipulation, then there are none. Detective Remo Wolf shot that man in the back, cold-blooded."

"Maybe."

"Your numbers are slipping with two weeks before the election. You need to..."

"Don't tell me what I need to do. I know what needs to be done." She stares at Remo's eyes in the picture. "Forgive me, babe. I need to win this for both of us."

"You have to go after Detective Wolf," Danny says. "Everyone in Chicago knows you two have a history."

She places the picture frame back into the drawer and closes it. She clears her throat. "Call for an impromptu news conference. I'll make an announcement."

Forty-five minutes later, in front of the courthouse steps, Maggie stands next to a microphone pole with three microphones taped together. "I have started an investigation into the Detective Wolf video. Yesterday, our department determined there was no manipulation of the video. It seems correct, even the out-of-focus part. I'm asking for Detective Wolf to report to my office for questioning concerning the shooting death of Johnny Rivera."

Hands pop up in the air, the press explodes with questions. "Miss McCall, when was the last time you talked to Detective Wolf?"

"The day before the video."

"Will you arrest him for the murder of Johnny Rivera?"

"At present, he is a person of interest. I...we want to talk to him in the CCSA office. As a Chicago detective, he needs to answer our concerns."

"Have you found the other suspect that escaped?" another reporter asks.

"We are still looking for Rolly Chang," Maggie says. "He is at large and considered extremely dangerous."

"Doesn't seem like you can find anybody," another voice calls out from the crowd.

"Need to ask Mr. Watters about that. He is still the CCSA. When I am elected, things will change. We will find Mr. Wolf and Mr. Chang promptly."

Brenda, the blonde bobblehead, raises her hand while asking, "How long have you been sleeping with Detective Wolf? If you are elected, will you protect him by releasing him or marrying him?"

Maggie knew this was coming. She prepared for it. Her eyes shift to the horizon as she answers, "I have no intentions of marriage. My life is keeping Chicago safe." She turns to a man on the front row and points to him.

"Miss McCall, what will happen to Detective Wolf when he comes in?"

"I have instructed my office to hold him until all questions are satisfied. This investigation will be thorough, with no partiality toward the detective. I will keep you informed of all activities. Thank you."

❖

"Smart girl," Richard Watters says as he watches the announcement on the television. "Blaming me for her inadequacies and her blinders." He adjusts the picture frame with Becky Lynch and him at the Willis Tower Skydeck. He purses his lips toward the picture.

Watters' adviser blurts out, "You can't let her do this."

"What do you want me to do? Tell the press that I won't let her pursue this? That she not investigate? What is that going to make me look like?"

"She scooped you two weeks before the election."

"No, she got it right," Watters says, "except now she will have to throw her lover, a psychologically injured man on the run, in jail. Maybe she's not as smart as she thinks she is."

Chapter 70

The John Hancock Center antennas cut through cumulus clouds like a Samurai sword slicing pork belly. It's sixty-eight degrees at half-past noon, with a soft breeze, an unusual October day in Chicago. People, embracing wonderful weather and good fortune, walk the beaches wearing shorts, t-shirts and sandals. Bicycle messengers dodge traffic and slice between cars, waiting for red lights to turn green.

Maggie's office commands a view of Lake Michigan's placid aqua blue water. Wearing her black heels, a below-the-knee gray pencil skirt and a red long sleeve blouse, she leans against the windowsill. It is precisely seventy-four degrees in her office every day.

Her thoughts wander to a warm beach. A half-naked man jogs toward her, toes kicking sand behind him. Firm biceps wrap around her. "Maggie," he whispers. "Maggie."

A knock on her door breaks her thoughts. Danny Williams's voice outside calls, "Maggie."

The beach fades away. "What, Danny? I'm busy." She slides the gold-plated letter opener through another envelope in her hand.

"I have someone here to meet you."

If he is interrupting her, it must be worthwhile. "All right, come in." She places the letter and opener on the desk.

A massive bodyguard sent from Truk, before he died, steps into her office. His gold cufflinks clasp white cuffs that peep out of his XXL black jacket. In Chicago, politics requires a personal bodyguard. "Do you need me to stay in the room, Miss McCall?"

"That's okay, Michael. I'll be fine."

A black male walks in with Danny following close behind. His head looks like a miniature football with two cauliflower ears. He looks to be early- to mid-twenties, with a red star tattoo above each eyelid. She guesses his weight at one-thirty-five. He wears the mandatory oversized bulky jacket that can hide a gun. She hopes Michael searched him before coming inside her office.

Maggie walks around the desk with a smile on her face and eyes, which beg for sleep, thinking every vote counts. "Hello, I'm Maggie McCall. Nice to meet you." She thinks twice about why she sent Michael out of the room.

The man steps between two chairs in front of her desk. She holds her hand out. Her grasp is firm, boxing strong, intentionally holding too long.

With a South Side accent, he says, "I got a cuz that was killed. Bet you can help."

She steps around the two black padded armchairs at a forty-five-degree angle to each other, motioning him to sit. "What's your name?"

"They call me Sizzle."

"Sit, Sizzle." Her hands sweep across her buttocks and thighs, straightening her skirt. She sits in the other chair and leans forward with her legs crossed. "Well, I do work in the Criminal Prosecutions Bureau. We try our best to get criminals sent to jail. How can I help you?"

He plops down in the chair and spreads his legs like a gangsta he has seen in the movies. "I know you hangin' with that cop on the run."

Her hand moves from her armrest to his forearm. Her ruby red lips smile. "What do you mean?"

His arm moves away. Fingers angled in different directions, his hands sway left and right like he's singing hip-hop. "Yeah, Che killed my cuz."

Her eyes flash to Danny and then back to Sizzle. "Danny, would you get me a couple of bottles of water, please? Sizzle and I have something private to talk about."

"Maggie, I think I need to be in here. You don't know…"

"Water, Danny."

Danny rubs his tightened lips. "Sure. I'll hurry."

She wants to break his nose. "Your cuz. You mean a member of your gang. And what makes you think this person you call Che killed him? Maybe one of the other gangs did it."

"I figured out what's going down. You and Che tight. But you messed up in the courthouse and didn't send him down, so you told Che to kill him."

"And what is the name of your cuz?"

"Effie."

"Effie? Do you mean Ferguson William Washington? The two-timer felon that got off on a technicality a few months ago. That's your cuz?"

"Yeah, Effie."

She steps away from the chair and leans against the side of her desk. Thank God for Chicago's ignorance. "Let's just say you are right." Her smile stays constant. "What keeps me from having Che kill you, and then nobody knows anything?"

"Because I got a proposition for you."

"A proposition," she says. "Go on."

"I also know Che is a cop, Remo Wolf. Ya see, I ain't as dumb as you think I am."

Her smile disappears. "Yeah, Sizzle, I do. It's all over the news the last few days. Everyone in Chicago knows Che is an undercover cop."

Michael steps back inside and hands a paper to Maggie. He stays in the room.

After a quick scan of the page, she nods. "Thank you, Michael. You can step outside and close the door."

Maggie stands straight next to her desk.

"You go by Sizzle. I see here, Mister Kerry Martin Carson, that you have a long rap sheet in Chicago: petty theft, burglary and selling to kids. Impressive for a man who may never reach thirty, but nothing about extortion." She wads the paper in a ball and bounces it off his nose. "You think you can walk in here and extort the office of an ASA? How about if I make you disappear tonight, forever?"

He stands to face her. "How about I make your little brother disappear?"

"You don't want to fuck with me," Maggie says. "And that includes my brother." She steps back in front of the desk. You have got to be kidding me. David again?

"I know where he is." Stepping in front of her, he leans forward. His eyes pinpoint on hers. "You give me Che, and I'll leave your brother alone."

Maggie pushes the letter opener to the back of the desk.

"Che or your family," Sizzle says. "You choose."

"How about I arrest you for the murder of, I don't know, anybody dead in the last few days? Resisting arrest, the police had to shoot you. Shoot until dead."

Sizzle pulls a bent picture from his jacket pocket and slams it on the desk next to her. "Recognize him?"

Maggie's eye twitches. "That's my brother, David."

"Your brother, in line at the grocery store." His hand slides on the edge of the desk. "See this man behind him? That's Dogface. He's been following your brother. He's waiting for me to call and give him the go…" He uses his hand to imitate a gun. "Take care of him. You tell me where Che is, and Dogface leaves your brother alone."

Maggie grabs the crumpled picture off the desk. "Wait. This is the same picture Jersey showed me. Did Jersey send you in here?" Her eyes shift to his arm moving across the desk.

Sizzle reaches for the letter opener. After two quick punches to his chest like she does on the heavy bag, Maggie shoves him back against the chair. Her hand pulls on his jacket as she swipes her foot behind his legs. He bounces on the floor like a deflated basketball.

"This is Chicago, you dumbass," Maggie yells. Her shoe presses against his nose and lips while her heel spike pushes against his chest. Her composure returns. "I'm not some quiet whitey that scares easily from a little piece of shit like you. Tell Jersey to back off."

His hand swings at her foot. Maggie lifts the shoe as his hand flies below it. The heel spike jams into his mid sternum. Sizzle coughs.

"If anyone hurts David, I won't just kill you. No, I will break every one of your fingers and then cut your dick off and stuff it up your…"

Danny opens the door. "Maggie? We got this." Michael drags Sizzle by the collar out of the office. Danny turns back to her. "What in the hell was that?"

Maggie fluffs her hair and clears her throat. "He said he wouldn't vote for me."

Chapter 71

North of Lincoln Park, the sky looms over Lake Michigan. An expanding accordion of black clouds charges toward the western moon. An electric motor whines inside a storage building, and a metal door rolls up. Icy rain feathers the concrete. The Indian rumbles forward with headlights piercing the darkness. The engine stops, doves coo in the rafters. He flips on the light switch. The door rolls back down as clouds slice open, and heavy rain sounds like a machine gun on the metal roof.

Abandoned spiderwebs knitted in perfect triangles cover each corner of the building. Remo has not been here in months, maybe a year. A large blue tarp lies across the middle of the concrete floor. He drags it away, revealing a kerosene lamp, two dozen cans of food, a can opener, a box of jerky packets, three six-packs of bottled water and five pints of Bulleit Bourbon. A thirty-six-inch television screen sits on a low table. A wood-burning stove stands in the corner with an exhaust pipe up to the ceiling. It's not his favorite safe house, but the best for a quick escape.

With the lights back off, a fire crackles from the stove as the cold air diminishes. The light flickers across Remo's face with jittery shadows. Open cans of beans and corn sit on the stove. The police scanner chatters—nothing about him. The television screen is split into four sections, with live views outside the safe house. He bites into a strip of jerky.

Propped on a hillside, a chain-link fence with barbed wire rolls on top surrounds the storage building. Dense trees hide the sides and back of the building. A back door opens to a concrete drain gutter heading down to a rarely used street.

He opens the back door and bites off a piece of beef jerky. Truk is dead, and Ton has taken over his work. What is Maggie doing? Whose side is anyone on? By now, Jersey must know who he is.

The pager on his belt trills. *darling, call me.* He finishes the second pint, then flips open his phone and pushes M.

"Remo, darling, I miss you."

He steps inside again. "Yeah, things are pretty messed up now. Where are you?"

Maggie sits in her office, lights off. Outside, a lighthouse swings a long, slow light around the harbor. Tall boat masts metronome in the evening. "I want you to come in."

"You believe me, don't you?"

"Of course I do. Come to me."

"Maggie, not now. Need to find the video that will clear me."

Danny sits in a chair in front of her desk with his arms crossed. The ON IT tracker app runs on his laptop. He needs more time.

"If Richard Watters wins the election, you know he will prosecute you," Maggie says. "If for no other reason than to get back at me. Come in, and we can get the news of us walking down the hall together. Something like that."

"You mean down the hall with handcuffs behind my back, and you walking next to me with a sign saying, 'VOTE FOR ME'?"

"No, that is not what I meant. You need to get cleared. After that, we can move forward."

"Move forward or move on? I thought this was a team effort. An effort to clear me, not to have you elected and me behind bars."

"I hear rain in the background. Is it raining where you are? It is not raining here. Can you come in on your motorcycle, or is it too wet?"

"Maggie, are you trying to locate me? I'm out." He throws the phone toward the wall, and it bounces against a cardboard box before it hits the floor.

"Damn it. Danny, did you get anything?" Maggie asks.

"Don't hang up," Danny says. "His phone is still on."

"What? He never leaves his phone on. Never."

Danny brushes his finger across the screen. "He is north of here, and I have him within a diameter of a mile wide."

Behind boxes, on the other side of the storage building, Remo's screen on his phone illuminates Maggie's number.

"We still have a signal. Give me three more minutes, and I'll have his location."

❖

With the back door open, he listens to the rain decrease to a hum against the metal roof. His boots balance midway on the threshold, he bends to a crouching position. Lightning crackles behind angry clouds. Remo stares at the black sky.

Three black all-wheel-drive SUVs roll slowly on an industrial side street with headlights off, east of a large sleeping community of Middle American houses. Inside each SUV, the front seat passenger watches a map on his laptop. Maggie and Danny sit in the back seat in the last SUV. She glances at Danny's laptop. "Can't believe he still has his phone on."

"Believe it. Take luck when you can," Danny says as he pinpoints to the storage building.

They turn off the street to a long, curved driveway and stop. A chain-link fence surrounds a metal storage building. The building's entrance is fifty yards past the gate. There is nothing between the gate and the building, leaving no protection from a blown surprise.

A man in full SWAT gear clamps the padlock shackle on the gate with his extended bolt cutters. He squeezes the handles together until the shackle pops in two. The two gates swing wide apart. The SWAT member's first step crosses over a metal traffic spike bar, which lies flat on the asphalt.

Remo's pager trills. Picking it up off the floor, it shows GATE. He glances at the screen which shows intruders. He flips the saddlebag open and grabs the two Sigs with suppressors. Slipping the night vision goggles on his head, Remo zips his leather jacket up over the vest. He promised Maggie, he would always wear it. Remo closes the stove and turns the lamp off.

Remo deliberately made the width of the gate posts too narrow for a car to drive through. The SUV rolls forward as the front tires pass the flush-mounted traffic spike bar in the ground, and the quarter panels scrape across the narrowed posts.

"I don't like this. The gate is too narrow," the lieutenant says.

She watches the first SUV stop as it wedges itself between the posts. "This is something Remo would plan," Maggie whispers to Danny. She snaps the walkie-talkie button down. "You got one chance, lieutenant. One. You mess this up, and we'll never find him again." No answer, only a fuzzy click comes back to her.

After the front tires roll past the flat spike bar, Remo pushes a button on the wall. A bi-directional spike bar pops up from the ground at the gate—spikes pointing both ways with barbs that look like spearheads big enough to kill a bear.

The driver of the SUV calls out, "I'm backing out."

From the back door of the building, Remo turns on his night vision goggles, then races around to the front. He fires, and two tires explode. Blackness surrounds the area, but the men light up green.

An SUV barely in the gate blocks the entrance. The spikes rip the spinning tires like paper in a shredder.

Remo's suppressor spits twice into the SUV radiator. The engine stops, steam rolls out of the grille. The headlights pop on, momentarily blinding him. He fires twice, knocking out the lights. Blackness again. The two SUVs in the back are trapped outside the gate. The doors of the first two SUVs open, and men flood out. Remo turns behind the corner. Blind return fire from the fence line pierces the metal walls.

"Don't kill him, damn it," she yells through the walkie-talkie. "I am a hell of a lot worse with him dead. I need him in jail." She lowers the walkie-talkie from her mouth. "Jail, damn it. Jail is the safest place for you, darling."

The middle SUV backup lights pop on.

"Oh damn," Maggie says. "What is that idiot planning on doing?"

The driver of the second SUV floors the accelerator. Maggie is thrown forward as her SUV is shoved back. Headlights from the second SUV expose Remo as he stands alone with night vision goggles on and both pistols pointed at them. A fastball hits his chest. He fires again, and headlights explode. Remo disappears in the black again. He fires and hits the front tire of the middle SUV. The engine revs. It jumps forward, but four-inch-wide posts standing every three feet along the fence line stop the SUV. Remo fires three more into the radiator. The engine belt flops inside the engine bay like a mad carp out of the water. Two SUVs down, gate still intact. His chest throbs.

The back door of the third SUV opens. A woman highlighted in green stands behind the window. The door stays open. A bullhorn squeals. "Remo, I can help you. Come out. Surrender to me."

Behind the fence, the police fire into the metal building.

"Stop it, stop it, stop it!" Maggie yells through the bullhorn.

"Maggie, you shouldn't be here," Remo yells. "Too dangerous. A stray bullet could hit you."

She hears him calling her name. She steps out from the door. She is in a dress, and her legs are perfect. With the bullhorn up to her mouth, she calls out, "Remo, stop."

He aims at her and fires, shattering the side window next to her. She screams.

"Time to go." Remo runs back around the building.

Maggie hears his motorcycle revving in the background.

"Remo, damn it, get back here." The bullhorn slams against the concrete. Her hand pulls her hair back from her face. "Come back to me, baby."

Remo's fingers pop the clutch. He flies out the back door down the gutter to the boulevard below.

Chapter 72

I n her office, Maggie sits in her chair, the heels of her hands rub her temples. "He got away. How? Six from the SWAT team and three SUVs. He takes it all out."

Danny brings her a cup of coffee and says, "At least he didn't kill anyone. He just killed three SUVs that cost fifty thousand each."

She spins the handle around and takes a sip. "Thank God for that."

"What's going on in that head of yours, Maggie? You've been off-center since you came back from the shooting."

Her hand combs through her hair. Should I tell Danny the whole story? Too messy. She waves her hand. "We missed on Remo. I will never catch him. Shit, I probably will never see him again." Should I warn David about Jersey?

Her phone vibrates on her desk. A text reads, *West Kinzie and Laramie. Midnight, alone. R.*

Danny sees the text. "Remo? Don't go. It's late, really late at night. He might want revenge for the ambush."

Maggie stands, her feet planted like concrete in the ground. Her eyes fixate on the message. "Maybe. Maybe the R stands for Richard Watters, and he is trying to pull a fast one on me." Her hand with the phone drops to her side. "Catch me in the act of sneaking around at night and trying to see Remo on the slide. Or maybe he wants revenge for me running against him." Maggie watches the steam rise from her cup. "Maybe it's the news reporter that hates me. Does she want revenge for her being a dumbass bubblehead and I'm not? Or maybe I am and don't know it yet." She looks at the message again.

"I don't see Watters doing this," Danny says as he lights a cigarette. "And Brenda Nielsen would probably put a smiley face next to the R."

Maggie shakes her head. "Don't smoke in here. It's bad for my health." She grabs the matches from his hand.

"Yeah? Bullets are worse. Don't forget, he shot at you and missed. You might not be so lucky next time."

She rereads the message. "No. Richard doesn't have the balls to send me a text. His primary interest is blow-up dolls and videos. And Remo? My sweet little man, he loves me too much. Even *with* that fiasco tonight. Who else would send that? Maybe it's Jersey. She wants me dead. She could do it." She puts the coffee cup on the table. "I'm going."

◆

Maggie's car door closes. The intersection sign of Kinzie and Laramie stands above her. Gloves clamped between her teeth, she bends down and sweeps her hair into a tight red ponytail. Skintight gloves slip over her hands. There is no need for fingerprints anywhere with bubblehead wanting Maggie's ass on a plate or a stick. Maggie looks at her watch, thin as a dime. It's midnight straight up. A late fog rolls in, clutching the ground, slashing her vision to a few yards. She follows Remo's lead and uses a thermal night vision monocular. She raises it to her eye. Cutting through the white envelope, she can see an entire block away. Empty, everything is empty. Not even the Chicago rats scurry the streets tonight.

The cold mist bites her cheeks. Maggie's heart pounds against her fleece jacket. At the corner of the intersection, a metal door of an abandoned, brown-brick building stands six inches ajar. Darkness past the door contrasts the pale fog outside. The point of her Beretta Pico .380 pushes the door farther open. A creaking hinge announces her presence. The monocular scans the room—no warm bodies. A rotting table lying sideways and two wooden chairs face each other with a paper folded in half taped to one. The tape shows red on the thermal lens. This happened seconds, maybe a minute ago.

She flips the paper open. I am watching you. Step outside, turn left, walk two blocks, then right one block. Three-story warehouse, door with an X. Better be alone.

The paper floats to the floor as she says, "I hate games." She steps outside and breaks into a run, trying to catch the host of this idiotic game. A quick look behind her reveals no one following. She charges toward the warehouse while looking for car movement.

She stops at the closed door with a red painted X and scans the area with the thermal monocular. She grabs another folded paper taped to the door. 'Why is someone following you?' She spins around. Is there someone behind her?

She stands in the middle of the street as the fog slowly rolls around her. She scans the street. About sixty feet down the road, a tractor-trailer is parked next to the curb. The engine bay and radiator are cold, but there is a red spot on the front bumper. A handprint? She sees red shoes hiding behind a tire next to the curb. This could be Jersey. She steps across the street close to the cars along the curb. The shoes are still behind the truck, not moving. Maggie holds the pistol in one hand and the thermal monocular in the other in front of her. Her breath is short and rapid. Please don't be Jersey. Maggie's body shakes from cold and fear. The shoes shift. The outline of a red body moves under the trailer toward the street. Whoever it is knows she is near. With slow, quiet steps in front of each other, Maggie reaches the front of the truck and looks under it with the monocular. The shoes are by the left tractor cab door.

Maggie spins around the bumper and yells, "Don't you move. I promise I'll shoot."

"Don't shoot. It's me, Danny." His hands go up.

She relaxes a bit, still aiming at his chest. "What are you doing here? Do you have a gun?"

"A gun? Hell no. And why do you have a gun?"

She drops the barrel down. "Because I'm in Chicago, and its night, and foggy, and I'm meeting an unknown person. Need more reasons?"

"I'm here to help you. I thought you might need some help…in case you need help."

"Danny, I thought you were Jersey. I might have shot you sneaking around here." She releases a deep sigh of relief. "Go home. I will be fine."

"Okay, my car is two blocks away." He looks around. "Think I will be okay walking back? Maybe I need your gun."

"No, you are not getting my pistol. Get your ass back to your car and go home. I'll see you tomorrow morning."

She steps back to the door with an X. It has another folded paper taped to it.

'Now you can enter.'

The middle of the door shines a bright red handprint. Someone's hand was on it seconds ago. A quick scan of the street reveals no red. Maggie pushes the door; it swings wide and bangs the wall. A sixty-year-old warehouse echoes back at her. She raises the monocular to her eye as a lump the size of an apple sticks in her throat. No hot spots inside. Knife blades and unfired guns don't shine red. Maybe this is not such a good idea. Maggie thinks what tomorrow's newspaper headline would be. "Maggie McCall Found Dead in Abandoned Warehouse" would sell quicker than hotcakes at a Rotary Club breakfast.

The vacant, three-story building with soot-covered brick and large framed windows cut high into the walls spook her. Rusted poles every twenty feet hold the metal roof three stories above. The thermal scanner finds nothing but cold dust. Her hand trembles holding the pistol.

"Wasn't sure if you would come," Remo's voice announces from behind her.

Her left hand lowers from her eye as she spins around; Remo is inches away and kisses her. She raises the Beretta to his chest.

"You think you need that tonight?" he asks.

Pupils fully dilated, trying to slow each breath, Maggie's finger slips away from the trigger. With a shaky breath, she holds it for a second before warm air flows between her parted lips. "No."

He kisses her again.

Her thoughts won't line up. Election, David, Remo, Jersey. To hell with the others. She tries to clear her head. My God, he looks good. A low hum rushes from her carotids to her dizzy head. "You need to...you...I want..." Concentrate, focus. "I want you to..." Take him in and win the election. "Give yourself up and come back to my office." Tell him about Jersey pushing harder. "I need to tell you about David, my brother and Jersey."

"I know about Jersey's threat. David is safe."

"What do you mean?"

"Safe, I sent him to a safe place until after the election."

"Promise?"

"Promise." His finger pushes a remote control button. A lamp with a red scarf over the top shines on a white tablecloth lying over a small round table. A table for two with a bottle of red wine, a square of white cheese and a loaf of French bread. On a small plate, olive oil and parsley sit ready to be taken.

"Your favorite."

"Damn you, Remo. Wine and cheese and bread? Suppose you brought a bed too?"

"A bed? Why would I need a bed?"

Maggie looks around the warehouse. There's a bed with satin sheets behind him. She looks back at Remo and taps the end of the pistol barrel against his chest. "How did you get a bed in here?"

Remo pinches the gun barrel between his thumb and index finger and slides it from her hand. "Better," he says. "Let's take those off."

"Wait a minute. I'm running for CCSA, and you should be under arrest. I am not taking my clothes off."

Turning his head, revealing a half-smile, he says, "Clothes? I meant the thermal camera in your hand." His hand gently wraps around her hand. "Are you going to take your clothes off?" He looks into her eyes. "May I?" A gentle push of his hands slides the night scanner off her hand.

Focus, damn it. Say no and take him in. "Yes."

They sit across from each other as he pours two glasses of wine. Remo tears a small corner of the bread, swirls it in the oil and parsley and holds it an inch from her lips. "Can I trust you? I mean, even with the safe house debacle and all?"

Her pursed lips pull the oil-soaked bread from his fingers. "I don't know. Can I trust you? You almost shot me at the warehouse."

"I would never *accidentally* shoot you. I never miss my target."

"Oh, well, that makes me feel better about the bullet that was inches from my head."

"You know there is more to the video. Jiang fired the shot, hitting Johnny, not me. I need you to help me find the rest of the video."

Her wine disappears in one motion like a shot glass. "Who is interrogating whom? You are the one in question, not me." Another bite of bread leaves a snippet of parsley at the crease of her mouth. She sighs, "This is good. Damn it, Remo. You are supposed to be on the run. You know, hiding from me, from the law."

He leans over and kisses the parsley from her lip. "Why would I ever try to hide from you?" He pulls her up from the chair; stepping closer, he slides her jacket zipper down, exposing a red lace camisole.

Looking down, his hands near her breasts, she says, "I hoped that note was from you. It would have been embarrassing if the R was Richard."

Remo's finger rolls her hair behind her ear. His lips graze her ear as he whispers, "You would have let Richard get this far?" Her jacket falls to the ground.

Lifting her head back, exposing her ear to him, she giggles. "Maybe after I broke all ten fingers and his balls stopped aching."

Remo's hand slips around her waist to the small of her back. The thin red strap slides off her shoulder. Their lips meld into one. She loses herself to his warm body. Her fingers fumble at the top button of his five-button jeans. A quick machine-gun burst of the buttons, and the pants drop, revealing his birthday suit. Moonlight reflects off satin pillows and linen sheets. She pushes him back as they fall onto the bed.

Maggie's head spins, the wine flows in her brain. The room is dark. Remo's black hair brushes against her pale breasts. His hands roam across all the secret places. Bliss envelops her.

Her eyes are closed, light and warmth surround her. "Remo, darling." There is no reply. With her eyelids feeling heavy, she wants to open them but can't. She reaches across the bed and touches his chest. Her fingertip smears blood on his skin. Her tongue licks the blood away. The taste is bitter. A tear rolls down her cheek, sadness clouds her eyes. The warmth of his body is gone. She pulls him toward her, but his firm muscles turn to a soft cloud. Her eyes open, and her arms are wrapped around a pillow.

Sunrise pierces through the soot-smeared windows above her, snapping her away from her dream. She wakes alone in bed; her perfectly painted toenails stick out from under the satin sheet. Last night flashes in her head. She wants it back. She wants him back in her arms.

An empty wine bottle and two glasses sit on the table. Maggie flips the watch around her wrist. It's 7:16 in the morning. "Oh, shit," she says. She has a nine o'clock meeting with the media about Detective Wolf.

She wraps her bedhead hair back into a ponytail. A square envelope lies beside her. Ripping it open, she reads as her heart pounds. *Maybe again. Later, R.*

Chapter 73

The automatic glass doors at Northwestern Memorial Hospital slide open to heavy snow floating to the ground. Donovan Fillard steps outside for the first time in over a week. His checkerboard hat is tight next to his ears, the uniform is clean and pressed.

Kenny McLemore, a close friend from the same police academy class, says, "Bet it feels good to be back outside again. Kinda strange letting you go this late at night."

A deep breath of Lake Michigan air swirls inside the lungs. "I love the snow. No place in the world better than Chicago. Heard from Detective Wolf?"

"You haven't watched the news?"

"No, been in the hospital with tubes stuck up every orifice for days."

"He's on the run," the fellow officer says.

"On the run? What do you mean?"

"Something about him shooting a suspect in the back, point-blank. Someone put it on YouTube. Internal Affairs wants to talk to him, but they can't find him."

"Wolf?" Donovan scoffs. "Nah, he wouldn't murder someone. Shoot someone if they tried to escape, maybe, but not in the back. I need to find him."

"Yeah? Well, get in line. IA, Captain Kimball, and the CCSA's office want him first." With a clap on the back of Donovan's shoulder, he says, "Come on, let's get some well-deserved pizza."

Donovan shakes his head. "Later, got to find Wolf."

Remo's pager trills. It's Donovan's number. He calls. "You still alive?"

"Yes, and I want to help you."

"Thought you were dead, or half dead."

"It's going to take more than two ugly men to do that," Donovan smirks.

Remo laughs. A long ten seconds pass. "Where are you?"

"Four blocks west of Northwest Memorial Hospital. Huron and State Street."

"I'm on the South Side. I know a place the two of us can meet. Stay there, and a slick top will pick you up."

"Who?"

"An unmarked car."

"Do I know him? How will he know me?"

"Bet you got a clean uniform on, right?"

Donovan's lips tighten like he blew his cover. "Yeah."

Remo laughs again. "Is your cap on your head or under your arm?"

Fifteen minutes later, an engine echoes like a church organ with headers. Tires crunch over fresh snow. The window rolls down. Davy says, "Get in, you know."

"No! This is not an unmarked police car."

"That cop ain't coming. Do you want to see Remo? Get in, you know."

As soon as Donovan's seatbelt snaps, the car surges forward.

"Hey, you need to slow down. I'm a cop." Donovan points to the badge on his shirt. "See?"

"Oh, is that because you're such a good driver, you know?"

"Uh, it doesn't matter. Slow down."

A hard turn to the left across oncoming cars. "I'll get you where you need to go without flipping the car over, you know."

"Heard about that, huh?" Donovan holds on to the shoulder belt and dashboard as car headlights race across buildings. "Slow down, too much snow out here." The red light zooms by overhead. "I just got out of the damn hospital. Don't put me back in it."

Davy drives through a maze, dodging cars, people and buildings. The front wheels bounce hard, the tires sing in harmony across a metal bridge. Davy's eyes scan the rearview mirror.

"Oh crap," Donovan snaps. "Stop sign. Stop sign, damn it." Donovan grabs the dashboard.

The tires slide to the intersection. "No car lights behind us, you know." Davy turns the wheel right. "Don't worry, almost there, you know." Davy blackens the headlights as the car ambles down his street. Streetlights shine through tree limbs like hands with too many fingers to count. The car turns into the driveway, past the house, and edges toward the unattached garage in the back. Remo's white Indian motorcycle is in front of the garage. Davy pushes the remote above his head. The garage door lifts.

"Is that Remo's bike?" Donovan asks.

"Yeah, he wasn't here when I left to get you. Why is he here now, and why did he block me from going inside the garage, you know?" Davy asks.

Chapter 74

Ton steps out of his car behind the police station. His car chirps as he unlocks the metal alley door. After wiping the snow off his shoes, he steps down the small hallway to the fire door to the lobby. Officer McDonald sits in a chair behind the front desk in the lobby.

"Donnie, are you here all night?"

Leaning back in the chair, he looks at his phone. "Yes, sir, Captain Kimball. All night long. It's snowing hard outside. You stay much longer, and you might be stuck here with me all night."

"That's an old man's job being here all night. Don't you have a wife and kids?"

"Divorced, no kids. I'm good right here."

Ton steps up and raps his knuckles on the desk. "I got a buddy that has a sister who needs a boyfriend. Maybe a husband."

"No, sir. Not sure which is worse, ex-wives or lawyers. I never want nothing to do with either, ever again. Happy playing the field, one-night stand at a time."

He snickers and says, "I'm heading upstairs."

In the office, Ton opens Truk's laptop and stares at the long list of department emails with nothing important over the last week. He taps the junk mailbox and rolls through weight-loss plans, lower mortgage rates and BFF requests. Back to the inbox, he types REMO in the search box and finds a mass of emails from IA with subject lines related to Remo and Bobby's ambush. Ton stops at an anonymous sender with the subject line of REMO VIDEO. He opens it. A single word in the message says READ, with two attachments below named REMO 1 and REMO 2."

REMO 1 is the video everyone has. Ton taps the REMO 2 attachment. It opens with the same scene, except the person recording on the phone shows a chrome revolver pointed at Detective Wolf. Sirens wail in the background. The words are clear, unlike the first video. Remo tells Johnny Rivera and Rolly Chang to stop and put their hands up. Remo steps back and away from the fire. To his side, a gunshot fires and hits Johnny Rivera in the back. Rolly Chang drops the bag and runs.

Ton backs up the scene and expands it. Remo's pistol aims high and straight. Ton taps through each frame. A gun flash spurts from the ground, not Remo's pistol. With the tip of Remo's gun visible, it turns and aims at the ground. Remo steps forward with his face looking down. Remo tells Jiang to drop his weapon. Two more gunshots fire at ground level. Remo fires back.

Ton watches the video again at regular speed. It's obvious, Remo did not shoot Johnny Rivera. Somebody on the ground did. He watches again and again. He snaps the laptop closed, slides it off the desk, and heads down the stairs.

Ton pushes the panic bar on the outside metal door. A white blanket of snow covers the alley. With the laptop in one hand, he flips up his overcoat collar. The door snaps closed behind him.

"Ton," a woman's voice from behind says.

His hand quickly reaches for the shoulder holster. Before he can grasp his pistol, two punctures from Jersey's knife pierce Ton's back. He falls to his knees. The laptop bounces on the ground.

"You're too close to all this." Her blade slices across his throat. "Need you out of the way."

Chapter 75

Inside Davy's house, Remo bends down and watches a car crawl past the kitchen windows; tires slowly grind against white gravel. Davy doesn't drive at night without a serious reason. Red taillights creep by the kitchen window as he hears the garage door rise. His bike is in the way. What kind of trouble is Davy in? Remo has enough problems for the two of them. He racks the slide of his Sig and listens as the car engine stops, then two doors close. Outside, Remo hears footsteps crunching the snow. Three metal bolts snap open on the backdoor that sound like a bank vault opening. Davy steps through the door as Donovan follows.

"What the hell is he doing here?" Remo asks. "I called Maddox, and he agreed to pick Donovan up and drop him off at the train station, to let him stew for a few hours." Remo stands and faces off with Davy. "How did you know where to pick up Donovan?"

"I tapped your phone. I heard everything, you know."

"I wish you'd quit that. Sometimes it bothers the hell out of me the shit you can do." Remo holsters his pistol. "I promise you, Davy, nobody knows about you. I don't want anyone to know about you. And now this, someone knows you."

"I brought him here. And you don't know everything about me, you know," Davy replies.

"You tapped my phone? How?"

"Easy for me, hard for you. Why is your bike out, you know?"

"Too many things going down the wrong direction," Remo says as he shakes his head. "Saw Maggie tonight, and she still wants me in jail. Jersey, Solido, Fedora, all want me dead. And I'm not sure if Ton is on my side or not."

"You need to go back to the detectives' office and get in Belly's laptop, you know."

"Why Belly's?" Donovan asks.

"Once upon a time, he never shut it down when he walked away. A few months ago, I sent Davy his IP address. He dropped a porn folder deep inside and hacked into his microphone and camera. I knew what was going on in the room anytime, day or night. I was going to open the porn folder later at an opportunistic time to embarrass him. Last week, I asked Davy to open the folder and send it to everyone. Trying to take some heat off me. Davy was looking for the folder, and he found a different one with my name on it."

"On Belly's laptop?" Donovan asks.

"Davy was listening when Truk walked in and told everyone to shut down. IT was doing an update that night. Belly shut down the laptop before Davy could copy the folder with my name. IT added new anti-spyware, made everyone change their ID and made them use an eleven-digit password. Can't watch or listen anymore because now he closes it every time he leaves his desk." Remo grabs the nylon handle of his backpack. "You're right, Davy. Got to figure this out."

"Take me with you. You need backup," Donovan says.

"Davy, you got that infrared camera from next door?" Remo asks.

He runs down the hallway to his bedroom, and a few seconds later, he returns. "Yeah, here, you know."

Remo checks the pistol shoulder holster over the armored vest he promised to wear. His thumb presses the magazine release lever. A second later, his palm snaps it back in. He pulls his pant leg up and taps the left and right ankle pistols around military boots.

"If you got a vest on, I know you need my help," Donovan says.

"Need you here. Besides..." Remo drops the camera in the backpack. The zipper hisses across the top. "...this is on me." He flips the pack over his back shoulder. "Call you in a few days."

"Remo, I came here to help." Donovan steps in front of the door. "Take me with you."

"And what do you think you're doing? Stepping in front of the door is not going to stop me."

"I was top of my class at the academy in self-defense. I can handle my..."

A quick fist to Donovan's stomach drops him to his knees.

"I wasn't ready for that."

"Sorry. Ready now?" He reaches for Donovan's shoulder. "Can you stand?"

"Yeah." Donovan's fist swings hard against Remo's knee. His fist bounces off like a Nerf ball. "Damn, that hurt. You got bricks for knees?"

"Come on, up you go." Remo grabs his shoulder and pulls him up.

Donovan swings his fist into Remo's stomach. "You can't go without me."

Remo doesn't budge. "Do I have to tie you up?"

"No. You have to take me with you."

A quick backhand to Donovan's stomach curls him to the floor. Remo pulls him up and sits him in a chair. "Davy, get me that rope in the utility closet."

"You need an extra set of eyes while you work on Belly's laptop. Take me with you."

Remo turns to Davy. "What do you think?"

"Take him. I don't want him here, you know."

A boot shoves the kickstarter down. The engine idles low as Donovan climbs on behind Remo.

"I feel like Easy Rider," Donovan says.

Remo scoffs. "Don't end up like Jack Nicholson."

The headlight is off as the bike rolls down the driveway and disappears down the street.

Chapter 76

Hexagonal snowflakes float across the dark city. The Indian glides down the alley as the engine rumbles.

"All this snow. I can't believe we made it," Donovan says.

"Ride in Chicago long enough, and you can maneuver in almost any kind of weather."

The bike stops a few feet from the back door. Donovan's footsteps crunch down the alley where the snow covers Ton's blood.

"Crazy, snow this early," Remo tells Donovan. "Don't remember the last time it snowed like this in November."

Donovan points to the back parking lot. "Two cars? Someone here?"

"Shit. One belongs to Ton, and the other is McDonald's. He's the night watchman."

"There's two inside? No good, Remo."

"Ton must have left with someone. He can't be here. Not this time of night. Come on, but quietly."

Remo twists a large key in a police station's metal door lock and steps into the narrow hallway. Donovan follows.

"Don't let it slam shut," Remo whispers. "McDonald is at the front desk. The city pays him to stay all night playing games on his phone."

Donovan slows the door while the pneumatic closer pulls it forward. The rubber weather strip scrapes across the wet threshold. He whispers, "Never been here before. Pretty old building."

"Yeah," Remo says. "Look up. There is an old laundry chute where, thirty years ago, the detectives would drop their suits to be cleaned at a laundry service next door. Rumor is the owner cleaned them for free if they left his weekly poker games alone."

"The chute is in the detectives' office?"

"No. It's inside the utility closet."

"Still use it?" Donovan asks.

Remo scoffs. "Not for suits. Now the cleaning service drops trash bags down and then throws the bags in the dumpster in the alley."

They quietly climb the staircase to the second floor as Donovan asks, "You sure nobody is coming to the station?"

"Yeah, yeah, it's four in the morning in the middle of a snowstorm. Who wants to be out in this mess?" Remo quietly pushes open the stairwell door to the second floor and steps on carpet needing to be replaced decades ago. The wind howls around the building.

The door has DETECTIVES' OFFICE printed in black across frosted glass.

Remo points down. "Careful with the floor. It squeaks right there." Remo shakes his head. "Someone is going to fall through this floor someday."

Remo fishes a flashlight out of his backpack inside the dark office. He snaps the button down, and a round ball of bright light shines on Belly's keyboard. The sixteen-inch monitor pops on when he moves the mouse. His thumb flips the phone open and taps D*. A voice answers, "Hello." He touches the speakerphone.

"Okay, Davy, I'm on Belly's laptop. You take control of it. Do your thing."

An empty white rectangle on Belly's laptop waits for a username. Thousands of random numbers and letters fill the screen, rolling too fast to read.

"Hate this part, the waiting," Remo says. "Davy, how much longer?"

"Few more seconds, you know."

The phrase 'BEER!' fills the username box. Remo snickers. "Should have guessed that one."

A second empty rectangle pops up, password, another roll of numbers and letters spin through. Two minutes later, it stops. Fedora60607 pops up in the box with the Chicago Police Department logo appearing as a background.

A hot buzz saw runs up Remo's neck. "You bastard. Are you Fedora?"

Davy opens the FILE EXPLORER folder and hundreds of pictures and files roll across the screen. He types 'Remo' in the search box. A single file pops up named GARFIELD-REMO.

"This must be it," Remo says. "The shooting happened at Garfield Park."

The arrow pops the folder open. Davy says, "It's empty, you know."

"Damn it, Davy. Where is it?"

"Wait, got an idea, you know." Davy goes to Belly's emails. "I'm looking for an email with an attachment. Maybe he sent it somewhere and then deleted it from his folder. Hold on. There's one sent to Truk's laptop. I bet he wanted Truk to see it, you know."

"Can you get into Truk's laptop?" Remo asks.

"Going to take a while with the eleven-digit password. Make sure the laptop is open, you know."

Remo drops Belly's laptop screen almost closed and steps to Truk's office door, where Captain Kurt Maxwell is still printed in bold white letters across the glass.

"Love you, man, but we need inside your office." He searches the room with no laptop found. "Davy, nothing here. CPD has a tracker on every piece of equipment. You have Truk's IP address. Break into CPD and find it."

Remo listens to Davy's fingers type on his keyboard a thousand times a minute. "Found it, about four blocks from the station."

"Ton must have taken it. Are we out of luck?"

"No. I'll pull up the deleted email on Belly's machine. Look there."

The email reappears with the subject line, WOLF IS GOING DOWN. THE VIDEO IS PROOF. Remo taps the email, then the REMO 1 attachment. After a few minutes, it's downloaded only fifty percent. Tapping his fingers on the desk, he watches the number slowly increase to sixty percent, seventy, eighty, ninety. The attachment finally opens. "This is the one the media ran," Remo says. "I need to look at the other one."

He taps the arrow on REMO 2. A circle spins around a picture of a video camera in the center of the folder. Ten percent, twenty, thirty…

"Why so long?" Remo's fingers comb through his hair. Is this the actual evidence that could clear him? Seventy percent, eighty, ninety…

The video opens. This time, the person videoing has a gun pointing toward Remo. It's Fedora's chrome revolver. The footage moves around as the camera bounces with steps toward the middle of the street. A thumb pulls the revolver's hammer back. Remo steps back behind the Escalade. A second later, there's a gun flash near Remo's feet.

Remo pushes rewind, then forward. "There." He freezes the scene. "The flash is low. Not from my angle. It's from Jiang's gun."

He pushes forward again. Johnny Rivera drops to the ground. The chrome barrel disappears. Remo turns and fires at Jiang. The video ends.

"This is great, you know," Davy says. "This is proof someone digitally altered REMO 1. Somebody knowledgeable with IT manipulation removed the chrome barrel and Jiang's gun flash. REMO 2 is the unaltered one, the real one, you know."

"This clears me. No doubts. Flames come from the ground, Jiang's gun."

Chapter 77

A sky full of white confetti floats toward Earth. A person wearing a black fedora with a red pin steps across the intersection, leaving boot impressions aiming toward the police station. One hand carries a five-gallon canister while the other hand brushes the snow off the shoulders of the black wool overcoat.

Fedora has found Wolf. "Remo Wolf, you are going to die tonight."

Inside the warm police station, a tall, dark-wood-paneled desk stands in the middle of the lobby, designed for intimidation. The sergeant-in-charge can look down, like God during the rapture, on whoever is in front of him.

Officer McDonald is happy to be alone in the police station. He leans back against the chair with his feet propped on the desk. His eyes switch from the phone to someone outside the glass doors.

Fedora stops and places the canister on the snowy concrete. The door opens, and a burst of snow and cold air rush as Fedora steps inside.

"Can I help you?" McDonald asks.

"Yeah, got a guy outside that needs help. Can you come down here?"

Feet not moving off the desk yet, McDonald asks, "What's wrong?"

"Says he is Remo Wolf and wants to turn himself in."

McDonald lays his phone on the desk and stands. "Detective Wolf?"

Fedora turns and fires a pistol with a suppressor. A single thud above McDonald's right eye drops him to the floor.

Fedora flips the lobby light switch off, brings the canister inside, and sets it next to the desk. Behind the sergeant's desk are two doors, one with an arrow pointing down and the other with an arrow pointing up. A pull on the upstairs door reveals a narrow hallway to the left with another metal fire door exiting the alley. A stairwell heads straight to the second floor. Seconds later, Fedora shoves open the metal door at the top of the stairs and gazes at a small light through the office's frosted glass door.

The floor creaks outside the door. Remo and Donovan's eyes pop up. Cold wind gusts as the windows creak behind him. Remo pushes the power button on Belly's laptop as he wonders if it was a foot or the wind that made the creaking sound.

Fedora stares down at the floor and then back at the frosted glass. The light in the center of the detectives' office goes dark. Fedora unscrews the lid to the five-gallon container. The smell of gasoline escapes from the mouth of the container.

❖

Downstairs, Maggie opens the glass front door to the empty police station. The lobby lights are off. She leans the umbrella against the door, brushes the snow from her knee-length wool coat and rubs the soles of her boots on the wet rubber mat. She keeps the fur-lined hood over her head. There are wet footprints in front of her. Someone else has recently been here. She shifts the shoulder strap of her purse across her chest. Her hand searches inside for her pistol. She cringes when she remembers putting it in the trunk of her car when she left the practice range. She grabs the umbrella and steps to the sergeant's desk.

"Hello? Isn't someone supposed to be here, twenty-four/seven?" Maggie calls out. "Assistant State's Attorney McCall here, and I'm going up to Detective Wolf's office," she says in a loud voice.

Still, no one comes to the desk. Maggie doesn't see McDonald lying on his side behind the desk with a pool of coagulated blood surrounding his skull. This is the first time she has been to Remo's station. She remembers he told her the detectives' office was upstairs and heads for the two metal doors behind the desk. Remo had talked about the downstairs door leading to a forgotten basement. For years, a rumor floated it was once top-secret down there, Cold War secret. The metal door creaks open. Cold air and moldy cardboard odor rush past her. She lets it go, and the door closes with a sealed thump. She opens the upstairs door and sees a narrow hallway, an exit metal door to the left and stairs going up in front of her.

Fedora's gloved hand drops the screw-top lid of the gasoline canister on the carpet. The downstairs metal door opens, and the sound of footsteps comes up the stairs. Who else is here? It can't be McDonald. He has a bullet in his brain. Down the hallway, there's a sign above the bathroom and a utility closet.

Fedora steps inside the utility closet and quietly closes the door as Maggie opens the metal stairwell door to the hallway. It's dark except for the dimly lit exit sign above Maggie's head. The carpet smells like cheap cigars. A black plastic lid lies on the floor in front of her.

Chapter 78

Blue lights swirl outside the second-story window. Snow falls like a scene inside a shaken snow globe. Remo steps to the window; an officer walks from his car to talk to a guy pushing a grocery cart stuffed full of everything he owns. It's the old man from the train crossing. He looks up at Remo through the window and waves, then points to his hat and back to Remo—Fedora. His hands move across his stomach like someone is pregnant—Belly. He points to a car parked at an angle across the street with tire tracks behind it. A white blanket covers the road except snow-crushed footprints pointing away from the car toward the police station.

"We've got company," Remo says. "Belly's car is outside."

"Think Belly made the creak outside the door?" Donovan asks.

"Not sure. If he's trying to sneak up on me, he knows where the loose board is and where not to step. He's a dumb Irishman, but not totally stupid."

"Maybe it was McDonald downstairs," Donovan whispers.

Remo shakes his head. "He wouldn't leave the desk." Remo squints at the snow blowing hard outside the window. "It's an old building. Probably shifting in the wind." Remo turns his attention back to the video showing Jiang firing, hitting Johnny Rivera in the back and falling forward.

"Watch this," Davy says. "Got it as a ten-second loop, you know."

"This has to clear you, Remo," Donovan says.

"Okay, great. Davy, hack into the CPD and CCSA websites tonight and loop it as the background of every computer. Send it to my phone."

Davy repeats the loop several times. "Okay, need five minutes. Beautiful, you know."

◆

Maggie's eyes stare at the words, DETECTIVES' OFFICE, printed on the frosted glass. She is sure the muted voice is Remo. She needs to tell him about Jersey extorting her, but her voice is frozen with fear. If she could get him in a jail cell, she would keep him safe and sound. Would he understand? Would he forgive her?

Fedora squints through the crack in the utility room door. There is a person in the dark hall. Is that a rifle in their right hand? Fedora waits in silence.

Maggie's eyes turn to the ladies' bathroom sign sticking out of the side of the wall. Instead of walking into the office, she must reorganize her thoughts. Retreating to the bathroom, she waits until the door closes before turning on the light. Maggie turns the hot water handle, then grasps each side of the porcelain sink as steam rolls over the mirror. Her eyes refocus on herself while her nervous heel taps the wooden flooring. "It's for your own good. Please forgive me."

◆

Stepping out of the utility closet, Fedora pours a line of gasoline down the hallway and stairs. Back on the first floor, she turns the can upside down and the flammable liquid splashes across the curtains and the floor. I got you now, Remo Wolf. Bobby is dead because of you. It's your fault, not mine. You made me shoot Bobby. You were supposed to die—not him. The empty canister bounces on the floor. Only one way out, Remo. Down the stairwell, and I will be waiting for you. You die tonight.

Chapter 79

Outside, Detective Belly Lynch and a young officer walk on the sidewalk a block away from the police station. Belly raises his coat lapel higher around his neck. "It's colder than a polar bear's tit." The Jameson whiskey inside Belly's metal flask empties down his throat. "When we get inside, you wait in the lobby, and I'll run upstairs and get my wallet. Can't believe I left it in my desk drawer again." He places a cigarette between his lips and says, "After that, Charlie's Bar stays open until 4 AM. We'll have a few." His thumbnail flicks the tip of a wooden match as his hands cup around the cigarette. Belly recognizes the automobile across the street. "Is that my car?" He takes a drag from the cigarette. "Let's get inside." They step through the front door of the station. The lobby is dark. "McDonald! Why are the lights out? Sleeping on the job?"

The smell of gasoline drifts across his nose.

"Gas," Belly says. "That smells like gas."

"Yeah, gasoline," the officer says as he motions toward the front door. "Get rid of the cigarette."

Belly opens the door and flips the cigarette outside. He points to the other officer's microphone on his shoulder epaulet. "Call dispatch. Something's up."

Across the lobby, a dark figure wearing a fedora and overcoat silhouettes in front of a plate-glass window. Belly's eye catches the pin on the hat glistening as the traffic light behind turns red.

"Who the hell are you?" Belly asks as he reaches for his service weapon.

Fedora's right arm raises shoulder high. The suppressor spits twice, dropping both to the ground. Blood spreads across Belly's shirt as he lies on the floor like a marionette with the strings cut.

Belly gasps for breath. He hears footsteps coming closer. Lights from outside shine across Fedora's facial features. Belly recognizes the eyes. "Becky? Is that you?"

Chapter 80

You couldn't do it, could you?" Becky crouches down over Belly. "You don't have the guts to kill Wolf. Well, I do."

"No." Belly raises his hand in front of him. "What the hell are you doing here?" He grimaces with pain. "I got to get out of here."

"You're shot in the chest, idiot. How are you going to do that?" She stands again and shoves her boot against his leg. "You think I'm going to take you to the emergency room on my way back to the house?"

Belly grabs at his chest and coughs. "Becky, where did you get a gun?"

She squats in front of him again. Her lips rise into a cruel smile. "Our closet. The gun safe is filled with your little arsenal, stupid. Remember, you like to go in there and pretend to play cowboys and Indians. You're always the good guy, and Remo Wolf is the bad guy."

A death moan rolls from the young officer's throat. She swings the barrel, a muted shot in the head squelches the noise.

"I took the machine pistol with the suppressor you stole from the evidence room last year. And this, I like this thing with the long magazine stuck in it. Tell me, how many does it hold?"

"Thirty, but you can't kill Remo. That's murder."

"Murder?" She points the barrel at the dead officer next to Belly. "You dumb shit. Don't you dare tell me what I can and can't do. That's the second cop I killed today."

Belly's chest gurgles with blood. "What do you mean, the second cop? Who else did you fucking kill?"

She swings the muzzle of the gun toward the cop next to Belly. "Well, this one, whatever his name is, and the one up there at the desk." Becky slaps Belly's hand away in a poor attempt to swipe at the gun. "Stop it."

Belly grabs her coat lapel. "Did you kill Truk?"

"Oh yeah, that makes three. I sort of did. I got Jersey to do it."

"Goddamn you. Why?" Belly coughs up blood. "You've gone bitch-crazy."

"Why? Because he was protecting Maggie McCall."

Belly grabs a handful of Becky's pants and tries to pull up. "Protecting McCall? What the hell did she do to you?"

"You dumb shit." Becky hunches over Belly. "I'm going to kill her, too."

The cop next to Belly gurgles once again.

"Damn. Die already."

She fires two more into the cop's chest.

She looks back at Belly. "I loved Bobby, but he was cheating on me. He was with a different prostitute every week. I told him to stop. I know Remo Wolf kept telling Bobby to screw anything and everything. It's his fault Bobby kept doing it. I was aiming for Remo, but Bobby jumped in the way."

Belly scoffs at her.

"What the hell are you smiling about? You got a hole in your chest, you dumb piece of shit." Becky snaps the magazine out. "I only brought one of these. Hope it's enough." She snaps it back in. "I paid good money trying to get what he loves killed. That stupid Euro missed McCall when he had the chance. And that Jersey bitch is no better. It's because of Remo my Bobby is dead, and now he's going to die tonight."

Belly scoffs at her, then coughs up a wad of blood before spitting it on the floor. "You're dumber than I am. Remo didn't care who Bobby was screwing. I'm the one who told my little brother to screw those hookers. He said you got fat and ugly after those kids, and I said you got fat from shoveling food in that pie hole all day long." He grimaces from the pain. "I told him to get all he can while he can. I didn't care if he was screwing you. I know those kids look like him and not me." He coughs up more blood and struggles with a deep breath. "But I'm seeing someone else too. You thought you were smart screwing two brothers, but both cheated on you. You're the dumb bitch."

She stoops over him and rams the end of the gun into Belly's chest. "Feel smart now with a bullet hole in you? I'm going to make you smarter." She steps back and aims the pistol at Belly. Two muffled shots enter his chest.

She can end all of this now when the stairwell door opens.

"Damn it, Wolf. Get down here. No more interruptions. You have to die now." Becky rushes toward the stairwell door.

A bloody cough spews bits of a lung on Belly's shirt. His fingers struggle inside his side pocket for a wooden match as the pungent smell of gasoline continues. His thumb rests on the tip, each breath aches. The thumbnail flicks the match tip—nothing. It flicks the tip again. Nothing.

Belly's eyes focus on the match head. He groans from the pain as his thumb rests on the tip of the match. He feels the weight of death engulfing him. He gathers the last of his energy. He snaps it again, white-hot fire explodes on the tip. It flies end-over-end as he rolls with a dead man's cough. A whump of yellow heat rolls across the dark lobby.

Chapter 81

Upstairs in the bathroom, Maggie runs water from the sink on a paper towel and dabs the coolness at the back of her neck. Her eyes gaze back at herself in the mirror. "Will he go with me back to my office? I love the bastard, but the election is a shoo-in if I bring Remo in." She pivots away from the sink and taps the metal partition door with her fist. "I will be the new CCSA if he's in jail, and Jersey can't get to him. I am the *only* one who can save him." Wiping the tears from her cheeks, she straightens her skirt and fluffs her hair. "I can save you, and you'll thank me for this later." As she reaches for the door handle, the floor rumbles below her feet. The room whipsaws like a ship on water.

Across the hall, inside the office, Remo and Donovan stumble. "What the hell was that?" Donovan asks.

Halfway up the stairs, Becky is thrown against the wall. A blast of heat and bright light strikes her as the fire door closes. The fire wasn't supposed to start yet. Her overcoat slides down her arms onto the stairs. A quick check of the magazine again and she snaps it back into the pistol handle.

Becky pads near the office door as she hears two voices mumble inside. A laptop screen is bright again behind the frosted-glass door. Two shadows move within the office. She feels the warmth of the barrel and chuckles. She raises her gun chest-high, fingertip on the trigger, elbows lock in place. She leans back, the floor creaks. "You need to die, you bastard."

Remo's eyes skim across the frosted-glass door as his hand snaps Belly's laptop closed. He whispers, "That's the second time the floor creaked. Someone's here. Get down."

Becky's finger jerks the trigger back. Glass explodes as bullets rip through the door and wall.

Inside the bathroom, Maggie crouches to the floor next to the sink as the building shifts. Smoke rises through the floor while heat penetrates the soles of her ankle-high boots. The building is on fire, and she's trapped upstairs. She looks up at the ceiling in panic. "No sprinklers? Cheap bastards."

A machine gun bursts outside the door. Someone returns fire. It must be Remo.

Glancing around, she surveys her shrinking escape options, with the two-by-three-foot window on the outside wall as her only hope. She wraps her coat around her hand and pounds on the window until it breaks. The icy wind catches her breath as snow tacks on her face. With her neck stretching up, she breathes deep, gasping for clean air. The snow-covered alley is below. She could jump out the window into the open dumpster. If she misses, there would be too many broken bones.

The overhead light flickers, then it's gone. A single alley light shines into the window. Maggie tries to muffle her smoke-filled cough.

Becky hears someone in the bathroom. She rips another row of bullets into the office. "Remo Wolf, are you in there?" She kicks the door open and sees a woman attempting to climb out the window. Becky grabs the waistband and yanks the woman back inside the bathroom.

Maggie crashes against the metal partition and lands on her back with her purse strap over her shoulder. The palms of her hands are bleeding from broken glass on the windowsill edges.

"Maggie McCall? It's you, isn't it? Now I don't have to pay that checkerboard bitch to kill you. You saved me a lot of money."

Maggie turns and sees Becky wearing a black fedora and holding a chrome revolver in her left hand and a machine pistol in the right. "Holy shit. You're Fedora?" Maggie tightens her bleeding hands in light fists while pushing up from the floor. She braces herself against the wall. "You're Fedora? You killed Bobby Lynch?"

"Shut up, bitch. Remo killed my Bobby. Well, technically, I did, but Remo caused it. And now I will take away what he loves most... you." Becky bellows toward the ceiling. "Do you hear him coming in here to rescue you? No. That's because I just killed him." The building rumbles beneath them.

Chapter 82

"You okay?" Remo asks as he shines his flashlight on Donovan clutching his bleeding leg.

Blood rolls down Donovan's left leg. "I'm alive. What the hell just happened?"

"Not sure." Remo crouches down and examines Donovan's leg. "Let's fix this and then go after the shooter."

Remo pulls out his knife and cuts Donovan's jeans from the cuff to his knee. Remo pops his head up for half a second and sees bullet holes racked across the wall with the front door glass shattered. With his hand, he wipes the blood off Donovan's leg.

"You got a half-inch hole in the calf. Lucky for you, it looks like it went through the muscle." Remo feels the bones. "Everything intact." Remo unzips his backpack and grabs a roll of duct tape. "This will put pressure on the leg and stop the bleeding, but it is going to hurt like a mother when you take it off."

"Find the shooter," Donovan says. "I got this. Go." He grabs the duct tape from Remo's hand and wraps his leg.

"Put Belly's laptop in the backpack and wait for me. When we get through this shit, I'll see that you become the first rookie detective in Chicago."

◆

Back in the bathroom, Maggie feels the heat in her boots. "Listen, you crazy bitch. I'm with the Cook County State's Attorney's Office..."

"And I'm going to kill you." Becky motions with her revolver. "Get up."

Maggie glances at the umbrella leaning against the wall next to her as she stands. Her fingers trail across the partition door toward the umbrella. "Yes, of course. Just be cool about all this, Becky."

"You don't need that." Becky steps on the umbrella and snaps it in half. "Heard you were some kind of tough chick." Becky sticks the revolver barrel against Maggie's neck. "Don't seem so tough to me."

Maggie swings her left hand against Becky's forearm. The revolver fires. Maggie headbutts Becky. "Remo, damn it," Maggie yells out. "Where are you?"

Remo hears Maggie's voice in the hallway. Like a bull, Remo charges through the broken door into the blackened hallway. His flashlight scans the hall. He smells smoke. The metal door to the stairs is warm. He hears another gunshot in the bathroom, turns back down the hall and calls out, "Maggie!"

"In here."

Becky swings the revolver, hitting Maggie across her face. "A little louder." Becky spins Maggie around and grabs her by the hair. "I'm going to let you watch while I kill him."

Remo kicks the door open.

Maggie's boot heel jams down onto Becky's foot. Becky cringes from the pain and fires high above the door.

Remo calls out from behind the wall, "Maggie. Who else is in there with you?"

"A crazy bitch named Becky Lynch," Maggie says.

"Come on in, *Detective Remo Wolf*," Becky says. "I got something of yours."

"You shot at me once. Don't think I should just step out so you can do it again."

"I changed my mind. I want you to watch her die, and then I'm going to kill you."

He steps from behind the wall. His flashlight scans the bathroom, finding Becky with a fist full of Maggie's hair with one hand and the chrome revolver pushed against her neck with the other.

"Drop the gun, or she dies. *Do it. Now.*"

Becky has a cut on her forehead. Blood rolls down the side of her face. Maggie has a swollen right cheek and upper lip.

"Easy, Becky." Remo holds his hands up and then slowly lowers the pistol to the floor. He decides it's too risky to reach for the gun in his ankle holster. Instead, he stands again. Sirens wail in the distance.

"You're a hard man to kill, Remo Wolf, but that doesn't matter now, does it?" Becky pulls harder on Maggie's hair. "I'm going to kill the one person you love just like you killed my Bobby." The red pin glistens on the black fedora.

Remo's flashlight shines on the chrome revolver. "Becky Lynch, I don't get it. You're Fedora? Why did you kill Bobby?"

"You killed him." She pulls Maggie's head back again. "And now she's a dead woman."

Chapter 83

I didn't pull the trigger, you did. You killed Bobby with that revolver in your hand." Remo's eyes can't stop looking at the red pin. "You are one psycho bitch." Remo watches Maggie's eyes shift back and forth to the sink, where the machine pistol rests on the countertop.

"Find what you wanted, Wolf?" Becky asks.

"You mean the emails on Belly's laptop?" Remo asks. "Yeah, found the real video. How do you know about that?"

"I did it. I sent it to Belly's laptop. Do you think my dumb shit husband knows how to do that? I was there at Garfield Park. I was going to kill you and send it to the world. I wanted to watch it every night before I went to bed, but Jiang changed all that."

"How did you find me tonight?" Remo asks.

"You're pretty easy to follow when you don't think anyone is following you. Before tonight, I never could find you, but you let your guard down."

"Why are you doing this?" Remo asks as he steps closer to the machine pistol. "I'm sure we can work this out."

"I changed the video and sent it to the local news," Becky snaps back at Remo. "They did exactly as I thought they would. Then I had this great idea to get rid of everybody. I put both videos on Truk's laptop. And Belly, my dumbass husband, never looks at anything on his computer that he didn't put there. He never saw it. I sent the folders from my laptop to his, emailed them from Belly's laptop to Truk's and then deleted them from Belly's, knowing how easy it is to find deleted folders on a hard drive. When Richard Watters is re-elected as CCSA, he'll prosecute you for murder. Truk and my shit-for-brains husband would have gone down for withholding evidence. But everything changed when Captain Kimball stepped in and screwed things up. Had to get rid of him. So, Truk is dead, Ton is dead, and that worthless piece of shit husband of mine is dead."

"You killed Belly?"

"Yeah, downstairs in the lobby. Don't worry about it. What you need to worry about is I'm going to kill you and Raggedy Ann tonight. After tonight, *all* my troubles will be gone."

"Except you still killed Bobby," Remo quips back. "You killed him, and he's never coming back."

"Shut up!"

Remo slides his feet closer toward the sink counter. "Got it all figured out, don't you, Becky?"

Shoving the barrel harder against Maggie's neck, Becky casts him a wicked grin. "Oh, you see it, the gun on the sink. That's my new favorite gun, besides this pretty revolver stuck in your pretty friend's neck. You're only five feet away. Think you're fast enough?" The building shifts beneath their feet. "Hands and knees on the floor, Wolf."

"The floor? It might get too hot for my hands. With all that work you did on the video, if you shoot me, then I won't feel the fire. I won't suffer as much as you have suffered." Remo turns and glances at the sink counter. "I'll just step back a little. Let me get some paper towels for that nasty cut on your head."

"Drop on the floor, or she's dead."

"Shoot her in the head, Remo," Maggie says. "I promise I'll duck."

"Yeah?" Becky's thumb pulls the hammer back on the revolver. "Bet I can kill her *and* you before you can get to the sink." Becky stretches Maggie's hair and head backward.

Maggie's bloody fingers fumble inside her purse.

Remo's eyes glance back to the revolver and then to Maggie. He needs a diversion. "What the hell are you doing here, Maggie?"

"I came to warn you. Warn you she was coming. Warn you Becky is Fedora."

Becky smirks. "You? You did what? You didn't know shit before you came here tonight. You came to put your felonious boyfriend in jail."

Remo's eyes widen. "That so, Maggie? Were you here to arrest me?" He leans toward the machine pistol. "Maybe it would be better if I left you here with Becky, and she can do what she wants."

Maggie mouths out to Remo, "Not me, darling." Maggie's fingers push her lipstick and cell phone to the side inside the purse. She feels her key ring and thinks the office and apartment keys might hurt if she hit Becky in the head. Remo glances between Maggie's satchel and Becky's revolver. Maggie sweeps her fingers inside for something else; her lip curls up as her eyes meet Remo's. Her hand wraps around what she wants.

"Becky," Remo says. "I'm sorry Bobby is dead. I wish I could do something to bring him back." Maggie nods at Remo. He shines the flashlight in Becky's face, and she blinks.

Maggie's right hand plunges the file into Becky's chest.

An electric pain from chest to back takes Becky's breath away. She releases Maggie's hair. A metal fingernail file is stuck deep into Becky's chest. Maggie turns, shoves Becky's hand with the gun up into the air and plants a right hook into Becky's jaw. Maggie slams her fist against Becky's nose. The revolver falls to the floor, and Maggie's boot kicks it away. Becky crumples to the floor, gasping for air.

"Don't you dare stick a gun to my head, you fucking psycho."

Maggie shoves Becky to the wall. Her bloodied hand pulls the nail file out of Becky's chest and raises it to stab again. Fire rages from hell below and deeper inside Maggie.

"Maggie, Maggie!" Remo shouts. "Stop!"

She sees Gerardo Hernandez on the floor, not Becky. Maggie's sister flashes across her eyes, dead in her bedroom, her wrists cut to the bone. She remembers the smell of the blood-soaked floor. She couldn't save her sister.

Maggie turns toward Remo. Her teeth clenched, eyes wide open, her breath hard and heavy. Her hand wrapped around the nail file, ready to plunge it into Becky. Maggie's blue eyes are gone. Red veins wrap around dilated black holes and black mascara smudges across her face. She looks back at Becky slumped on the floor. She remembers her sister's tombstone read, GOD FORGIVES. REST IN PEACE. Gerardo Hernandez killed her sister. He needs to die, now.

"Maggie, don't do it. She's finished. I'll take her in."

Maggie's bloodied hand squeezes tighter on the file. She raises her arm, ready to plunge. Her heart burns with hate, with regret.

"Don't, Maggie. I know what you're thinking. It's Becky, not Gerardo. Let her go."

Her hands relax, and she drops the file down on the floor. She pushes Becky away from her.

Water pounds on the roof. Remo looks up. "The fire department is here. We need to get out now." He points to the ceiling. "The water from the hose is going to collapse the roof." Remo holds his hands up. "Donovan is lying in the detectives' office. I can get him over here, and we can jump out the window."

Satan kicks the building, and fire roars below. The walls bend, and the windowsill twists and flattens like the moon in Remo's dream.

He remembers Maggie floating away on a burning cloud, a sign of death. He can't let that happen.

The floor cracks like a broken tree branch. A four-foot-diameter section of the floor between Maggie and Remo drops out of sight, shooting a volcanic ball of fire up from the first floor. The bathroom fills with black smoke and ash.

Maggie coughs as the fire below roars. "Remo, I'm trapped. I can't get out this way." She scans the damaged floor, then pushes against the metal bathroom stall with her shoulder. It doesn't move. The pilaster, the corner of the stall, is still bolted to the ceiling. The floor groans death. She shakes her head at him. "I can't jump to you. It's too far."

Remo points to the metal stall. "It looks sturdy. Use your hands and pull yourself across the top of the partition."

Rust and peeling paint are across the top of the metal. Maggie shakes her head. "My hands are cut from the window glass. That metal file hurt like hell. I don't think I can do this."

"Got to. The only way out, girl."

Damn, this is going to hurt. Maggie's hands grab the top of the partition as the floor beneath her boots capitulates to the fire. She hangs from the partition and screams from the pain. Her hands slide across, leaving bits of skin on the rusted metal.

"Come on, Maggie. Slide a little farther. I'll grab you."

She coughs as she breathes black smoke into her lungs. "Remo, I can't." Her skin rips from the rust as her feet dangle. Heat surrounds her body. A bolt in the ceiling holding the pilaster pops out from the extra weight.

Remo's hand stretches out. He scoots his boot to the edge of the jagged floor in front of him. The sole of his boot melts on the floor. Stretching his hand out as far as he can, Remo reaches for her. "Come on, Maggie. We only have a few seconds more."

Her hand slides across the top of the partition. "Goddamn, my hands," Maggie screams as her skin peels off from her sliding hands. Flames lick around her legs.

"Keep sliding, almost got you. Come on, Maggie."

Becky lunges forward. Her fingernails dig into Maggie's legs, scraping off blistered skin. Maggie lets out a bloodcurdling scream. Becky's fingers wrap around the top of Maggie's ankle-boot tops. Another bolt pops out from the ceiling.

Her hands feel the extra weight of Becky. She curls her toes in, and one boot slips down her heel and falls off.

Becky's fingers grasp Maggie's other ankle, holding on for life.

"Get off of me!" Maggie screams. Her fingers weaken. Maggie's toes curl inside the boot as it slips off her foot.

Becky falls toward the burning hellhole as she grabs for the edge of the floor. Her elbows are holding her up as her legs dangle into the fire pit below.

Maggie gasps for breath. Her arms feel like rubber.

A voice from behind Remo calls out, "Lean forward. I got you." Donovan grabs the waistband of Remo's jeans.

Remo stoops toward Maggie. She stretches her right hand toward him. Their fingers are as close as Adam and God's, while hell roars below.

"Let go," Remo says. "Come to me. I'll catch you."

Maggie releases the partition. Remo's thick fingers grab Maggie's wrist as she falls toward the flaming hole. Donovan drags Remo backward as he slides Maggie's exhausted body to the hallway.

"Help me, Remo. You're a cop." All three turn back toward the burning bathroom. Sirens blare outside. Becky's elbows rest on a small section of the floor. Her shoulders weaken. "My legs are on fire."

Remo stands at the edge of the bathroom and takes the machine pistol from the countertop. He points it at Becky. "I'm done with the Killing Club. It didn't go like I thought it would. Grab the end of the barrel, and I'll pull you out."

"Thanks," Becky says. "I will tell Jersey to back off."

He pulls the barrel back just out of her reach. "What do you know about Jersey?"

"Your ambush. Jersey was the one on the motorcycle and wanted to kill you in the parking garage. I said no. She drew you into the storage unit, but she never saw your face before she jumped over the fence. She knows all about you now."

"Of all the people dead," Remo says, "you're the one that deserves it, but I'm not going to kill you."

Becky's fingers wiggle at the gun barrel. "Jersey and Solido are coming to kill you. I can help you."

"Funny what people are willing to grab to save themselves. You're willing to grab the wrong end of a gun barrel. Brave or stupid? Which is it?"

Becky's elbows squirm on the hot floor. "I promise I'll send Jersey away. Just help me!"

"Maybe this is a little taste of hell for you, Becky. Eternal shit and all that."

Becky looks at her elbows as the floor cracks again. "Help me." Her face falls blank. The floor drops, Becky disappears as a volcanic ball of flame engulfs its victim.

Chapter 84

"How do we get out of this hell hole?" Donovan asks. The office window shatters from a hose full of water flowing inside the office, across the hallway, and blocking the door to the stairs. "We can't get out that way."

The building shifts more. Remo turns and looks down the hall. "Down the laundry chute."

"Not me." Maggie holds her hands in the air.

"Come on." Remo points to the utility door in the hallway. "Down the chute and out the back door." He opens the door, with the chute angling forty-five degrees to the first floor. "Looks clear. I'll go first. It's a straight shot down one floor. After me, then Maggie."

"Whoa, wait," she says. "You want me to jump one floor down with shredded hands and burnt feet? That's going to hurt like hell."

"Slide not jump. I got you, I promise."

Donovan asks Maggie, "Do you trust him?"

"Bullshit on the trust. I'm worried about the pain."

"No other choice, girl. This way or follow Becky," Remo says. "Donovan, you help Maggie down, and then you follow."

"Damn, this is going to hurt so much," Maggie says.

Seconds later, Maggie leans against the wall on the ground floor, holding her hands against her chest. Remo feels the heat as he touches the lobby door.

Donovan touches the outside door. "This door's not hot. We could go out this way, out the alley."

"Don't forget what Becky said. Jersey and Solido are nearby. They may be out in the alley waiting for us to open the door."

"You aim the machine pistol outside when I crack open the door." Remo shoves his shoulder against the back door, but it's not opening.

"What's wrong?" Donovan asks.

"The door is stuck. The building shifted."

"Come on, both of us can open it," Donovan says. They both try, but no luck.

Remo looks around. Flush against the wall, a rusted steel water pipe hangs from the ceiling to the floor. "I bet this water pipe hasn't been used in years." He wiggles it. "It's loose from the wall. Stand back. I'm ripping it off the wall. We can use it as a lever."

He tugs hard. A three-foot section snaps off, and water pours down on top of them.

"That was not a good decision," Remo yells above the noise of water pouring out. "Maggie, you push on the panic bar, and we'll ram the door." Remo looks at Donovan. "On three. One, two, three."

The two charge into the door with their shoulders. A crack of outside light seeps at the top of the door. The water is up to their knees.

"Again. One, two, three." They ram against the door. It opens an inch. Water flows out and air rushes in.

From outside, a knife blade sweeps up and down the crack. "I'm here waiting for you," Jersey calls out.

Maggie pitches the machine pistol to Remo, and he fires through the crack. "We have to get out of here."

Jersey and Solido shove the door closed. "You're going to drown like sewer rats."

Water is back to their knees. The outside door rocks back and forth. Water rolls down the stairs from the fire hoses.

"If she opens that door, we're dead. No escape," Donovan says. "The only way out is through the lobby door where the fire is raging."

Jersey and Solido bang on the outside door.

Burning debris falls from the second floor. "We have no other choice. Let's go," Remo says.

"Out the lobby door?" Maggie yells. "Are you crazy? There's a fire on the other side of this door."

"The basement door is right next to this door. We're soaked. We only need a few seconds to get downstairs," Donovan says.

"All this water will rush out and push the fire back just long enough to get downstairs," Remo says. "We have to go. The walls are going to collapse any second."

The building shifts, knocking all three against the wall. The lobby door snaps open. The fire roars its dominance while water sweeps them into the lobby.

Chapter 85

The metal basement door slams shut behind the three of them. Remo flicks the light switch on.

"Thought we lost electricity," Maggie says.

"Separate circuits, in case a Russian bomb dropped on us," Remo says.

A brown cloud of suspended dust hovers in the air. It hasn't moved for years. Rows of industrial overhead lights hang down from the ceiling. Each light has a four-foot-wide cone shining bright enough to be seen from Wisconsin.

"The electric meter must be spinning crazy," Donovan says.

Parallel lines of electrical conduit and rusting HVAC pipes are bolted to the twelve-foot ceiling.

Remo leads the way down the concrete steps. A rusty catwalk eight feet above the basement floor goes straight for sixty yards, then splits left and right. The chill brings clouded breaths.

The massive basement under the building is as large as a football field, running from under the street to the next building. It looks like a corporate labyrinth of 1980s office cubes, each filled with cardboard boxes stacked three and four high that should have gone to the dump decades ago.

"What the hell is this place?" Donovan asks.

"During the '70s and '80s Cold War scare, the Feds made an underground shelter against ICBM attacks," Maggie says. "They shut it down when the Soviet Union dissolved in 1991."

"Looks like everybody got up and walked out," Remo says.

"It's five hundred degrees up there and less than forty here. Is the roof going to hold up with the fire, or is it going to crash down on us?" Maggie asks.

"Don't know, but enough of the history lesson," Remo says. "The quickest way to the other side is to take the catwalk. Where it Y's, take a left to the other end of the basement."

"What about that forklift over there in the corner? We can pile on it, ram boxes out of the way and shoot down the middle," Donovan suggests.

"Good call," Remo says. "Let me check it out."

"I need my boots back." Maggie's bare toes are blanching. "I feel like I'm standing on an iceberg."

Two minutes later, Remo returns. "No good. It's got a heavy-duty chain wrapped around the steering wheel and a metal post with a lock on it. Has a propane canister on it for fuel, probably empty after all these years."

He looks at the hole in Donovan's leg and Maggie's injured hands and feet.

"If we take the catwalk, we can be on the other side in ten minutes. It would take over an hour to cross through that maze on foot, and I don't think either of you can walk through that zigzagging maze." Remo grabs Donovan by the arm. "Donovan, you first. Use your arms and hands to pull you up the ladder. Next Maggie…"

"I can't grab the railings," Maggie says. "My hands, they're shredded."

"Use your wrists and forearms, and I'll help you up."

Donovan goes up like he is doing twenty pull-ups. His right foot bounces on each metal step, and the catwalk sways. "Be careful. Must not be bolted to the wall well, if at all."

"Your turn, up you go."

Her wrists squeeze the railing while her bare feet take three painful steps. She feels Remo's two hands clasp on her buttocks.

"Now I know why you wanted Donovan first. A quick feel me up, darling?"

"Later, much later."

The three stumble twenty yards down the catwalk when the basement door bangs against the concrete wall.

"Che, or Detective Remo Wolf, or whatever your name is this week, you can't get out of here alive."

Jersey stands at the bottom of the stairs and fires her Uzi. Bullets ricochet sparks off the railing.

"Betcha' wondering how I got here. Fedora called me as she came into the building. Got your best buddy with me."

"Che, baby," Solido says. "I'm gonna scalp that fucking head of yours. Maybe show it off at the next meeting 'cept you won't be there, 'cause you being dead and all."

Remo's machine pistol bursts five bullets toward the door.

"How did she get here?" Maggie asks. "The building is on fire."

"Maybe she's the devil and can walk in fire," Donovan replies.

"Go." Remo motions forward.

The catwalk sways like a rope bridge. Jersey fires again. Two more bullets clang off the metal rungs near Donovan.

"Get down," Remo says. Donovan slides across on his right side, keeping the injured leg up. Maggie hides the pain each time her bloodied hands crawl across the corrugated steps. Remo slips the backpack off. He pulls his Blackhawks t-shirt over his head, rips it in half and wraps her hands.

She looks straight at the eagle tattoo looking back at her. "He's saying you have to make it," Maggie says.

He slips the backpack over his shoulders. "You too."

"Come on, get up, got to go," Donovan calls. His feet pound the corrugated steel as it swings wide. Jersey fires another lightning burst with bullets pinging off the steel. The catwalk's left side breaks loose from its ceiling bracket and turns ninety degrees like a dying ship at sea. Donovan's injured leg hits the rail, shooting searing heat down his hip to ankle. He rolls off, crashing on a desk below, and feels his ribs crack.

Maggie tries to grab the rail with her t-shirt-covered hands but slides through and lands on stacked boxes.

Remo drops to the floor like a bare-chested paratrooper. "Maggie, where are you?"

A painful voice replies, "Here, behind the desk."

He looks at the boxes full of shredded paper. "They must have spent days shredding and stacking. You're a lucky woman."

She moans. "Don't feel too lucky right now."

"Up, up you go. Got to get Donovan and make it to the other side." He grabs her by the waist like a ragdoll. "On your feet."

"Donovan landed on that desk across from us," Maggie says.

He's still lying on his right side, breathing hard, gasping for air. Donovan turns toward Remo. "Not good. Feel something in my side."

"Can you roll and let me look?" Remo asks.

A pool of blood stays on the desk as Donovan rolls onto his back.

"Damn, a paper spike is stuck in you," Remo says.

"I don't know what that is, but it hurts."

"You know, one of those spikes that stood straight up on the desk and secretaries would shove papers on it. It's shoved up to the base."

"Pull it out. Can't breathe."

"You got a pneumothorax. If I pull it out, it'll make it worse."

A bullet shatters wood from the desk drawer inches from them. "Listen, Remo, I can't run anywhere. You two go. I'll stay and fight her off."

"No, I can carry you," Remo says. "We can make it."

Boxes bounce on the floor and fly in the air as Solido shoves through, like an angered linebacker.

"No, it would be too slow with me. Run like hell straight down the middle. I got this."

Remo slips a pistol off his ankle. "It has nine in the mag." From the backpack, Remo hands Donovan a single grenade. "These, plus your gun, should keep them at bay."

"Yeah, man," Donovan moans. "Forgot to reload. I only have three bullets left. Don't worry about me. I'll see you on the other side."

"I'm sorry, Donovan."

Donovan fires twice in Solido's direction. "Sorry for what? Go on, get out of here."

Remo grabs Maggie's wrist, and they run. He counts the ammo as it's fired three times. Donovan's standard-issue police weapon is empty. Jersey replies with a row of thumps through cardboard boxes. Remo hears three more from the ankle pistol.

"Maybe we should go back for him," Maggie says.

A thousand pins prickle Remo's face from smoke and ash an hour ago. Steel wool grinds under his eyelids with each blink. They turn behind a desk as Jersey's machine pistol burps twice. Donovan fires again. Remo knows the ankle pistol is empty. Jersey's pistol fires once. No response, nothing from Donovan. With no grenade blast, Remo knows she has it now.

Chapter 86

"Che," Jersey's voice echoes across the large basement. "I will cut you down and that bitch you got with you."

Remo gently places his finger on Maggie's lips. "Don't talk, don't reply to her. She'll know where we are."

"You got a long way to go to the other end," Jersey calls out. "Can't go back, too damn hot up there." Jersey turns right, down an aisle with boxes stacked six feet high on each side. "Solido is circling to find you. When he does, you're both going to die. Dead. You hear me? Dead."

Remo and Maggie run left into the cardboard maze.

"Where are we going?" Maggie asks.

"Can't run down the middle, have to zigzag through the boxes and desks." Remo opens desk drawers as he turns back and forth while looking for some kind of help. He grabs a thin rope and puts it over his neck. Another desk has a yo-yo.

A glass bottle shatters in front of him. Another one breaks on a desk ten feet away.

"Found me some Coke bottles, Che," Solido says. "You thirsty? Almost as good as my DDT."

Another hits ten feet away, another ten feet in the other direction.

"He doesn't know where we are," Remo says. "He's pitching them to get us flustered."

"Well, he's doing a damn good job of it." Another bottle breaks across the desk next to them, spraying sticky syrup on them. "Damn it." She stops moving. "Remo, I'm barefoot. There is glass everywhere."

"Never expected shrapnel in Chicago. Hop on." She jumps on his back, his arms wrap around her legs. He shuffles through stacks of boxes like a running back smelling the end zone. He turns a corner and finds a baseball bat laying across a desk. "Grab it."

They run into a sea of twelve-foot-tall metal lockers, with most of the doors open.

"Here, get off and look for something useful."

"Something? Like what?"

"You'll know if you see something. Here, like this sack of marbles."

Maggie finds a dust-covered mirror on a desk. She picks it up and looks at it. She's not sure which is worse, the mangled hair or her face from mascara and lipstick in the wrong place. "Oh, Jesus."

Remo turns around and looks at Maggie. "What? Did you find something?"

Maggie turns to Remo. "Yeah, the ugliest girl in the building."

He smirks. "Not by a long shot. Put that down and find something useful."

She drops the mirror facedown and opens a locker. "How about this? I played with this when I was a child."

Remo opens another locker door. "What is it?"

"A slingshot. I was fairly good with this back in the day. Hit frogs and lizards with it."

"Stick it in your pocket. It might be of some use."

A row of lockers bangs against each other in front of them. Remo fires through the metal doors.

Solido groans. "Son of a bitch."

A big thud hits the ground. "Solido, did that hurt?" Remo calls out.

Solido kicks a locker. "Not done with you."

Jersey's pistol fires behind them. "I'm coming."

There is no time for Remo and Maggie to run as Jersey comes around a cardboard column. Remo takes advantage and charges into her, knocking her against the boxes. In one motion, Jersey grabs Remo's arm and swings him a half-circle into another column. He staggers as his gun slides across the floor. Jersey's massive hand grabs his hair as Remo throws a violent uppercut. It should have knocked anyone out, but Jersey absorbs it and headbutts him instead.

Instinctively, he throws both arms out, blocking Jersey's punch to his face. His right fist pounds her ribs. Her hands slap his temples and then a fist drives into his chest harder than any man has hit him before. He buckles to the floor while Jersey's boot pounds into Remo's ribs. He rolls onto his back, breathless.

Standing over him, Jersey raises her foot to stomp him again. Remo jackknifes his leg and kicks at the side of her knee, bringing her down within reach. She lands hard on her back, mumbling. Two-fisted, Remo slams his fists down on her solar plexus. Jersey rolls to her side and moans. He reaches for his gun, but when he turns back, Jersey is gone.

"We got to get out of here and cross the main aisle," Remo says. "See where the catwalk is? If we get to the other side, we can climb up and run across to the exit in a few minutes. Can you make it?"

"Burned hands, a bleeding leg and bare feet standing on freezing concrete? Sure, why not."

He slips the magazine out, three cartridges left. It snaps back in. He feels almost naked with no extra bullets or pistols and no grenades. He's sure Jersey took the grenade from Donovan.

Remo and Maggie run left to right between desks and boxes. The lockers rumble behind them.

Jersey shoves a column down and finds Solido lying on his back. "Solido, damn it." Two bleeding holes leave his left arm limp. "Get your fat ass off the ground and go get them."

Remo and Maggie zigzag, being careful not to move any of the columns of cardboard boxes. Remo wants to go faster, but Maggie's bare feet slide on the ice-cold concrete, slowing them down.

They stop and huddle against a stack of boxes, waiting for noises. Maggie's chest heaves. She covers her mouth with her elbow as white clouds expel. Tears drip onto her forearm. Fighting tunnel vision. Fighting fear. Fighting pain.

Remo pulls the infrared camera from the backpack and shows it to Maggie. "A gift from a friend." He flips the switch, changing from screen to lens, and looks through the eyepiece. He sees columns of boxes and a red body, maybe twenty or thirty feet away, with a red gun moving near them. Jersey is walking with a red hot gun in her hand. Remo points his finger to the ground, telling Maggie to stay where she is. Handing her the camera, he shows her how to turn it on. She understands. He stoops low and disappears.

Where is Jersey? Does she still have her knife? Are those footsteps behind her or the pounding of her heart? It must be Jersey. Remo's are big boot sounds; he wouldn't sneak up on her. These steps are quieter.

A surge of adrenaline flows like Niagara Falls in Maggie's arteries with each approaching footstep. She hears them—one footstep, three seconds later, another. The sole of a shoe taps the concrete. Again, again.

Every hair on Maggie's scalp leaps to attention, skin tightening like shrink-wrap. Her hand pushes down on the bat to stand as lightning shoots up her wrist and feet. Her teeth grind the pain away. She holds the camera in her hand and pushes the power button again. Electric shocks fire through her bleeding finger.

Maggie's pupils dilate as large as .50 caliber. Remo's blood-soaked, torn t-shirt is wrapped around each of her hands. Red drops splat on the concrete. The nerves in her hands scream. Her moist breath swirls around the camera as a trembling hand tries to steady it close to her eyes. Her feet burn against the ice-cold floor. She's not sure which hurts more, the raw meat or the frostbite.

The camera scans columns of boxes. A red body appears. The head turns left and right, with a long red gun held in the right hand. It must be Jersey. Where is Remo's body? Maggie hears heel steps two columns away. The body turns toward her. How does Jersey know where to look? Jersey's left hand moves back and forth. What is she doing? Cold steel won't show on the infrared camera. A blade is invisible.

Maggie buries her mouth into her elbow, trying to hide her breath. Blood rolls down the shaft of the bat. She clenches her teeth, trying to make panic disappear. There's a roar in her head.

The camera shakes in her other hand. The red body comes closer to the column of boxes five feet away. Maggie's vision blurs from tears too cold to flow.

Maggie places the camera on the ground and grasps the bat. Fear smothers her pain, heartbeats pound her ears. Jersey is on the other side of the column. Maggie charges, her shoulder plows into the column of boxes. Jersey falls backward and cracks her head against the cold concrete. She moans and rolls to her side as her hand releases the gun.

Maggie swings and slams the bat against Jersey's back. The sound is the same when she hits the heavy canvas bag. Another swing, and the bat cracks against Jersey's right wrist. The knife clatters across the floor.

Maggie raises the bat to strike again. Jersey's leg sweeps behind Maggie's legs, knocking her flat on her ass. The bat clatters on the floor.

Jersey grabs Maggie's leg and pulls. A tsunami of heat explodes from her ankle.

Jersey screams as she grabs at Maggie's leg. "I'm going to kill you."

Maggie launches herself toward Jersey. Her fist swings hard and connects against Jersey's temple.

Jersey yells, "Fuck you, bitch." She pulls on Maggie's leg.

Maggie's bloody fingers stretch for the box camera only inches away. She feels the camera against her fingertips. Quiet screams rush through her head.

She remembers her core exercises, knee fold tuck, oblique reach. Her thumb flips the camera closer and grabs it. With a quick trunk rotation, she smashes the camera onto Jersey's head. Her hand releases Maggie's leg. She will kiss her trainer.

Maggie stumbles away. "Remo, help!" She turns left, then right, then left again, pushing columns of boxes to the floor.

Two hands grab Maggie, one at the waist and the other around her mouth. She reaches above her head and grips a handful of hair. The two of them roll to the floor.

"Maggie, I got you," Remo says. "You're safe."

Her forehead wrinkles, eyebrows raise. She exhales. "Jersey was right behind me," she says with a quiet laugh and equal cry. "The camera, it was great. I pushed her away. I think I broke her wrist. I broke the camera."

His arms wrap around her. Her forehead falls to his shoulder as tears roll down his bare chest.

"I got a plan," he says. "You still have the marbles in your pocket?"

Chapter 87

Heartbeats pound every half-second in her head. Maggie lies across the top of two columns of boxes with a cauldron of witch's brew boiling inside each of her feet. Fireballs shoot up her legs with each pulse. Blood drips from the bloody t-shirt wrapped around her hands.

Twenty feet away from her, Remo calls out to a crazed animal. "Hey, fat boy. Come get me." He rattles a column of boxes. Solido rumbles down the aisle. Maggie lies still as she watches Remo's eyes. "Solido, I got nowhere to go. You got me. I give up." Remo stands in front of a wooden roll-top desk with the bat lying on top.

"I'm gonna snap you in half, asshole." Solido walks down the aisle, his shirt a sopping mess of blood. His left arm swings like a twenty-pound sausage casing.

Remo's eyes flick a quick look at Maggie peeking down as Solido passes by her. The yo-yo on her finger rolls down the string toward the floor. She swings it in big circles.

"Hey, Solido," she yells.

He turns and looks up. The yo-yo smashes into his forehead, making him stumble backward.

She aims the slingshot at his head. Her bloodied fingers hold the pocket with the marble, then a quick release. Blood explodes from his nose. She fires again, and the marble slams against the center of his neck. He grabs his throat and charges into the column, throwing Maggie to the floor. Columns spill between them, with empty Coke bottles falling out of boxes and shattering. Shards of clear glass surround her bare feet. On her back, she grabs the neck of a broken bottle.

"I'm getting tired of this shit," Maggie yells.

Solido's boots crunch through the glass. With his right hand out in front of him, he charges at her like a bull elephant.

Remo smiles. "My money's on the girl."

She snaps up like her trainer taught her and swings the broken bottle in a wide swath at his face, ripping a chunk from his cheek. His hand aims for her hair, but she dodges and jams the glass into his palm, twisting it and feeling tendons and blood vessels snapping.

Swinging a hand that looks like fresh roadkill, he slaps the broken bottle from her grip.

"Hey, Solido. Behind you." Remo slams the bat against Solido's ribs with a sound of dried branches snapping, echoing off the walls.

Jersey fires the last rounds of her pistol. Wood splinters around them, as Remo and Maggie zigzag out of sight.

"You and your bitch, you're dead." Jersey throws the empty pistol behind her and finds Solido moaning on the floor. Receding footsteps pound the concrete floor. Flipping the machine pistol off her shoulder, Jersey rips a line of bullets across the boxes. The magazine empties. "Damn it." She looks at the moaning blob on the floor, blood flowing from his nose, face, hand and shoulder. "Damn it. Solido, get up and do something right."

"Stop, I have to stop," Maggie pleads. Icy mist rolls with each hard breath. She leans against a box. "My hands. I've never felt pain like this. They look like bloody sponges. Using the slingshot ripped the last of the skin off." Her shoulders shiver, her neck tightens. "Can't feel my feet."

"Get on your hands and knees," Remo says as he checks the magazine in his machine pistol, hoping for more, but there are only three cartridges left.

The corner of her mouth turns up. "Darling, I love it when you talk that way."

"Good God, Maggie. Is that all you ever think about? I meant hands on the floor to cool them and feet off the floor."

"That damn eagle on your chest is staring at me. It was not a good idea when Johnny put that one on you. Besides, why aren't you cold, wearing no shirt and all?"

"I was in Afghanistan. This is a heat wave to their winters."

A motor whines at top speed twenty yards away.

"What the hell?" Remo says.

Towering boxes fly in all directions, desk legs screech across the floor. Thirty-year-old dust swirls above the columns.

Forklift blades slice through the gray cloud ten feet in front of them. Solido's bloody head turns toward them as he passes by. He spins the forklift hard, tripping columns as the broken chain whips across the floor.

Solido aims the forklift's metal blades at them.

Remo shoves Maggie to the floor and runs across the aisle. "Hey, crazy man, this way," Remo says.

Solido follows, his face swollen, nose pushed to the right, his face and shirt covered with blood. The motor whines, Solido raises the forks decapitation-high. Remo snakes between the boxes and desks. Solido shoves the accelerator to the floor, a bull in a china shop charging straight ahead.

Two metal blades stab boxes; books and shredded paper explode into the air as he misses Remo's head. The forklift turns a hard left. Remo grabs hold of one fork blade while body-blocking cardboard boxes and boots sliding on the concrete.

"Die, you bastard." Solido aims at the metal file cabinets ahead.

Remo holds the pistol with his right and lifts his body with his left. "You first, fat pig." Remo fires, Solido ducks, a spark pings off the metal frame. No clear shot. His left arm is losing its grip on the fork. Twenty feet from the metal cabinets, Remo swings off the speeding machine. The blades pierce the cabinets with a harsh metal clang.

Solido shifts to reverse, and the forklift beeps loudly as it charges at Remo. He fires at the propane can strapped to the back end. Propane spews a white cloud. Remo has one bullet left. He fires again, an orange fireball envelops the forklift. Solido screams as he frantically slaps the fire surrounding his head. Burning clothes melt onto his skin. Remo covers his nose and mouth as the smell of burning flesh fills the air.

He spins back to find Maggie. With columns of boxes strewn everywhere, he's lost direction. Where is she?

Jersey's vexing laugh echoes within the massive room. Maggie sits on the floor, facing Jersey. Barely able to hold the bat, her hands shake like hummingbird wings.

"Well, well. Are you going to hit me with that bat again? I don't think you need it anymore." Jersey pulls out a serrated hunting knife from her boot. "Drop it!" The bat bounces against the concrete. Jersey's foot sweeps it behind her. "When your two-faced scab of a boyfriend comes back here, he will find you dead. You see this grenade? This is a present from him, but I can't keep it. Oh, no. Have to give it back to him. Going to put this under your back, and when he picks you up, boom, you'll both look like pulled pork. Speaking of pork, I don't hear Solido anymore. I'm expecting Remo here pretty damn quick. But I got to slit your throat first. I promise this is going to hurt you a lot."

"Not today, Jersey," Remo calls out from behind her.

She turns with a smile as the grenade handle pings into the air.

Chapter 88

R emo's face is cold. A blurry white vision moves back and forth. His eyelids hurt. Half-open, his eyes try to follow an out-of-focus hand holding a glistening sword. He can't move, defenseless. A voice mumbles. No. More than one. There are two voices, muted like people on the other end of a deep cave. Someone raises Remo's eyelids. A sudden headlight charges forward like a train in a tunnel. Just as quickly, it's gone. Everything's black again. His eyelids feel like anvils.

"Mr. Wolf."

He hears his name. Someone is calling for him. He tries to turn his head toward the voice, but something holds it still. Who's calling his name? The headlight charges toward him again.

"Mr. Wolf, can you hear me?"

◆

A thousand clicks from cameras snap before Maggie in the hospital hallway as several CCSA employees stand behind her in support. Danny stands faithfully by her side, bracing her arm for balance. Her feet, wrapped in lidocaine gel pads and stuffed inside fashionable boots three sizes bigger than usual, are numb and temporarily free of pain. Her hands, except for two fingers on her left hand, are wrapped in bulky medical gauze. They resemble white boxing gloves ready to fight the media. Maggie points toward a reporter.

"Ms. McCall, are you going to pursue charges against Detective Wolf?" the reporter asks.

A strand of red hair falls past her ear. "The CCSA office has reviewed both videos. Each of you has seen both, the altered and unaltered, a hundred times by now. The evidence of the second video appears Detective Wolf has always told the truth. CPD has cleared him of any wrongdoing, and I, as CCSA, will drop all charges against Detective Wolf. A full report will be completed and released in the next few days. There are many brave officers involved in this case," Maggie says. "I promise you, each of their stories will be told."

"Was there another officer killed in the basement?" a person calls out from the crowded group.

"Yes, he was killed in the line of duty. We are withholding his name for now until his family can be contacted."

Another reporter yells out a rhetorical question, "How do you feel about the election results?"

Maggie finally cracks a smile. "The people have spoken, and I am happy that sixty-four percent agreed with me. A lot has happened in the last few days since the election. Hell, a lot has happened in the last two weeks."

This will probably be the first and last time Chicago reporters laugh *with* her.

"The day after the election, Mr. Watters was gracious enough to hand over the CCSA reins to me." A hand from behind her touches her shoulder. A nurse whispers in her ear. She holds her gauzed hands in front of her like she won a heavyweight fight. Her two fingers point a V for victory. "Thank you for all the questions. I promise my office will give an official report about Detective Wolf soon. Excuse me, I'm being called."

Remo's eyelids are closed. His mind wanders and swims between dreams and nightmares. Remo's father floats near him and pours bourbon out of a bottle onto the ground as he whispers, "Reconcile. Remorse." He hears muffled noises and faces again. Bobby sits next to him in the police car, smiling, and then the two of them laugh while running toward the Navy Pier. His mind shifts to Donovan standing next to the Shelby.

A doctor lifts both eyelids again. Light streaks across Remo's eyes. The doctor nods his head with the satisfaction of the pupillary response.

Remo's arms feel like concrete. Eyes of the dead stare at him. He screams inside his head, "What do you want?" Incomprehensible words jump from ear to ear, sounds as blurred as his vision. A bottle of bourbon explodes in the air.

The doctor rubs his knuckle into Remo's sternum. "Mr. Wolf?"

Slow-motion gunshots echo in Remo's mind. His chest hurts, and he tries to push the pain away.

"He's waking, doctor," a nurse says.

Maggie's oversized boots clunk down the hospital linoleum floor. Her new entourage of wannabe politicians follows. She motions for her staff to wait outside the door as she enters Remo's room.

"He's waking, ma'am," another nurse says.

"Yes, but slowly." The doctor flips the ophthalmic light off. "But he does respond to painful stimuli. All the vital signs are stable."

"Excuse me, doctor, I can wake him." She looks at the nurse and says, "I can do this, and no one else, understand?"

The nurse nervously shakes her head.

Maggie sits on the edge of the bed. Her bandaged hand with the two free fingers slips under the sheet. "Remo, darling…"

He feels two fingers on his ankle. They are moving to the inside of his thigh and then higher. The heart monitor quickens.

She reaches a little deeper. "Darling? Time to wake up."

Remo's eyes pop open to red hair and red lips in front of him. "Maggie?"

Chapter 89

There is an unusual warm front expected to reach Chicago today and tomorrow," the television weatherman says. "Better get out and do your thing this weekend. Late Sunday night, it is back to freezing temperatures again."

Remo finds an open spot on the Millennium Park grass. Balloons drift with the breeze, and a progressive jazz band plays on stage. He snaps the wool blanket open, and it floats to the ground. He opens the wicker picnic basket and pours a glass of white wine for her. His gray Cubs t-shirt is tight.

Maggie has progressed to loose surgical gloves, with the bulky cotton gauze bandages finally gone. Her fingertips gingerly hold the wine glass.

"We haven't seen each other since I got out of the hospital," Remo says. "I've missed you."

"I've been swamped fixing all the problems Richard Watters left behind. And you? What have you been doing?"

"Phone calls are not the same. They're all asking how I'm doing, not telling me to die or go to jail." Remo slices a small square of cheese for her. "They call it administrative leave. I call it avoidance." He looks at her hands. "How much longer for the gloves?"

"The doctor said the last skin graft will be in a few weeks. The good part is I don't have fingerprints anymore."

"So, no one will know you have been in my apartment if you decide to kill me."

"Crossed my mind." She bites her piece of cheese in half.

He opens a bottle of water and drinks most of it.

"No wine for you?"

"Not today," Remo says. "Water will do for now."

"Interesting," Maggie says as she shifts on the blanket. "You never told me how you got the full video."

"We found pictures on an aberrant website. Becky Lynch made it look like it was a North Korean site, but it was here in Chicago. A friend of mine tracked down the house where the computer was."

"A friend? Do I know this friend?"

"No."

"Tell me who it is. Maybe I can have him work for me."

"No." He cuts another slice of cheese and bites into it. "I checked the house out and found it empty. No computer, nothing, except I found an empty bottle of beer, Killian's Irish Red Ale."

"Belly?"

"His fingerprints were all over the place, but we didn't get confirmation until after the fire. The bottle had five fingerprints, but they were all from the same finger. Becky must have taken his fingerprint and put it on the bottle."

"So, Belly was just ignorant of everything?" Maggie asks as she sips her wine.

"Belly wasn't clean. He and Rolly Chang were in on the heroin. The reason Chang kept slipping away is that Belly warned him every time. After Belly's death and the fire, Chang was without a warning system. They found him in an Asian strip club, arrested him, and he quickly gave up Belly."

"Still haven't said how you found the video on Belly's laptop." She bites another piece of cheese. "You knew about both videos before you came into the bathroom. How did you get Belly's password?"

"A friend helped me. It was FEDORA60607. His zip code."

"Fedora? You mean, as in Ambush Becky, the crazy psycho bitch who almost killed me? Do you think Belly knew what Becky was doing?"

"Belly was an idiot. After both were dead, Internal Affairs raided their house. There was a picture hanging on the wall of a black fedora in the living room. I don't think he ever connected Bobby's killer, who wore a fedora, and the picture in his house. The detectives searched and found a loose panel in the bedroom closet. The black fedora and the chrome revolver would fit in fine. Becky's fingerprints were inside and out." Remo finishes his water bottle and opens another. "Belly was clueless, as always. She must have convinced him to use the password, and then she could use his laptop anytime off-site."

"She logged into his computer from her office?" Maggie asks.

"Pretty easy for someone who knows how to do it. The police searched Becky's laptop at home and her office. There were multiple logins to Belly's laptop."

"And Ton?"

Remo's hands rub across his face. "He discovered both videos and took Truk's laptop. He left a voicemail to IA that he had additional evidence. Jersey caught him in the alley and killed him. They found him in his trunk along with Truk's laptop."

"You're not techy enough to get that password. Who helped?"

"Friend."

"More friends? You seem to have a lot of friends I don't know about."

"Hey, by the way," Remo says to change the subject. "I still don't have any remembrance of what happened with Jersey."

Maggie takes a sip. "I was sitting on the floor, scared shitless, with Jersey towering over me. Her right hand held the grenade, and her left had the knife. I tried not to look past her, kept her stare at me. Out of the corner of my eye, I could see you behind her. You bent down and picked up the bat. You took a Javier Baez stance in the home run competition. Your left leg rose, knee bent, and you looked like you were swinging at a fastball as you said, 'Not today, Jersey.' Her head turned, and the grenade handle pinged away. I knew I was dead. When the bat hit her in the head, I swear, it looked like the top half of her skull shifted two inches. The grenade rolled out of her hand to the floor. You twisted her as she fell and landed on top of the grenade with you on top of her. When it exploded, both of you flipped at least ten feet in the air."

"Hate what happened to Donovan. The kid deserved more," Remo says.

"With all the postmortem accolades, they named the main garage after him," Maggie says. "The mayor changed it to the Donovan Fillard Fleet Management Facility."

Remo takes another swallow of water. "I'm done with this revenge thing. It didn't go as I planned. Ton, Truk and Donovan are dead because of it. You were almost killed."

"Twice!" Maggie says.

Two teenagers step by them. "Hey, look, it's that cop on TV."

"Kick some ass, man."

"Guess my undercover position is blown with all the media coverage."

"I think as the new Cook County State's Attorney, I can find a position for you in our department."

"I can't go undercover. Those kids know me. Everyone knows me."

"'Special investigator' has a nice ring to it. Cook County is twice the size of Chicago with twice the bad guys. You arrest them, and I will send them to jail. Deal?"

"Deal."

"The governor's election is in two years," Maggie says. "I might have to look into that." Her hand rubs the soft wool of the blanket. "A gift from her?"

"I don't know what you are talking about." Remo squirms a bit.

"This beautiful blanket. I can tell it's handmade. Did she give it to you?"

"Don't think I have ever seen a jealous Maggie McCall. Interesting, but yes, from her."

Rolling on her back, Maggie spreads her hair across the blanket. Her eyes watch clouds drifting above. "When did she give it to you?"

"You're asking when I saw her last."

"I didn't ask that. Just, um, what exact day did she hand it to you, and where were you, and how long did the two of you...talk?"

"That's what I thought you asked." He pulls two red grapes from the basket and pops one in his mouth. His fingers place one on her closed red lips. "She mailed it to me with a note, a goodbye note."

Her lips open, allowing the grape to fall into her mouth. After rising back on her elbows, her eyes search for the truth. "Was she your first love?"

"High school crush, puppy love." His water bottle empties. "After high school graduation and my parents dying in a car accident, I joined the army. We wrote to each other regularly. The letters started getting longer apart, and then they stopped."

Her red lips take another grape. "Well, everyone needs to fall in love at least once." Her hair spreads across the blanket again as she lies back down.

"I agree, at least once, maybe twice," Remo says.

A dimple retracts as her lip curls up. "Have you been in love more than once?"

"I think so."

"And when was the second time?"

"I think maybe now."

Her arms swing around Remo's neck as she pulls him down on top of her. Her warm sigh races across his lips. She pushes his shoulders back. "I have a problem with you. That damn eagle on your chest will look at me forever. Those eyes are too much."

"Thought that was the case. I made some adjustments." He sits up and flips his shirt off, revealing sunglasses covering the eagle's eyes. "Only want one set of eyes in the bedroom looking at you."

"I love it when you talk that way."

Epilogue

Rosie holds a wrinkled black and white Polaroid picture of her daddy strapped to the electric chair. On the other side of the plate-glass window, her sister was holding her pregnant mother's leg. She remembers the story her momma told her and her sister a hundred times. Rosie's momma always held the picture in her hand when she told the story.

"At Holman Prison, Atmore, Alabama, yo daddy sat on an electric chair, inside a brick room with two windows. He had played out his time. He was convicted of killin' a cashier at an all-night convenience store. The warden stood with his arms crossed as he watched through that window. He acted like he had other things to do besides watch yo daddy die. All those witnesses sat outside the window, just a 'waitin'.

"They called the chair 'Yellow Momma.' Another inmate got the job of slapping on another coat of paint for the show. Bright yellow paint splattered on the concrete floor surrounded the electric chair, same paint as the 'Do Not Pass' stripes down the middle of a road.

"A sponge soaked with saltwater sat trapped between his shaved scalp and a metal bowl with an electric cord stickin' out toward the wall. His sweat and water drippin' from the sponge down his cheeks on his leather-strapped forearms. His eyes shifted at me and Clarice's big black eyes. His chest a 'heavin'. His lips quiverin'.

"Outside that death room, Clarice held my leg tight. Her eyes watchin', unblinkin' on her daddy. Flames a' fear rose up my neck.

"Clarice's smooth face blended into her dress she wore, except that small white spot on the left side of her forehead. I tried to wipe that white spot off her head again and again. It never would rub off.

"The warden took a picture with his fancy Polaroid camera. That round clock with big black numbers hanged on the wall above Clarice's head. The second hand tickin' away. Clarice's eyes were closed. We both wanted it to stop. When I heard the warden's camera snap, panic clawed inside me. My chest was jumpin'. It hurt to breathe.

"Inside that small room, a policeman stood against the wall. One hand held the phone waitin' for the governor to call, but he never called. Instead, that policeman used his forearm to shine his police badge on his chest. It flickered against the light overhead. He motioned to the executioner with the black curtain pulled halfway shut. They put a black hood over yo daddy's head.

"The minute and hour hand were waitin' at twelve. The policeman was watchin' the second hand click until all three hands on the clock snapped together in one row. He shook his head and hung the phone back on the lever and then looked at that black curtain.

"Clarice buried her face deep in my dress. My ears roared as Clarice's prayers disappeared. A bolt of lightning seared through yo daddy's head to his ankles. The man with the badge killed him. Don't you never forget it."

Rosie remembers, the cops killed her daddy. The cops killed her momma years later for no good reason. A cop killed her sister. Jersey is dead and Remo Wolf killed her.

Jersey's house is a mess. One leg of the couch is missing, and two bricks are there instead. Plastic takeout sacks and pizza boxes cover the plywood table. Dirty glasses are piled on the kitchen counter, pans piled high in the sink. Cupboards are empty. A constant fuzz hisses on the television. A fifty-yard pistol practice page is taped to the wall with dozens of cuts in the silhouetted head.

Four boxes of knives lie on Jersey's unmade bed, varying in length from four inches to twelve inches long. Each one inside hermetically sealed bags. Rosie lying sideways on the bed, her hand slips under the pillow and grips the handle of a large, serrated hunting knife. Dried blood taints the edge of the blade. She rolls off the bed and returns to the main room with a box and the serrated knife.

Talking to the practice target on the wall, she says, "That damn cop killed my sister. Jersey's dead and it's all his fault. Him and that bitch." She drops the box of knives on the couch cushion. She slips a knife out of the bag and flings it toward the target. It cuts the ear on the target. She tosses another, cutting the other ear. Another sinks into the forehead. Another in the throat. Holding the serrated knife above her head, she rushes the wall and stabs the heart again and again. "Remo Wolf, you must die."

The End

About the Author

Patrick Hanford has lived in Texas most of his life. He graduated from the University of North Texas, Texas College of Osteopathic Medicine and recently retired from family medicine after more than thirty-five years. He interjects his past experiences of daily medical clinic life throughout his stories.

With two novels published and The Creation of Marla Adams reaching Amazon best selling status in four countries, he has continued with the Marla Adams series. A third in the series is planned to be released in the Spring of 2024.

He lives with his wife, plays golf, walks in West Texas wind, and travels from one end of Texas to the other visiting children and grandchildren.

Acknowledgements

For the help on this novel, I want to thank the Chicago Police Department, Cook County State's Attorney's Office, Lubbock Police Department, Dan Spencer, K J Waters, and Jody Smyers. Thanks to my Beta readers encouraging me to continue during challenging moments. I especially want to thank the Lubbock Write Right Critique Group for ripping my first draft to shreds and allowing me to rebuild a better story. And to Sharon, my wife, who has tolerated my ups and downs and downs and downs with writing this story.

Stay in Touch

Please visit my website at www.patrickhanford.com.

You can find me on social media at:

Facebook: PatrickHanfordauthor

Instagram: @patrickhanford.

Twitter: @patrickjhanford

If you'd like to receive the updates, contests, and exclusive excerpts, please sign up for my newsletter on my website. I'll share occasional updates on my writing, upcoming releases, sales, and special offers.

www.ingramcontent.com/pod-product-compliance
Lightning Source LLC
Chambersburg PA
CBHW051306300726
48976CB00002B/287